SUMAYAH

DENICE GARROU

Cover Model, Whitney Jo-Ellen Henson
Dragonhorse logo by Michael Bailey
http://michaelbaileyart.com
Cover background picture by
http://janeeden.deviantart

ISBN-10: 1497305748
EAN-13: 9781497305748

The Dragonhorse Saga
Dragonhorse and Seeker of the Forgotten Knowledge, Book 1
Sumayah, A Gypsy Celtic Love Tale, Book 2
Talion, Book 3   *Coming Summer 2015*

And only the poet
With wings to his brain
Can mount him and ride him
Without any rein,
The stallion of heaven,
The steed of the skies,
The horse of the singer
Who sings as he flies.
~ Eleanor Farjeon

CONTENTS

ॐ

PREFACE

I must confess that when I was writing book one, I never thought there would be a book two. But in finishing up book one, I soon realized there was a much bigger plan at work here. I thought I was done speaking my truth in book one, but lo and behold, I have much more "truth" to tell. I don't write for the commercial aspect of it. I write as my responsibility to the world, joining other like-minded authors in the new age of writing consciously. We write under a new genre, which is called Visionary Fiction.

Many lessons and messages are woven in the storyline, a story rich with emotion and beauty, a fairy tale in an enchanted realm.

Love is the main ingredient in my saga—how the heroine must sacrifice all to save those she has never met! Most humans have yet to experience the truest form of love, for I believe if they had, our world would be a much different world. I like to think we would still be living on the lost continent of Lemuria, our lost Garden of Eden, our utopian society.

One can only surmise as to what happened to our ancient and spiritually evolved lost civilizations. But my theory for Lemuria and Agartha is that they are still here, but in a much higher dimension than where mankind has chosen to live.

I had the best time writing this book; it was a journey of self-discovery, an awakening. Is that not what life is truly about, reaching for our next level of learning and growth?

In book two, I have gone back to Shion's past life as a young girl struggling to become a priestess of Lemuria. Her life in Lemuria is more complex, and she realizes it is not her own, that she has come to the blue planet, which they lovingly call Mother Earth, to help humankind, who has been led astray.

We learn how the dragonhorse was created, and we go into lost worlds only thought of as legend or myth. I will bring the realms of Lemuria and Agartha to you like you have never read before. I pick up where Jules Verne left off, but in keeping with the magic and wonder of this gypsy fairy tale: the love affair between a Lemurian priestess and her Fae, her dragons, and her horses.

If you loved book one of this saga, I promise you will love *Sumayah* as much as I do. You might even find yourself reading book one again, right after you read the last word of *Sumayah*.

For those of you who have not read *Dragonhorse and the Seeker of the Forgotten Knowledge*, I recommend you do so before reading *Sumayah*.

CHAPTER 1

DRAGON SCENT

ⓒℛ

The earth throbbed. The beat, quick and continuous, was a dead giveaway to what Sumayah knew approached. Holding her breath, she squinted and focused on the early-morning horizon in anticipation, waiting and watching as the growing, pale cloud of dust rolled right toward them. A tingling sensation coursed through her whole being, and her skin prickled. These beings had a hold on her, always had, but she knew not what the connection was.

Riva fidgeted noisily behind her. Sumayah jerked her head in the direction of the big-boned girl, narrowing her deep, sapphire-blue eyes in warning, and Riva obliged.

Sumayah turned her attention back to the approaching cloud. A hand tenderly sneaked its way into hers, and she smiled, knowing it was Jaylan.

"Is this what Mergus spoke of?" Jaylan whispered, barely audible over the thundering sound.

The question snapped Sumayah's thoughts back to the wizard's classroom so fast, she thought she felt her neck pop.

The tall wizard stroked a lock of his cascading white beard, a perfect match to his waist-length head of hair. He walked a few feet in one direction, spun on his silent booted heel, then seemingly floated in the opposite direction. His gray-blue eyes sparkled knowingly as he gazed at the two crystal pillars that towered fifty feet in the air as sentries to the gates of Lemuria. Twin dragons held fast to each pillar, long golden talons gripping the luminous obelisks as if only death would lessen their hold.

His gaze averted, he cleared his throat. Sumayah shifted nervously on the soft woven carpet beneath her backside as the wizard chose her to rest his sights on. A slight twinge to his lips hinted of a smile.

The wizard cleared his throat again and spoke. "They came long ago—in the beginning—one of only a few species allowed to come to Mother Earth along with us, from the realm of Arcturus. They had passed the Grand Inquisition and were allowed entrance, along with the phoenix, our most sacred bird. But be forewarned before you try to conquer these great beings, for they will test you. This will be the final and hardest test that you will be given before you can continue on to the teachings of the Goddess..."

"Oh, I pick that one," said Riva, pointing her long finger over Sumayah's shoulder, yanking her from Mergus's classroom.

"We can pick all we want, but it is up to them to choose us," said Sumayah, her words forced out between pursed lips of annoyance. Jaylan's grip on her hand tightened, and she turned to look into the pale sapphire eyes, then down to the slight smile on the girl's overly plump, pale-pink lips.

"They are beautiful," Jaylan said in a breathy whisper.

The rhythmic beat to the earth slowed, and the billowing cloud of dust began to clear as the massive herd slowed one by one to stop a few feet away from the treelined edge of the lake. The leader snorted at the tempting waters, making sure it was safe to drink—that no hidden dangers would suddenly spring from the glistening depths to clamp its massive jaws on her slender neck.

The girls knew what dangers lurked. Lemuria, a floating island secluded from the outside realm of the human race, was beautiful beyond words, but it harbored the most ferocious flesh-eating beasts one could only imagine. Lemurians, a gentle, highly spiritual race foreign to Earth, had come as a rescue mission over three thousand years ago to help the humans. They, the guardians of the skies who kept their ever-watchful eye on the evolution of man, had made the agonizing decision to intervene, even though it was decided prior to the birth of man to never interfere with its goings-on. The human was to be left alone with a will of its own, to create as it wished, but the unauthorized influx of the Reps, a violent, self-seeking race, had plunged the course of man into a downward spiral of self-destruction and planetary destruction.

Suddenly the leader of the herd snorted, then reared into the air, forcing a loud scream from her lungs. The whole herd flinched and turned, an instinctive response ingrained within them from a thousand years of being preyed upon. They did not wait to see what overshadowed them, and with a flurry of hooves grinding the earth, they tore with lightning speed under the cover of the gigantic weep trees. The trees, with their tendrils of silvery-green, slender limbs caressing the ground in the gentle breeze, made a natural cover for the herd.

Sumayah saw the shadow too, and her first instinct was to run, but she found that legs turned to stone did not move so well, unable to respond to her command as momentary panic overtook her. She felt Jaylan's fingernails dig deeply into her palm. She tried to pull her hand away, but a surprising and sudden jolt to her body sent her and Jaylan to the ground. Jaylan landed heavily on Sumayah's face, pushing it into the moist soil. The pungent smell of dampness and rotting leaves filled her nose. With her mouth and nose now full of earth's flesh, she could not speak. Her mind screamed, *I'm going to be eaten!*

Feeling another push of her face into the earth, she caught a glimpse of a plump ankle before the soil once again blocked her vision. Gathering her remaining strength, Sumayah rolled to the left, unsettling Jaylan, which in turn sent Riva onto her nose.

"Riva!" Shion yelled, digging dirt from her front teeth and nostrils and quickly scanning the sky for what had spooked the herd.

The ominous, black form collapsed at the edge of the lake. Sumayah's breath caught in her throat as she struggled for words. She grabbed Jaylan and yanked her close, then pointed to the figure and put her finger to her lips, shushing any comments that might startle it. She breathed in as a tiny breeze carried the scent of what she could only describe as a mixture of musk and lemons. The smell was unmistakably dragon scent.

All three girls squatted behind the cover of a hibiscus bush with flowers the size of their heads. The heavy, sweet aroma of flower now masked the scent of dragon.

3

"I saw it first!" rasped Riva, pulling one flower head to her nose.

"Well, why in the name of the Goddess did you jump on us?" Sumayah fired back, trying to keep her anger under control.

Just then the raven-black dragon lowered its long neck into the lake, plunging its head into the glistening waters. After a brief moment, it lifted its head out, sending the water cascading noisily back to the lake. It suddenly let out an earsplitting roar, making the girls cover their ears. They had never heard a dragon vocalize in such a manner before.

Sumayah's vision suddenly went blank, replaced with a veil of red light.

"It's wounded," she whispered. An uncontrollable urge freed her legs of stone, and she took one step toward the dragon. Two hands grabbed at her shoulders, forcing her around.

"You cannot go near a wounded dragon," pleaded Jaylan. "This one must be an outcast—a loner."

"Hush, the Goddess has given me vision; I must heed her urgings and go to it."

"Sumayah, I'm scared. Don't leave us here alone," whispered Riva, wavering a bit on her shaking legs.

"Riva, don't you dare faint!" ordered Sumayah, putting out a hand to steady her.

The dragon belched out another agonizing roar and collapsed at the lake's edge with a loud thud, sending up a wide spray of water as its head disappeared under the lake.

"Oh, it will drown! Come on, we have to save it!" ordered Sumayah, running to the beast and dragging the girls with her. They half struggled against Sumayah, but the excitement of possibly healing a dragon surpassed their fears.

They reached the lake's edge. The herd, still under the shelter of the weep trees, watched with wary but curious eyes.

Bubbles gurgled to the surface of the water and popped.

"It still lives, but not for long if we don't drag that head out," said Sumayah as they crept cautiously toward their patient.

They maneuvered to the front of it, Jaylan and Riva hugging on to her like a wet cloak. Sumayah slowly reached her shaking hand out to rest on the glistening black-green scales. It surprisingly was not hard or rough, but smooth and yielding under her hand, and as she rubbed harder, dragon scent wafted to her nose. Braver, she poked at it, which sent up more

4

bubbles from the bottom of the lake. Suddenly realizing the urgency, she splashed into the water. Searching with her hands, she followed the neck until she reached the head.

"Help me, girls!" she groaned, yanking at the boulder-size head. It gave slightly, and she tried again with a grunt. Suddenly the heavy load became lighter as Jaylan and Riva each grabbed a hunk of dragon flesh.

"Together, girls, on the count of three! One, two, three!" ordered Sumayah. The head came out, and they struggled with the weight, bending it to the warm sand of the lake's edge; it landed with a heavy thud. The jolt of the landing sent water pouring from its mouth, and it made an eerie gurgling sound. This frightened Riva and Jaylan, sending them scrambling away on all fours to hide behind a red standing stone.

Sumayah scanned the dragon. She had been this close before. She loved to visit Drakaous the dragon lord that lived in Crystal Cove right outside of Lemuria. He was a wise and kind dragon and loved to tell her stories of his journeys on Earth. But this dragon seemed different. Besides the obvious, something about this one made her heart feel different. She couldn't put her finger on it. When she stepped closer, something glinted and flashed, blocking her sight for a second. Changing her position brought it into sight. It was a long-sword, belonging to humans. *What would a human sword be doing in this dragon so far away?* She knew from Drakaous that human men had begun to hunt dragon flesh. As to why, he could not tell her, but those young, loner dragons that left the island of Lemuria never returned.

"This one must have been to the realm of men," she explained to the girls still camped behind the boulder. "It has a long-sword behind its shoulder. I really should pull it out. You two look for comfrey and yarrow." She turned her sapphire eyes on the two. "And be quick about it!"

I wonder if I even have the strength to pull the sword from its wound, and worse yet, will it be so angry and hurt that it will awaken and eat me?

"Goddess, help me," she said aloud and tried three hand grips on the sword before she felt she had the right combination to yank it out, hopefully without awakening the large beast. A small bead of sweat ran down the side of her face. She ignored it and slowly, steadily, began tugging on the sword. *Oh, come out, please come out.* Then, with a strange squeaking sound, it slid out an inch, releasing the flow of dragon blood. *Oh, no—no, don't do that.*

"Please hurry with the yarrow, he's bleeding badly." Once again she pulled on the sword, and this time it gave much easier. She backed away from the dragon until the sword dislodged completely. Another bead of sweat ran down her face to pool at the corner of her lip. She licked at it, tasting the salt.

Riva came panting with exertion, shoved a large handful of herbs into her hands, and then quickly spun on her heel and dove behind the stone.

"Some priestess you will be," Sumayah chanted over her shoulder as she carefully packed the green medicine into the gaping sword wound. Not knowing what else to do, she backed away from the dragon to the shelter of the rock.

"I think we should send it healing...Do you think we have the power to do it?" asked Jaylan, looking down at her hands.

But before the question could be further explored, the winged beast shifted its weight.

The sound of a gasp reached Sumayah's ears, and she realized it was her own, for Riva was lying in a heap behind her, with Jaylan kneeling at her side.

Oh, Riva! Sumayah smirked, then watched as the dragon shifted again, then rolled slowly to a half-sitting position. It turned its massive head to look directly at her, then beyond her. Its large crimson-rimmed nostrils sucked in the air from her direction. The expression in its deep amber-orange eyes changed from wonder to recognition and widened, exposing white rims as panic set in. It struggled to its hindquarters and let out a long hiss.

Sumayah's heart filled with sorrow, for she did not feel danger from the beast but only fear. She knew it wanted to put as much distance between her and itself as it could. *What happened to you? What did the humans do to make you so fearful—well, besides running you through?*

A whistle behind her alerted her. It was Mesha; he had come to check on them. The whistle startled the dragon all the more. It limped along the lakeshore, gaining speed, huffing and puffing as if to conjure more strength with its fiery breath. Then with a mighty groan, it went airborne, catching and riding the late-morning breeze into the blinding rays of sunlight.

Mesha was upon them in an instant. Jaylan ran to him, panting. "Did you see it?"

6

Mesha frowned down at the raven-haired girl. "You were supposed to be letting the herd get used to your scent. Not mingling scents with a dragon."

"Mesha, we were watching the herd when the dragon practically fell out of the sky onto them." Sumayah pointed into the weep trees. "See, they are hidden there still."

Sumayah watched as he dismounted from his white stallion. She remembered the day he had stumbled half dead into Lemuria almost two hundred years ago. He had been her constant companion ever since. To this day no one knew of his plight, for he would not speak of it. Though she had tried many a time, he would not "go there." His black hair glinted like freshly polished onyx, and his brown eyes bore into her, sending a slight shiver through her body. He was the catch of Lemuria; all upcoming priestesses wanted him, though Sumayah did not know why. Maybe it was his mysterious past? Or maybe the strange sensation she felt in her stomach when he was near was felt by all the young women in Lemuria.

His voice brought her from her thoughts. "Tell me of this dragon…"

"It had a man sword in its—its side," interrupted Riva, brushing sage from her crumpled skirt.

"I pulled it out, Mesha—it did not harm me," said Sumayah. "It was more scared of us than we were of it! What would terrify a dragon in such a manner?"

"Reps." Mesha spit the word. "I have heard from the Fae that Reps have a bounty on all dragon flesh. They have the humans killing every one that comes to their land. I fear once they have them eradicated there, they will leave their lands to look for more…and come here."

"Why on this Earth would they want the dragons dead?" asked Sumayah. "I don't understand such thinking."

"I do not have an answer, but I do know the lord of the Fae is very worried and seeks council with the king—your king."

Sumayah could not stop the excitement in her voice at Mesha's statement.

"Lord Fallonay is coming! Will—will he be bringing his son, Ryven?" Immediately she put her hand to her mouth. Speaking the name *Ryven* in front of Mesha always seemed to make him simmer inside…as it was doing right now. Wanting to take the scowl off his face, she quickly added, "I bet Princess Elspeth will attend also."

The last sentence only made his scowl grow all the more, until his right nostril flared into the most unappealing manner.

"Come, enough of the Fae...you were sent here to mingle your scent with the king's herd. Have you picked any yet?" he asked, bending to look in the forest of trees.

"We were afraid to get too close...we didn't want them to dimension shift," replied Jaylan, also bending to look into the forest. "You know how easily they do that."

"Well, if you were up on your studies, you would shift right with them, wouldn't you?" Mesha said in exchange.

Sumayah interrupted. "Mesha, you know we are not yet ready for such a magic task. Why, even Mergus shifts only for dire circumstances and not just to follow a herd of horses."

"Well, do what you must or mustn't, but for you girls to pass into the level of priestess, you *must* bring a horse."

"I don't really like horses all that much," Riva chimed in. "They make me sneeze."

"Riva, you know that the horse is the only being that can project your true inner self, expressing outwardly your—what's the right word I'm looking for—readiness," lectured Sumayah. "And it is the only being that will allow your companionship if you can raise your level of vibration to its own, a level needed to be reached in order to become priestess," she continued, reciting the words of her mother, Lhayan, a master at horsemanship who had several companion horses of her own.

Sumayah puffed out her chest. "I will go first. I have been practicing— it cannot be that difficult. Why, just look at Mesha and his stallion. If he can do it, I can do it."

Mesha snorted at her statement. "Well, get on with it, little priestess-to-be." He grabbed her by the shoulders and shoved her toward the trees where the herd watched contentedly, chewing on sweet grass.

Jaylan stepped forward with her, but Mesha stayed her with his arm. "Let her go first...would be best if one at a time went."

Sumayah took a deep breath. *Think like Mergus—think priest, but in my case, think priestess. Yes, I'm raising my level of vibration now...I can feel it.* She stepped forward once, than stepped forward again. *Maybe if I whistle a nice tune, they won't shift.* She puckered up her lips and blew. Nothing. She blew again much harder. The sound was not sweet and lulling. It came out loud, long, and raspy like a beast snort, which in turn sent the herd deeper into the trees.

She felt her determination wane; she could feel the stares of Mesha, Jaylan, and Riva searing her back. She had to move forward, had to keep pushing on. *Forget the whistle, that was stupid. What would Mother do?* Taking another step, then another, brought her closer to the herd. She saw many pairs of golden-brown eyes peering through the cover of leaves at her. One of them stomped its foot. She froze in her tracks.

A bead of sweat ran down the side of her face. She ignored the temptation to wipe it away. But it was strong. The sweat traveled farther and farther down, tickling all the way. The urge to wipe was much stronger now, and it tickled. *No, don't do it, don't put that hand up*, she screamed within herself! Ah, but too late. The temptation became too strong, and up went her hand. And as she had figured, in the blink of her eye, the herd shifted into the next dimension.

"Mind control, Sumayah, and today you did not exhibit the control over mind that was needed," lectured Mesha. "If you cannot stop your body parts from flailing needlessly, you will never move up to priestess."

Sumayah heard none of Mesha's bantering. A vision of Ryven, his waist-length, chocolate-black hair, and piercing, crystal-green eyes flooded her mind. She had only seen him one other time. But that was all it took to forever etch the young Fae into her mind and heart.

CHAPTER 2

RYVEN

❦

"**W**ho are you watching, Ryven?"

Ryven, startled, felt his heart beat in his chest. *Thump, thump, thump.*

"Elspeth, why do you insist on sneaking around? I could have run you through. It's not like the old days, you know!"

The elegant Fae stepped from behind him to see what had his attention. "Ah, I *see*...she is sprouting like a well-tended rose, is she not?" she teased.

Not wanting his sister to see his blush, he did not look at her when he spoke. "I was watching Mesha." Than it dawned on him what she might be doing here, and he spun to face her.

"Why, Elspeth, what might you be looking at? Might it be the *handsome,* raven-like creature with them?" He let out a chuckle, knowing he had her this time.

"Ryven, whatever do you mean? We know that Sumayah is promised to him. So why would I waste my time?" She ended her sentence by flicking an invisible speck from her luminous gown.

He knew all too well whom Sumayah was promised to. But today, watching the two of them interact made it all too real. Besides, he knew his father, Lord Fallonay, would never consent to a communion between a Fae and a Lemurian, even though she *could* live for another nine hundred years or more. He sighed and looked at his sister.

"I was tracking a loner—a big male. He must have wandered to the realm of men." He paused a moment, watching Sumayah and her entourage leave. "It was badly wounded and even very fearful of the Lemurians. I fear his dealings with the humans did not bode well."

Elspeth rested her hand on his arm. "As would be expected. I cannot believe he made it back to our island. What happened? Where did he go?"

Ryven couldn't suppress his grin as he recounted how the girls had administered to it.

"Sumayah did display a great show of courage when she pulled the long-sword from its shoulder. Once the sword was dislodged, it gathered enough strength to fly."

Elspeth frowned in concern. "Come, brother, Lord Fallonay awaits your presence. The dragon will most likely make its way to Mergus and Drakaous, or he could be in Faeria right now."

Ryven turned to see Black waiting patiently for him. Ryven patted the big horse lovingly, then swung himself on his back. Elspeth whistled to her mount, which was grazing quietly. The pearl-white mare nickered in answer and trotted to Elspeth.

"I just don't understand why you chose a unicorn. They are so independent, Elspeth."

Elspeth chuckled softly at his comment. "Ryven, it takes a female touch to acquire a unicorn. Yes, they can be as unpredictable—as a woman. We understand each other. And besides—she picked me."

The mare nodded her head at Elspeth, whose pure-white, silken tresses flowed in motion almost to her knee.

Ryven patted Black. "Black and I have an understanding too. Let's go, boy," he urged, and all four took off at a healthy, ground-eating canter.

Faeria was within the realm of Lemuria; the Lemurians and the Fae harmoniously shared the island. You knew when you arrived in Faeria by the change in atmosphere and landscape. Faeria was the mecca of three-hundred-foot-tall willow trees...unlike the weep trees, the willow trunks were doubly wide, with far-reaching, intertwining roots that came above, then went below in the soft green earth like some elemental work of art.

Some of the Fae lived within the trunks of the trees and the weavings of the gray-brown, intricately carved-out roots and limbs. Some even chose to live fifty feet or higher in the swaying coolness of the enormous and thickly leaved canopy. The leafy limbs interlocked in such a way, they became a perfect roof for the inhabitants.

The climate, though temperate, had been known to bring sudden weather changes that could be unpleasantly wet. The forest and its dwellers were also protected by the Faerian Ridge, the northern end of the mountains of Lemuria, raggedly sharp, jutting skyward as barrier to the often-savage and relentless beating the island took from the waves of the endless ocean that stretched beyond the island, separating them from the realm of man.

Ryven loved his home and could not suppress a smile as the ever-present smell of jasmine flowers sensuously swaddling the feminine curves and lines of the willows filled his nostrils with a heady sweetness. It naturally calmed him as he and Elspeth entered the city.

Tial, a winged elemental was there to meet them. Ryven swiped at her lavender and pale-yellow iridescent wings as they fluttered too close to his face. She easily avoided his halfhearted movement and closed one bright aqua eye in a quick wink.

Pushing a strand of white-blond hair behind her ear, she said, "Welcome back, Ryven and Elspeth. The lord is waiting for you. He instructed me to watch for your return and bring you to him without delay."

"Why, thank you, Tial," replied Elspeth as she dismounted, letting the unicorn amble away.

A short while later, Ryven and his sister stood before the council of Lord Fallonay. Lord Fallonay was a proud, striking man. His jet-black hair, braided with eye-catching strands of ribbon, hung thick and heavy to his waist over his elegant robe of iridescent green and black. The sleeves were long and deep, his hands gathered at his solar plexus in a white-knuckle grip.

Ryven gulped, noticing the ever-present twitch of Lord Fallonay's left cheek. He knew he had inherited the same telltale sign, warning everyone how serious or urgent the matter at hand was. Elspeth pressed her warm hand in his. This comforted him, and together they stood in front of the stern, yet compassionate ruler of Faeria.

"I am so *very* honored that you two took time from your day to grace me with your presence." He winked at them, his meticulously groomed left eyebrow arching downward.

Must be very important since all of the Faerian court has been summoned, Ryven thought. He looked about the room as his father addressed the throngs of beautiful beings who stood hanging on his every word. Each one dressed much the same as the lord, some in a lighter shade of green or a deep orange gold. Some choose to plait their untouched, never-cut locks of hair, and some let them hang in a long continuous wave of glistening mane.

Those who were too short to watch this most important gathering, hovered silently as if they were standing on an invisible strand of hair, extended from one end of the courtyard to the next. It was quite a spectacle of brightly colored wings, in every hue imaginable. The constant flutter reminded Ryven of the hummingbirds that lived near the honeysuckle and jasmine. Just the thought filled his nose once again with the sweet musk of jasmine.

Lord Fallonay motioned for his two most prized possessions to sit next to him on ornately carved and polished stools of oak wood.

There was a sudden hush as attendees of the meeting began to separate, leaving a long and wide opening to the courtyard. *What is Drakaous doing here? He hasn't been seen in court for many years.* Ryven watched the dragon, even with his great size, nimbly come forward, making sure to keep his enormous silver-black wings tucked in and out of the way. Drakaous's large blood-orange eyes spied Ryven, and he gave him a slight nod. Ryven could not stop the feeling of his hair trying to crawl off his head as the grand beast proudly walked by. Dragons always had this strange effect on him. Something about the communing of energies, he was once told. Not only did the presence of the dragon make his hair prickle, but dragon scent was also unmistakable. He admitted he did enjoy the smell.

"Drakaous, it has been much too long!" Lord Fallonay said, walking up to the towering dragon. He held out his hand to give him an affectionate pat.

"I know why you have summoned me," Drakaous replied, his proud stance softening a bit. "Times are changing, Fallonay. T'is not the same. Too many beings have conjured their way to the realm of Earth, even though uninvited. All of the careful designing and planning now means nothing."

Lord Fallonay patted the strongly molded flesh. "Drakaous, don't look so defeated. We knew from the very beginning there would always be a chance that it would not go as planned. We must make the best of what comes our way—and if it be bad—so be it. I am ready for a good challenge!"

The silent courtyard became alive with chatter. Lord Fallonay stood listening for a moment, then held up his hand.

"Please, please, our times have not yet become so desperate. This is why I have summoned Drakaous." Slowly he turned his head, scanning the gathering.

"We must remember who we are—and why we have come to dwell upon this chosen realm. We have been here from the very beginning, for we *are* the air, as sylphs that flutter in the breeze of our breath. We *are* the earth, as gnomes that bring body and foundation. We *are* the fire, as salamanders of the creative flames that we live and learn by. We *are* water, as undines, the tides of emotion that rock to and fro. We *know* that we are what holds our Earth from separating into nonexistence. We *are* the elements that have created her! Without the elements there is nothing. But how do you make a human understand this? Their minds have been shut by the self-seeking tutoring's of the Reps..."

His last words trailed off as he stood in deep contemplation. His hand went up, and his finger smoothed his thin right brow.

"Fallonay, the Reps have control over the humans, though the humans are in the belief that *they* are in control," explained Drakaous with a heavy sigh. "Their illusion of life will surely bring them to an end, and all will be lost!"

Ryven did not like what he was hearing, and a vision of the wounded dragon filled his mind. He rose from his wooden stool and turned to his father.

"What part do the Lemurians have in this?"

Drakaous's slumped form straightened once again to his enormous stature. His nostrils flared as he looked at Ryven, and then took in a deep, long breath. His gesture unnerved everyone, and most took a few tentative steps back. The dragon could not help but let his lip curl up into a grin.

"Master Ryven, they *now* have a great part in this. Even though they had come only as a scouting party in the beginning..." The dragon's voice trailed off, and he stared into the distance.

This is new information, and noteworthy, thought Ryven. *Can I use this information to my advantage somehow?* After watching Sumayah today, all he could think about was finding a way to get to closer her, to know more about her.

"There was an accident...," Drakaous began again. "It was most tragic, and something had transpired, though I must confess I do not have knowledge of what that was, but those left behind after the accident were told they must now become part of the 'scheme of things, the goings-on of Earth."

Lord Fallonay turned to Ryven. "Then we must have council with the Lemurians. Whether they wanted it or not, they are part of this world now, and must take their role in the original design."

Ryven's heart quickened. He knew what that meant. "Will we be going then? Will I go too?" he asked.

Lord Fallonay's eyes narrowed at his son in thought. "Yes, both of my children will accompany me to Lemuria."

Before Lord Fallonay could utter another word, Ryven blurted out, "I watched the king's daughters today!" He felt the questioning eyes upon him; he knew they all wondered why he would be watching the Lemurian priestesses. Speaking quickly to appease their stares, he said, "I was on the trail of a loner. It was wounded—had a long-sword stuck in its shoulder. Sumayah tended to it!"

Drakaous, finding Ryven's blurting's most interesting, stepped closer to him and put one long, black talon on his shoulder.

"Tell me of this loner."

"The king's daughters were shadowing the king's herd in hopes of gaining trust. The dragon literally dropped out of the sky—almost on the herd! It would have drowned had not Sumayah and her sisters pulled his head from the bottom of the lake!"

"It must have gone to the realm of man. Impudent, young fool! Did he not know what he would find there?" Drakaous spat out angrily, his blood-orange eyes rolling wildly.

Ryven had never seen the dragon so upset. The big guy was always most amicable and much more soft-spoken.

"Once Sumayah pulled the sword free, the dragon soon awoke and took flight—to where, I do not know."

"And what of the girls?" the dragon asked, leaning in closer, his hot breath settling on Ryven.

Elspeth stood from her stool and took the few short steps to the conversation.

"I found Ryven still watching as the herd dimension shifted. Once the herd was gone, the girls left. But Ryven spoke of the dragon's great fear of Sumayah. Why would that be?" she asked.

"Because he had gone to the realm of man!" answered Lord Fallonay, now pacing the front of the courtyard. "Does this mean they come closer?" he asked, stopping in front of Drakaous.

"That is precisely why I have come. They have been spotted in boats nearing our shores. I fear the Reps are behind this."

Tial took this moment to flutter close to Fallonay and interjected, "We have heard they cut and burn the great living forests. Some of our relations who must tend to the four elements in the realm of man have come back to us with many harrowing stories..." Tial paused and took a deep sigh before she began again. "The worst that has been reported is...is that most humans no longer gather or grow their food—they have turned to eating flesh."

The last word sent the room into a moment of shocked silence. A few gasps could be heard, and one Fae woman even fell to the earth in a dead faint.

The winged Fae left their respectful distance and now hovered near the lord. Their voices droned on about the many atrocities.

"Drakaous is right. If we do not take note of what is happening, our world will collapse around us," added Tial. "I fear my relations will soon leave their homes. If they do, we know what will happen to the lands. We know what terrors will ensue from the imbalance."

Drakaous stepped toward the crowd. "We do know what will ensue. The great Earth Mother will begin to pull apart, with us hanging on for one hell of a ride. A ride I fear I do not want to partake of." He turned his head to Fallonay. "I leave for Lemuria. I will prepare the king for your arrival.

Lord Fallonay put his hand to Drakaous. "Make sure he does not bring...her," he whispered.

CHAPTER 3

THE VISION

Ᏸ

*T*he sudden rapid pounding of hooves awoke her with a jolt. Feeling dizzy, she scrambled up the slippery, hot rocks, hurriedly gathering her scattered clothing. A curse escaped her lips as she tripped, trying to get her foot into the opening of her skirt. The rider had come upon them so fast, she could only yank up her skirt and hold her tunic in front of her. The wolf growled loudly as the horseman approached, giving her only a slight sense of protection. She noticed with a frown that the knife kept in her skirt pocket had fallen out and was halfway down the rocks.

Seeing the wolf and half-naked girl, the muscular, black horse came to a sliding halt, his deep, red nostrils flared.

"Steady there, my friend. I do doubt this half-naked waif can harm us," soothed the young rider. The great horse spun; the raven-haired young man craned his neck around. His crystal-green eyes locked on her. His thick, dark brow came together as he studied her and her wolf.

"Are you not afraid of the ghosties?" the young man asked, a slight grin spreading across his face. The black steed reared, pawing the air. "There, there, Black, tis rude not to stop and chat when you come upon a true and lovely faerie of the woods!"

So he thinks he is charming, *she thought. Sticking her nose in the air to peer at him sideways, she replied, "I have no reason to fear the spirits at this place. I have been coming here since I was a wee girl."* She could feel the heat in her face rise from *the fluttering sensations of attraction. Besides his elfish—yes, that's the word—elfish good looks, she had never seen a man handle a horse in such a controlling, yet gentle manner. That intrigued her more than his appearance—granted, he did have great appeal sitting so confidently upon his stallion, but it was his horsemanship that made her forget she was half dressed. She was so lost in her self-banter, she was startled when he spoke to her.*

"Well, my lady," he said, then let out a loud laugh, *"I will carry on and leave you to your—endeavors. Might I give you a warning first?"* He flashed a toothy *smile, his eyes expressing the enjoyment of her manner of undress. "I would cover yourself...you just never know who you might meet in these woods. Not all are as honorable as I."* With that said, he clucked to his black steed, and they loudly cantered off. He managed to turn his head to take one last look before he disappeared into the tag alders...

Sirius took that moment to land with a flapping flurry next to Sumayah as she lay in her altered state. The slap of the feathery wings on her face wrenched her from her vision.

"Sirius!" she hollered at the golden-red phoenix staring at her intently. Sitting up, she stroked the raptor, loving the silky softness of her gold-tipped hackles. "If you would have given me just a short while longer, I would know who this mysterious horseman is," she said, planting a light kiss on the large raptor's head. The raptor, loving the attention, nuzzled closer.

Just who is this horseman that keeps appearing in my visions? He seems so very familiar to me. I must talk with Mergus about this. He will help me. But, her thoughts were taken away by a shrill whinny off in the distance. Standing quickly, she searched the shadows beneath the weep trees. The usual rhythmic pounding of hooves on soil could not be heard. *This one is alone. But why? This could work to my advantage.* Her eyes watered as she concentrated on the shadows. She blinked once and then blinked again. Her vision soon returned, and she saw a filly standing at the lake's edge.

Sumayah sucked in her breath at the beauty before her. She had never seen such a color. Gold was as close as she could describe it, but a pale gold—not yellow, but an iridescent white gold. The filly was young—three, she guessed. But she was exquisite, with a snakelike neck attached

20

to a well-balanced frame and the longest, finest legs Sumayah had ever witnessed on a horse. *Who was your mama? The king would be most pleased to see you!*

The filly must have spotted Sumayah, because she jerked her head up, ears twitching to catch any sound. She let out a snort. Her tail raised, and she spun. But instead of running off into another dimension, she relaxed and turned. Her large, soft eyes connected with Sumayah.

Sumayah held her breath and walked out from the cover of the house-size fern. It brushed at her cheek as she walked past. She tried to recollect Mergus's instruction. Something about matching energy...or more like matching one's level of frequency or vibration to the other. She knew from listening to her father that horses were very sensitive. They can hear a sound coming from far, far away. They can even hear your heartbeat, so you must always maintain a steady, calm beat. Her heart pounded uncontrollably. *Steady, steady there, Sumayah. Take a deep breath and will your heart to slow.* To her amazement it worked. Her heart calmed, and she took one step closer, then another. By this time Sirius had become bored and had flown off to find something else to bother.

The filly stood as if mesmerized by Sumayah's approach. Her delicately molded lips played with the air as if to catch a scent of the nearing Lemurian.

Just a few more steps, and I will have you in my grasp. Sumayah's hand itched to feel the softness of the filly, and she took another step, but something suddenly changed. The filly snorted and reared straight into the air. Not wanting to lose her, Sumayah ran the last few steps, sending her right under the filly. The filly's flailing front legs came down with a heavy thud. Sumayah grunted as one sharp hoof landed squarely on her right shoulder. The impact sent Sumayah face-first into the soft soil. *Oh, dirt tastes awful.* The filly whinnied again and circled Sumayah twice.

Something else was here, and Sumayah twisted her body; her flesh prickled in warning. Panic rose, and she feared looking up at what it might be. The filly ran around her as if trying to protect her. Then a hair-raising, hideous scream pierced the air, ending in a toothy hiss. The filly bolted and dimension shifted clear out of sight.

The foul smell, the scream, and the hiss told Sumayah exactly what she needed to know. She braced as she slowly came to her knees and looked over her left shoulder. The twitching of the tail gave up its hiding spot. Her mind raced. *Long-tooth cat, brought to our world by the Reps. I have no protection. I cannot dimension shift like the filly yet. I don't have the learned powers yet. I am too young, too young for power, too young to die. Why, I am only three hundred years old!*

The horse-sized cat crouched behind the overgrown wild roses, twitching with the anticipation of a kill. Claws extended and dug into the moist soil. The strong scent of musk and foul breath made its way to Sumayah, unnerving her all the more. Her heart pummeled her chest painfully. Her body convulsed, and her teeth chattered loudly as she prepared to leave this lifetime. *Mergus will be so disappointed in me.*

The cat once again let out a low growl that ended in a hiss. It took two steps, exposing itself fully. Muscle on muscle twitched and bulged. Its upper lip quivered, two dagger-like teeth protruded from its mouth. It took another step closer to her and crouched lower.

Sumayah felt her stomach roll and threaten to come up her throat. She knew the cat would be on her now. She held her arms in front of her, hoping to hold off the gigantic beast as it leaped so easily, so gracefully, right at her. Her eyes automatically closed in defense...

Suddenly a great *whoosh* of air hit her—well, she thought it was air, until it knocked her to the ground. A clump of dirt hit her square in the face and splattered into her peeking eyes. She blinked the dirt away, listening to the horrendous sounds of guttural growls, snarls, and a sort of bellowing that ensued around her.

Desperate to see, she wiped at the dirt, glimpsing bits and pieces of the carnage before her. Never in her life did she think she would witness a battle between a dragon and a cat. She knew this one would be till death.

The silver-black tail of the dragon lashed out and slammed into the cat and sent it airborne. It wildly grappled for something to hold on to as it landed heavily. Its enormous claws desperately clung to soil as the dragon latched on to it, dragging it backward. It let out a hideous cry and twisted toward its attacker. The black beast clamped its massive jaws around the neck of the cat and chomped down. The sickening crunch of yielding flesh and bone sent shivers through Sumayah. She stood frozen, not sure what to do. Her palm pulsated with energy in response to the battered creature that stood only a few feet away.

The cat was dead silent. The dragon pushed at it one last time, then lifted its head to gaze at Sumayah. Trails of blood ran down the fresh wounds near its large blood-orange eyes. A stench of rotting flesh filled the air, and with a mournful cry, it hefted itself into the air and flew into the amber glow of the setting sun.

It still lives, but by the smell of it, not for long. But why on Mother Earth did it save me, it seemed so afraid the last time it saw me? Her hand still pulsated with energy. It might be alive now, but that smell meant trouble. She knew the old sword wound needed more tending to. Grateful for what it had done for her, she felt strongly compelled to search for it, to help it. But how do you follow something that flies, just like how do you follow a filly that can dimension shift?

She noticed the sun sinking farther into the horizon, and that was her sign to get back home. Carefully she tiptoed up to the mangled cat and gave it a good kick. The muscles twitched in response, which sent her into a run. She would explain to her father that they must search for the dragon, the dragon that saved her life.

As she neared the crystal pillars at the city gates, Mesha ran out to meet her. His handsome, dark face was etched with worry, his heavy brows were knitted into a deep frown.

"Don't look in such a manner, or your face could stay that way," she said to him with a laugh.

"Where have you been?" He grabbed at her arm and stopped her to give her the once-over. "By the looks of you, you got yourself into trouble again."

"How am I to become a full-fledged priestess if everyone is always so concerned about my whereabouts? If you must know, I was looking for the herd. And I found the one. Oh, you should just see her. She is magnificent, exquisite. Father will be so pleased!"

Mesha let go of her arm and began wiping away the soil still smeared under her eye. "You do not look like a priestess with all this dirt."

She pushed away his hand and stomped her foot. "Well, Mesha, not only did I find the one, but I was attacked by a long-tooth!"

Mesha's jaw dropped, contorting his handsome face once again. A strand of silken black hair fell in front of his bulging eyes. He roughly turned her around one way, then the other.

"I see no wounds. Are you hurt? What—how?" He grabbed her to him in a snakelike embrace.

Sumayah *let* him hold her for a moment. It felt safe. He felt strong, and he smelled pretty darned good, like lavender and rosemary after a fresh rain.

"Mesha, it was that dragon again," she mumbled into his chest. "It killed the long-tooth!" She pulled from his crushing embrace and looked into his deep-set black eyes. "It is not mending from the sword wound. I want to look for it, to see if I can help it." She studied his expression and what little she saw made her wonder. He *was* hard to read.

"Sumayah, it is a loner. It came from the realm of man. It is not like the dragons here on Lemuria. It could be a rogue."

What is he talking about? Rouge? If it was a rogue, why did it save me? This was the first she had ever heard about rogue dragons. Somewhat angered, she turned and walked into the inner city without a word.

Mesha followed her, and they walked through the glistening city of pearl-white buildings. Each home had its own smaller crystal pillars, which gave the city its energy. It was pure and clean. Between each home ran a sparkling stream of fresh water, which also helped control the atmosphere in the city. The air was not dry and harsh, but temperate and soft upon the skin. Dust and grime were unheard of. The Lemurians fit their city, for they were as beautiful as their city.

Mergus lived on the outskirts nearer to the sea; he wanted to keep clear of the "commotion" of city life. His home was humble; some say it was a mix between a tree dwelling in Faeria and a Lemurian home. He liked to dwell closer to the trees—said they were the best and fastest route of information past and present, with a little future thrown in.

"Why must you bother Mergus with this, Sumayah?" Mesha ran in front of her, giving her one of his "looks," raising his eyebrow in disapproval.

"He knows the dragons the best. He councils with Drakaous and his brothers and knows all there is to know about them."

Mesha put out a hand to try to slow her, but she pushed past it. "You know he does not like unannounced visitations."

This time Sumayah stopped. She looked questioningly at Mesha. *Why does he not want me to talk to Mergus?*

"It is getting late, Mesha. Do not slow me any longer, for I will not be able to see the wizard...or is that what you intend?" She gave him a long look, then spun and walked even faster toward the wizard's dwelling.

"Then I leave you to your endeavors," was all he said and let her go the rest of the way alone.

She paid him no mind. She had had two encounters with this one drag-on and knew there was magic behind it. *I wonder if the old wizard will tell me of this dragon. He must surely know something.*

Seashells dangled from a thin cord hung in a tree on the path just before the wizard's door. Sumayah gave them a flick, and they bounced off one another with a merry little tune, alerting the magician within.

Sumayah stood waiting for him to come out and was rewarded by his twinkling eye and knowing smile.

"Ah, Sumayah, always so good to have your company. I was just playing my flute," he said, holding up the hand-honed, polished wood instrument. He put it to his lips, and his fingers expertly touched each hole, bringing forth a sweet melodic sound not unlike the shells she had just passed. He did not play long and abruptly pulled it out of his mouth. His one eyes narrowed in thought.

"You have come for answers, and I am afraid I will not have those an-swers that you seek."

How did he know what I am going to ask? But then again, maybe he does not know what I will be asking. She hoped for the latter and walked forward to receive his embrace.

The old wizard smelled of sea spray and nettle water.

Sirius pulled another impromptu appearance and landed on the tree holding the seashell chimes. She plucked at it until it tinkled sweetly.

"See, Mergus, even she knows how to announce her presence." She walked to the raptor and stroked the long black feathers that sprung out of the top of her head just above her black-rimmed eyes. "Where have you been, sweetie?"

"She has been with the black one. The one you seek answers about." He smiled, and winked then said, "Sirius just told me."

"We must find the dragon. It is dying—I must find it and save its life like it saved mine." The words tumbled quickly out of her mouth, hoping he would not just send her away.

His somber expression changed when she mentioned it had saved her life.

"Child, tell me what happened." He motioned for her to come and sit by him on a small wooden bench.

She recounted the story, and when she finished, she sat watching him closely. His only expression was that of his left eye narrowing. She knew that he was pulling up memories or conjurations from somewhere in the deep and ancient recesses of his mind.

"I knew a dragon long, long, ago. His name was…" The wizard paused and lowered his head and gave her a slight smile, then said, "Nero was his name, but this could not possibly be the same dragon."

CHAPTER 4

HOW TO FIND A DRAGON

☙

"How could you be so certain this is not the same?" she asked. "Let's not speak of this dragon, for…he…he fell," Mergus whispered.

Suddenly a shadow cast upon them, and they both looked to the darkening sky.

"Looks like I have more company!" Mergus said with delight at the intrusion and shuffled quickly toward the shadowy figure that landed with a loud *whoosh* of air.

"Drakaous? What is he doing here?" she asked, following Mergus.

"Why, old friend, what brings you to us this night?" he asked, putting his hand up to pat the large frame of the ebony dragon.

"I come to seek council with you. I have just come from Faeria and have spoken with Lord Fallonay. There is much unrest in the realm of man. Word from elementals in that region has alerted us to trouble heading our way."

"We must take your news to the king immediately." Mergus turned to Sumayah. "Would you be so kind as to prepare the king for our arrival?"

Sumayah nodded. *Unrest in the realm of man. What would that mean for them?* She hurried past the king's stables and up the winding and steep pathway to the king's private chambers. As she approached, she could smell the ever-present scent of burnt sage, a daily ritual performed by her mother to keep harm from their sleeping chambers.

She could hear murmuring as she pulled aside the silken drapes that separated the chambers from the outdoors. Two tall crystals the color of the early-morning sun glowed brightly throughout the room.

"Rupert, my dear, we have a visitor."

The king turned and smiled warmly, his golden eyes sparkled brightly in the glow of the crystal light. He reached out one brown-skinned arm to receive his daughter.

"Sumayah, you look worried. Why have you come?"

"Mergus sent me ahead to tell you that he and Drakaous would have council with you." She let her father hug her close, and she pressed her head to his broad chest. He was not a tall man, but he was strong, and some would say overly kindhearted.

"I saw this coming, Rupert; I felt the nearness of Faeria this morning. It involves them too," replied Lhayan.

All three walked beyond the curtains to see wizard and dragon already at the base of the smoothly honed coral stairs.

"It must be very important to see both of you here. What news have you from Faeria?" Rupert asked with a welcoming smile.

Neither looked fazed at the king's question. It was Drakaous who spoke first.

"I have just come from council with Lord Fallonay. There has been word from elementals from the realm of man. The Reps, with their uninvited arrival on Earth, have greatly altered the original plan. Lord Fallonay would like to come to Lemuria and speak with you about it."

Sumayah perked at the mention of the Fae coming to see them. "You mean the Fae are coming here...to Lemuria—when?" she asked.

Drakaous turned to her, then turned back to the king. "They come as soon as we will have them."

Rupert clapped his hands with glee. "Well, send them word. We will make ready for them. Or better yet—we will go to them! It has been far too long since I have set my eyes upon the beauty of Faeria." He turned to Lhayan. "I think I shall take Lhayan with me."

"Oh, could I please go too?" Sumayah asked excitedly.

Before the king could answer, two girls ran from the bedchambers and down the stairs.

"Oh, can we come too...can we?" It was Jaylan and Riva. They had been listening in the shadows.

Mergus laughed at the display, then cleared his throat and with a more serious tone asked, "Rupert, do you dare take Lady Lhayan with you?"

Lhayan walked to Mergus. Her golden halo of hair flowed like mist around her with each step. She put a comforting hand on the wizard's white robe.

"Mergus, it has been too long. I think it is now time."

"Lhayan," Drakaous said as he walked to her, his long tail scraping behind him. "Lord Fallonay expressed he was not ready to see you."

"Oh, that lottenberry-stuffed old faerie can just deal with her coming," said an exasperated Rupert. "It has been far too many years."

Sumayah wondered at her father's words, but only for a moment. The form of the black loner filled her mind, and she hurried to her father, almost tripping over Drakaous's tail.

"Father, I have to tell you what happened to me today!"

The king turned and gave her a quizzical stare. Everyone gave full attention and listened as Sumayah recounted her long-tooth attack and the reappearance of the loner.

Drakaous found this information most interesting and inched his hugeness closer to Sumayah and leaned down to her level.

"Lord Fallonay's son spoke of this loner. He was watching when you freed the dragon from the long-sword."

Ryven saw me with the dragon, but how and why? Her mind filled with images of the handsome Faerian.

"Mergus, I know you know something about this one," said Drakaous, shifting his attention to the wizard.

"I am not quite sure. We were just chatting...Sumayah and I—I have no idea who this loner could be until I see him."

As the two exchanged words, everyone listened. Sumayah devoured every morsel of information on both the Faerian and the dragon. *What is so mysterious about this one? Why is Mergus so reluctant to talk about this dragon?* The sudden stench of death filled her nostrils, and her hand pulsated. The rest of the conversation was now a puppet act with no sound. She was so lost in what her body was feeling, she did not notice when the cold, polished coral steps reached for her face with a hard joining, and all went black.

She awoke a few hours later. The strong, earthy smell of rosemary leaves and lavender permeated the room. She knew it was her mother's workings even before she opened her eyes.

"Everyone has gone to bed," whispered Jaylan. "Mother said I could stay with you, that you would be fine. *Are* you fine?"

Angry with herself, she sat up with a jolt. "What happened? Did I pull a Riva?"

Jaylan chuckled at her reference to her sister's tendency to faint. "Mother thinks it is the same. Your body could not withstand the intense emotion and energy running through it. She felt it too, and said in time you will learn to control or adjust to the strong feelings."

The stench of death once again overcame the pungent smell of herb, and she scrambled out of bed. Her legs, still entwined in the bedcovers, sent her to the floor with a thud. She rolled to her back, gripping her knee to stifle the sharp jabs of pain.

"Jaylan, I have to find that dragon, or it will die!" she gasped out.

Well then, I am coming with you," she replied, lowering her voice.

"No, you must stay here...in case I...I don't return." Sumayah felt the urgency and fear in the very center of her stomach. She felt in her bones that she and this dragon had some sort of connection. She had to listen to this feeling, which was part of the Goddess's teachings: Follow your guidance. She was stepping into her role as priestess.

Jaylan gave Sumayah a long look as she helped Sumayah off the floor.

"I worry about you, Sumayah. You seem so driven lately. Though it is against my better judgment, I will stay here. But you better be back by sunrise or else!"

Sumayah grabbed Jaylan and gave her a hug. Worry gripped her, and she held on for a moment longer as if to gain strength from the embrace.

"I will take Sirius with me. She will be my watch."

"You better not let anything happen to her either. The priestesses would come unraveled, not to mention what that wizard would do to you if you got one of their sacred birds killed."

Sumayah anxiously rummaged through her room, grabbing bottles and herbs. As she searched for the right remedies, she could hear Lhayan telling her how her room was more like an apothecary than a sleeping chamber and that she was just like her. Sumayah knew her mother was right except one part; she still did not have the wisdom, the full knowing that whatever she administered was the right thing and would bring healing. Sumayah knew she had a long way to go before the sureness that her mother possessed would come.

Jaylan walked to her sister then pressed an indigo colored stone into her hand. Sumayah tried to push it away and said, "This is your favorite one. I can't take this."

"No, I have charged it with protection for you. I want you to keep this…I have a feeling you will be gone longer than you think."

It was not long before Sumayah and raptor were out of the city. The sun was a long way from cresting the horizon. The moon in the night sky eerily followed her as she wound her way around the red standing stones outside the perimeter of the city.

"How she follows you," she whispered. "She is everywhere you go." Grateful for the company, she watched as Sirius flew silently above her, like her shadow, but a shadow that could attack with cunning and lightning speed if provoked. Even though the phoenix were vegetarians, they had learned to use their dagger-like talons for protection, and Sumayah was happy for her very own set of flying daggers.

The energy in her hands pulsed stronger as she crossed the River Crystal. She soon realized her hands were leading her to her destination—well, so she thought anyway. The odor of rot still prevalent in her every inhalation also told her she was going in the right direction, along with what she thought was a new sign: a dull throb in her right shoulder.

She walked for another hour, watching the sun make its climb, bringing with it the mystery of a new day. What would this day bring her? What new experiences? She hoped the experiences would be kind to her, but also knew from the Goddess's teaching that you can learn the hard way.

Worry suddenly gripped her, knowing her family would be out looking for her soon. How long would Jaylan hold out before she told them? Mesha's frown of disapproval flashed in her mind also. *Mesha, Mesha, what would he do if I never came back?* It made her feel sad to think he would be most likely devastated. She wondered about her feelings for him. They were strong, but there was something else there. She couldn't quite put her finger on it...trepidation, maybe. She wasn't sure. She knew her father wanted to see the two of them as one, though she did not understand why. She knew she would be happy with Mesha; she guessed she would anyway. But there was another face that haunted her.

She walked alone with her thoughts. Her stomach grumbled, and she soon found a rosebush. The flower heads as big as her own head beckoned to her to taste of their fruit. It was too early for rose hips, so she reached for a few blushing, pink petals. Quickly she snapped a few off and stuffed the succulent, smooth petals into her mouth. She chewed to bring out the sweetness and swallowed.

"Did you ask first?" came a tiny voice deep within the darkness of the bush's leaves.

Embarrassed for forgetting her manners, she felt the heat rise in her face. She need not see it to know it was probably as pink as the petal she had just so rudely shoved into her mouth.

"I am so sorry. I know it is no excuse, but I have been walking for some hours and forgot my manners. Please accept my apology." She held her breath, waiting for an answer, searching the shadow realm from which the voice had emerged.

"You look for someone...we all know and are watching you. It knows you seek it out. It wants you to find it."

Sumayah could not suppress the urge to put her hands into the bush to reveal the wise council within. Her fingers slowly pushed away a lush branch of deep-green leaves, and there she was, a shimmering, floating ball of energy with only the essence of a form. Her essence was an outline of a slender female. But her eyes were enormous, reminding Sumayah of big, blue almonds. *Oh, almonds. I could use a handful of them right now.* Sumayah knew she was face-to-face with an elemental. This elemental was most likely the keeper of the flowers; she could not be exactly sure, since there was an elemental for everything on Mother Earth.

"Well, if you know what I seek, tell me; am I on the right path?"

The peering elemental replied, "We think you already know the answer. Do your hands not guide you?

Is there nothing they don't know? She did feel the heat growing stronger, and she clenched her hands, keeping the energy within. The urge to move on strong.

"Yes, you are right, and I feel the urgency. I bid you a good day, and...I will be more mindful when partaking of your food."

Sirius flew overhead, then swooped down to land on Sumayah. Sumayah extended her arm, letting her land, sharp talons gripping a little too tightly.

"Not so hard, Sirius, my arm is flesh—soft flesh at that. Now what have you seen on your journey? Did you see the lone one?"

The beautiful bird cocked her head to look with one eye and then let out a raspy screech. Effortlessly she lifted herself from Sumayah and sailed up and away.

Sumayah felt the heat again in her palms. *I just have to be close.* Chewing her bottom lip, she scanned the beauty of the landscape. The Faerian Ridge that separated the Fae from the Lemurians and the ocean beyond was fast coming into sight. The mountains jutted mightily into the bluing sky. She walked around a towering mushroom, brightly colored orange, and wondered what elemental tended this one, for it was a beautiful specimen. She ran her hand along the stem that was as tall as her but canopied out into a natural protection. The stem was smooth in her hand but cool to the touch. It felt soft, almost as if it has been slathered with one of her mother's special balms.

This thought brought her back to her family, and she felt their worry. She could feel within herself the anger of her father and of her mother. A tiny voice spoke in her ear, and knew it was Jaylan begging her to return.

I cannot return yet. I feel I am very close, and I am not far from Faeria. She hoped Jaylan received her message and closed her mind to any more messages.

The air suddenly changed as she entered closer into the realm of Faeria. It was cool and moist; she guessed it was from the now abundant fungus and ferns that were sheltered under the three-hundred-foot-tall canopy of trees blocking the warming rays of the sun. It did not smell of sea spray as Lemuria did, but of a pleasingly pungent and sweet scent. The "sweet" was from the jasmine that grew in abundance like long, tendrils of hair around the trees.

Suddenly feeling renewed and restored in this new realm, she walked faster and with more determination. The ground was very different here and seemed to steadily rise and roll, then descend again, leaving many interesting gullies to explore. Sumayah thought it would make a nice place to dwell. How cozy it would be to live with and hear the thoughts of these massive trees. What stories they would have to tell.

Her thoughts we interrupted by a sound in the distance. It was loud enough to catch her attention yet not enough to identify it or pinpoint its location. She scrambled and pulled herself to the top of a knoll. Once at the top, the knoll seemed to roll gently down and flatten out into a valley, wide enough for the lazy river that meandered around the bank of trees and foliage.

Forgetting the sound, she couldn't resist the urge to go down and explore the river. She quickly slid to the bottom of the valley and stopped at the edge, watching the water flow past her. It glistened and sparkled as tiny wisps of sunlight beamed through the tree roof down upon the water. Swimming things darted quickly past her. Some sort of fish, she thought or hoped. She mindfully stepped back, allowing the swimming things to pass, and walked along the river's edge. Frogs larger than her foot leaped out of her way and landed with a splash into the river, quickly engulfed by the deep aqua-green waters.

Then that strange sound echoed again through the throngs of tree limbs and gigantic boulders. She craned her neck the direction she thought it came from. She noticed the river forked off in that direction and wound around a dwelling-size, moss-covered boulder. Having no fear whatsoever, she trotted across a row of flat rocks in the river that looked like they had been carefully placed there just for her. Once on the other side, she followed the liquid path into a canyon. It was not much wider than the river but left her enough room to follow without getting wet. The canyon walls traveled up much higher than she could climb and were also blanketed with moss. Her hands pulsated again, and she trotted on.

The sound this time was unmistakable. *What on Mother Earth would one be doing way down here?* It snorted and blew again. *Oh no, it caught my scent.* She slowed her pace and left the river and hugged the canyon wall, thinking she could hide among the walls of moss.

The slap of hooves meeting water made her hug closer to the moss; she had nowhere else to go.

They saw each other at the same moment. The mare halted in the river, water dripping off her chest. She snorted and shook her head. The white gold of her mane billowed heavily around her long neck.

It's my filly. Why is she here…and alone? Feeling brave, Sumayah took a step toward her and was promptly greeted with flattened ears and bared teeth. Sumayah halted instantly, knowing that warning all too well. *This isn't going to be easy. And I have no apples to offer her.* Uncertain what to do next, she just stood in silence watching the filly. The filly stood her ground and did not flinch. Her nose made a rattling sound as she breathed in, then snorted in her direction. *I can wait all day, sweet one. Take in my scent all you want. I'm not going anywhere.*

After both studied each other for a while, the filly's eyes began to shut, and it looked like she was dozing. Sumayah, taking this as a good sign, stepped forward as softly as she could.

Nope. The filly's eyes flew open, and her head jerked up. She lunged forward so quickly, all Sumayah could do was dive for the canyon wall. Before she could think of what to do next, the filly spun and splashed back down the river.

"Now what was that all about?" she said aloud. Not wanting to lose the filly, she trotted along the river's edge behind her.

It was not long before she caught sight of the horse. She had stopped where the canyon had widened to almost double its width and just ended there. The canyon walls shot straight up past her line of sight, and water tumbled down the cul-de-sac as if pouring right out of the sky. The sound was deafening. The water emptied into a large, sky-blue pool filled with lotus flowers and pads so large, she could easily use one to sleep on.

The golden filly watched her with a wary eye and munched a tall blade of grass that grew out of the pond. She kept herself between Sumayah and the pond.

Sumayah sat and watched the filly, not in any hurry. But a sudden, low roar snatched her attention. She swore it came out of the waterfall. Forgetting the filly, she stood and headed in that direction. The filly, having none of it, charged Sumayah once again, large, long teeth gnashing at her with a loud *clack, clack.*

Sumayah had no time to turn and ran backward as best she could with hot horse breath on her face and white teeth filling her vision. A few more paces back, the filly stopped and turned, then trotted back to the pond's edge, munching grass as if nothing had happened.

"I'm not daft. I now realize you are protecting something beyond that wall of water," Sumayah yelled. "But how do I tell you that I mean you no harm? I would like to have your trust." Her hands tingled as she finished her last sentence. The sensation was different, lighter, tickling her hand instead of burning it.

"Is this energy meant for you?" She remembered Mergus's instruction that Lemurians could use the inherent energies within them for many things; all you needed to do was use your imagination. "Well, why not?" she said loud enough for the filly to hear. Holding her hands forward, she let the tingling sensation build and swirl.

"This is for you, golden one. This will tell you I mean no harm, and that whatever you guard, I do not want to take from you. I am here to help you—and to become your most trusted friend." With her intention verbalized, she willed the energy in her hands toward the filly.

It was not long before the filly felt the change and stopped munching the grass. She didn't even lift her head but let it hang.

It is working; a horse is most relaxed when its head is lower than its shoulders, a very vulnerable position. Steady there, Sumayah, don't get too excited. Just wait...

Sumayah could feel a wash of relaxation enter her. She was certain this was what the filly was feeling. The filly's eyelids began to close, and she let out a deep sigh. Holding her breath and not wanting to break the flow of energy, Sumuyah carefully and mindfully took a step forward. The filly did not react. Sumayah took one more step, then another and another. One last step, and she could put her hand on her. She hesitated, but the filly's eyes were fully shut, so she let out her breath and gently laid one hand on her mane. It was softer than she had imagined. The proud smile of her father filled her vision. She knew he would be pleased with her this day.

The filly stirred and began licking her lips in acceptance. Slowly the filly lifted her head to Sumayah's face and this time did not bare teeth. Sumayah ran her hand along the long arched neck and circled her jaw and up over the filly's amber eye.

"See, little one, I bring no harm."

They stayed that way for a few moments more, just touching each other and letting the filly breathe in and remember her scent. The filly nosed her everywhere and nibbled lightly at her tresses.

"Oh, that tickles."

So caught up in the presence of the golden one, Sumayah forgot what lurked in the pond. A few tiny bubbles popped along the surface and went still. Then larger bubbles made their way to the surface and snapped. The calm, bottomless pond came alive with bubbles and churning water. This time Sumayah noticed. *Where is the phoenix when I need her? Probably eating grapes with that wizard!*

CHAPTER 5

CIARA

☙

A familiar scent filled the air. Sumayah's nostrils naturally flared, taking it in. *Dragon scent!* The huge, black form emerged, spraying water in all directions. Sumayah could not believe her luck and took a step closer.

The filly pushed at Sumayah and walked between her and what rose from the watery depths.

"It will be fine, golden one. I will not be harmed."

The pungent lemon scent was strong. The black form surfaced with a loud snort, its blood-orange eyes blinking away the last of the water. It craned its neck in one direction, breathing in deeply; the sound was weak and raspy. Then it saw her.

Sumayah tried her best to calm her racing heart. Her hands pulsated with heat. The dragon froze, his eyes widened, and his lips curled tightly back as if it was getting ready to spit something distasteful. Before she could act, the dragon turned and floundered toward the cascading waters spilling from the sky above, then disappeared into the liquid curtain.

The filly paced the water's edge, calling out with a shrill whinny. "So, this is who you protect. And by the looks of him, he needs it."

The filly trotted up to her, and Sumuyah put her hand to the fillies face, resting it there.

"What is the connection between you two? Why would you leave your herd to be with this dragon?"

A sudden flash of many images filled her mind. Chaotic, gruesome, and red sprays of blood. The agonizing screams of anguish and death made her stomach roll, and she quickly shut out the vision. But one last picture remained. It was men, but not real men. She could see right through the mask, knowing it was Reps. *What are Reps doing here? And why did they slaughter those poor horses?*

Her question was answered by the next vision that blindsided her. The motionless carcasses of the horses were being dragged toward a large gathering. This gathering was not Reps, but the many forms of true man. Oh, Goddess help us, they were consuming the flesh of the horse! The vision was more than she could comprehend. Her mind and body rejected it, and all went black. Her legs could no longer support her, and she fell to the earth. As she lay in the throes of darkness, another vision persisted. There was one horse left; it was the golden one. She fought wildly at those who would consume her, striking and screaming. Sumayah suddenly felt as if she were one with the filly. She had *become* the filly.

Terror filled her body, and blood coursed rapidly, pumping through her heart with such power, she felt as if someone had reached inside her chest and was trying to rip it out. She screamed in confusion and unknowing. *Why is this happening? I don't understand. What is that smell? Who are they? What do they want with us?* She kicked and lurched. She gnashed her teeth so violently, pain exploded in her head. *I must fight...I will not let them take me. I want to live, let me live!*

Just as she felt it was over and she could no longer kick or bite, a dark shadow descended upon her, and it scattered those who were trying to kill her. She heard words she did not understand and screams, but this time it was not her screams, nor screams from her herd. It was the screams of men.

Suddenly the vision was gone, but the shock of it remained. Sobs of pain and sorrow surfaced, and she let them spill forth. She had never experienced such emotion. She did not even know such emotion existed. Wiping the hot tears from her face, she turned to the filly that stood watching her.

"I understand now, I understand fully, that dragon saved your life." Sumayah felt the bond between them grow. The filly had shared her darkest hour, yet she still did not understand why it had happened. Sumayah knew this sharing had made her different. She had experienced the horror of evil, and it made her feel tainted in the knowing.

Reaching up, she stroked the filly. She had fulfilled her requirement for becoming a priestess. Now she understood the rite of passage, and she was ready to take her place alongside the other priestesses. The young girl she had been had stepped aside to bring her closer to the realm of wisdom, the kind of wisdom that comes only with experience.

"There is a much bigger picture here, my golden one. You have shown me that my small world is not the truth of all that is. We are sheltered in our own living, unaware of what waits beyond our boundaries, beyond the walls of our dwellings. I feel the story has just begun, and you and I are a big part of it...and the poor creature that lies dying beyond that wall of water."

The filly perked up at the mention of the dragon and trotted off to the far edge of the large pond, where heavy mosses and large-leaved vines hung to the earth. The filly darted between the vines and was gone.

"Wait. Where did you go?" Sumayah hurried to where the filly disappeared and stopped at the heavy curtain of vines. Slowly she extended her arm through the tangle of greenery and was not surprised when her hand was not stayed by the never-ending wall of the canyon. She waved her arm back and forth, separating enough to put one foot through. With her leg, she pushed aside the branches and tucked her whole body through.

It was a hidden path, and by the ever-changing shadows flickering along the canyon wall, she knew it wound its way to the waterfall. She hurried along the path and was not surprised to see the pond extended far beyond the waterfall. She followed the lake-like pond until it ended in front of a large, ominous cavern. *Where did the filly go? If she thinks I am going to go in there, she is wrong.*

Her hands suddenly heated up, and she looked down at them. Tiny golden ringlets of energy popped from her palms. She watched them in awe, having never seen this before.

A sudden thump on her back sent her heart into a frenzied pump. And she almost choked on her own saliva as she spun to face her attacker.

"Geesh! I am so happy it's you. Where did you go off to, my little one?"

The filly snorted again, and a flash of the sleeping dragon entered her mind.

"Do you want me to follow you to where he sleeps? Only a short while ago, you would have rather taken my face off than let me near him."

Another vision of the dragon hit her. This time severe pain wracked her body. She doubled over, and her leg went out, sending her to the damp earth.

The filly nudged her. "Give me a minute...and please don't send me any more visions of him. I hear you loud and clear."

The pain subsided, and she stood, putting her right hand on the filly's neck as together they walked behind the veil of darkness into the cavern.

The *drip, drip* of water could be heard as it silently slid from the stalactites descending from the ceiling of the cavern. The air was cool, and she kept her hand on the comforting warmth of the fillies neck.

They walked that way for some time. "I am amazed how large this cavern really is. I had no idea things like this existed," she said, making conversation with the filly.

Seeing had not been a problem either. The canyon walls sparkled and twinkled bright enough to light the way. An occasional clear crystal jutted sharply from the canyon floor, also lending its own luminosity. The colors bounced off the cavern walls in glistening hues of purple, violet, gold, and orange. Sumayah wondered if there were elementals at work here.

Suddenly the cavern opened up and doubled its size in width. A bright beacon of sunlight streamed down from the high ceiling to the floor. The light brought warmth, and water dribbled down the cavern wall, feeding a pool that brought life to the back of the cavern, with tiny pink and yellow flowers growing along the bank. The air was not so stifling, and a gentle breeze made its way down, riding the beam of sunlight pouring in. The pungent, familiar smell of dragon scent wafted to her nose.

He is here. I can smell him. But where? I can't even hear him breathe. She searched the jagged outcroppings of the cave, looking for the black form. The filly suddenly trotted to the left. Sumayah followed.

And there it lay. A horrible stench overtook dragon scent, and she covered her face. Her stomach rolled and threatened to rise. Sensing the urgency, she stepped closer until her toe touched flesh.

"I think we might be too late," she whispered.

The filly nudged the dragon in response. The dragon moved, and its long neck slowly turned so that it could focus on what disturbed it. A low hiss rose from its belly and came out its nose. It struggled feebly.

42

"You poor, poor thing. How long you have suffered," she said, trying to use her most soothing voice. She felt a strong pain in her heart, and the desire to help him overcame all else.

Too weak to fight, it lay back in submission. A low moan rumbled deep within. Panic set in. She had not had much practice at healing; no one ever got sick in Lemuria, or even hurt, for that matter.

The heat in her hands pulsed, and she looked to see the golden spirals of energy swirl in her palm. Slowly she knelt to the side of the dragon and let her hands hover over its body. She knew she didn't have to touch him, and only needed to keep contact with the beast's energy field, which expanded to a few feet beyond his body. Her hands felt what she could only describe as a weak energy field. It did not sizzle or pop. It felt very dense and heavy beneath her searching fingers.

Her hands came close to the old long-sword wound, and with her fingers, she tested the energy of the wound. Her fingers pulsated strongly, so she let her hands hover.

"Goddess, help him if it be his desire," she said. She let the golden threads of light spiral out of her hands and into the gaping, oozing wound.

It was not long before she felt a great rush of calmness wash over her. She *knew* she was helping. It gave her courage to stick to it, and with renewed determination, she willed the energy to encompass the whole being of the dragon. As long as she felt the energy flowing, she kept her hands hovering over his body. Without warning her eyelids drooped, and the form before her faded from sight.

Awhile longer something warm blew against her cheek. It roused her, and she realized she had been asleep. She opened her eyes to see the filly staring back at her. *Where am I? Where did the cave go?* Visions of the dragon flooded her mind, and she scrambled to a sitting position. She was no longer in the cloaked darkness of the cave. She was back at the large pond with the crashing sounds of the waterfall.

"How did I get out here?" She gave a stern look to the filly, who had been watching her intently. "Did you bring me out here?" Before she could ask another question, the small lake churned wildly. Bubbles burst on the surface. Sumayah took a few steps back as the water opened and spit out the dragon.

He energetically glided to the bank and gave Sumayah what she could only describe as a smile. He dipped his large black nose into the water and playfully splashed it at her.

"Hey...I'm not ready for a bath," she yelled. *Why not? I am pretty dirty. I cannot think of the last time I was this coated in dirt!* She quickly untied her silken sash around her waist and pulled off her calf-length tunic. She tested the water with her big toe as the dragon, still smiling, watched her.

"It's like my bathwater!" She scanned the surface for a clear spot and dove straight in, just like she would have done with her sisters. As she hit the water, thoughts of them flooded her mind taking away a little of the joy of her swim. Pushing the thought aside, she surfaced right next to the dragon. His large form overshadowed her, making her feel a tad vulnerable.

Then she heard the words, *"My name is Nero,"* pop in her head.

In shock she replied, "But Mergus said you fell!" Treading water for a few more moments, she hoped for a reply, but got nothing, so she just talked to him anyway. "I am just happy to see you are feeling better. I was not sure you were going to make it—well, at first. I have really never used my abilities before, until you showed up in my life. And you don't have to worry about telling me your story. I am sure you will trust in me soon enough. I will wait until you are willing to share." She finished her one-sided conversation and swam a little longer.

She saw the horse tasting grasses here and there, and the last couple of days hit her. How much things had changed in such a short while. She would return home a different girl. Thinking of her family made her hear them searching and calling for her. She was not ready to go to them just yet. She was having more fun than she could ever have imagined. Besides, she felt totally protected by her dragon named Nero and her teeth-gnashing filly—what's her name.

I think it is time I give you a name, or at least let you tell me what your name is. She swam toward the mossy bank and pulled herself out of the water. She shook off as much water as she could, pulled her silken tunic back on, and tied her sash. The filly stopped her feeding and trotted to Sumayah.

"Can you tell, my golden one? Tell me your name, or I can give you a name," she said, resting her hand on her delicate yet dangerous face.

Then the word *Ciara* filled her head.

"What? Is your name Ciara?"

In reply she heard *Ciara* again.

Sumayah laughed. "Well then, Ciara it is! That is a very pretty name for a very pretty girl."

The filly nodded her head up and down in agreement.

They were promptly interrupted by Nero lumbering toward them. She took this time to inspect his old wound. She was thankful the stench was gone, and the oozing hole had now shut, leaving only a tiny tear-shaped, indigo-blue scar.

"How strange is that," she said aloud.

Later that night she lay next to the dragon, with her filly not far from them. It seemed the two were intertwined somehow, inseparable. *What is your story, Nero? I know Mergus said you fell, but how, from what? Who put that long-sword in your side, and why did you come back to Lemuria?* These questions whirled around her mind, keeping her from sleep. But the dragon's breath was long and deep, the rhythm lulled her, and soon her eyelids became heavy…

"Kill that one; he is no longer of use to us. He is one of the enlightened." The loud clang of iron chains startled her, and her eyes flew open. In front of her hung a large cage swaying from a boom in the strong wind over a bottomless cliff. Inside the cage was a black dragon. The dragon hissed at the dark-haired man standing with his back to her.

He unsheathed his long-sword from the scabbard at his side. It rang out loud and clear, even above the roar of the wind.

"You are weak. We no longer require your services, Nero! It's too bad; you could have been one of the great ones. Even Mergus could not hold fast your power." The man paused and looked down at his sword. He brought it up and put his finger to it, lovingly running it along the glinting blade.

"Is there nothing I can do or say to bring you to us?"

"Might I ask you the same question?" the dragon hissed out. "I have never worked for you, but for the original plan." The dragon then lunged at the man, hitting the iron bars. The man reacted swiftly, plunging the long blade into the dragon. The dragon roared and fell back. He moaned loudly, and the sound echoed over and over, carried on the breath of the wind.

The man tried to retrieve his blade from the flesh of the dragon. The dragon snapped his large jaws, and the man withdrew his reach.

"Tis no bother; my family has others of the same make, forged from the fires of the Draconians themselves. You may keep that one...as in remembrance." The man lifted his arm up and yelled, "Release the floor of the cage!"

A moment later the squeak of iron on iron filled the air, and the bottom of the cage fell out. The dragon did not try to hold on. He tumbled out, taking with him the sword with the brilliant-blue, tear-shaped crystal, flashing at the hilt.

She cried out as the dragon plunged out of sight. There was no sound except the howl of the wind and her sobs. She waited for the raven-haired young man to turn so she could see his face, but he did not.

CHAPTER 6

RYVEN'S DREAM

∞

The ground trembled as the Sky Spirits boomed out their thunderous tones, evoking the Wind Spirits to awaken. The Wind Spirits awoke and whirled wildly, awakening the Water Spirits, who in turn let loose a sheeting fury of rain upon her olive-skinned, slender frame. She lifted her head, letting the warm liquid slide across her thin, pink lips into her mouth.

The black horse stomped impatiently. He reined him deeper into the woods to watch the girl undetected, as he had done for the past two weeks. "Soon, boy—soon," the rider said, stroking the horse's large, muscular neck. The sky trembled, and the rider looked up at the rolling, black clouds, heavy with moisture. For a few moments more, the rider watched the girl dance beneath the threatening sky, then he silently turned and rode away.

Ryven awoke perturbed. He had had this dream most of his life, and he always woke up at the same moment. The beautiful wildling dancing under the turbulent sky was always too far away to make out who she was. All he had was a feeling and familiarity and a deep desire to find out who possessed his hours when he slept.

The noise from the courtyard told him the new day had dawned. This day was to be different, and he quickly jumped into his knee-length olive tunic and matching breeches. He reached for his sword. As he grasped the cold, unyielding handle and ran his hands along the intricate heavily woven sheath, he thought about a time when there was no need for such an instrument. There was no fear in the land, only cooperation. Slowly things changed and new beings appeared, bringing fear and the need for protection. These beings, like the long-tooth, had come with the secret influx of a race that had not been permitted to come.

Ryven pushed away his thoughts; he did not want to be reminded of the true reason for the arrival of the Lemurians today. A young girl who had captured his attention from the first sight was on his mind right now. He had no idea what he saw in her. She was Lemurian, and he was Fae. It would never be permitted.

"She intrigues me, that's all," he said aloud to convince himself that was all it was. *A girl who was not afraid to pull a long-sword out of an injured and angry dragon.* He chuckled. *I wonder what else she has attempted.* He guessed a girl such as her was probably in all sorts of mischief.

The realm of Faeria was busy making ready for the king of Lemuria and his entourage. Accommodations were being readied with all accoutrements that a Lemurian would need on his stay. Musicians were practicing for the night's entertainment. The music was soft and echoed throughout the canopy of trees in a mysterious melody.

Ryven hurried through the melee, dodging this way and that, barely missing the shoulder of one of Elspeth's oncoming unicorns.

"Hey, who let the unicorns out!" he hollered in exasperation at nearly being run down.

Tial fluttered close to him. "Good morning, young master. Can I get you anything to break your fast? A wonderful peppermint and lemon tea, perhaps?"

"Thank you, Tial, I have need of nothing. Have the Lemurians arrived?"

"They were sighted not but a few hours from here, a large procession. The king has brought his whole family!"

Ryven couldn't stop the smile that curved his lips. "The whole family—good, good!" *That means she will be with them.*

"Drakaous has already arrived early and roused your father out of his chambers. They are in the east courtyard catching the morning sun and partaking of hibiscus tea."

Hearing this, Ryven increased the speed and length of his steps. *Why would Drakaous already be here, ahead of the Lemurians?* As he got closer to the east courtyard, he could hear them talking.

"Mesha has been searching for her since she left. He has yet to return, and that was well over a week ago," said Drakaous as he shifted his large head away from the bright sun.

"Who is missing, Father?" asked Ryven as he entered and sat on a long, cushioned bench.

Fallonay turned to his son. "Why, it's Sumayah, the oldest of the king's daughters. She left searching for that wounded dragon. Mesha is out with a search party looking for her as we speak." Fallonay put his strong tan hand on Ryven's shoulder. "Have no fear. The king will arrive shortly. Our meeting will go on as planned."

Ryven was not worried about the rest of the Lemurians. And the thought of Mesha out looking for her made him feel—well, it made him feel uneasy.

"Father, I would like to help look for her. It is the least I can do to help out our allies. And besides, I have an idea where a wounded dragon might hide."

Fallonay slapped Ryven's back. "Proud of you, my son! Yes, very compassionate of you. Why didn't I think of it myself?"

Drakaous eyed Ryven, his left eye narrowed in thought. "Yes, Ryven, so very *considerate* of you."

Drakaous's long look did not go unnoticed. Ryven tried not to look so enthusiastic. He picked at an invisible speck on his tunic.

"I think it is the least I can do, since they decided to travel all the way here and save us the bother."

Drakaous smiled, as much as a dragon could, and replied, "Why, yes. Yes, of course."

Suddenly the low roar of a horn sounded. "Looks like our Lemurian caravan has arrived earlier than expected. Come, let us greet them," urged Fallonay.

Drakaous used his tail to block his steps. "There is something I neglected to tell you."

Fallonay turned to glare at the tail impeding his path, then up to the dragon. His left cheek muscle quivered.

"Come, come, Drakaous, what is so important that you would keep me from my guests?"

Ryven wondered also and waited to hear what the dragon had to say.

"One of the reasons I came early was to tell you that *she* is with him."

Fallonay stared blankly at the words. Then suddenly his expression changed.

"What do you mean *she*, dragon?"

Ryven perked up, knowing his father was not too pleased with the information.

"Yes, it is Lhayan—Rupert thought it was time to end this—this *tiny* rift between Fae and Lemurian."

"Rupert thought it was *time*? Since when is the king of Lemuria now ruler of Faeria?" Fallonay spat.

"Please, Lord...Fallonay," Drakaous lectured calmly, the tip of his tail twitching nervously. "I must admit I agree. Times are much different now. The original plan has been changed. We cannot control all events any longer. If Lemurians and the Fae are to work together, there are things you all must put aside."

Ryven wanted to hear more. *Was there a joining of Fae and Lemurian he did not know about? This was good!* He stepped closer to the two, waiting anxiously for the next words.

The horns sounded twice more, interrupting the conversation, this time telling of the entrance of the caravan. All four courtyards became as busy as a beehive before a summer rain.

"Drakaous, I cannot discuss this now. I will be welcoming, and I will be most courteous to *her*. But I will not forget that she went against our law. And that when she left, she took our most sacred knowledge with her! But for now I will humbly welcome my guests. We will have plenty of time to reopen this old wound."

Fallonay spun on his heel and made way for his guests. He suddenly stopped and looked back at his son.

"Ryven, are you coming?"

"Yes—yes, after you," he said, giving the dragon a glance before he followed. *How do I find out more of this? I did not know any of it. I have a feeling not many of us do. So the daughters of the king of Lemuria are half Fae...most interesting.*

It was not long before all guests were settled and everyone was sitting comfortably within a great hall constructed of intricately intertwined branches and leaves of the giant willow. These trees had been groomed and lovingly urged to grow in such a fashion that they made a natural ceiling over a lawn of thick mosses, soft to the touch of a bare foot. The area was long and large enough to easily entertain three hundred guests. A small waterfall trickled soothingly at the north end of the great hall and emptied into a large, brilliant, blue pond. It emptied again into a small babbling stream traveling around the north, then on to the southernmost end of the hall. The water kept the air cleansed and just moist enough to make the skin feel soft as newly spun silk.

Ryven sat next to his father, eyeing Lhayan. *So, she is Fae.* She sat in silence next to her husband, Rupert, and never let her eyes leave her lap; her halo of white-blond hair almost hid the beautiful, impish face.

"I am sorry to hear about your daughter's disappearance," said Fallonay. He turned to look at his son. "My son, Ryven, has offered to look for her. He was also scouting this lone dragon and might know where he might hide."

Lhayan perked up at the words. She looked at Ryven and spoke.

"Ryven, you were meant to find her. I already know this."

Ryven choked on the jasmine tea he had just taken a sip of. Everyone looked in his direction, and he could feel the heat rise in his face.

"Why—why, yes, I think I might already know where he would be." Not quite sure what to make of the message he had just received, he stood. "If you all will excuse me, I would like to leave immediately."

"Yes, of course, Ryven," said Rupert, jumping from his seat. "I would give anything to go with you, but..." He hesitated, looking at Fallonay. "A king's duty is to his people first, I am afraid. And Mesha has been looking also. I am sure either of you will bring her safely to me."

"She is safe, Father," Jaylan said. "I know it. She is with that dragon and is not yet ready to return. Ryven *will* find her. I can even tell her you look for her right now."

Lhayan grabbed her daughter and made her sit back down. She leaned into her and whispered something Ryven could not make out.

51

"Ryven, you are permitted to leave," instructed Fallonay. "And please do bring the young Sumayah back, quickly. We have much to debate and discuss about the fate of our world, and it will be so much easier if all were safe...at this moment."

Not wanting to be held up any longer, Ryven quickly turned and strutted out of the great hall. Before he made it to where his horse was, he was stopped.

"I will go too."

He did not turn around and walked on, knowing the voice. "Elspeth, let me go alone. I can travel much faster and should not be gone more than a week's time. If I do not return in that time, you have my permission to come and rescue me."

Elspeth hurried after him. "You go to the cavern, do you not?"

"You know it?" he asked halting his steps. He turned to his sister, sensing the worry. "Don't worry about...Mesha. I think he can take care of himself."

He spun back around and left her standing alone. *What hold did this man have on her? Does she not know he is just a man? Father would rather die than permit her to be with a mortal.*

A short while later, he was doing what he loved best: riding with his friend and heading into the realm of a new adventure. He wondered about the girl he sought. Wondered what hold she had on him, and why he felt he needed to rescue her. Did she not have someone already looking for her? That was the problem, but why? What was it about this Mesha he did not trust?

Black snorted and pranced excitedly as they left the common area of Faeria. He too knew they were on an adventure.

"Steady there, my friend, we will find her soon enough."

The black snorted again in reply and tossed his head.

"Oh, so you want to be the first to find her? Do you feel the same reservations about Mesha as I?"

Black bobbed his head in response.

"And you are not afraid of this new dragon that we will most certainly be meeting?"

Black pranced higher in the air and shook his head from side to side.

Ryven laughed. "Have no fear, my friend. Dragons do not eat horseflesh."

The terrain was soft, and Black's steps made no sound within the heavily canopied forest. Ryven watched as elementals tended to their charges. They paid him no mind, knowing Ryven was of them, and let him pass with only a slight nod or acknowledgment as they busily pruned, plucked, and fluffed.

The smell of fresh, sweet orange berries filled the air. The thumb-sized fruit hung heavily from the long wispy branches of their trees. He plucked a few that were reachable from the back of Black and quickly thanked the elementals that tended them.

He popped one in his mouth and bit, savoring the burst of sweetness. Nodding to the elementals, he said, "They are the best I have ever tasted. Thank you!"

Black snatched a few stalks of sweet grass along the way, keeping himself happy and sated.

They traveled for a few hours more, but the brightness of day soon waned, and the sun began its descent behind the jutting peaks of the mountains. As the sun sank, it illuminated the tops of the mountains, making them glow as if somehow crystals had been activated within, shining out and around. He knew that the base of the mountains were in fact large beds of crystal. Elementals tended and harvested the smaller ones for everyday use, since the crystals were a life-giving part of every being upon Mother Earth. He even knew it was a very important part of the blood that coursed through his body.

A shadow beyond the expanse of the tree roofs caught his attention. It was a dragon, the color of the ocean in the late morning as the sun hit it. He wondered what this dragon was doing and tried to make contact with it. He opened his mind and tried to call him down. He waited for a reply and received none.

"That is strange," he said aloud, watching the dragon sail easily along the wind trails.

Riding up on a stream bed, he decided to climb off and rest a bit. Black walked to the edge of the stream and drank deeply. Ryven followed and knelt at the stream. As he drank from the waters, he could feel the sensations of someone having been here not long ago—the essence still flowing within the stream. He breathed deeply, trying to capture any scent or anything that would tell him who or what it was. His hand naturally went to his side and grasped the hilt of his sword. Feeling the cold within his grasp somehow made him feel more at ease, and he once again relaxed. After swallowing the water, he felt drawn to follow the stream as it wound into a narrow canyon. The walls of the canyon were too high to climb out if need be, and it unnerved him to have to go in there. But the draw was too strong, and he forced his caution aside.

"Come on, Black, we will be going in there," he said, pointing into the narrow and darkening canyon.

Black took one tentative step back and snorted, then shook his head back and forth.

"Come, come. I have my sword, and you have...well, you have those deadly hooves. I will watch your back, and you watch mine—don't act like a unicorn. What say you, my boy?" He knew the word *unicorn* would get him.

The horse pawed the ground three times, then extended his neck and butted Ryven hard.

"Oh, *not* a unicorn? Well then, prove it."

Black raised his head and stared down his nose at Ryven. Ryven couldn't help but laugh.

"You win."

The way was narrow and dark. The canopy of trees even covered over the wide berth of the canyon. The illumination of the moon this night was of no help. Only tendrils of radiance streamed through the thickness of cover above. The darkness made him feel alone. The vibrations of the busy day had long since ceased. The occasional warmth on his arm from Black's breath told him he was still behind. The last time he had been to the cavern was not in the dark. This must be a different way, since he could not quite remember how he got there the last time. A memory from long ago of what lurked deep within came bubbling back to the surface. His skin prickled in response to the vision that suddenly flashed in his mind.

The narrowness suddenly opened, and the trees gave way to the brightness of the full-moon night.

"Black, we rest here. I do not feel like exploring any farther. The dragon and the girl can wait one night longer."

Black seemed happy with the decision and nibbled on a few blades of sweet grass. Ryven pulled another thumb-size sweet orange from his cloak and popped it into his mouth. The juice dribbled down his chin, landing on the bare skin beneath his tunic. He wiped at it and searched for a place to rest for the night. Mindful of keeping his back protected, he went to the canyon wall, which had a thick blanket of ivy hanging from it. He pulled it away, revealing a small opening in the wall, big enough for him to lie down, unseen and protected.

Black did not seem so worried and grazed farther away. The moonbeams shone down upon him, illuminating his black coat to a color of liquid celestial crystal.

Ryven felt his thoughts stray. A girl with long, black hair and penetrating blue eyes filled his mind. He revisited the time she dislodged the sword from the dragon, and the countless other times he sat in secret watching her swim with her sisters in the ocean not far from where the wizard dwelled. And he remembered the last time the Fae and the Lemurians came together all those many years ago. There had been an upheaval. They would not tell him what about. But he remembered watching Sumayah ride into Faeria, sitting so proudly on her horse right next to Mesha. He remembered how Mesha had noticed his stare, and they had locked on each other. That was all it took, one long look—a moment but an eternity. Energies were exchanged between the two, and they were not welcoming but challenging. Ryven remembered nodding in acceptance to this silent agreement. He will never forget the feeling as he and Mesha became adversaries.

Ryven wondered if Mesha even remembered. Maybe he did not even feel the same as him; maybe he didn't even know he existed, and all of this was in his mind.

A sudden *whoosh* of air alerted him. He sat up and searched the darkness for Black. The horse had wandered too far. Using his thoughts, he called to his horse.

A sudden shadow loomed and circled right above where Ryven sat. He pressed himself as close to the side of the canyon as he could, hoping he was not seen or smelled. The hair on his arms prickled. He held his breath and tried to slow his heart. The shadow came closer and closer. Carefully he dug at the ground for his sword, but found no familiar feel of metal. *Damn, I took it off. Where is it?*

Suddenly the pound of heavy hoofs to earth could be felt beneath him. *Good boy, Black.* The horse whinnied loudly and sped up, coming closer to where Ryven hid.

The searching shadow left at the sound of the approaching horse and was replaced with the bright cast of moonlight.

Black slid to a stop right in front of Ryven.

"Where did you go?"

Black gave him a blank stare, then sniffed him.

"I'm not scared. I was just worried about you...Something was out there, and I was fearful—for you."

Black lifted his head.

"Don't you give me that look, I *was* concerned..." He paused, then smiled. "Well, I was worried that I might have to walk out of here alone."

In response, Black snorted loudly, spraying Ryven's face.

Ryven wiped off the snot, then proceeded to wipe it back on Black. "Here, you can have this back."

The horse's back twitched in protest, and he walked off in front of Ryven.

"Fine, be that way. But my sword will not wield in your defense, that I can promise you!"

Black loudly broke wind.

CHAPTER 7

THE RESCUE

☞

Sumayah awoke sobbing. Her face was damp, and she had dirt in her mouth. Sitting up, she wiped her mouth and looked over at the dragon as he slumbered peacefully.

"Thank you for showing me," she whispered. She wondered who it was that had so cruelly tried to kill Nero.

Ciara was bedded next to the dragon. She opened her eyes and looked at Sumayah.

Sumayah turned her head. Nero was awake and watching her also. The sun was just beginning to peek through the opening at the top of the high cavern; a single beam of light streamed down to the floor of the cavern.

No one seemed in any hurry to arise and just lay watching the beam glisten and sparkle as tiny particles of dust floated through. It was Ciara who stood first and sniffed the air. She pawed at the dirt floor and snorted.

Misunderstanding her signal, Sumayah stretched her arms up and said, "Just wait a minute, Ciara, we can go out in a little while. I am enjoying the peacefulness. No classes to take, no tests or questioning stares from Mergus this morning." She rolled over and pressed her face to the coolness of the moss beneath her head. The smell of vegetation wafted into her nose, making her stomach grumble.

Ciara snorted again and jumped to one side, taking off in a circle around the cavern. This alerted Nero, who in turn stood, sucking air into his large lungs.

Sumayah rolled to a sitting position and sat listening. To her left she saw a black shape spring from one rock to another. *Thump, thump, thump*, wildly beat her heart.

Nero turned his head in the direction of the lunging form. A low rumble-like growl emanated from within him. The shadow appeared once again, and in a blink of an eye, it jumped from the large rock to another rocky ledge.

Ciara made a run toward the shadowy figure, ears flattened and teeth bared.

"Ciara, get back here right now!" Sumayah screamed. The mare spun and returned to her side.

Nero suddenly raised his neck and head, making himself larger. A puff of steam escaped his left nostril. He roared, and a thick stream of hot smoke aimed at the intruder rolled out of his mouth. The steam hit it just as it sprang forward, at the dragon.

Sumayah could not believe her eyes as it easily sailed the long distance from the ledge to her dragon. Ciara charged, colliding with Nero as he spun his neck away from the attacker. The horse skidded and tumbled to her knees.

The shadowy form suddenly grew piercing green eyes and dagger-like fangs. It snarled and screamed. The sound reverberated throughout the cavern, echoing back and forth.

"Long-tooth!" was all she could muster from her constricted throat. Nero spun with a loud hiss and tried to grab the long-tooth before it landed on the prone filly.

The filly, sensing and smelling her attacker, scrambled on all fours, trying to stand. But it was too late; it landed with a heaviness that even shocked Sumayah, sending the delicate filly back onto the ground. The filly screamed and thrashed.

Nero charged into the fray, snapping at the cat, snagging one back leg. With leg in mouth, he violently jerked his long neck up and swung it to the left. A strange sound, as if forced, came out of the cat's mouth and ended in a vicious snarl.

Sumayah saw another movement from the corner of her eye.

"Help us!" she screamed, unbelieving that someone would have found them this far back in the canyon.

Ryven and Black rushed in. The horse ran to Sumayah, standing between her and the battle of beasts. Ryven swung his sword at the cat just as Nero let go. The cat landed and rolled, then sprang to its feet and spun, facing Ryven and his sword. Its ears flattened, and its mouth snarled, exposing its own weapons.

"Come on if you dare!" Ryven yelled and swung his sword. The cat, suddenly feeling outnumbered, spun and with three bounds reached the top ledge of the cavern and escaped out of the opening.

Sumayah studied her deliverer from death's door. At first she did not know who he was. The dark cavern hid most of his features.

"I am so relieved I found you!" he said to her. "Is everyone unharmed?" He walked to the filly, which proceeded to flatten her ears at him.

"Oh, don't go near her. She has very big teeth too," Sumayah said, still trying to get a better look at her lifesaver.

Nero came closer to the group and sniffed at the intruder. Ryven stepped back, holding up his hands.

"What about this one. Is he unsafe also?"

Sumayah walked to her dragon. "Oh, he is safe enough…It's a long story, but I have been searching for him for quite some time." She finished her sentence and walked around to the other side of her rescuer, where the beam of light was the brightest.

"Well, the story gets more interesting, because I was sent—well, ah, I volunteered to come look for you," he replied as he slid his sword back into the sheath.

He walked right into the beam of light. The clear sight of him struck her like a bolt of lightning. Her mouth dropped, and her heart fluttered wildly. She opened her mouth to speak but nothing came out.

He bowed his head to her since she had nothing to say and said, "My name is—"

Suddenly finding her voice, she interrupted, saying, "I know who you are." Stepping closer, not believing he was standing right in front of her, she silently thanked the Goddess, uncaring why he came. She felt like laughing out loud at her good fortune.

"You are Ryven, son of Lord Fallonay, are you not?" She tried to sound calm, even though her heart thundered against her chest. She was positive he could hear it.

"I am. We have only met once before, a long, long time ago. So I was not sure you would remember."

"Oh, yes—yes, I do…" *Shut your mouth, you sound too eager.* She shifted her weight to her other foot and put her hand to Nero, scratching the warm texture of his skin, trying her hardest to look nonchalant.

He smiled, grabbing at the hilt of his sword, suddenly feeling awkward. "I must tell you, your family has made it to Faeria. They are there to—"

Once again she cut him off. "I know why they have come." *That's better, my heart is slowing…just take a deep breath. Stay calm.*

Ciara took that moment to walk to her and nudge her in the back, which caused Ryven to chuckle.

"Mine does the same thing when he is impatient. I think everyone is ready to leave the confines of this cavern. If you are ready, we will lead the way." He put his hand on Black, and together they walked out of the cavern.

The sun hit them with such might, she had to take a step back. She had not realized how dark that dark could be. Everyone blinked until they became used to the light once again. The waterfall at the other end of the large pool tumbled loudly, spraying water toward them. The shower refreshed her, and she welcomed it. She walked to a spot undisturbed by the cascading water and dipped her cupped hand in for a drink. It was cool to her lips, and she let it slide down her parched throat. After a couple more handfuls, she began to feel the refreshing effects.

Everyone else did the same. Ciara waded in almost up to her chest and playfully shook her face in the water.

"She is a beauty—never saw that color before," Ryven said.

"I know, me neither. Not sure what to call it. But she is the most exquisite thing that has ever come out of my father's herd. He will be so pleased to see her. Well, when I *go* back, that is." She let her voice trail off with the last words.

Ryven looked at her in question. "What do you mean, when you *go* back? I am to take you back directly."

"No you're not!"

Ryven puffed up like a peacock. "Yes I am! I have other things to do, you know."

Sumayah could not help but let a smile form.

"Let me explain, Ryven." She paused, looking behind her at the dragon watching his reflection in the pond. "You have no idea what I have been through these last few days. Or ever since I met him," she said, pointing at Nero. "I am a changed girl; my life back in Lemuria is dull in comparison. I have experienced emotions and have challenged myself with things I have never done or felt before."

She sat heavily on a moss-covered rock next to the quiet end of the pond. She put her finger in the water, tracing it in a spiral motion.

"Have you ever felt like you had something in your life you just had to do, but could never put your finger on it?" she asked. "Or what you believe to be true was only an illusion?"

Ryven shifted his weight and looked at her with searching eyes. He sighed deeply.

"I do think I know what you speak of. I have seen things, had visions of things that either were or have yet to pass. I search for the meaning of those visions. So in essence, yes, I do know what you are saying."

"Ryven, I want to keep experiencing this…I want to go out and explore. There is a whole world out there waiting!" she finished, spreading her arms out.

He stood quietly, his right cheek muscle twitching, and one dark brow dropped. "Sumayah, I do believe in what you say. And I believe that your world is now different to you. But I must remind you why our families have joined. I must remind you that there is someone else out there searching for you right at this moment."

Mesha. I knew he would be out there. "I know who and what you speak of, Ryven. We are in trying times." She got up and turned toward Nero. "I believe this dragon came to me on that first day for a reason. Ryven, he showed me what had happened to him! There is no good coming our way. I believe this dragon knew of the evil out there and how they plan against us. There was one who would conspire against us. I saw him but did not see his face. He was the one who put the sword in Nero. They are connected somehow, because, look"—she pointed to the tear-shaped blue scar behind his right front arm—"this scar is the same shape and color of the jewel on the sword that pierced him."

Ryven knelt to look at it. He put out his hand and traced the shape with one finger. "Do you think he has come to warn us?"

She nodded her head up and down. "I *know* it."

Nero snorted, and a rumbling sound deep within him surfaced.

"That's right, my friend, I do know why you have come." She patted him, and he purred in response to her attention.

"Why, I have never heard a dragon make that sound before!" said Ryven.

Nero suddenly left them and scrambled along the path next to the waterfall and went out to the other side.

"Where is he going?" Sumayah asked, chasing after him. She trotted out beyond the waterfall in time to see him easily lift himself into the air. The sun blocked her view, and she put her hand to her eyes.

Ryven pointed past Nero. "There! Look, another dragon!" He moved to the canyon wall to stand in the shadows where he could see easier, with Sumayah following.

"Oh, I see it. Nero must know it." They both watched in silence as the two joined in air and did a conjoined roll and ascended toward the sun. "Look at them fly!"

They were like twin eagles catching the waves of the wind, hovering together, then rolling and diving.

"Wait, I know this one. Well, I at least have seen this one before, just last night. I do believe this dragon knew all along what was going on here in this cavern, Sumayah."

She walked away from the canyon wall as the two flew out of sight. Her heart sank a little, seeing Nero fly away.

"Sumayah, do not worry. You are connected, I can see that. He will be back, I am sure of it. Like you said, he is here for a reason; he must have a purpose too."

His words were true, and she knew it. She forced a smile at him.

"Thank you, Ryven." She took a deep breath. "Well, I guess we should make our way back to your home. How far away are we?"

"We should be there at the morrow. Tis not too far. The way is easy, and I think you will enjoy the sights." He turned and started walking along the narrow path following the stream out of the canyon.

Sumayah followed, with Ciara right behind her. The filly played in and out of the water, nibbling tall sweet grass here and there. Sumayah itched to ride her, but knew it was too soon. This filly had plenty of spirit, and she did not want to end up on her backside in the dirt. So they just walked together and played hide-and-seek behind the towering trees that canopied above them.

They walked for quite some time, both Sumuyah and Ryven deep in their own thoughts. Sumayah watched the sky where there was no covering of treetops. She did not see the dragon, but she felt him. Her hand, which was still warm, told her he was near.

"We stop here tonight. Do not worry about the long-tooth. We have never seen them this close to Faeria. I do believe the elementals do their best to scare them off," explained Ryven with a laugh.

Sumayah studied her sleeping chamber for the night. The trees were much closer together, and if you moved back far enough within the curtain of branches hanging to the ground, there was protection also. The smell of sweet orange berries caught her attention. She turned to see Ryven grinning broadly at her, holding them almost beneath her nose.

"Why, thank you, I love sweet orange berries. I love how they pop in your mouth." She grabbed them out of his hand and tossed one in and quickly bit. The nectar exploded, filling her mouth.

Awhile later they sat, happily filled with berries and sleepy eyed. Ryven stayed close but respected Sumayah's space, not wanting the king of Lemuria to have any reason to come down on him. They watched the moonlight flicker between the rustle of the leaves overhead, but did not see any sign of her dragon.

Sumayah could no longer keep her eyes open and succumbed to the call of sleep, with the sound of running horses in her mind...

Suddenly the horses snorted and ran, frightened by the loud baying of hounds. She quickly scanned the woods, knowing that sound always meant trouble. Wondering why they were so close, she quickly sneaked through the woods to see more. She jumped the stone wall. The baying of the dogs became louder, combined with the sound of thundering hooves. The earth began to tremble as they came nearer. She put her hand to her eyes to see, blocking the setting sun. She thought she saw movement and realized they were coming right at her! With a shriek she tried to run away from the confusion as dogs brushed past her legs. Then she felt someone roughly grab at her waist, yanking her to the top of a horse.

Hearing the loud, "Whoa," the horse came to a jolting stop.

Before her assailant could speak, she yelled, "Let me down!" Her voice was nearly drowned out by the chaotic noise of hounds, horses, and the intimidating crack of whips as they all continued by.

With a chuckle and an "As you wish," her captor let go of her, and she slid with a thud to the unforgiving, damp ground.

She stood and brushed twigs and leaves from her skirts. "Since when do you need hounds and other riders to hunt stag?" she asked angrily.

He urged his mount closer and bent low to face her. His thick brows came together as he narrowed his eyes. With a snarling whisper, he said, "We are hunting witch tonight..."

"Sumayah, wake up, wake up. It's only a dream."

She felt hands on her shoulder, lightly jostling her. She opened her eyes to be met with Ryven's concerned stare. His thick brows came together as he narrowed his eyes. Startled by his look, she bolted upright, pushing him away.

Confused by her actions, he sat a few feet away from her and watched her. "I'm sorry if I startled you, but you were moaning and thrashing in your sleep."

The vision that was still fresh in her mind kept her silent. It was the same person she had seen in her visions before. But what scared her was this person in her dreams had a striking resemblance to the person staring at her at this very moment. She could not stop the flood of questions that filled her mind. What were these visions, why was she having them, and why were they always the same person? The world in her vision was not the same as her own world, but she felt like she had been there before. Was there a connection somehow?

She needed to see Mergus. He would know; he could help her. But in the meantime, she would not tell Ryven what she suspected. Something inside told her this was not the time or the place. The look Ryven gave her made her feel bad. She could tell he was confused and had questions too. She had to give him something and searched her mind for an answer that would relieve his questioning look.

"I'm sorry, Ryven, I was dreaming about Nero again, same horrible dream. He is trying to tell me something in my sleep time, and I must not be hearing all that he has to say." *There, that should do it. I can tell by the relieved look in his stare. That was close.*

Black alerted them with a snort and shot through the dense cover of the forest. "What the—" Ryven said before he took off after him.

Ciara ran to Sumayah. Her ears twitching this way and that. She snorted and stomped her hoof.

"There, there, golden one, do not be frightened," she crooned to the filly, stroking her silken mane. Both of them jumped at the sound of thrashing branches not far from them.

Sumayah's skin prickled, and Ciara charged into the chest-high ferns along the tree line, but quickly turned and came back trembling.

There went her heart again, trying to outrun herself, since she could not manage to make her limbs move.

"Ry," was all that came out of her stonelike lips. The ferns began to wave and shake as a dark, crouching form stumbled toward them and collapsed with a moan.

"Ryven!" she finally yelled, keeping her eyes on the creature that lay before them.

Ciara snorted and took a tentative step. Sumayah grabbed her mane.

"Hold on, wait for Ryven."

Where is he? What is keeping him so long? The creature moved again, and it began to tremble violently. A ray of moonlight peeked through the trees, concentrating on the form that trembled beneath. Sumayah sucked in her breath. *It's a black long-tooth!* As soon as the words filled and left her head, the black form of the lion in front of her changed, and in its stead lay a beautiful young woman.

"What on green earth?" whispered Ryven behind her.

She jumped at his voice and spun to face him. "Do you see it? It—it was a black long-tooth," she hissed beneath her breath.

Before either could say another word, another young girl walked out of the ferns and knelt beside the woman lying on the ground.

"Her name is Leesabeth; she is a shapeshifter from the realm of Avalonia. My name is Pennyann. We mean you no harm and ask for sanctuary. It has been a very long trip to get here. We were told to find Faeria, and they would take us in. We have much news. We have..." The young girl crumpled to the ground.

Sumayah ran to the girls and put her hand to the one who spoke. Cold to the touch. She put her hand to the one called Leesabeth. Also cold.

Ryven knelt beside her. His left cheek twitched, and he fumbled with his black hair, uncertain what to do.

Heat built in Sumayah's hands. She allowed the glittering line of gold to split, each strand connecting with a girl. She sat that way and let the energy flow as long as needed, watching Ryven out of the corner of her eye. His eyes were as large as two full moons in the sky.

"I did not know Lemurians could heal like that."

She giggled lightly. *There are many things you do not know about Lemurians, especially this one, and I am going to show you...*

CHAPTER 8

WITCHES

⚭

It had been a long night healing the two girls who fell into their camp. Sumayah awoke feeling the heat of a stare. She knew it was Ryven. The thought of him sent her straight back to her dream from last night. The mysterious young man would not leave her mind, especially his last words. *"We hunt witches tonight."*

"Did you sleep well, Sumayah?" asked Ryven in a lowered voice, not wanting to wake the two young girls slumbering peacefully not far from them.

She nodded to him and stretched her arms overhead and yawned. She ran her fingers through her tussled chocolate-black hair, which had fallen out of its plaiting a while back. *I must look a fright. My tunic is torn and dirt smudged. I am sure I have dirt on my face too.*

"I could use a bath," she said apologetically.

He smiled back at her. "If I might say, I think your wild-haired look is quite appealing."

She giggled, feeling her face warm. When she saw that the girls were stirring, she sat in silence, waiting for them to rise.

The two stood and smiled sheepishly.

"Thank you for your help. We had nowhere else to turn," Leesabeth said.

"You gave us quite a start with your—ah, appearance," replied Ryven, running his hand through a lock of hair that insisted on hanging in his eye. "We were just happy you were not a long-tooth—not the kind that wanted to eat us anyway."

Sumayah patted the mossy earth next to her. "Do come and sit. We have many questions."

Ciara took that moment to come in greeting. Pennyann ran her hand down the filly's face.

"She is a beauty. What is her name?"

"It's a long story, but she told me her name is Ciara," answered Sumayah.

The girls sat down next to Sumayah, and Leesabeth said, "We saw two dragons shortly before we found you. We saw only a few more on our travels. But I must say they are far more abundant here than they are in the realm of man."

This bit of information shocked Sumayah. "You came all the way across the waters from the realm of men?"

"Leesabeth and I are from a small island called Avalonia, where I was born," said Pennyann. "Avalonia is a small land separate from the realm of men, but is under the watchful eye of men who do not like the teachings of the priestess of Avalonia. And in those teachings, we were told the legend of an island called Lemuria, that it was a very magical place, and the beings that lived there were not of our world. Since our realm is of a lower dimension then Lemuria, we had to work very hard to reach your higher dimensional world."

"Wait a minute, Lemuria is just a legend in your world?" asked Ryven.

Leesabeth nodded her head. "It is legend only because it is unattainable to all except those of us who practice magic and learn how to rise up to a different dimension."

"We also dimension shift," added Sumayah. "But like you, only those who are a priestess or priest can do so. Our horses dimension shift, and I am beginning to think the dragon also."

"We believe they can too," replied Leesabeth. "We were told something happened to the dragon. Once they shifted to our lower realm, they could not shift back and were stuck in our world. There are other beings that have come from another star far from us. It is told they were not allowed in, but came in after a great battle in the sky. Those that made it here have taken control of men through a great deception. They cloak their true identity and call themselves the messengers of the one God."

Sumayah turned to Ryven. "Ryven, they speak of the Reps, I just know it!"

Ryven's left cheek twitched, and he dug his booted heel into the soft pliable moss.

"Yes, Sumayah, we do now know. That is why your family has come to Faeria—to discuss what to do."

Sumayah stood, brushing a loose tendril of hair away from her face. "Then we must hurry back to Faeria. These two girls have important information."

A half day of travel finally brought them to the entrance of the inner city of Faeria. Tial and Elspeth were there to greet them, both wearing questioning looks.

Ryven slid from Black's back, letting him meander off. "We have just as many questions as you, so please hold your questions for court."

"I will inform them of your arrival. I am sure they will meet in the north courtyard," said Tial before she sped away.

Elspeth grabbed Ryven's arm and whispered, "I don't see Mesha." Turning to the girls, she softened her expression and formed a welcoming smile. "My name is Elspeth. I am Ryven's sister. Please, I am sure it has been a very tiring journey. We have chambers ready for you..." She paused and searched the sky above. "I see no dragon with you?"

Sumayah answered. "He is well and has joined another dragon. They are close by." She knew it by the heat still in her hands.

"Elspeth, I would like to see my family," Sumayah said. "Are they near?"

Elspeth smiled sweetly. "Why, yes, of course—follow me." She turned to Ryven. "Brother, would you be so kind as to take these young women to their chambers? They are beyond the south courtyard."

Everyone was so happy to see her. They greeted her with tight hugs, then promptly backed away.

"Oh, Sumayah, why did you not bathe first?" exclaimed Riva, pinching her nose to block out the wild aroma wafting from her sister.

Jaylan hugged Sumayah again. "I can deal with the smell; I am just so very happy you are back!"

"Well...my brave daughter, you have much explaining to do," Rupert said, shaking his finger at her. "It was a very hard decision to leave you out there while we traveled to Faeria. Now, tell us, was it all worth it?"

"You should be so proud of her, King Rupert," interrupted Ryven, entering the courtyard with Mergus behind him.

"Ah, so the dragon is well then?"

Sumayah let go of Jaylan and went to her father, who backed away.

"Sorry, Father," she said, taking a step away. "I have so much to tell all of you, and that is why I have forgone the bath—well, for just this moment."

Mergus stepped forward, a beaming smile upon his face. "Not only did she save that dragon, but they have also stumbled upon two very interesting souls...from the realm of men!"

A hush went around the room. Ryven quickly spoke.

"Yes, *they* are bathing at this time. We will all convene in the courtyard. What they have to tell us must be heard by all. Now, please excuse me. I must go to my father."

Sumayah watched him leave; she could not suppress the smile that crept across her face. Jaylan caught her sister's look and gave her a wink.

"We all can wait awhile longer before the news. Sumayah, please go take a bath. Lemurians are not used to so much dust and dirt and...odor. Why, if I didn't know better, I would say you slept *in* the dragon chambers!" said Rupert with a large smile.

Sumayah smiled as she made her way to the bathhouse. *Little do you know, Father.*

Candles lit the courtyard, illuminating the room to a golden-amber glow. Leesabeth and Pennyann retold their stories with a quiet and captive audience.

Fallonay, pacing the moss-laden ground of the courtyard, was the first to speak. "So, we are correct in surmising that the Reps are truly behind the slow destruction of men, leading to the destruction of all."

Both girls nodded their heads yes in unison.

"It appears that the Reps have been able to teach the chosen few of men the art of dimension shifting," said Mergus, keeping pace with Fallonay.

"And they have found a way to keep most of those dragons that have shifted to the lower realms."

"But what would they want with the dragons?" asked Rupert. "Most have already shifted to the higher realms, even higher than us."

"I think they mean to use them in a war against us," Lhayan quietly interjected.

Fallonay shot her a stern look.

Ignoring Fallonay's stare, Lhayan continued. "I believe the dragons have been teaching them how to shift into our dimension. They must have found a portal in the waters and have sailed right into it. If they can teach their army of men to do this, they can bring their war to our shores."

"What is it the Reps want?" asked Sumayah.

Mergus stepped forward to answer that question. "They want slaves; they want to enslave our whole world for their personal gain and greed." He pulled away the sleeve to his robe, revealing a thin golden cuff that encircled his wrist. It was molded in the shape of a thin tree branch.

"This is what they come for; gold is what binds them to Earth. This is why they were not allowed here and why the battle in the sky took place. They forced their way in, knowing that the realm of man was young and could easily be controlled to mine this." He shook his gold-wrapped wrist at all of them; a look of disgust covered his usual smiling, contemplative expression.

Rupert got up and walked to Mergus. "You are correct, my friend, but they miss one thing. They did not realize that we were here."

"So true, at first. That is why they come...now," replied Drakaous, entering the courtyard with Baratheous and Drakemon behind him.

Everyone's attention went to the dragons. "This must be most serious to have the presence of all three of you," said Fallonay.

"Our brethren, those who have already risen to the higher dimensions have sent out a calling to us here," answered Baratheous, the mirror image of his brothers, except his eyes were black-red, almost black with a flicker of red. "They watch us in hopes that the original plan for Earth will still be successful."

"Volunteers," said Mergus. "I have been hearing of this new plan. And yes, I feel there will be a great need for more of them as man's greed grows to match those who control them."

Drakaous moved to Mergus. "We had no warning that the young souls of men would be so easily guided—guided in the direction that was not intended."

Lhayan moved forward past Fallonay, who frowned. She ushered Leesabeth and Pennyann to the three dragons.

"They have come from the realm of man; they have risen above the mind control of the Reps and have made the journey here to us."

Sumayah jumped into the conversation. "They happened to come upon us as we"—she pointed to Ryven—"traveled back here. Leesabeth here, told me they are witches.

"Witches?" asked Mergus. "Is that not the same as our priestesses? I have heard once, long ago, that some of our priestesses—"

Leesabeth interrupted the wizard. "You are correct, Mergus. And I have heard many great things from three of *your* priestesses who have chosen to come to us, seeking out men of quality and heart so that they may raise children who will have the abilities to learn the ways of the higher realms." She pulled Pennyann closer to her. "We are both children of your priestesses. The gentle folk of our realm call us witch, simply meaning wise woman."

Riva and Jaylan moved in closer to listen to Leesabeth.

Sumayah studied the four girls now standing together. Something about them stirred a strange feeling deep within her. The feeling started in the pit of her stomach and escalated. She felt the buzz form in her head, and her hands began to pulsate. She looked down at them and swallowed hard, trying to clear the darkness that enveloped her as a new vision formed blocking out all else . . .

"We shall assemble the circle here, within the ring," instructed the beautiful young woman with the look of great wisdom. "I have already asked permission from the diva of the faerie ring, and it has been granted. They ask only one thing, and that is we enter in our natural state, bringing nothing of the human realm with us but our skyclad body."

She felt a moment of shyness and hesitated. "Shion, our bodies are a temple of the goddess within us, so be not so modest," said the woman leading. Seeing the others disrobe, she quickly followed. She studied the women who were present besides the beautiful woman and young woman with the billowing red hair. The third young woman standing next to the redhead was tall and somewhat large in stature—not overweight by most standards, but bigger of bone. Her hair was long and black, with three streaks of silver running down the middle. Her skin was olive-tan, and her eyes were black-brown. She was comely but had an air about her, somewhat unapproachable.

The other woman was much shorter, even shorter than herself. She too had long, black hair that hung in thick, long curls. Her petite face encased two of the largest brown eyes she had ever seen. Her body was rounded and curvaceous in stature. As she watched her, she felt a sweetness about her connect with her heart center.

Her attention shifted back to the redhead. She guessed she was only a year or two older than herself. The woman's very pale skin almost glowed against the dark backdrop of night. Her wild mane of fiery red hair and deep-set green eyes hinted of a willful personality.

They all gathered facing the east, waiting for the circle to begin. The dark-haired leader held a large shiny shell filled with herbs that she had lit from the center fire. A plume of smoke spiraled up from the shell, smelling strongly of earth. She knew and loved the smell of sage, breathing in the spiral of smoke as it came to her.

The dark-haired leader took each woman one by one, saying the words:

"Know you, it is wiser to leave now than enter with mistrust, anger, and cynicism within your heart. Knowing this, how do you choose to enter?"

Each woman answered with:

"In perfect love, in perfect trust."

After being swept from head to toe with sage smoke, each woman entered the circle walking widdershins—clockwise. As the women entered, the first woman began a chant, joined by each woman after:

"Earth our body, water our blood, air our breath, and fire our spirit...

"Sumayah. Wake up, child."

Sumayah felt the coolness of a compress on her forehead and the smell of lavender flower and chamomile. Her body responded to the magic of those plants, awakening her from the darkness, bringing her back until her eyes opened naturally.

Lhayan held the compress to her forehead. "What did you see? Can you tell me?"

Sumayah could not find words, feeling a little shocked that her mother had known about her visions.

Lhayan smiled sweetly down at her. "I can tell by your expression you are surprised that I know. There are many things about you that are special, my dear, and things that have yet to be discovered."

Sumayah completely awakened with a renewed vigor at her mother's words and sat up in the enfolding softness of the bed.

"When I saw all four of the girls standing together, it awakened something in me, and I felt a shift within myself." She retold her vision. Her heartbeat quickened as the realization hit her. "We were there, all together as witches. They called me Shion."

"This might be a good question for Mergus. But, I do think you shifted into a different time, a time to come. I am happy that you and your sisters were together in the different time. It confirms what I have always believed; that we travel through time, dimensions and lifetimes together."

Their private conversation was interrupted as Elspeth entered the room, her silken gown swishing behind her.

Sumayah felt a slight twinge watching the beautiful young woman come toward them. She was the most beautiful Fae she had ever seen.

The Fae settled herself on a beautifully carved wooden seat next to Lhayan.

"Sumayah, I am most interested in what it was you saw that caused you so much discomfort."

Sumayah squirmed, unable to bring a single thought to her lips. Telling her mother was one thing, but explaining her strange vision to Elspeth was a little uncomfortable.

"Sumayah, please answer Elspeth," lectured Lhayan. "They have been such wonderful hosts to us, the least you can do is hold polite conversation."

The tone in her mother's voice snapped her to. She clenched her hands together and spoke.

"It was the strangest sensation, and yes, I have had them before, each one different—except one that has been recurring."

Elspeth smiled broadly, pushing a thick length of black hair behind her. "Oh, I love a mystery. Please, do continue."

"It is always the same. I am lying on a large rock that was dug out and smoothed by water. I lie there naked, and I feel like I am in a vision even in this vision. I cannot explain it, but, as I lie there watching that other vision, I am startled by a horseman. He is riding up hard and fast—until he sees me. I struggle with getting my clothing back on, and he is amused by my manner of undress. I cannot see him clearly, but he is on a horse. Why, he is on a horse much like Ryven's Black."

Sumayah paused, letting the words spring forth a picture within her mind. She studied the man on the black horse, but could not make out his face. It is always the same; his face is in shadow.

"I cannot ever see him clearly enough. It perplexes me!"

Elspeth's face changed from a smile to a more somber expression. She leaned closer to Sumayah, her bosom strained against her gossamer dress.

"Did you say he rode a horse much like Black?"

"Elspeth, I do know where you are headed. I think this conversation should be saved for another time. All will be revealed in its own time," said Lhayan, standing.

Sumayah wanted to understand what her mother was talking about. Her mother and Elspeth had gotten on to something, and it frustrated her that her mother would not shed more light. Sumayah flung her bare legs over the bed, letting her feet feel the coolness of the polished floor.

"But Mother...I think Elspeth knows—"

Lhayan put her finger up to her mouth. Sumayah knew that gesture all too well and reluctantly refrained from letting her next words out.

Elspeth chuckled softly and stood. "You are correct, Lhayan. But, I find your glimpse into another lifetime interesting." She stood, brushing at the slight wrinkle in her gown. "I do want to say that I am happy to see you. It has been far too long. And have no fear of my father. He might be gruff and staunch in his ways, but he is the lord and he has only our best interests at hand...even though I think sometimes he can be a bit unyielding."

Sumayah watched the exchange in frustration, knowing her mother would not tell her more of what she heard.

"I know he has a heart the size of a rosehead. And that is why I chose to come this time. It is time for old ways that no longer serve us to die away. Mother Earth has to make changes as well, so we must live by her example."

"Once again, you express the wisdom I wish I had, Lhayan. We are riding the wave to difficult times. It is time for all of us to come together, for there is much uncertainty. I see it, Lhayan, when I peer into my crystal globe of truth. It tells a story that I do not want to unfold. And in this vision, I also know we have the power to change the course of time."

By this time Sumayah felt as if she did not exist. They talked over her. What was all of this talk of uncertain times and difficulty ahead? Just then her hands began to heat, and she pulled her feet back onto the bed, afraid she was about to experience another of her visions. She closed her eyes and sucked in a deep breath to calm her heart. There in her mind's eye was a picture of the golden mare; she had forgotten to tell her father about her. She snapped her eyes open and looked at her mother.

Lhayan stopped her chatter and gave her daughter a questioning look. "Sumayah, have you something to say?"

"I had almost forgotten, what with all the commotion going on. Mother, I was accepted by one of the horses! She was very difficult at first, and she has a bit of a temper. But you should see her, Mother, she is exquisite. I think she might be one of Father's fillies, but I could not be sure. She is pale gold, but a gold that shines with the iridescence of the most precious pearl ever!"

Lhayan's eyes widened. Her pursed lips relaxed to the point where you could see her bottom teeth. She looked at Elspeth, and Elspeth mirrored the look.

"What is the matter?" she asked, feeling a rush of worry overtake her. "Did I do something wrong?"

"Where did you see this filly?" Elspeth asked.

"Yes, Sumayah, where was it you went when you were gone? Where did you really go off to?" inquired her mother, narrowing her eyes at her.

Their stares seem to beat her down, and she sank further into the softness of the bed. *Better be careful how I answer this. I think I am in enough trouble. What would make them look as they do?* The heat in her hands intensified and rose up her arms. She swore she could hear the filly calling to her.

"Sumayah, we have asked you a question," her mother said.

"I was at the lake with Riva and Jaylan. The same time we saw the wounded dragon. The filly was with them. Then I saw her again, but she was alone. She was there when the long-tooth attacked me. And again she was there when I found the wounded dragon. She would not let me get too close; she wanted to kick and bite me at first, but then she relented," she finished, the words tumbling uncontrollably out of her mouth.

The expressions of the two women changed again to recognition. She was sure of it. She stopped talking, waiting for either of them to respond to her answer.

It seemed a long time before either spoke; they looked at each other as if to dare the other to speak first. Slowly both turned their stare to Sumayah. Sumayah watched them, watched the word slowly form on their lips in unison. And together they spoke it.

"Bethia."

CHAPTER 9

A LESSON IN MAGIC

CR

Frustration was the only word Sumayah could use to explain her emotion. *I just don't understand! Mystery and secrets, everything is hidden, and you must find your own answer. If I am to become priestess of Lemuria, I need answers!* She was so alone in her thoughts, and paid no heed where she stomped. The city had been left behind her. The soft, whimsical melody of a flute could be heard ahead of her. Knowing whom the tune belonged to, she quickened her pace.

Mergus sat comfortably upon a boulder laden with thick moss sprouting tiny purple flowers.

"I knew it was you," she said.

"And I knew you would come," he replied, putting aside his flute. "I called you to me...there is much aflutter these days, and I wanted to chat with you alone." He winked at her, and his tiny mouth, barely exposed beneath the groomed beard, curled up into a smile. He patted a spot next to him.

"Mergus, I have so many questions. I am told to move forward in my abilities and am tested and tested. During this, things have been happening to me—things I cannot understand. Mother will not give me any answers." She picked a tiny purple flower and gave it a flick.

"Patience *is* another test, something we all must learn to conquer. Otherwise it will just keep coming back for us to learn and relearn. Everything comes to us when we allow the flow. It is much easier to float with the current of the river than to paddle against it. Is it not?"

"That's not fair, Mergus. How do I know if I am floating or I am paddling?"

"By how easy things come to you. Yes, we must be responsible in our learning, but in doing so, we must also do the work. If we do not do our own work, we will have only learned on the surface and not within here." He put his hand to his heart.

Something in his words seemed so familiar; it was as though she had heard this same conversation once before, but long ago.

Mergus waved his hand in front of Sumayah. "Where have you gone, Sumayah?"

She giggled at him. "I felt as if I had heard this before—how can that be?"

"It is all an intricate part of the magic we live. Our lives and the 'time' it takes is like riding a spiral. It goes around and comes back to where it started, only a little higher; then it goes around up into another layer, but always comes back. It is hard for a young mind such as yours to understand such things and even harder for me to explain in words you can understand." He paused, thinking of a better way to explain. "Today you look at your life like it is happening one day at a time. You have no notion of what it will be one hundred years from now, do you?"

She thought a moment and replied, "No, I cannot imagine one hundred years from now."

"Part of learning magic or wizardry is the understanding of time. Child, time does not happen in a linear fashion. It does not happen like you perceive. You look at your lifetimes thinking one life happens after another, like a book...page one is the day of your birth, page twenty is your first word, and so on and so on." He narrowed his gray-blue eyes until creases formed around them. "When in fact, all of your lifetimes are happening at the same time, beginning to end and end to beginning. If you lived three hundred different lifetimes, page one would be turning at the same time for life one as it is for life three hundred." He stopped and looked at her with expectation.

Sumayah thought about it, but it only hurt her head and made her eyes cross. She put her hands to her face.

"Ugh, I cannot think of it."

He chuckled. "You will learn soon enough. But the best advice I can give you is to always trust your heart. Know that there are forces greater than you who are with you and guiding you. These forces know more about you than you know of yourself. Learning patience and trust is powerful magic, my young goddess."

"Mergus, some of the words you use are different than our words. Why is that?"

The wizard studied her for a moment. He shifted his weight, then studied her again.

"Because I know the greatest magic trick of them all, and one day you too will know it, for you are special, Sumayah. You are not who you think yourself to be. I have learned and have known that trick for a very, very long time. I know who I truly am, and that knowing has opened me up to the knowledge of all that there is."

Something inside her stirred. She could feel it awaken. "Mergus, I think I know what you speak of—well, part of it. You see, I have had many visions, visions of different times, different lives, and if what you say is true, there is more than one of me! So that must mean I am beginning to learn who I truly am and that who I am today is not...*all* of me. There are many more of me than what is right here." She held out her hand in front of her, turning it this way and that.

Mergus laughed, clapping his hands. "Good for you, Sumayah! You are beginning to awaken to the real magic of our existence! Once you understand this fully, there will be nothing that can stop you from what you want or want to be. The only thing that can stop you is your belief. Never let anyone change what you believe in your heart. And never become something someone else wants you to become."

He then clammed up and narrowed his eyes at her. After a moment he perked up again.

"Sumayah, once you learn to access all that you are—" He tightened his lips. "Well, soon enough you will know the rest, but for now I think you have had enough *awakening*."

Disappointed that he did not finish his sentence, she plucked at another poor flower. "So tell me, Mergus, why do I feel something is coming? I cannot explain it, but what comes is dark."

He put a hand to Sumayah's shoulder; the radiating warmth calmed her. "You are correct, your power is beginning to build. There are things you will be able to do that we have yet to know, Sumayah. And it is up to me to make sure you do not fall into darkness."

His words scared her. A lump formed in her throat. But she had to ask, "How will I know I am heading into the darkness?"

"Sumayah, if I do my job, you will never have to know."

Suddenly Ryven appeared with the filly behind him. "Ciara has been searching for you, so I tracked you here," he said, his face slightly red, knowing he interrupted an important conversation. "I am sorry to have disrupted your—ah, well, I assume lesson?"

"You assume correct, Ryven. She did learn today, and no, you have no need to apologize." He waved the intruder closer. "Come, Master Ryven; let this beautiful specimen come to us."

The filly playfully trotted the short distance to Sumayah. She pawed at the boulder and pushed her nose into Sumayah's chest, almost unseating her. Sumayah giggled.

"She is something, is she not?"

Ryven walked to the filly, rubbing his right arm. "She bit me but good on the way here. I think I was not moving fast enough for her!"

Sumayah laughed. "She got me a few times too, so I have learned to watch her and never turn my back on her."

The filly flattened her ears at Ryven as he approached. "She is very protective of you too," he said.

Sumayah noticed that Mergus was watching the filly intently. "What do you see in her, Mergus?"

The old wizard jolted as if startled by her question. He coughed as if to clear a blockage in his throat.

"There is something about this filly, something about her energy. She does not seem to be of your father's herd."

Sumayah bounced on the boulder, remembering the word that her mother and Elspeth muttered.

"Mergus, can you tell me who Bethia is?"

This one single name seemed to have startled the wizard all the more. His eyes widened, and he slid from the boulder, choking once again. His eyes began to tear up and spill forth as he violently coughed.

Ryven, fearing for the old soul, ran to his aid and hesitantly began to pummel his back, shooting a questioning look at Sumayah.

Sumayah slid from her spot and rushed to help. Mergus held up his hand and swallowed loudly. He sputtered once and then tried to express the word *Bethia* from his trapped throat. It came out raspy and almost incoherent. He swallowed.

"Who, who has used this name in your presence?"

Surprised by his reaction, her answer was delayed.

"Come—come, child, who spoke this name?"

"My mother and"—she turned and pointed to Ryven—"and his sister, Elspeth."

The wizard's expression of shock soon softened back to its jovial self. He smoothed his beard and spoke again.

"It seems as though a time of long ago has come full circle. But in order to keep things sacred, there are names we do not speak of in this dimension."

"Who is she, Mergus?" asked Sumayah, again afraid that he would not tell her either.

"What did Lhayan tell you?" He peered down his nose at her.

There it was, avoidance. "She did not tell me anything," she muttered in reply.

"Well then, it is as it should be for now! Remember when I said there were many forces at work here, unseen forces, and some need to stay that way."

Sumayah just nodded her head yes.

"This is one of them. And with the coming of men to our realm, we must be careful what names we utter, for there are those forces working against us also."

Just then the filly tore away, almost knocking Ryven to the ground, her tail waving in the air behind her. She nickered loudly.

The shadow above alerted them to what approached. All eyes went up as he settled himself into a landing. The filly met the dragon, and they touched noses. The dragon made a deep purring sound.

"I'll be dipped in honey and fed to the bears," muttered Mergus. "I have never seen such an exchange before by two different beings in my life."

The dragon perked up at hearing the wizard speak. His eyes locked on the wizard. Sumayah suddenly felt the emotion of recognition.

The wizard stumbled forward. "Is it...you?"

The dragon moved forward to meet the wizard. Mergus tentatively reached up to touch the dragon's face. He did not cough or sputter this time, but tears flowed, and a muffled sob escaped his lips.

"My dear, dear old friend, I thought you had fallen," Mergus said. "When Sumayah told me of such a dragon, I had hoped in my heart it was you, but knew in my head it could not be!" Mergus spread his arms around the large dragon in as much of an embrace as he could.

Sumayah wiped her nose and looked at Ryven. He gave her a half smile, then looked back at the reunion.

The wizard suddenly remembered he was not alone and wiped his eyes dry. He turned and with a beaming smile said, "This is my oldest and dearest friend, Nero. I have known him since my childhood. We were among the very first who came to Earth from our homes"—he pointed up to the brilliant blue sky—"there."

"Mergus, why did you think he had fallen?" Sumayah asked suddenly, remembering the vision she had of Nero. "I must tell you of my vision the day I found him...before Ryven found us!"

All listened as she recounted what she had witnessed.

"Tell of that blue stone," urged Ryven.

Puzzled by his request, she said, "All I can recall is that it had a very dark...the darkest blue stone in the hilt I had ever seen. I remember hearing the one who held the sword say it was forged by his family."

"And you pulled the sword out of him, did you not, the first time you saw him?"

Still puzzled, she answered, "Yes, but I do not know what happened to it afterward."

"Hmm, I swear I have seen a sword such as that before, but for the life of me, I cannot remember where or when." Ryven's left cheek twitched as he narrowed his black-lashed eyes in thought.

"I think in time it will be revealed," said Mergus. "I'm afraid, though, my friend here has lost his ability to communicate with us with his voice. I fear it must be the residue of living in the lower realm of man."

"Will he ever regain his voice?" Sumayah asked, walking to the ebony dragon and giving him a pat.

"Only time will tell, but apparently he can communicate with you in your dream realm. I have many questions for him, but for now I am willing to wait. In time he will tell me, tell us, what has happened."

The filly barged in once again, putting her ears back, driving everyone away from Nero.

"I have never seen such a joining before," exclaimed the wizard, scuttling out of her way.

"They have a story. Her story is of how this half-dead dragon saved her life from—" Remembering more, she grabbed Mergus's white sleeve. "She and her kind were attacked by Reps and men! They are much closer than we think, and they are eating the flesh of..." Her voice trailed off as her mind replayed the horror.

Mergus put his hand to her shoulder. "You need not finish. We already have been told."

Her stomach lurched. A feeling like she had never felt before enveloped her. It was as if a fire in her stomach was rising up, burning her throat.

"Reps have found more than one way to control man," spat Ryven. "Feeding from flesh dims the mind."

"Well, Sumayah, Ryven, this has been a very enlightening moment. I am glad I stole Sumayah away. Lords and kings, though they mean well, have a way of compromising all conversations. We must warn of this news. We have preparations."

Mergus then turned to Nero and whispered something to him. The dragon bowed to the wizard, then with two flaps of his immense wings lifted into the air. The filly ran after him, calling, and soon they were both out of sight. Mergus stood and watched the empty sky, deep in thought.

"Mergus, you haven't told us why you thought Nero fell," Sumayah bravely said. She was determined to get information. This "wait, see, and learn" attitude was not setting well with her.

Mergus sighed heavily and walked to them. "I do understand your questioning. And there is a connection between the three of you. Though why, has not been revealed to me. I feel Nero is keeping a very dark and important secret. He has been gone more than two hundred years. It was not long after the great battle in the sky. We had and still have our mission, but he just disappeared one day, and I feared the worst. I had heard rumors of his sighting in the realm of man. I did not know what to think, for I knew him and could not believe he would have gone..."

The wizard did not finish his sentence and grabbed Sumayah's arm warmly. He forced a bright smile.

"That was when you began your lessons in the Goddess teachings. My mission was to teach you and watch over you. I think the same is true for that dragon, though his mission took him elsewhere, where he got into something he could not get out of."

Slowly they made their way back into the inner dwellings of Faeria. Ryven did his best to walk right next to Sumayah, attentive to her every need. He helped her when she tripped on a branch and lent a hand when crossing the River of Mirrors that meandered around the inner city.

The inner city was alive with chatter; the intricately carved wooden horns blasted an eerie tone. This was the announcement of visitors. The three of them quickly made their way through the throngs of Fae to the south courtyard where Mesha stood waiting.

Sumayah's heart pounded as he caught her stare. His raven-like eyes, black and keen, bored into her. She had missed him after all. Gone from her mind was the Fae who stood next to her, and she trotted to Mesha, who met her halfway.

"Mesha, I have been so worried about you!" she said, pressing her face into his chest. Their hearts beat as one, and they held each other until someone cleared his throat loudly behind them.

"I am most pleased that you two are reunited," said her father, "and you will have your chance to catch up later, but first, Sumayah, we must talk with Mesha."

Everyone walked to the far corner of the courtyard and sat once again around the circular wooden tables, polished to shine like glass. Sumayah felt a hand at the small of her back and turned her head to see Ryven. His cheek twitched rapidly, and he gave her a strained smile.

"May I assist you, Sumayah?"

She felt her face blush, suddenly feeling herself caught in the middle of something she had no control over. She gave him a smile and allowed him to usher her to a bench next to the table, next to Elspeth, who shot her a smile.

Sumayah glanced around the table. She saw the usual occupants: Fallonay and his assistants, her father, mother, Drakaous, and his two brothers. Mesha was seated between the lord and the king. Tial tended to everyone's needs. She had shifted so that her size almost matched Sumayah's. She knew elementals had the power to do so.

Once everyone else left the courtyard, the sound of voices lowered. Fallonay spoke first.

"We are grateful you made your way to our great city. As you can see and I am sure are most relieved, Sumayah has been found by my son, Ryven, and brought back here safely."

Sumayah did not miss the slight change in Mesha's expression as his gaze shifted to Ryven. Mesha, doing the honorable thing, gave Ryven a stiff nod of acknowledgment, then averted his look. Sumayah tried to quell a strange feeling, nervous and jittery; she noticed that Ryven too squirmed in his chair. Was she picking up his energy, his emotions, or where they her own?

Mergus entered the room. Sumayah had forgotten that he was not at his usual place at the round table.

"Ah, Mergus, so good that you have come," said Fallonay, standing to give a half bow.

Mergus returned the gesture and sat at the left side of Lhayan.

"Mesha, we know you have been out searching for Sumayah and have been gone for quite some time," said Fallonay. "Please tell us where you have been."

The smile on Mesha's face faded and was replaced with a questioning look. He shifted his weight and narrowed his left eye, which raised his left nostril up. He put his right fist to his mouth to cover a slight cough.

"Why, Lord Fallonay, I was out along the Valley of Horses, about four days ride from the eastern shores of Lemuria. I thought Sumayah might have gone that way, knowing she also had to fulfill her task of joining with a horse. I did not see any of the king's herd, nor did I see a single dragon."

Fallonay studied Mesha for a moment; he kneaded the smooth table top with his fist. "So you are saying you saw nothing?"

Mesha nodded his head. "That is correct."

Rupert took this moment to stand; he placed his right hand on Mesha's shoulder and patted it.

"We all know how hard you searched for my daughter. That is not the question, my son. The question is, did you see or suspect anything out of the ordinary? Did you see any tracks of men in the dirt or sand?"

Mesha's eye narrowed again, and this time his mouth sagged open. He turned his head to Rupert and asked, "Men, sir?"

Mergus shot up from his chair. "Come, come, Mesha, did you or did you not see an army of men out there on your wanderings?"

Stiffly Mesha replied, "I did not."

Sumayah began feeling nervous for Mesha; she wondered what information they were searching for.

"Mesha, we have had much news during your, ah, excursion. Two women from the realm of men have made it to our shores and into our dimension. They bring us news of an impending invasion of our lands. Reps, Mesha. They have found a way to bring men here to mine the gold that still lies beneath our mountains."

Mesha squirmed. "I am sorry, Mergus, but I did not see or hear anything while I was out there. I was looking for Sumayah, for she is promised to me!"

Ryven shot up from his bench, startling Sumayah. She saw a bead of sweat escape down his brow.

"King Rupert, may I approach? I would like to talk with you in front of this whole assembly."

Rupert smiled and waved him forward. "Why, of course, young man. I would be delighted in hearing what it is you have to say. After all, you did bring my daughter back safely. I owe you at least that much."

Ryven stepped forward, his sword slapping against his thigh. Sumayah watched him, tasting her bottom lip.

What is he doing? She could tell he was nervous, and his left cheek twitched to match his quick steps. Mesha stood, and the two stood eye to eye. No one spoke; Mesha inhaled, making his chest puff out like a peacock. Ryven's hand went to the hilt of his sword.

Mergus broke the tension. "Mesha, do sit down so that we may hear what Master Ryven has to offer."

Mesha's brow came together, displaying his displeasure.

"King Rupert," Ryven began, "I know you have great heart and honor. I understand that by your union with Lhayan, even against my father's approval." He stole a look at Fallonay, who sat frowning. "You have a vision and are searching for a way to bring more harmony in our world. Now more than ever, I realize how important it is for our people to join. And you have shown great example by your union with Lhayan." Another bead of sweat fell from his face, and he paused to wipe his brow.

I think I am going to empty my stomach right here. She was not sure what Ryven was up to, but had her suspicions. She glanced at Fallonay, whose nostrils flared in anger, then glanced at her father, who sat calmly waiting for Ryven to finish.

"Ryven, my son, be very careful with your words," Fallonay said in a low tone of warning. "Do not go against my wishes or my commitment to Faeria."

Ryven put up his hand. "Father, this *is* for Faeria!"

Fallonay stood from his bench with such force, the heavy seat fell over with a crash. "My son will not join with a Lemurian!"

The silence broke, and all in the circle gasped, then chatter ensued. Above the chatter Mesha yelled, "Sumayah has been promised to me!"

"What a wondrous plan," Mergus roared. "I wish I had thought of it myself!"

"If you do this, Ryven, you will no longer be my son," raved Fallonay.

Sumayah sat in stunned silence. She looked at Ryven and Mesha, who were eyeing each other like peacocks in the springtime. She had yet to absorb the moment.

Drakaous let out a roar, silencing everyone. "This is enough! Have we forgotten why we have gathered in the first place? Let us settle once again, and let young Ryven here speak his truth!"

Fallonay ignored Drakaous. "If you ask the words, Ryven, you will leave Faeria, never to return. It is your choice."

Ryven looked at his father, then looked at Sumayah for a moment. Sumayah had lost all feeling and sat empty like one of the rag dolls she had played with as a young child. She could not even bear to look at Mesha.

"Father, there are forces at work here greater than ourselves, greater than our old and outdated rules and beliefs. The very first time I saw Sumayah, I knew there was a connection. I do not know what it is, but I feel that in our time of great need, I must ask"—he turned to Rupert—"King Rupert, to be joined with your daughter, Sumayah."

The only sound was Fallonay's rapid footfalls as he left the courtyard

CHAPTER 10

THE DECISION

CR

Sumayah could feel Ryven's defeat. She wanted to go to him and tell him everything would work out. But his surprise kept her mind racing. This was something she too found herself wondering and dreaming about. But one thing stood in the way. Mesha.

"King Rupert, this is an outrage," roared Mesha. He rubbed his hand at the hilt of his sword. "You do not mean to go against your word? We do not need an alliance with the Fae. We can take care of the Reps on our own!"

Rupert walked over and put his hand on Mesha's shoulder. His smile was genuine and seemed to steady Mesha.

"My son, I have much to weigh. Things in our world have changed; the original plan has been abandoned. I believe as much as Ryven does that it is imperative at this time that all come together." He looked at Ryven, patted Mesha's shoulder once again, then sighed deeply and walked to Sumayah.

Sumayah watched him come; her heart leaped, for she suspected what her father would have her do. *Damn you, Ryven, I don't want to be put in the middle of this.*

Rupert grasped his daughter by the arms and bent to look into her eyes. "My daughter, you come from bloodline that has yet to know its limits or boundaries. I am wise enough to know that our future is always just a probability, that many things can happen along the way to change that probability. It has taken Master Ryven great courage to come forth with his proposal. And there is much merit in what he speaks. I know you, my daughter. I know what is in your heart, and therefore I..." He paused a moment and took another deep breath. "I must leave the decision up to you."

A loud gasp filled the silence; it was Lhayan as she hurried to her daughter's side. Jaylan came forward and put her hand in Sumayah's. Sumayah found comfort in it. The smell of sweet grass and rose oil filled her nostrils as her mother embraced her.

"You have the power within to do the right thing," she whispered into her ear.

"I cannot choose between them, Mother," Sumayah pleaded quietly, only for her mother to hear. "I do have a great love and admiration for Mesha, but there is something between Ryven and me. My mind whirls. My thoughts will not gather, Mother...I need more time. Please don't make me make this decision now."

Lhayan hugged Sumayah closer. After a few more seconds, she let go and turned to face Rupert.

"Rupert, my love, this is a most delicate matter. Sumayah does not wish to hurt either Ryven or Mesha at this time. She respects Ryven's offer and his wisdom in doing so. She has great love and admiration for Mesha, someone she has known most of her life. Therefore, Sumayah cannot make a decision at this very moment."

"But she belongs to me!" Mesha replied and pointed to Rupert. "There is no decision to be made; it has already been made—by the king himself."

Sumayah turned to Ryven. His expression stone, he turned on his heel and left the courtyard, with Mergus shuffling behind him.

Mesha took his leaving as a sign of defeat and stepped to Sumayah. She could not read his expression, but this time she did not like how his eyes narrowed, causing his lips to curl and his nostril to flare.

"Sumayah, I know in the end, we will be together. It is the small annoying stones along the path that make us realize what matters most."

Drakaous came forward, cutting Mesha off. "I feel our time of welcome has run its course. We must make our way back to Lemuria and prepare for the imminent coming of men."

Mesha perked up and said, "Drakaous, is it not time to consult with the…one?"

Lhayan shot Mesha a disapproving look and said, "Mesha, that will not be of your concern. Please remember your place."

As the Lemurians made ready to leave, Elspeth approached Sumayah with a tense smile.

"I do not know what possessed Ryven to speak as he did; my father has locked himself in his chambers and sees no one. Ryven is gone."

Sumayah felt a stab to her heart. "He is gone? Why? Why would he leave?"

"He has greatly disappointed my father, and since you did not choose him."

"Oh, Elspeth, poor Ryven. I did not mean to hurt him. I have come to admire him so in these past weeks. But his offer was so sudden, it was a shock."

"What will you do now, Sumayah?"

"We go to prepare." Sumayah grasped Elspeth's hands. "What will your people do?"

"There is talk that we will leave this dimension and leave only the elementals alone here to tend to the outer dimension of Earth."

The vision of a dead and dying Earth filled her mind. "Elspeth, Mother Earth will not survive without your presence, for you are of the Earth herself, and *we* are mere visitors here!"

"I have yet to fully understand what it is we do, Sumayah, but I wish you well. I must go now. I will find Ryven."

Sumayah watched as the elegant Fae walked from the caravan, which was packed and ready to travel back to Lemuria. She could not stop the wonder in her mind. *What would it have been like to pick Ryven?*

The trip was tiresome, and Sumayah was somewhat thankful that Mesha rode a day ahead to make sure the way was clear. She spent most of her time searching the skies above for her dragon. His telltale shadow never crossed her path. The filly stayed close and watched the sky too. Sumayah wondered about the connection between dragon and horse...and if it entailed the person named Bethia. She knew that name was connected to the realm of magic. And since she had passed her test, she could move forward into the teachings of magic.

A day later the dragon-wrapped pillars at the entrance of the city were in sight. It was good to be home.

An hour later five girls sat on large, overstuffed pillows in the center of Sumayah's sleeping chamber. The chamber was built in a semicircle, and off from the circle were individual rooms. Each had a door of its own to the outside world. The center of the chamber was a gathering area where stories could be shared and food eaten.

"What a beautiful bird. What is her name?" asked Leesabeth.

Sumayah stroked the very happy raptor. "Her name is Sirius, for the star home in the sky, her original home."

"I do remember the priestesses teaching us about that," replied Leesabeth. "She also told us you are not of the Earth, that you have come from a different star home."

"That is true, and since you are half *us*, that means part of you is also from that star home," answered Jaylan. "So you see, we are related. We are all one!"

The young women giggled, except Riva, who sat pouting.

"Riva, what is making you look so sad?" asked Jaylan.

"The priestess ceremony is soon, and I have nothing. I will not become a priestess," she replied, tugging at a corner of her pillow.

"Riva, I have not fulfilled my test either," replied Jaylan. "Now that we are back, we can go in the morning and bring Leesabeth and Pennyann with us for help."

"Don't think it will be much help," Riva fumed. "I might never become priestess."

"Riva, it will not be the end of the world if you do not become priestess," said Sumayah. "Besides, if you do not make it this time, there is always next season."

Riva moaned. "I could not sit through another of Mergus's lectures."

"There is too much fun coming from this chamber," interrupted Lhayan as she entered. "Your father cannot sleep."

"We were just talking about the priestess initiation," whispered Sumayah. "Riva fears she will have to go through her studies again if she does not meet her requirement."

Lhayan sat next to her and pushed on the floor pillow to make it more comfortable.

"Riva, just what will we do with you? Have no fear, my darling, we will find another way. And if not, then you can come and learn all of my Fae secrets."

Riva perked up. "Oh, I would much rather do that—can we start soon?"

Lhayan put her finger to her mouth and shushed the buxom young girl. "Yes, but first off to bed, all of you. The morning dawns soon enough, and we have much to do."

Lhayan rose from the pillow and on silent feet left the room. The girls each went into their own rooms, and all went silent.

A warm ray of morning sun peeked through Sumayah's bedchamber window down upon her face, waking her. Sirius rasped out a squawk and pulled at a tiny crystal bell that hung from her perch. The whimsical melody filled the room, and Sumayah opened her eyes.

"Are you ready to be let out for the day? Is that what you ask?"

Sumayah held out her arm, and the large raptor stepped on and rode it to the door. Sumayah yanked hard on the handle until it opened with a high-pitched creak. She stepped out and lifted Sirius into the air, and away she went. A large shadow overhead covered the red-gold raptor as she lifted higher in the air.

Sumayah studied the shadow, realizing it was a dragon, but which one? Shrugging it off as Drakaous or one of his brothers, she went down the soft pathway, which wound down around the bedchamber to another set of polished steps leading to the morning room. There she found her family already discussing the day's activities.

"I know Sumayah will come with us," said Jaylan as she shoved another pomegranate seed into her mouth. "Her filly can help me. I saw a beautiful bay with a half star on her forehead. I think she might be the one."

"I know just the one you speak of," replied Sumayah as she sat on the cushioned wood bench.

"You girls be very careful, and do not leave Lemuria," said Rupert, wiping the fruit stain from the corner of his mouth. "Drakaous has sent out sentries to watch the surrounding area for anything suspicious, and so far it is quiet out there. But for how long, we cannot tell."

"Well then, let's finish and go," Sumayah said excitedly as she downed her last bit of lemon and honey tea.

It was not long before the girls, except Riva, who chose to stay back with her mother, were nearing the edge of the forest of weep trees. They were not far from where they first saw Nero, and Sumayah glanced above, looking for any sign of him. *Where are you, my friend? I miss you.*

"Let's go into the forest away from the lake," Sumayah said. "There is a circle of stones not far from here." She turned to Jaylan, who was walking next to her. "I have an idea. Have you been practicing the priestess pyramid?"

Jaylan gave her a wink. "I know what you are thinking, sister, and yes, I am ready, as long as stuffy old Mergus isn't peering and fuming over me."

The sisters laughed as they skipped deeper into the woods. Pennyann and Leesabeth bounded playfully behind them, excited about the new sights and sounds.

"Our realm is much different than yours," said Leesabeth. "Things here are bigger, brighter, and have more fragrance. Your weather is much more temperate, and I do not think you get snow here."

"Snow? What is snow?" asked Jaylan.

"You have never seen snow before?" asked Pennyann, giving a wide look of amazement.

"Well, I think not, unless it is something we have that you have a different name for," replied Jaylan.

"Does it get cold enough here for things to freeze?" asked Leesabeth.

Sumayah stopped in her tracks. "What is this strange language you speak? I do not know this word *freeze* either." She then pointed. "There, see the standing rocks? It's just a short climb up the foothill. It is not far, but is worth the effort."

The girls huffed and puffed all the way to the top, and as promised there was a large circle of pink flowered moss. Sixteen towering pillars of stone edged the circle. They were crudely carved, not polished smooth like the crystal pillars at the city's gate, but as if someone had hammered them and stood them upright, so they could point toward the sky.

As they entered the circle, Ryven flashed in Sumayah's mind. *Where are you? What could you be doing? I wish you were here so I could tell you not all hope is lost. I need to explain...*

"Sumayah, does this ritual require a pentacle to be drawn on the ground, and does this pentacle symbolize the four powers of the magus?" asked Leesabeth.

"You know of this?" Sumayah asked. "I guess you would, since you were taught by our priestesses."

Jaylan had already found a long stick for the ritual. She pulled out one of her crystals, and it glittered brightly in the sun.

"This will act as my altar; I will lay it here at the point of the pentacle, the Goddess point."

Giggling, each girl pulled out her own crystal. "We are definitely what you call witches in your realm!" said Sumayah with a laugh.

"Yes we are!" replied Pennyann, taking her position in the east.

All girls stood next to Pennyann in the east. Jaylan held up her stick. "This stick, my staff, is an extension of my inner power. I will trace the pentacle upon the ground, illuminating the power from below and from above me. Here my cause, for I seek the one who would join me, fulfilling my task."

Each girl walked to her spot within the circle, waiting for Jaylan to begin her tracing of the pentacle. She started in the east and said, "Element of air, I seek your blessing and *to know*! I trust the process of your teaching."

Pennyann held out her crystal as Jaylan pointed her staff at it. "What I ask has been given!"

All the girls repeated the chant three times, each time getting louder: *"What has been asked has been given!"*

The girls went to each direction of the pentacle, charging their crystals; Sumayah could not get the thought of snow out of her mind. It was making it hard for her to keep her concentration on the ritual at hand. She felt Jaylan elbow her in her side. Startled, she looked at her, noticing the look of exasperation.

Quickly Sumayah held up her crystal and recited, "To go! Goddess, I live in your truth, and I believe! What I have asked has already been given!" She waved her crystal into the sky, noticing the telltale shadow of a dragon. As the girls finished chanting the final sentence, the sky suddenly changed. The shadow had disappeared, and she felt cold—very, very cold.

She looked down at her feet, and the pink moss was gone, replaced by something white that crunched beneath her foot. *What is this,* she thought, kicking at the white substance.

She felt a hand grasp her and roughly pull her around. Leesabeth stared back at her wide-eyed, mouth agape. Her mouth began to move, but Sumayah had to strain to her words.

"...done, Sumayah? What were you concentrating on during the ritual?" asked the shocked Leesabeth.

At first she did not understand her question, but as white, liquid crystals filled the sky and landed on her face, she began to put it all together.

"Leesabeth, is this snow?" She looked up into the falling crystals and opened her mouth, feeling the tiny, cold bursts of wet. It was more a feeling than a taste. Disappointed, she shrugged at Leesabeth.

"You were thinking about snow? Oh, Sumayah, I think you have shifted us, shifted us here," said Leesabeth, kicking snow at her in frustration.

Surprised at Leesabeth's words, Sumayah replied, "We don't yet have the power to dimension shift. I don't know what has happened. This should not have happened."

"You have not been tested, Sumayah. No one knows what inherent powers you possess. If you can get us here, then you can get us back... right?" Pennyann asked, walking closer and grabbing the girls, pulling them closer.

All girls huddled together, feeling the chill of the air. "Where are we? Where is the warmth of the sun?" questioned Jaylan as her teeth began to chatter loudly.

"This could be our realm," replied Pennyann. "We have snow, and you don't want to be out in it dressed like this." She held out her thin tunic.

Suddenly a loud roar ending in a raspy hiss echoed across the snow-covered valley. Jaylan jumped, and all girls screeched. Sumayah looked behind her at what she suspected to be a lake, now covered in snow. In the other direction were trees, thick, black trees. They did not look inviting. Another scream filled the air, making her skin prickle.

"Long-tooth," she said. The words did not sound like her own, and terror gripped her. Her stomach twisted, sending nauseating waves of fear throughout her body.

"We have no choice but to escape across the lake, but I fear it will not hold us," cried Leesabeth.

Sumayah, not accustomed to such landscapes, backed to the lake, keeping a keen eye on the shadows of the woods. Movement caught her attention, and she focused. The border of the forest seemed to awaken; emerging from the shadows came two very large cats. Their eyes glowed eerily against the opaqueness of the snow. They walked in unison, low and calculating. One sniffed the air, then hissed, tail flickering.

"Better get us back, Sumayah," said Jaylan, her voice shaking as her body convulsed from the cold.

Sumayah's mind whirled, she couldn't think, couldn't recall what it was that brought them here in the first place. She stepped in front of the three girls, holding out her arms, watching the movement of the cats.

"Let's just back up slowly," she whispered. "Leesabeth, will this hard water hold us?"

Using her foot, Leesabeth carefully brushed away the foot of snow covering. "I cannot be sure, but as deep as the snow is, I feel it could hold. What choice do we have?"

"Forget about the ice—Sumayah, just get us out," rasped Jaylan.

"Just keep moving backward, and call upon the element of fire," Sumayah ordered under her breath. "Feel it gather in our hands, but it had better be hot." Sumayah felt the intense heat build; it was much stronger than her healing energy.

"I don't think I can hold on to this element much longer. It is burning my hands, Sumayah," said Pennyann.

"Just a moment longer. We need to be able to melt the hard water in front of us, and quickly," Sumayah coached, watching the cats approach, matching step for step.

Suddenly, out of the corner of her eye, the blinding white of the sky opened, and a black figure appeared, swallowing the paleness surrounding it. With lightning speed it shot into the haze of the stormy air, a shrill roar escaping from its mouth. It rolled into the misty air, puffing billows of blackened smoke. The cats slunk to the earth, melding into the snow. Their ears flickered this way and that.

The black vengeance swooped down, spewing a fiery stream of red death. It hit cats, burning and shredding flesh and hair, mingling with the liquid crystals and spreading a canopy of red, a bright contrast against the noncolor of snow.

The cats howled and hissed. Turning, they ran, stumbling over each other in an attempt to reach sanctuary within the black forest.

"It's a dragon!" cheered Sumayah, releasing the fire from her hands with a shake.

"And just in time, look at them go!" replied Pennyann, jumping with elation.

They were so intent on the appearance of the dragon, they had not noticed the form that also appeared out of the hole. It was male, and his black hair hung lifeless from the onslaught of the heavy, wet snow piling fast. He struggled, lifting his feet higher to keep from tripping.

Sumayah felt his approach, and turned suddenly, uncaring that she was soaked to the bone, and ran toward the figure. The snow impeded her progress, but she worked and worked, her breath now heavy rasps. She would not stop until she felt his arms encircle her.

With the last of her energy, she lunged for him and yelled, "Ryven!"

CHAPTER 11

THE WIZARD'S APPRENTICE

❦

"I've been—we've all been looking for you!" Ryven said excitedly into her ear.

Her knees felt weak and buckled under her weight. Ryven held her to him. His tight embrace did nothing to chase the chill away.

"We need to get you out of here," he said, turning to the other girls. Their tunics clung to every curve of their body, leaving nothing to be imagined. Out of respect Ryven turned his head. "Come, I know the portal that brought you in. Can you walk a little farther?"

The sound of chattering teeth was the only answer he got. Ryven pulled Sumayah behind him. His tracks had made a narrow path through the mounting snow. The girls kept to the tracks, making it somewhat easier to travel. With the two cats chased back to the darkness of the forest, Nero flew near them, keeping his eyes on them until they made it back to the portal.

He was the first to enter, and with less than a blink of an eye, he was gone.

"Come on, girls, we can enter all at once," ordered Ryven as he grabbed, then shoved, one by one into the portal.

The relief was instantaneous; the heating rays of the sun took away the searing pain and ache of cold. Their chattering teeth silenced, and their hair began to dry. The moss beneath Sumayah's feet told her they were back in the standing stone circle. She looked up at Ryven, who was watching her. His eyes softened a bit as she gave him her best smile.

"Thank you, Ryven. If you were only a moment longer, we would not be standing here."

Leesabeth touched Ryven's shoulder, and he turned to her. "How did you find us?"

He looked up into the sky for the familiar shadow. He turned to Sumayah with a frown; his thick dark brows came together.

"It was Nero; you were gone so long, there were many out searching for you. I got word from one of your Lemurians and joined in the search."

"Gone so long? We were gone but a few minutes," replied Pennyann, pushing her unruly red hair out of her face.

Ryven looked surprised at her words. "You were gone well into a week's time."

"It is no matter," Sumayah said. "We are safe, and my dragon found us, though how he knew I had shifted us, I cannot tell."

Jaylan walked out of the circle and looked back and said, "I did not meet my challenge because of you, Sumayah. How you shifted us is another question. Now I will not be part of the priestess initiation, and I am going home."

Sumayah followed her sister as she stormed out of the circle.

"I am so sorry this happened. I thought our ritual would help you. Let me talk to Mother. Maybe I can convince her."

"It is not Mother...Mergus will need convincing," she replied, speeding along the wildflower path.

They bantered back and forth for a few more moments. Everyone trotted behind, trying to keep up.

Ryven suddenly stopped; the silence in the air became alive with the sound of thundering hooves.

"Here they come. Might not be too late after all, Jaylan."

Everyone halted and watched as the herd approached. Ciara was in the lead. She tossed her pretty head and snorted. Her white-gold mane framed her long neck, reaching below her chest. Right behind her ran the pretty bay mare with the half star on her forehead. The mare, slightly larger than Ciara, pranced forward next to Ciara as they came closer.

"Look at that! Ciara is bringing her right to you," cheered Sumayah. "Nobody move a muscle. Just let the mare go to Jaylan. I am sure Ciara has already told her why she is here."

A short while later, the group returned to the city, receiving a warm and cheerful welcome. Sumayah was with her filly, and Jaylan proudly entered with her bay mare.

Rupert eyed the new mare with great approval. "She will make a great companion for you, Jaylan," he said, giving his daughter a hug.

Rupert then turned to Ryven and grabbed the young man to him in a bear-like embrace. "Once again, Master Ryven, you have brought my girls back to me. I am forever in your debt."

Ryven's face turned a deep shade of red. "Thank you, but I must confess, it was not all me. It was that dragon who knew where to take me... him and that filly."

Rupert turned to Sumayah, giving her a wink. "Looks like Sumayah has more than one guardian watching over her."

Lhayan rushed forward to hug her two daughters, "What will I do with you girls! I cannot let you leave my sight!" She eyed Sumayah strongly. "You are never to leave the city gates again!"

Riva came forward and hugged the girls. "I'm glad you're back. Come, I have made medicines for all of you. I am sure you will need tending, since you have been gone so long."

Sumayah laughed at her sister. "Riva, it was a good thing you did not come this time. I don't think you would have liked snow."

The smiles and chatter suddenly stopped, and all eyes were on Sumayah.

"Snow? Where have you seen snow?" asked Lhayan, narrowing her eyes.

Rupert grabbed Lhayan and pulled her along. "Come, we have plenty of time to hear about their venture. Mergus awaits us. He is eager to hear also."

Sumayah slowed to let Ryven catch up to her. She gave him a smile. "Have I thanked you yet?"

He puffed out his chest and smiled in return. "Many times."

"Ryven, where do you go now? You are always welcome in our city... and I would like it if you . . . stayed." She had plenty she wanted to say but here was not the place, and quickly changed the subject. "What news have you of your family?"

His broad grin diminished. "Elspeth found me. My father has taken the Fae into the middle dimension of Earth. It is another dimension where hopefully the Reps and humans cannot follow."

"What, they have left? There is no one in Faeria?"

He put his hand on her shoulder and gave it a reassuring squeeze. "The elementals are still here, and there are enough of the Fae left behind to tend to Mother Earth. Though things will not be the same."

"And your sister?"

"She is...well, she is still here. She waits for someone or something. I fear she waits in vain. And she has volunteered with the others to stay behind, as I have."

Before another word could be said, they had made the climb to the seaside chambers. A slight warm breeze filled the air with a tangy, fresh scent. The Lemurians knew well the positive healing properties of the minerals in the sea and used them in abundance. The moisture from the sea water kept the skin dewy soft and the hair silky to the touch

Mergus was seated, his robes pristine and white as his beard. His look was quizzical as if he had many questions plaguing his mind. Sumayah noticed for the first time that Mesha was nowhere to be seen. She shrugged it off, thinking he was tending to one of her father's wishes, as usual.

Mergus stood as everyone got comfortable. Refreshments were served and greatly appreciated.

"So, you went to the lands where Mother Earth sleeps, young Sumayah. Tell me, young priestess, how did you shift through the portal?"

He knew? How did he already know? She fidgeted with her artichoke, the spiny top poking at her finger. Needing time to think, she slipped a leaf between her teeth and scraped the hearty pulp from the petal. She chewed once, then twice, all the while staring at Mergus. He tapped his crystal-encrusted staff next to his foot.

Knowing he was running out of patience, she said, "We were doing the priestess pyramid ritual—to summon a mare for Jaylan. Leesabeth mentioned the word *snow*, and I was curious about it, and the word was stuck in my head, so during the ritual, I could not keep my attention where needed, and, well, you know the rest."

"And you shifted to the winter lands. How marvelous!" he said with a beaming smile.

Not amused, Ryven interjected, "Mergus, they were almost eaten by two cats. If Nero and that filly had not found me and led me to them, I fear we would not be having this conversation."

"Ah, well, that answers my next question." The wizard paused, eyeing Sumayah again. "Could you tell if you were in the past or the future, Sumayah?"

She had never thought of it. The thought of being impaled by those dagger-like fangs, still fresh in her mind, made her shiver.

"There were none but us there. I could not tell." She turned to Leesabeth. "She thought we were in her realm."

Mergus walked to Sumayah. "Just knowing you can dimension shift and with all who are with you is enough for now." He bent to her and put his finger under her chin. "We will have great need of your abilities."

"Speaking of which," interrupted Lhayan as she gathered her daughters. "We have the rite of passage pending for two of my daughters."

"You are so right, Lhayan, and the timing could not be better, for there is a dark moon tomorrow and the tide will be out. I can access the cave and bring forth the One...the Holder of Light and Knowledge."

The next day everyone prepared for the ceremony. Sumayah looked for Mesha and was told he had yet to return. He was never around these days. It was frustrating to her, since she had much to discuss with him. With Ryven here she did not want any bad blood between the two. She had yet to give her father her answer, and it was becoming increasingly harder, since Mesha was never around.

Sumayah and Jaylan took their horses to the warm springs to bathe them. They had to shine brightly before they could take them to the shores of the crystal cove, which happened to be close to where Drakaous and his brothers resided. She loved it here; the air seemed lighter and much cooler. The water was tepid. She knew this because she had stolen away one day on her own to bathe in its magic waters, even though it was for priestesses and initiates only. But today they were initiates, and it was required of them to be here with their horses.

Sirius flew overhead, with another of her kind; they rolled playfully in the air and dove down in a high-speed chase, then shot up again to catch the flowing currents that would carry them, letting them hover effortlessly above.

Sumayah and Jaylan laughed at the raptor games. "Oh, how much fun would it be to fly," Jaylan said.

"That we can do, once we learn and control the art of shifting."

"As soon as I am priestess, I want to learn to shift," replied Jaylan. She stopped pouring the water over her pretty bay mare and studied Sumayah for a moment. "I think you could do it right now, Sumayah. I dare you."

"It is very tempting, Jaylan, but since I took us to the winter lands of another realm, I think I will wait for instruction first. I fear what I might shift into. Controlling my mind has been a great challenge for me. Can you just imagine if we instantly manifested everything that came into our minds? I for one am glad we cannot perform any magic until we have total control of our thoughts first."

Ciara suddenly perked up from her meditative state while being washed. She whinnied loudly right in Sumayah's ear.

"Oww, Ciara!" she cried out, putting her hand to her right ear, which rang loudly.

A large, looming shadow suddenly filtered out the sunlight above the cove. The scent of lemon and sage wafted down to Sumayah's nose. *Dragon scent. It's Nero!* The filly took off out of the water, racing for the shadow as it glided to the earth in silence. Nero purred loudly as the filly nickered and pawed at the ground.

"They have quite an affection for each other," said Jaylan, holding her mare from also taking off.

"Where one is, the other is not far away," replied Sumayah. She stepped out of the bath-like water and walked to her dragon. She held out her hand and waited for him to lower his head to her. She extended her hand to his nose, and his kind, amber-red eyes blinked at her. She felt sucked into his eyes, as if she were looking straight into his very being; she could not resist the feeling and let herself fall into his gaze. The love that enveloped her could not be measured. Further and further she fell into his gaze, and farther and farther she seemed to float away…

A sound in the distance made her freeze in her tracks, and she listened. Hearing it again, she slowly inched forward through the waist-high grass that crackled crisply under her feet. The sound, more audible now, was a long, low moan. She tried to see through the long grass, searching for what it could be. She took a few more steps, and suddenly her foot connected with a large mound of white hair, sending her backward on her butt with a grunt. She scrambled to get away as the mass struggled with long, flailing legs. Then an overpowering stench filled her nostrils. She had smelled this before; it was the stench of death. Flies buzzed noisily around the white mass as it rolled itself with great exertion, and after three tries, yanked itself to a standing position.

"Oh, you poor thing!" The words just flew out of her mouth at the horror before her. It stared at her with large, sunken, black-rimmed eyes. Those eyes, she thought. Empty. Bottomless. Its nostrils flared and blew at her as if trying to figure out if she was friend or foe. She gulped back the emotion as she took in the sack of bones. The overpowering stench hit her again, and she put her hand to her nose. It was quite evident this horse was dying. Large, fleshy protrusions hung from the front limbs of the suffering animal. A low, tired nicker came from deep within as it took a tentative step toward her. She held out her hand, and immediately it began to pulsate. A swirl of white energy lifted from her hand into a stream of glittering gold as it connected with the horse. She stood silently, letting it flow where it was needed. A long, heavy sigh came from the horse as he lowered his forehead right to the center of her palm and closed his eyes.

The immediate heart connection caught her by surprise. The strong emotion coursed through her body and streamed in uncontrollable tears down her face. In that moment they stood together and became one.

"Oh—there you are," a voice said from behind her.

Startled, she spun around to the direction of the voice to see a short, plump, gray-haired woman with kind eyes standing before her. The woman smiled, walked to the horse, and brushed at his long white mane.

"I see you found poor Nero. I was afraid he had passed during the night."

She stepped closer to the lady and introduced herself. "Hello, I am Shion—I came across the river from the little village of Dragonwyck."

The lady looked in confusion. "I didn't know there was a village across that river, and I have lived here for over thirty years. Well, I guess that tells you I don't get out much.

"I found him down the road this summer. He was just standing alone in the livery stable, no life to him. They were going to...put him out of his misery. But I wouldn't have it; I saw a spark in his eye. I believe he told me he was once a great horse, of noble breeding. I decided to call him Nero after the dragon apprentice of the great wizard Mergus..."

"Sumayah!" yelled Jaylan.

Her eyes flew open. Annoyed at the intrusion, she reluctantly willed herself from the vision. She tightened her mouth as she turned and gave Jaylan a glare.

"Jaylan, why did you wake me? I was in a vision. I must have gone to a different realm. I think I went ahead in time—with an old woman, and I found a dying horse." She paused to catch her breath. "The old woman referred to the dying horse as Nero, the same name as *my* Nero...what do you think it means?"

Jaylan just stared motionless, her mouth agape.

"I think I was looking at another of my lifetimes! Mother said time as we know it is an illusion. It does not travel in a long, straight line. It travels like the tide...all at once, along the whole shoreline!"

Jaylan tried to take in the words, her eyes almost crossing in thought. "It does hurt the head when one tries to think of it...But I do know what you speak of. Sumayah, this means we can see our past and our future whenever we want. How powerful is that!"

A little of her excitement waned. "I have yet to conquer it. It comes when it pleases, leaving me with many unanswered questions. Who is this Shion, and if the old woman was talking about an old apprentice of Mergus's, was she speaking of my Nero? If it was, the *Nero* in my vision was a dying horse."

Nero took that moment to gently poke Sumayah with his large, hot nostril, regaining her full attention.

His indigo scar pulsated from the touch of a sunray. The color flashed, and Sumayah felt the dragon's lingering pain enter her body. She grimaced from the unexpected feeling and clutched her side. The picture of a dark-haired man flashed in her mind. It was the same man she saw plunge the sword into him. She could not see his face because it was in shadow. But there was a sudden intense familiarity about it. She could not put her finger on it. Ryven came to mind and stuck with her.

"Sumayah, are you not feeling well?" Jaylan asked, her voice soft with concern. "Your face just drained of color."

Sumayah shrugged off the picture and the pain. "I am fine. Maybe the warm sun is too much for me..." Her voice trailed off as Ryven entered her mind once again. Was Nero trying to tell me something? Could that man have been Ryven? Feeling protective over her dragon, she clenched her hands so tightly, her nails dug painfully into her palms. So help her, Goddess, if she found out it was Ryven.

CHAPTER 12

THE RITE OF PASSAGE

☙

The moon was but a thin shard in the indigo sky. Stars flashed and pulsed, some like crystal droplets and others in colors of red, yellow, and bright violet. The other side of day enveloped the landscape, joining in a dance of shadows emphasized by the soothing, mystical ballad of the elementals and faerie as they tended to Mother Earth. It was a perfect night for the initiation.

The procession followed Mergus. Tonight he did not wear his usual white robes, but his finest purple, which melded into shadow, with only his white beard and waist-length tresses giving hint to his location. He walked along the shoreline. The waters had receded, revealing the white sands, soft and pliable beneath everyone's bare feet.

Sumayah enjoyed the walk along the shores. The cool, wet sand squished between her toes, splashing up to her gossamer tunic, tied at the waist with a golden sash. At the end of the sash hung tiny bells that jingled sweetly in tune with her and her sister Jaylan's step, blending with the wind song of night and faerie.

Sumayah could just make out Mergus at the lead, with Lhayan behind him. Although her father was king, he was not a priest, so he had no need to join this night's rite of passage. Tonight was just for the wizard and priestesses of Lemuria. This was Sumayah's night. She was ready, had been ready for quite some time. Her filly, Ciara, walked next to her, surprisingly calm, with the bay mare and Jaylan behind them. Ciara was not being her spirited and willful self; she too knew how special this night was and acted accordingly.

Both horses wore cords of silken gold, white, and dark blue, symbolizing the trinity, the three phases of the Goddess power. The horse, which symbolized birth, death, and resurrection, held the Goddess energy within it. The horse, able to mirror the energies of the one they choose will reveal the true inner light of the priestess initiate, if the horse begins to act in a negative manner, it is a sure sign the initiate has work yet to do.

Jaylan and Sumayah had both passed that final test. Their horses walked calmly and knowingly alongside them as if they had done this one hundred times before.

Behind the initiates walked nine other priestesses. They wore their hair straight and unbound. It fell to their waists, touching the silken sashes wrapped there. They too wore the gossamer tunic, thin and revealing, hiding nothing from the Goddess.

They passed the secret cove where the ceremony would commence and followed the wizard to the cave only a few yards away. The cave loomed above them, the shadow of night making it all the more ominous. Sumayah hoped she didn't have to enter there alone. The eerie sounds that echoed and bounced off the cavern walls floated to her ears almost as a warning. Her skin prickled in response. Ciara nudged her, and Sumayah knew she was telling her not to fret.

Mergus stopped at the cavernous entrance. The two initiates and their horses walked to him, with the rest of the procession standing in a half circle around them.

He held up his staff.

"Element of fire, keeper of the light in time of shadow, I command you to come forth." He stood for a moment staring at the large crystal at the tip of his staff. The stone began to flicker and then burst into red, gold, and lavender light. It flickered and fanned as if it were actually fire.

Sumayah had never seen this before, and she was amazed at the expanse of luminosity it offered.

"Only I have the right to enter and summon the Holder of Light and Knowledge," said Mergus and turned, entering the cave.

So, this is what wizards do. They crawl around in creepy caves to dig up old skulls. Better him than me.

All kept silent, listening for sounds in the cave that would reveal the wizard's progress. Suddenly the light of his staff announced his return, casting shadows on the ceiling of the cave. Mergus slowly emerged, grasping what appeared to be a small chest.

They followed the wizard back to the cove and walked farther, entering an inlet that had been dug perfectly round by ancient tides. Large flat stones were set a few feet apart, keeping with the circle. An altar stood at the north end of the circle; it was made from the stone of the sea, and shone a brilliant white even in the shadow of the night. The altar had a much wider, flat, circular stone balanced on top, and engraved within the circle was a five-pointed star.

Mergus walked to the altar with Lhayan. Lhayan carried a satchel, and she pulled a light violet cloth out of it and laid it on the altar, where Mergus then set the chest.

He turned to all and said, "Have all here cleansed and anointed themselves according to the rule of the Goddess?"

Everyone chanted in reply, "We have come as new, bringing only our pure golden light, those of the chosen few who have gathered for this magic rite!"

Lhayan pulled a large flat shell from the satchel. She placed it on the table, and then she took out a long athame. The inlaid stones were amber and indigo in color. A small pouch of salt from the sea and a small bundle of sage leaves were laid on the altar as well. Lhayan pulled out a crystal chalice and a tiny curved knife. She laid them all out and then picked up the small bundle of sage, untying it and putting the herb in the large white shell. She walked to Mergus, holding the shell out to him. Mergus pointed his still-flashing crystal at the bowl, igniting the sage. With a *puff* billows of smoke swirled from the bundle. Its pungent and earthy scent made its way to Sumayah, and she breathed deeply.

"May the priestesses take their rightful places forming the circle, and may the initiates come forward to me with your mares," Lhayan said.

Everyone did as bid. Sumayah and Jaylan stood in the center of the large circle, holding their mares. Lhayan walked to them, waving the shell of smoke around them.

"May fire and herb bring you passion, creativity, and the love of the Goddess." She turned back to the altar, set the shell down, picked up the chalice, and placed it in front of her. Finding the small pouch of salt, she took out three pinches, placing them into the chalice. Picking up the boline, she held it out to Mergus, who pointed his flaming crystal at it, heating it until it glowed red. She turned to the priestesses and nodded to a pretty blue-eyed priestess to her right. The priestess walked forward and took the chalice from Lhayan.

Lhayan walked to Sumayah and took her hand. Holding it up, she chanted, "Earth our body, water our blood, air our breath, and fire our spirit." Sumayah held out her hand and Lhayan grabbed it and quickly sliced the tiny boline across Sumayah's opened palm.

Sumayah sucked in her breath at the sharp pain. She watched as her palm filled with the crimson liquid, the blood flowing with each beat of her heart. Lhayan took her palm and folded it shut so that the blood would not escape, and in the blink of an eye, she was by Ciara. Ciara stood calmly as if in a trance, letting Lhayan lightly nick the place where her jowl met her neck. Blood ran, and Lhayan grabbed Sumayah's hand, putting it under the trickle to join with Sumayah's blood.

Lhayan put her hand to the mare's neck for a second, and the blood flow stopped. Lhayan directed Sumayah to dip her finger from her other hand into the small pool of blood in her palm and draw the pentacle on Ciara's forehead. When she was done, Sumayah held her hand over the chalice, letting the remaining blood drip into it.

Lhayan then turned to Jaylan and her mare and repeated the ritual. When she had finished, she took the chalice that held the blood from the four and walked back to the altar.

Mergus picked up the athame and walked next to Lhayan.

"By this rite of joining earth, air, fire, and water, these initiates are now one with the Goddess, to be of service and to do the bidding of the Goddess for as long as she is living her lifetimes upon our Mother Earth." He then plunged the athame into the chalice. "It is done. The joining has birthed anew! May the newborn priestesses, born of the God and the Goddess, forever hear their call and fulfill all deeds asked of them."

Lhayan then took the chalice with the athame still within and set it on the altar. Mergus walked to the altar and put his hands on the mysterious chest. Slowly, almost deliberately he creaked open the lid.

The air was still and silent. Everyone took a tiny step forward in antici-pation of seeing the Holder of Light and Knowledge.

Sumayah stood on her tiptoes to get a better look but could only see a smooth, rounded shape peeking from the chest. She turned to Jaylan, who also stretched to see. They eyed each other and then shrugged.

"Behold, the Holder of Light and Knowledge," Mergus said, his voice booming loudly. He stepped back and pointed his staff at the chest. The crystalline flames shot forward and connected with the chest. "I summon you, arise and awaken; we have children of the Goddess who wish to walk the path to all knowing."

A golden light within the chest sputtered as if trying to catch fire. It sputtered once more, shooting amber and lavender rays of light out the top. A low gasp went round the circle at the spectacle. The rays seemed to have enough power to reach the Arcturian galaxy. They climbed higher and higher, then burst into a million tiny specks of light illuminating the blackened sky.

Hurry, Mergus; take it out of the chest. Sumayah felt the excitement rise. Then finally he leaned his staff against the altar and carefully reached into the blazing box, his hands disappearing into the incandescence. With a half grin, he lifted his hands and stepped back with treasure in hand. He turned.

"Behold, the Holder of Light and Knowledge, one of thirteen like it in our world."

Sumayah stared, feeling the pull of its gaze. *It's looking right at me.* With a gulp she kept her eyes locked on the hollow eyes of the crystal. It closely resembled the shape of a human head, but did not have the normal features. Where there should have been eyes was large cavernous holes, illuminating amber sparks of light. It seemed to grin at her but did not have lips. Her attention was held on the colors and movement within the head-shaped crystal. The only way to describe it was it was like looking into another universe. The stars seeming to talk to one another, shooting rays of light back and forth between them. She felt it was communicating—watching her, gleaning information from this moment and sending its interpretation to its universe. She wasn't afraid, but intrigued. She felt an uncontrollable urge to hold it, to talk to it. She wanted to know.

Mergus walked to the girls. "Please do sit," he urged. He waited until they were seated and held the crystal head up. "All priests and priestess of the Goddess have joined with our most sacred one, and all have come away with knowledge and insight according to their level of understanding. Sumayah and Jaylan, in order to seal the rite of passage to the Goddess, both of you will have a chance to look into the universe of all universes and tell us what you know." He walked to Sumayah and handed her the crystal.

She could not stop the instant heat that coursed through her body even before she touched it. Her hands shook as she reached for it. And he gently passed it to her. It was much heavier than she could have imagined, and she let it settle into her lap, unable to take her eyes off it. She was pulled into the inner world of the head-shaped crystal, and the stars within pulsated more. They suddenly joined and rotated in a circle, spiraling up and up until the universal line hit her square between the eyes.

The force snapped her head back, and a violent flash of golden light blinded her. She did not feel afraid, but instead a great feeling of love wrapped around her. The love was stronger than she had ever experienced before. It consumed her. She felt safe, and most of all, she felt like she was home.

Then suddenly in front of her stood a wooden ladder. It needed no support, and as she looked up at it, she saw that it was not straight, but twisted round and round like a spiral climbing higher into the stars. The urge to climb was strong, so she put her foot on the first rung and grasped the side rails. She took a few steps up, and as she climbed, visions began to swirl in the shadows. They were visions of her childhood, beginning with her birth, then progressing through her life as she stepped on each rung. Then all went dark, and the visions stopped.

She climbed higher and higher, wanting to see more. She came to a small platform and stood on it, grateful for the rest. She sat down and watched the stars around her. The feeling was like no other, as if she had been given an herb to help her see the otherworld. But she knew she was not given such an herb this day. There were many clusters of stars. Some had form, and she tried to recognize the shape in each of them. The colors were not just different shades of blue, but brilliant greens, violets, reds, oranges, every color imagined. They swirled and intermingled, yet kept their own vibrancy.

Suddenly a beam of light came toward her until it hit her between the eyes. She had the sensation of falling. The stars fell with her, and the sky changed, and she knew she was back in Lemuria. She knew she was seeing her land, but she knew she was still on the platform of the ladder. Looking down at the ground, she felt it tremble. This aroused her curiosity, since she had never felt the ground move like this before. The trembling grew louder and stronger. Everything around her shook and swayed. The crystal pillars at the entrance to the city seemed strange without the dragons.

All forms of life were gone; the city was quiet as a tomb, except the sound of Mother Earth herself. The low growl beneath her feet built until it was so strong, she had to cover her ears. She watched in amazement as the pillars began to sway, farther and farther. *Surely they will fall and crumble into many pieces*, she thought. The buildings shook and the walls cracked. The ground opened with an earsplitting sound, and foul-smelling air shot up out of the cracks in the earth. It grew longer and wider, swallowing house after house, sliding in one by one, followed by great clouds of dust and more offending smells. The pillars never toppled, but slowly and silently sank into the growing abyss.

Her heart plunged at seeing her beautiful city slowly being consumed. And when all was gone, leaving just a gaping hole, it suddenly dawned on her that the whole city was descending, taking Faeria with it. She could no longer look nor could she bear the wail that filled the empty air. It permeated her whole being. Her heart felt as if it suddenly turned to stone. The sorrow was so deep, so heavy, she did not think she could carry this burden of knowledge, and she willed herself back down the ladder, spiraling down and down until she felt the crushing weight of the Holder of Light and Knowledge in her lap.

She opened her eyes to see Mergus peering at her, his lips pulled so tight together in question, they almost disappeared into the white expanse of his beard.

"Come, girl, what have you?" he asked in a voice much louder than usual.

His tone helped her out of her trance, and she began to feel life come back to her limbs. She felt as if she had slept for one hundred years. She was not sure how to approach the knowledge that had just been handed to her. She slowly looked at all those who loved this land more than life itself. Their feelings of expectation could be felt and made it even harder to open her mouth.

She turned to Jaylan, whose face was pale and drawn. Her eyes revealed that she too had received the knowledge.

Sumayah suddenly heard Jaylan's unspoken words. *"You saw it too, I know it. I am not sure I want to have this power of sight, and I wasn't even holding the crystal."*

"We are *one now, after the joining ceremony. That was all that was needed. You are here sitting with me, and I just had the burden in my lap,"* she replied, using only her thoughts.

Lhayan walked to the girls, bidding them to stand. She carefully took the skull-like crystal from Sumayah and handed it to Mergus, who placed it lovingly back in the chest.

"What you saw tonight was not what we had hoped. I know, my girls, for I saw it too. Be not afraid. You must tell us." Lhayan pushed her long golden braid of hair behind, leaving a few wisps of hair to frame her face.

How beautiful you are, Mother. I want to be just like you, Sumayah thought, staring into her crystal-green eyes and immortal beauty.

Ciara, still standing quietly behind Sumayah, took a step forward and nudged her in the back. Sumayah knew what the mare was telling her and turned, giving her a pat.

"You are right, my sweet one. Have courage, push through it, and reveal." Sumayah's voice cracked, and she took a second to clear the blockage from her throat. She felt Jaylan grasp her hand and give it a hearty squeeze. Sumayah searched for the words, words befitting a new priestess of the Goddess, words of great wisdom and understanding.

"Our world as we know it will come to an end. Lemuria and Faeria will sink into the waters—our beloved home, the only home we have known since our immigration so very long ago."

The priestesses behind her gasped, and a few murmurs followed. Mergus held up his hand.

"I know of this already..." He sighed deeply and stoked a tendril of his beard. "I have been informed, and now it has been confirmed. I do not doubt for an instant the validity of their gained knowledge." He stepped closer to the girls and asked, "Was there anything else?"

Both girls shook their head no. "I feared not," he said.

Sudden movement at the shoreline caught everyone's attention. Mergus and Lhayan walked the circle to the side of the shore. Six beautiful beings walked to them, as if out of thin air.

116

Mermaids, I know they are, just without their tails. It seemed odd to Sumayah to watch them walk upright, but she had heard they had the power to shift also; with the tide out, they had need for their land legs.

The leader, a very tall, handsome merman with silver hair and matching eyes, came forward with a bright smile. There were two other men, looking quite similar, and three beautiful mermaids with hair like spun white gold, almost the same color as her Ciara. The women were much shorter than the men, and all wore nothing, not even the covering that a tail would have given them.

"Ah, Malaya, what brings you to our ritual this night?" asked Mergus, returning the leader's smile.

"Greetings, Mergus, wizard of the realm of Lemuria. The one who dwells within has sent us to give you word that the time has arrived, and those who would do our world harm have come to the shores of our realm."

Lhayan smiled at Malaya. "Malaya, we have seen this night what comes. Our homeland will soon become part of your world...I fear."

Malaya stepped to Lhayan, putting his hand to her forearm. "The one who lives within wants you to remember that what was shown tonight is but only a glimpse of the truth of it. All is but an illusion. It is a means to the end, and to the beginning once more."

As Sumayah listened, a vision began to form in her mind's eye. *Yes, I did see the land submerge, but it was deserted. There was no one there. Where had the beings gone? Why were they not in the city?*

She had to speak up and interrupted, "My vision showed no one in the city when she fell into the waters. Where had we all gone?"

Malaya nodded to Sumayah. "This one will lead the way. She is like the great phoenix that rose out of the fire. She is the summoner of dragons. The wisdom will come, and you must listen...Priestess."

Mergus gave her a sideways glance. He pulled on his beard, and his eyes narrowed in contemplation.

"Yes, Malaya, you are correct, and tell Bethia that once again, she knows well. Tell her we will meet again one day, and that day seems much sooner than was written."

With that said, Malaya and his entourage walked back to the sea. They walked out of sight as silently as they had come, spiriting away into the opaqueness of night.

When they had gone, all attention went to Mergus and Lhayan. Lhayan was the first to speak.

"Sumayah, I would like to hear what is in your heart. How do you interpret your vision now?"

She thought a moment and looked at Jaylan, who gave her a smile and a nod. "When they said our world will end as they know it, I do not believe it means we will end. I believe our world will change and that we must change with it or perish. I think we have a choice. I choose to stay here on Mother Earth...There is another world within this world, like the realm of winter. Why can we not do the same, go into another realm—another dimension—like the horse and Fae, taking all our knowledge of Lemuria with us? We must go into another dimension. When the time is right, we can resurrect her, just as the phoenix resurrected out of the fire!" Sumayah studied the faces around her then set her eyes upon Mergus. "But I have just one question, a question I have asked before? Who *is* Bethia?"

CHAPTER 13

THE CRYSTAL KEY

ର

Sumayah stood alone watching the herd. She spied the frisky young colt as he playfully harassed his mother. The deep-golden mare was a favorite of her father and the colt testament to Sumayah's healing powers. She remembered back to that time, the time of his birth when he was too afraid to leave the protective womb of his mother and enter into this realm of unknown and uncertainty. It was her abilities with the plant realm and oils that eased him into the world.

"You were right to be fearful of coming here, young one," she said aloud to him. He heard her voice and nickered back to her in reply.

She searched the herd for Ciara, only seeing Jaylan's pretty bay. *Hmm, where are you off to today? I bet you are with Nero somewhere. Everyone seems to be missing these days; Mesha is out scouting for Reps for her father, and Ryven, where has he gone to?* Her stomach constricted at the thought of him and the vision of the dark-haired man plunging his sword so viciously into Nero.

Suddenly Sirius appeared, trying to land on her shoulder. Thankful for the distraction, she held up her arm.

"Where have you been, sweet girl?"

The raptor nuzzled Sumayah, nibbling softly at her ear.

"Stop that. It tickles, you silly bird," she said, turning her ear away from the assault with a giggle. She stood for a while stroking the silken hackles until a darkness, like a thundercloud ready to rain down, loomed overhead. A shrill whinny came from behind her, and she knew it was the inseparables.

Ciara skidded to a halt in front of Sumayah, nosing at Sirius, who tried to bite her in return. Ciara stomped her foot and squealed, trying to knock the bird from Sumayah's shoulder.

"Ciara, be nice. There is plenty of love to go around," she scolded, watching Nero settle silently on the ground before them.

His eyes seemed to shine as he walked toward her. Sumayah felt his lightness of spirit and reached way up to touch his neck.

"How are you today, my love? I see you two have been out already this morning."

He lowered his head and breathed deeply, and exhaled a deep, relaxed sigh. She left her hand on his neck, feeling the intense warmth at her palm.

"I haven't had the chance to thank you for helping us get out of the winter lands. How the two of you knew where we were is a great mystery. It is as though there are more than just your eyes watching over me." *Hmm, I wonder if this has anything to do with Bethia. No one will tell me about her. I don't know what the big mystery is.*

Nero purred deeply in response, closing his eyes as she stroked him softly. The vision of the white horse filled her mind; she thought back to the eyes of that horse and looked at Nero, who opened his eyes to stare at her. For a moment she thought the eyes were the same. *How can that be? Standing in front of me is this enormous dragon, and my vision held the picture of a white horse. Was the same name just a coincidence?* There was so much more to life and magic than she could comprehend. Yes, she was beginning to learn and understand, but there was always so much more.

"Will you leave with us, Nero, when we go?" she asked him. A sound in the distance announced an intruder, and Nero scrambled along the ground with a grunt. He gave her one look back before he caught the wave of air and lifted away from her. Puzzled at his abrupt exit, she turned to the intruder.

Her heart lifted as she realized it was Mesha. Forgetting Nero's reaction, she ran to him, disrupting Sirius, who had to take wing and fly.

"Mesha!" she yelled as she ran to him. She grasped him, hugging him. For an instant she thought he bristled at her touch, but her exuberance to see him overshadowed her thought.

He set her apart from him. "Let me look at you, Priestess Sumayah."

She felt the heat rise in her face. "Yes, I did it, Mesha, I am now a priestess. I have claimed my inherent powers and more!"

He frowned at her. "I have heard. Things change so quickly around here, I cannot keep up!"

"Well, if you weren't gone all the time, maybe you could," she teased him.

"You know I work in the best interests of your father. Since we were to be joined, and I was to become..." He did not finish.

Sumayah put her hand on his arm, feeling the strength. "I know things are much different now. I do not know what to do or how to act—"

"Where's the Fae?" Mesha interrupted. "Have you not chosen to join with him?"

Sumayah did not know how to answer his question and could only look at him.

"Or does he not want you now that there is no country to rule over?" he sneered.

Surprised at his remark, her voice caught in her throat. *Why are you being so cruel? I don't like your look. You have changed somehow.*

"Come, come, Sumayah, priestess of Lostworld. What say you?"

Anger welled within, and she felt heat gather in her hands. "Mesha, I don't understand. I have made no decision while you have gone. But yes, you are right about what is left to rule. We leave Lemuria, and I hope she sinks to the bottom of the waters before the Reps can take anything from her!"

"Well, if Mergus and your mother have anything to do with this, that is exactly what will happen!" spat Mesha, his expression hard and tight, making his nose curl up in that most unappealing manner.

"What have *you* to lose, Mesha? This land was not yours; you just washed ashore one day. And from where, we still do not know. What have you been hiding all these years, Mesha? Is there another reason you have come here?"

Sumayah watched his face contort. His usual bronzed skin turned an angry red, nostrils flaring, eyes narrowed. She suddenly felt fearful. The hair on her arms prickled in warning, and she gasped as he lunged for her. His grip was like iron as he crushed her to him.

"I came for you. You're mine," he said, his voice husky with emotion. He bent his head and crushed his mouth to hers, squeezing her tighter.

Sumayah's head swam. Emotion overtook her like a strong wave crashing upon the shoreline. Something within her stirred. It felt ancient and overpowering. She wanted to succumb to it, to explore this burning sensation within her. *Wait a minute,* her mind screamed, *he has no right to attack me uninvited.* Her hands began to build heat as she became filled with anger at his advances; she fought him to no avail. His grip held her.

Suddenly the heat within her hands expanded. She could not take the pain from the searing heat and pressed her hands to his chest, giving him a shove with all her might. This action sent the fiery ball of energy into Mesha, jolting him off his feet, backward away from her. *Oh no, what have I done?*

He stood, slack jawed, eyes narrowed and fists clenched. But something instantaneously within him changed.

Sumayah watched as his face softened. He walked to her to grasp her hands. She pulled away.

"Sumayah, accept my most sincere apology. It is just all this uncertainty. Where will we go, and can I follow you? I do not want to leave you; I have agonized over this since after our meeting with Faeria. Please, Sumayah, understand my position." He paused, giving her a half smile.

Hearing his pleas softened her heart. She could never be mad at him for very long. "You are right, Mesha, we are all fretting...the anguish is unbearable."

She held out her hand to him. "Come. Does anyone know you are back?"

He took her hand. "Yes, I have already seen the family. They prepare, gathering all sacred items for the...departure."

Out of nowhere Ciara appeared, trotting behind Sumayah. Flipping her head in annoyance, she flattened her ears back at Mesha and bit at him.

"Ciara, please mind your manners," scolded Sumayah. "I don't know why she does that. She does not like men very much."

The mare made another pass at Mesha, this time making contact. He swiped at her with his arm.

"Away with you, beast!"

Sumayah could not help but laugh at the two. "Maybe you should walk ahead of me. I will stay back with her so she does not partake of more of you."

He quickly obliged and moved ahead of Sumayah. Ciara seemed quite happy to have won her new position, but kept a wary eye on him.

When they finally reached the city, it was as busy as bees trying to protect their precious nectar during harvest time. Lemurians, normally a quiet and reserved race, were now hustling along the glistening streets, gathering, rooting up, and taking down. All sacred items, including sacred plants and stones, were to be gathered and packed for the journey.

Mesha and Sumayah hurried toward the palace, dodging and ducking the fracas around them. As they climbed the gleaming white staircase, Sumayah could hear a familiar voice.

"Rupert, you cannot possibly think about leaving the island unattended," argued Ryven. "We have word from elementals to the north they are fast approaching."

Not sure if she wanted to see Ryven at this moment, she hesitated on the step.

Mesha stopped. "What is it, Sumayah? Come, let's greet them." He grasped her elbow and ushered her in.

"Ah, Priestess and Mesha, we were just talking, Master Ryven and I. So glad you have come. Master Ryven does not want us to leave the two cities unattended after we leave. He feels there is too much of our culture within these walls to leave for the Reps, which could be used for ill gain."

Sumayah tried not to look at Ryven; it was much too difficult. She wanted to not only look at him, but she also wanted to feel his embrace once more. *Maybe I am putting too much into the vision Nero showed me. Maybe I am wrong, and it was not him.* She was torn. She loved her dragon and would fight to the end for him, but she was falling all too fast for this Fae, and then there was Mesha. She still did not know how she felt about him. To her surprise, Elspeth stepped from behind Ryven and her father and rushed forward to meet her.

"Elspeth, what—why are you here?"

"I had to find Ryven. I had important news for him, and his trail led me here." She grasped Sumayah's hand warmly and then smiled at Mesha, lingering a bit. "Always good to see you, Mesha. You look quite well."

Mesha tipped his head to her. "As do you, Princess Elspeth. How fares your father?"

"Why, thank you for asking...they are all gone but a few of us. Some could not bear to leave Faeria, and some have jobs here as well. We are of the mother, and we must tend to her. But this—these times of great undoing—are foreign to us. We are unsure what to expect and how to proceed once we are...overrun."

"You will go underground," said Mergus, walking toward the small gathering. "Another realm has been made ready for the Fae that men and Rep will not be able to access...well, very easily, that is. Only those pure of intention and in service to Mother Earth will be allowed into that realm. The Fae, of course, will always be able to walk between the worlds."

Elspeth seemed inspired by the news. "So we can go where you go, but also keep our connection here?"

Mergus smiled and nodded his head. "Yes, my dear, how powerful is that! This is your reward for sacrificing your choice to leave; all who have chosen to stay in service will have this power, and with it comes great responsibility." Mergus then turned to Rupert. "When will the city be ready?"

"All sacred objects and texts are being prepared by the priests and priestesses as we speak. We should be ready tonight. Have you received guidance on what to do with the cities after we are gone?"

"The cities will be destroyed," answered Mergus. "There is too much at risk to leave behind."

Sumayah could not help but feel Mesha bristle from the news. She looked up into his face, and his eyes seemed darker. He gave her a half smile, trying to clear his expression. It made her wonder all the more. *He must really love Lemuria. I cannot imagine seeing my beautiful city gone either—all the memories, all the years.*

Everyone slowly ascended the stairs to the middle chamber so they could discuss further. As soon as they reached the chamber, a large shadow materialized above, blocking the light of the sun. All eyes watched three dragons settled to the ground.

Drakaous came forward, bowing his head to all. He hesitated in front of Rupert, bringing up one claw to scratch at the corner of his large head just below his ear.

"Rupert, I fear I bring disturbing news. Your herd is gone. We cannot locate them. All have vanished."

Sumayah rushed away from Mesha's grasp. "Why I just saw them. They cannot be far. They cannot be left behind. They must come with us!"

Rupert put his hand up on Drakaous's thick shoulder. "Tell us. I have known you far too long...there is more?"

It was Baratheous who spoke, blurting the information out rapidly, "We have word that the Reps, with the help of the humans, have them. We do not know how they keep them from shifting, but they have them for food sources."

The room erupted in gasps. "How do you know this?" roared Rupert.

Sumayah felt unease in her stomach that began to spread. Her head swam, and she wavered as the room spun around her. That horrific vision shown to her by Ciara flooded her mind.

She swallowed, finding her voice. "It is true, I saw it...Ciara showed me in a vision. They have already taken many of the horses, not of our herd, but others." Reliving the horrific vision of the slaughter was too much for her, and she turned and vomited on the floor. *At least my Ciara is safe with her dragon.*

Lhayan ran to her, her face contorted in shock. She embraced Sumayah and said, "Killing another is inconceivable. Lemurians are not capable of taking another life. They feel the pain, the anguish. It is like killing themselves."

Drakaous shuffled closer. "It is time, Rupert. We are not capable of withstanding the darkness of those who descend upon us. There is no choice for us but to leave this realm."

"You are correct, Drakaous, we have just been discussing it...we leave tonight and take the cities with us," replied Mergus, his voice heavy and deliberate.

Lhayan clapped her hands to attain attention. "We must prepare now. Girls, go to your chambers and retrieve only your most sacred items."

Everyone scrambled about. Sumayah watched Ryven from the corner of her eye as he walked with his sister to his sleeping chamber. He gave her a quick glance. His left cheek twitched as his gaze then turned to Mesha.

Mesha turned to Sumayah. "I will meet you at your chamber, but first I must have a word with Rupert." He nodded to her and quickly left her side.

Dismissing him, she turned toward her chamber, Pennyann and Leesabeth fast on her heels.

"Sumayah, where is it we go?" Leesabeth asked.

"We go to Agartha, middle earth…have you not heard of it?" she replied, somewhat surprised.

"Yes, we were taught of it during our priestess training," Pennyann answered. "But we never imagined it was a place *we* could go."

"Sounds like you two might know more of it than I, for I have just learned of it myself. It seems there are many secrets kept by Lemurians." Sumayah stopped at the entrance to her chamber. "I will meet you with the family as soon as I have retrieved my items, and Sirius. And speaking of Sirius, where have the other raptors gone to?"

"They are all with the priestesses," replied Leesabeth.

"That is good; I will meet you girls shortly." Sumayah entered her sleeping chamber; Sirius was on her perch, cocking her head at her. She nodded her head up and down.

"There you are. You better stay close, we are leaving." Sumayah rummaged through her belongings, tossing or gathering her many tiny bottles of medicines, unsure what she would need in Agartha. Sirius watched her, sensing the urgency, and squawked at her.

A bang at the door to the outside entrance of her chamber alerted her. She walked to it and pulled on the latch. It was Mesha, and by the look on his face, it was important.

"May I enter?" he asked, pushing by her.

She stepped aside, noticing he carried a cloth. It was indigo blue, the sacred color of the Lemurians.

"This is from your father," he said quickly, unwrapping the cloth. "He wanted you to have it, just in case—in case something should go wrong."

What was he talking about, in case something should go wrong? How could anything go wrong? They were leaving, simple as that. Her thoughts suddenly ceased as Mesha revealed his prize with shaking hands. He grasped the latch of the door and closed it, but not before the sun caught the object, sending out a prism of light in his hand. It glittered and sparkled as if alive, dancing with a myriad of colors. Sumayah could not take her eyes off it, and the urge to touch it was powerful.

"I did not think this truly existed!" she said, excitement ringing in her voice. She went to touch it. Her hand shook as the crystal and she connected.

Mesha dropped it in her hand. "Here it is, one of the thirteen crystal keys. It is the true connection to all that is. It is the receiver of the Holder of Light and Knowledge."

How did he know all of this? He is not a priest. Her thoughts left as the crystal pulsated warmly in her hand. The tingle it created spread throughout her hand and traveled up her arm. The enormity of what she held frightened her.

"I cannot keep it; it is too dangerous for me. I do not want this responsibility!"

Mesha frowned at her, his eyes narrowed and glinted. For a moment she thought she saw anger.

"This is *your* destiny, Sumayah; do you know the power you hold in your hand, the power that is within you? Where else could be safer?"

I don't care what he says, I do not want to keep it. It is far too risky. "I know where it would be safer, and we must leave right now!" She wrapped the cloth around the crystal and shoved it in the pocket of her tunic. She grabbed Sirius off her perch and went to the door.

"Come on, Mesha, we have to go right now!"

He hesitated. "Sumayah, do you know what you are doing?" he asked, trotting after her as they quickly made their way out of the city.

A short while later, they were near the shoreline, the smell of salt filling the air. The waters crashed wildly against the red rocks piled and scattered here and there. They ran along the shore until it emptied into a large cove. The cove was calm and peaceful; the waters were a clear blue, and the bottom shone a brilliant white from the bed of coral beneath. At the far end of the cove, the weep trees and towering evergreens stood like a living barrier. Quickly they trotted and huffed beneath the canopy of trees. Sumayah spotted a few elementals peeking at her, and she thanked them for staying behind. She wondered how they were going to use their new gift of traveling between the worlds, for that was how she saw their new power—a new gift given to those who earned it.

"This is where the dragons reside, is it not, Sumayah?"

"Yes, I used to come here often when I was young. There were many more dragons that lived here, but all have long since disappeared." The mountain loomed before them, and the entrance to the home of the brothers came into sight. The entrance was open, and she walked in, expecting to see them waiting for her.

"Ah, Sumayah, should you not be preparing?" It was Drakaous.

She trotted the last few steps to the dragon, and stood for a moment trying to catch her breath. She bent over, filling her lungs with air; the pungent and familiar scent of dragon filled her nostrils. It was much stronger here, and she attributed it to being in the dwelling of the dragons.

Sirius landed on Drakaous, who chuckled in response. "Ah, Sirius, I see you have come also."

Mesha stood silent and brooding. Sumayah knew he did not want her to give up the crystal. She dug in the folds of her pale-gold tunic, unwrapped the crystal and held it up to him.

"I want you to keep this. I do not want the responsibility, nor do I care at this point the power it possesses. I am not yet ready for this. It is far too risky." She shoved it closer to the dragon, whose eyes widened.

"Interesting...she has passed the test," said Drakemon, stepping out of shadow.

"Did you think otherwise, brother?" hissed Drakaous.

"Quickly, take it from her," insisted Baratheous, also emerging from the curtain of shadow. "She is offering it to you."

What test? What are they talking about? More mystery. It is too late for this.

"I know not what you speak of, but please take this, and please keep Sirius with you, she loves you so Drakaous. Our lands are already changing, and the air is cooling with the immigration of men."

"Yes, we go to the top of the Mountain," explained Drakaous. "We will not follow you to Agartha, for we have our own duties to fulfill. We will be safe there; men and Rep alike will have no need to go there. Sirius will be safe with us. We will keep her until you're...ah...we will keep her safe for you. Lest we remind you, the power of this key can only be wielded by the one true holder. No one can open the gate unless you open it for them. Are you sure you do not want to take Sirius with you to Agartha?"

The question seemed to puzzle Sumayah. "I do not know why I leave her with you. It is a strong feeling...like it is something I must do. And if the time ever comes when I need to retrieve that key, I know it will always be waiting with you."

"Sumayah, Mesha, you must get back to your people," ordered Drakemon. "The window is closing. Soon the cities of Lemuria and Faeria will be gone."

Drakaous ushered them out of the entrance. "He is right, you must leave. We too will be gone from here as soon as you are out of the cove."

Sumayah flung herself at the towering dragon; his hide was warm to the touch. She could not stop the tear that ran down her face. Her world was collapsing around her; all that she knew would be gone.

"Take care of yourself and keep Sirius safe from harm. And please do not let *them* get the crystal key."

"Sumayah, we must leave!" ordered Mesha, suddenly in a big hurry.

It did not take them long to get out of the cove. And they ran the shoreline. Sumayah felt the urgency. She had to get back; she had to find Nero and Ciara.

Mesha abruptly halted on the shore. He put his hand above his eyes and looked out to the unending expanse of water. He pointed to the horizon.

"It's too late."

CHAPTER 14

FINDING SUMAYAH

☙

His left cheek twitched as he watched the invaders approach. From where he stood he guessed the army was a mere three hours from the city. The urgency to vacate ran rampant, and the Lemurians scurried about gathering the last vestiges of their great city. Sumayah and Mesha were nowhere to be found. Her mare had also disappeared. His brow furrowed with worry, and his mind filled with thoughts, things he should not be thinking. He had a very ill feeling about all of this and had already made up his mind that if she was not here when the rest of them dimension shifted to Agartha, he would stay behind to find her.

"No one has seen her, nor Mesha," said Elspeth, standing behind her brother.

"I will stay. I will find her if she does not make it."

"Ryven, you cannot stay. The cities will be destroyed, and we cannot say how much of the island will be spared, if any."

"They cannot destroy the *whole* island, not if she is still out there!"

"Come, it is time. We must go to where they gather."

Ryven let his sister lead him away, and soon they were standing with the gathering. Everyone congregated in a continuous circle, a spiral of beings ready to leave their beloved city.

Mergus held up his hands for silence. "The spiral of ascension will take all who are connected to it. Those of us who have the power to shift will make sure all will come. Be not afraid, for if your choice is to go, so shall you go." He stopped to scan the crowd as if searching for someone. "There is a place for us. It is called Agartha. The elders know about it and who awaits us. . ."

Mergus's voice faded as Ryven pushed past the people. He had to reach Lhayan. She would stop the destruction of the city. All of Sumayah's family was there, and he was going to make sure Sumayah was with them when they left for Agartha. He squeezed past two tall Lemurian men who frowned as he pushed toward Rupert and Lhayan.

Reaching Lhayan, he touched her arm and whispered in her ear, "Sumayah is not back. We cannot destroy the cities."

She gave him a wide-eyed stare, then searched her family. "I will talk to Mergus," she said, and hastily went to the wizard, interrupting his speech.

She whispered to him, and his look mirrored her same look of surprise. He grabbed a lock of his beard and tugged, then nodded and bent to whisper to Lhayan. Rupert looked concerned and joined in the private conversation. Heads nodded, and Lhayan walked back to Ryven.

"Ryven, it is your choice. If you choose to stay behind to look for her, you will have only two days to find her before the cities are destroyed. As heart-wrenching as it is, we cannot risk the whole race for our daughter. Rupert is the king for all the people. He must take them away even if it means leaving his own daughter."

Lhayan grasped Ryven's hands and squeezed. "I believe you will not fail. Prove me right and bring her to us." Lhayan hugged Ryven to her and held him tightly. She then whispered, "You must save her from the dark one."

Ryven pulled away and frowned, but before he could ask her what she meant, she had sneaked away, back to her place next to Mergus and her king.

He stood watching for a moment longer, wondering if he would see any of them again. Would he find Sumayah, and who was the dark one? Feeling the change in the air, he knew it was time for him to leave or shift to Agartha. Light-headed, he hastily left, his legs became as unyielding as if they were pillars of stone. Lifting them took great strength. He pressed on, finding determination in Black as the stallion whinnied shrilly for him, pawing at the ground outside the city. *I'm coming, Black, just a few more steps.*

As he reached Black, his world suddenly disappeared.

"Ryven, you have only two days to find Sumayah before Lemuria is destroyed."

The words were distant, but enough to rouse him from the darkness. Slowly he opened his eyes. Black nudged him.

"What happened, boy?" He stood. The silence behind told him they were all gone. Slowly, afraid of what he might see, he turned.

The city was dead. The crystal pillars at the city's entrance were void of dragons. It was eerily quiet, and his skin prickled at the realization that he was alone. Even Elspeth was gone. But he knew of her new power and knew she was not far and could still hear him.

"Looks like just you and me, boy."

Black nodded in agreement and pushed into Ryven, then pawed.

"I know, we must hurry," he said, putting his foot in the stirrup and easily swinging himself onto Black's back. "Have you any idea where to go?"

Black trotted off in answer.

Ryven searched the hazy blue sky. It seemed to have lost its vibrancy. Looking about, he noticed the whole landscape was not as bright, and the air seemed heavier.

"They were right, Black; all is not as alive with them gone. The upper realm of Mother Earth will no longer be what she once was."

He didn't bother looking for dragons, knowing the few that had been left were also gone. This was the new Earth, and he must attune to the new energies or lack thereof.

A bead of sweat ran down his face, and it seemed much warmer. Matter of fact, it seemed hot! No, he was not liking this new Earth and wanted to find Sumayah all the more.

Something on the horizon caught his attention. Black saw it too and stopped, giving a snort in question.

"Looks like they have arrived. We will have to change our plan. We cannot be seen by them, and since they eat horseflesh, we must keep you out of sight.

Black shook his head and nickered quietly.

"I will do my best. You have my word, no one will be eating my friend as long as I have breath in me."

Changing direction away from the shoreline led them to the mossy grasslands. It too was empty; not a single horse could be seen. They headed for the cover of the weep trees; their advantage over the newcomers was they knew their world, and *they* didn't. The entangled curtain of hanging tree limbs gave him the cover needed, but he knew what else lurked here. Nestled and piled high into the trees was a mountain of moss rocks, which was home to the long-tooth. *I wonder if they are still here, I cannot imagine they were allowed to enter Agartha.* Bethia would not stand for a flesh eater in her realm.

Though he had never met the queen, he had heard enough to know she was not to be trifled with, as she wielded strength and knowledge not known before.

Black knew exactly where they were going. Ryven never needed to guide him; it was as if they were one mind. The horse steadily climbed higher and higher until he could not do it carrying Ryven and stopped.

"You are right, I walk from here," Ryven said, sliding down. Together they climbed the last leg. Ryven held on to the horse's chest-length mane, letting the horse pull him to the top of the ridge. Once there the land leveled off, but was still covered by another eighty feet of treetops. Ryven picked a spot where he could see down to the bottom.

Black ships dotted the waters beyond the shore like fallen pinecones in a small pond. They were close enough to anchor; squinting, he could see tiny boats being lowered into the water. It would not be long before the island was overrun with men and Reps.

Where he stood, he got a bird's eye view of where he thought Sumayah would have gone. He followed the shoreline around rocks, up and down ridges, in and out of coves. To his frustration he saw nothing. With the waning of the sun, he felt the pang of worry, nagging at him like a thorn in his thumb. He had to find her soon.

A picture of Mesha entered his mind, and he felt the twitching of his cheek. *Why were you together? Where has he taken you, Sumayah?* He took the tight feeling in the pit of his stomach as a warning. He scanned the sky, hoping to see Nero. He figured the dragons went with the rest to Agartha, but that one was a loner, and he was tied somehow to Sumayah and that blasted mare of hers. He craned his neck to peer at the bite welt still on his arm.

Black stirred behind Ryven. He turned and was surprised to see an elemental petting the big horse. She was of the air, slight of build, with long flowing whips of pale hair. Her large eyes glowed a transparent blue, almost white. Her lips were thin and curved upward in a smile as she ran her hand down Black's thick neck.

"His name is Black," Ryven offered. "The color of black is a combination of all colors, so he holds the energies and magic of all colors within him."

"He will be with you always, from this lifetime on. He was chosen special for you. You both have a long journey ahead…more years than you can count. But he will be there until the last." She turned from Black and gazed upon Ryven. Her eyes widened, and she smiled brightly.

"The one you seek is not safe; her dragon tries to get to her, but is afraid. Her mare travels with the dragon. The dragon will not let her away from him."

This news energized him, and his heartbeat quickened. "Please, where is she? Can you tell me? I have but a short time to find her."

"You must travel back down to the Crystal Cove, where once the dragons three lived. Beyond the cove is the trail of sand. It expands beyond the waters and is unyielding and treacherous."

Ryven knew the trail was put there to deter travelers away from the realm of the cities. "Can you summon the dragon? He goes by Nero. Maybe together we can get her back."

"The one called Sumayah has been taken; those who eat of the flesh have taken her, and many others like her."

"You mean the Reps have taken her?" His heart slammed to a halt and caught in his throat, the slow and deliberate beat making his head swim.

The sylph nodded. "They have taken her and the one."

He knew she meant Mesha. *Some protector. He got both of them caught.* He felt the heat rise within as he seethed with anger. His left cheek muscle twitched, and his jaw ached as he ground his teeth.

"I will help you find both of them," said another female voice from behind him. He spun and was relieved to see Elspeth. Gone was her normal gown of gossamer silk. Instead, she was dressed much like him, in a tunic with vest and thin breeches, that held tightly to her legs. He had to admit she did look quite handsome in his attire, her long black hair hanging over her shoulder in a thick braid. At her side was a sword. *A sword! She could not possibly know how to wield a sword. Whatever is she thinking?*

She smiled and grasped the hilt. "I know what you think, brother. I too have been practicing, I too know of the future, and this is now part of it... unfortunately." Her eyelids lowered, expressing her sorrow.

"Well, sister, let's see what you know." His eyes glinted as he pulled his sword out. He held it up to her and winked. "Ready, Princess Elspeth?"

"Brother, do you dare?"

"I dare!" He lunged at her, slicing his sword with one expert swoop toward her.

She sidestepped back and to the left, swinging her sword up in answer. The clang of metal was sharp and loud.

"Very impressive," he said as he sliced the air at her again.

"Oh, there is much more where that came from," she grunted out, lunging at him with lightning speed.

His eyes widened in surprise as he hopped backward, staving off her unending attacks. *Clack, clack, clack* rang steel to steel. Forward and backward, right and left they went—a duel to the death!

"Good show, sister, but I have had enough!" Ryven caught her arm under his and with one strong upward push, her sword flew out of her hand to land in the moss. He bowed to her, giving her a wink. "Well done, princess of Faeria."

At the word *Faeria,* they both got quiet. Elspeth picked up her sword and sheathed it again at her side.

"I wish it was Faeria we fought for."

"We do, Elspeth; we fight to bring her back. I know in my heart that one day Faeria will return."

Elspeth turned to her unicorn to hide the tear that slid down her face. "I stay in a hope that it is true. But I have seen what is ahead, Ryven; man will become a slave to the Reps. They will turn from the Goddess, from Mother Earth, and will replace all of it with their one God shrouded behind its crystalline mask of gold."

Elspeth's unicorn suddenly nickered. Elspeth looked up, her face shadowed by the descending form, which glided with a flap of its mighty wings and settled onto the soft ground.

"Nero, am I happy to see you! This pretty sylph said you..." Ryven looked around for the elemental. "Well, she was here a moment ago."

"She was not particularly fond of our swordplay, Ryven," said Elspeth with a giggle. "Where is the mare, Ciara? Aren't the two joined?"

Ryven snapped his head around to avoid any unpleasant surprises. "I suspect she went with the rest to Agartha. But if Nero did not, then she must not be far."

"Everyone made it safely; all Faerians and Lemurians are in Agartha. They anxiously await your return, Ryven. That is why I have come; Lhayan and Jaylan want Sumayah back safely. That wand-wielding wizard is quite content with your abilities, but seems much too smug for my liking," said Elspeth with a laugh.

"I have a feeling Mergus knows more than any of us could possibly understand. The way he shifts here and there...why, he reminds me of Mesha, never around, always off on a mission."

Elspeth lit up hearing Mesha's name. "Do you think the two of them are safe?"

Ryven frowned at his sister. "We must be on our way...I have wasted enough precious time already, what with swordplay and all. I should be after Sumayah." He stomped to Black and gave him an affectionate pat. "Come, my friend, let us be on our way."

"Wait, where do we go?"

"Did you forget how to speak to elementals of the air?" Ryven yelled over his shoulder. "That sylph just told me to go to Crystal Cove and turn onto the trail of sand."

Elspeth did not speak again and followed Ryven, with Nero overhead and her unicorn next to her.

As they descended the mountain, still hidden in the shadow of trees, they watched the shoreline. More intruders had made land and resembled a colony of ants as they busily darted this way and that, like some sort of preattack performance.

Ryven looked into the air, hoping Nero had cloaked himself. He did not see the large black shadow.

Suddenly, from the bottom of the mountain, just where the trees joined in a curtain of darkness, came the golden glow of Sumayah's mare. She whinnied frantically and with tail flying high, sped her way right up to Ryven and Black.

She reared into the air; her coat was matted with sweat. Upon further inspection Ryven noticed an open and bleeding slash at her left shoulder.

Elspeth quickly came forward and put her hand near the wound. "Sword?"

"Looks like it to me, and by the sweat caked on her coat, she had quite a fight on her hands."

The mare jigged back and forth nervously; she bobbed her head up and down, with her ears flattened against her head. The more she jigged, the more the blood seeped from her wound.

Elspeth calmly put her hand to the forehead of the mare, and with her middle finger traced a five-pointed star. She held her finger there for a few moments more. The mare immediately calmed, and the wound stopped dripping.

"There, that should help her; Lemurians are not the only ones who can heal."

Nero had landed and pushed his way toward the mare. He nudged her and nosed the wound, taking in a deep breath. The mare nickered quietly and pawed playfully at the dragon.

Ryven chuckled. "I just don't get it."

"Never saw such a joining either, Ryven. But something has me wondering about this. I noticed that the few remaining dragons are staying much closer to the herds. It's as if something is afoot."

"Rupert's herd is gone. Did they make it to Agartha?" Ryven asked, putting his hand on Black to lean against him.

"They never appeared. I do fear the worst."

"I do too; I think we might find Sumayah and the herd together. It is apparent Ciara had to fight for her life, and I think this is all connected somehow." Ryven turned into the cover of the forest.

Ciara, sensing where they headed, promptly pranced her way to the lead, her feet barely touching the ground. They followed her through the forest, the back door to the trail of sand. Nero flew out of sight, staying cloaked in the air.

Then suddenly the trail was there, bone dry and dusty. Not a tree was in sight; only tall standing rocks, red in color, jutted out of the sand. Some were almost as tall as the trees in Faeria.

The sun beat down on them. Ryven dripped sweat. This was the hottest he had ever felt it. His tongue stuck to the inside of his mouth, and his eyes burned from the sweat dripping in them. He rubbed his forehead and watched the sky. Nero was nowhere to be seen, nor could he feel the breeze from his flapping wings.

"I fear the dragon has deserted us."

Elspeth trudged alongside him; she had already taken off her heavy vest. "I don't blame him. This heat and sun are unbearable. Without the balance of nature—with everyone having left—I fear the weather here will become very unpredictable and more extreme."

Suddenly Ciara stopped, her ears flattened, and she jigged in a circle as if afraid to go forward.

"Hold on, girl, let me take a look," Ryven said as he walked ahead of her, hugging a trunk-like standing rock. Slowly he inched his way around, ignoring the sweat that dripped onto his chest. He flattened himself to the rock, willing himself to become the rock. When he felt he was cloaked, he peeked out.

He estimated the camp to be no more than two miles away. The ground was flat and straight enough to see almost to the shoreline, which helped him gauge the distance. This was not the same group he had seen earlier on the shoreline. It worried him that there were more. They had tents, hundreds of tents, already dotting the white sands. Only a few hundred yards from the tents was a makeshift enclosure. It was made of trees that had washed up on shore. Rupert's herd was enclosed in the makeshift corral. Some had already been made ready for food, and he could not help but stare at the skin-stripped carcasses hanging, while men uncaringly cut huge chunks of flesh. The stench of what he could only describe as death carried to him, making his stomach roll. It was like nothing he had ever seen or smelled before. It was a new sensation, a feeling he did not like.

Elspeth pushed behind him. "What do you see?"

He pushed her back behind the stone. "You must not look. They are there, but you must not look."

She muscled past him and abruptly stopped and turned back to face him.

He watched her face drain of color and the crystalline green of her eyes turn deep brown.

"Your eyes. What has happened to them?"

She put her hand to her mouth and gagged. She tried to compose herself and walked to her unicorn. She whispered into the pretty mare's ear, and the mare promptly turned and walked a few steps before she dimension shifted safely back to Agartha.

"I feel tainted by what I just saw...I will not let her become food for barbarians."

"You are right, Elspeth; they are no help to us if we worry for their lives." He turned to Black and rubbed his ebony face. "It is better for you if you leave us, my friend. Take that mare with you. She has already been hurt enough by them." He pushed on Black's face, turning him around, and pushed on his shoulder. "Go, do not turn back. I will call for you when I need you. Now go, and take her with you," he finished, pointing at Ciara.

Black flattened his ears at the mare, and she trotted in front of him. He bit at her rump, keeping her moving away. Before long they both were out of sight. A dragon shadow suddenly appeared, flying toward the retreating horses.

"He has been here all along," Ryven said. "Look, see how he follows the mare."

They watched the sky as it swallowed the dark shadow and became whole and blue once more.

"If Sumayah is in that horror, how do we get her out? It is us against"— Elspeth pointed toward the tent city—"all of them."

"We have a plan."

Ryven and Elspeth turned to see Leesabeth, Pennyann, Jaylen, and Riva smiling at them.

"Why are you here?" asked Elspeth as she ran to them and hugged each one.

"It was Bethia who sent us, and Mergus was worried that time was running out. Lemuria will be gone soon," answered Jaylan, hugging Elspeth.

"Mother felt you needed our help too, and I have been studying with her closely, so I have much magic up *my* sleeve," boasted Riva, pointing her finger to her chest.

Ryven walked up to them, and eyed their manner of dress suspiciously. "Is this something Bethia has cooked up?"

"This is part of the plan, Ryven," Pennyann answered, shaking her hips and making her skirt of many bells jingle sweetly.

They all did look very enticing, the colors bright and vibrant. The music that came from their every movement kept his full attention. This was not the usual long silken tunic; this caught his eye. He looked from their bejeweled pointy-toed sandals, up to where shiny pieces hung in a rope around their hips and then to the tightly fitting bodices, exposing rounded flesh that threatened to pop out of the fabric at any moment. He felt the heat rise in his face as he could not help but linger. They were stunning.

Leesabeth walked forward with a bundle of clothing very much like their own and handed them to Ryven. "These are for the both of you."

Elspeth pulled at the pile of clothing and picked what she wanted. "Why is there clothing left?" she asked.

"Bethia told us of the tradition of her people, and how the women would dress and dance in honor of the Goddess," answered Leesabeth. "She has been watching the Reps and their men; since they have appetite for flesh, she thought they would enjoy a dance from us!"

"You mean a dance that is specifically to honor the Goddess will be used to lure men?" asked Ryven. He could not believe this was the *plan*.

"This is just to keep the attention of these flesh eaters as we dance for them. We will also be serving them a special drink," replied Riva, holding up several drinking vessels. "All they really have to do is smell it, and they will be asleep in minutes." She pointed to the clothing in Ryven's hands. "And that is *your* dress. You will also dance for the men."

Ryven dropped the clothing as if it were on fire. The expression on his face made everyone break out into strong laughter, jingling of bells sounded in perfect rhythm.

CHAPTER 15

ROPES OF IRON

☙

S umayah's heart sank, and her throat constricted. *They're here, between us and the city. How can we get back to the city without being noticed? If only Nero were close, he could—well, maybe he could help somehow.* But then her mind suddenly changed at the sight not far offshore, closer to the tree line. Hot tears cascaded from her eyes, sliding to the corner of her mouth. She knew why they were in there: food for the barbarians that came to their sacred lands. Quickly she wiped away her sorrow so Mesha would not see.

"There must be more already on the island, more than what is still in the boats." He pointed to the makeshift enclosure. "They keep horses for…"

He did not finish and looked at Sumayah. He could tell by the look on her ashen face she had already seen them. He looked back at the captives.

Not used to being penned, they milled around their prison, nipping and biting at one another in frustration and fear.

"Why don't they dimension shift?" Sumayah mumbled. "The Reps must have some sort of magic to stop them." Sumayah could feel their confusion. It hit her heart like someone had swung a bag full of rocks at her. It was excruciating. She could not bear this burden, nor could she separate their pain from her thoughts. She put her hands to her ears to block their thoughts, thoughts of great anguish and the strong urge to be let free. One simple word rang in her head over and over, as if all of them were screaming it at once. *"Why?"*

She felt Mesha's hand on her shoulder; it was warm but not comforting. She shrugged it off, suddenly very, very angry. Was it the anger of the horses or her own anger? She could not tell.

"Don't touch me," she hissed at him. "Why is this happening? I do not understand."

"But look, I don't think they are your father's horses."

"They are horses nonetheless! They were once free and were never, ever intended to fill another's belly. They are sacred, given to us by the Goddess. Their blood is not to be spilled by anyone!" She backed off, suddenly hating him. Her fingers clenched, nails digging deep. The pain felt good to her. This was at least her own pain, and it helped to block out the pain of those captured. She wanted to run to him and pummel his chest until he hurt as much as her. She wanted him to feel what she felt. Then she heard and felt a loud *snap* on her head, and all went dark.

It was the second day of her capture when she awoke to water being poured on her. The initial shock made her jolt upright. The salty water stung her eyes, and she rubbed them with her fingers. The reality of the situation suddenly flowed back into her mind. She looked around surprised to see others like her; how they got captured, she did not know. She thought they all had gone to Agartha. But some of them she did not recognize. They could be from another tribe from another city. She had heard of them, but had never seen them.

Screaming caught her attention. These screams she had heard before. She did not have to look to know what it meant. The barbarians not only ate the flesh of her beloved and sacred horses, but they also took great pleasure in beating and pleasuring themselves with the women of her land. Out of the corner of her eye, she saw three of them; the first one clubbed the poor girl on the side of her head until she stopped screaming, then savagely ripped her paper-thin tunic from her. Sumayah turned her head away hearing the girl's last gasps, trying to hold on to life.

Sumayah had never witnessed death in this matter before. Lemurians lived to be over two thousand years old, and death was a time of great celebration. It was time of ascension to a higher realm. Sumayah wondered if these men had taken away this girl's right to a sacred passing into the next realm.

Sumayah rolled onto her back, the sand scratching her tender flesh. Sand was everywhere: in her eye, in her hair, rubbed into her exposed flesh until she bled. Her feet were cracked beyond recognition, and the pain was unbearable. Her stomach lurched, and bile rose to her mouth. She let it flow onto her chest, hoping the stench of vomit would deter them from attacking her.

The heat was unrelenting, and it parched her so that she was always dizzy and tired. She looked to see Mesha talking with other men; they were of another tribe from the island.

"They take us as slaves, to build their city of gold," said one of the dark-skinned prisoners.

"Do they not know that they cannot mix the tribes?" another asked.

Mesha answered that question. "They do not care of your beliefs, for they have a god of their own, one who overrules all other gods."

"How can there be balance if there is only one god?" asked a petite, pale-haired girl. "There cannot be balance without a god and a goddess; their world will spin out of balance, as did Atlantis."

Sumayah noticed that one of the barbarians caught sight of the conversation and walked to the small gathering. He yelled something she did not understand and raised his long, heavy sword. Panic overtook her, and her heart thumped. She grasped her chest and opened her mouth to warn Mesha.

Mesha looked at Sumayah and gave her a half smile before the blunt end of the sword connected loudly with his head. The look of surprise widened his eyes. His left nostril curled upward as his mouth tightened in a grimace and he slumped to the ground.

The scream built in the pit of her stomach. She could feel it rush upward to her mouth. She opened her mouth, and it filled the air, cutting the silence, blocking all other noises. She watched unbelieving as Mesha lay in a pool of his own crimson blood, the sand greedily soaking it up.

The barbarian grabbed Mesha by his arm. The barbarian was very large; his energy was gruff and unapproachable. His eyes were small slits on a large, melon-size head. He sneered at Sumayah and grunted, then dragged the lifeless Mesha out of her sight.

No one else dared look at her, for they feared they would be next. She searched the sky over and over, hoping for the black silhouette, but it never came. She was alone. She felt such emptiness and despair, she no longer cared if the barbarians singled her out next. It surprised her that they did not even give her notice. It was as if she did not matter.

The sun began to thankfully set, which meant the searing heat would no longer burn her flesh, but she knew in its stead would be the chill of night. At this point her flesh, blistered and red, could no longer stand the intense heat of the day, and she welcomed the chill.

She looked longingly throughout the camp, its usual tents grasping Mother Earth like ticks on the back of a long-tooth. She wished one of the tents were being readied for her, with a nice tepid bath waiting.

Suddenly a scent carried to her nose. It was subtle, and she breathed in again. There was no mistaking dragon scent. Her heart jumped with the thought of a dragon. Was it Nero? Was he lurking nearby? She hoped Ciara was not nearby.

It was not long before all captives, all twenty-six of them, were set in a row, their hands bound with thick, flesh-piercing rope. The men bound them to one another so if one wanted to escape, he would have to take all with him. The ground was still warm, and as night overshadowed day, the chilled breeze began its nightly dance. She sniffed the air and could smell the dragon scent again. It was close, but where? Suddenly the empty air was filled with an earsplitting bellow, a most mournful sound of unending pain. Everyone muttered as the sound blasted the air once again. The camp suddenly exploded with action. There was a great commotion, and men scampered this way and that, some yelling commands, others obeying. A new sound could be heard in the already congested air. This was not organic, but something that squealed and creaked along. The sound got louder and more annoying, the closer it got. Everyone on the rope line watched in anticipation, looking for what approached.

The crack of a whip sliced through the air, and the scream of horses answered its sting. Finally it came into sight. Six sweating, snorting, and groaning horses bound together with ropes and strange lengths of wood pulled a towering wooden cage. From where Sumayah sat, she could barely see what was inside. As it got closer, she saw that it was tied with many ropes, and pieces of thin iron looped together, forming a long rope of iron. The iron ropes held the straining beast within the moving house of wooden poles.

The prisoner within the cage suddenly went silent and strained its head in Sumayah's direction. For a second it was able to look at her. The name *Sterling* filled her head, and an overwhelming feeling of knowing. *I know you, dragon, but how? I never saw you before. And why are you tied within the cage?*

Then she remembered. This could be the dragon they spoke of, that could teach men how to dimension shift. *It must have been forced to bring this swarm of evil to our lands, no matter the reason. Maybe they were going to eat his flesh too.* Anger began to build and flame within her. She strained at her tethers as a man walked to the cage and stuck his long-sword within, poking and jabbing at the beast until blood ran.

"Stop it, you barbarian!" she yelled at the top of her lungs.

Her twenty-six fellowmen gasped at her outrage.

"Leave him alone, you stinking barbarian." She struggled at her ropes, her mind on fire, wishing her hands to burn. She could see her fingers turn to flame and feel the searing heat against her back. Just before she could stand it no longer, the ropes separated and fell behind her. She jumped up, looking at her flaming fingers in surprise. The flames spread up her arms, enveloping her whole body. She walked toward the man, watching his face contort in astonishment.

Her twenty-six supporters chanted the word *phoenix* over and over, adding to the frenzy of the moment.

"Take another step, and I will send this sword through her belly and slice open her gut," came the steely and deliberate voice behind her.

She could hear a nervous nicker; she knew it was Ciara without even looking. The heat of the moment was extinguished like someone had thrown a bucket of cold water on her. Her fiery tentacles diminished, and she turned to see a hulking man. His boulder-size fist clamped around the hilt of his sword and pressed it into the petite mare's belly. Ciara's eyes rolled until the whites flashed. Her nostrils flared, and she quivered with fear. The man had a rope in a stranglehold around her delicate neck. The skin wrinkled where it was pulled tight. She fought for air as he twisted it tighter.

"Stop, you're killing her," Sumayah said, taking one brave step toward the man with her arm out in front of her and palms facing up. "What do you want from me?"

"Someone wants you for himself, and he is keeping this mare to ensure you obey by not using magic," the man said gruffly. He yanked on the rope and spat at Ciara. "Though she be too puny to eat!"

147

The dragon in the cage suddenly roared and threw himself against his restraints.

"Shut that beast up!" the man bellowed. The man nearest the cage promptly poked his sword at the dragon.

"Who is this man? What does he want from me?"

"Oh, never you mind, you will see him soon enough. But in the meantime, we have a city to build, and you are going to help us by leading us to *your* city. We hear there are enough jewels and gold there to build five cities!"

"There is nothing left there. Everyone has gone and taken what you seek with them!"

"We have reason to believe otherwise, little priestess. Now get back over there, and just remember, she dies if you try anything." He yanked on the rope, turning away. Ciara tried to fight back, but the man hit her hard with the flat side of his sword between her ears. The force almost sent her to her knees. As the man dragged her away, one nicker escaped from her constricted throat.

It tore at Sumayah's heart, and tears of frustration and anger ran. She slumped to the ground.

She felt a comforting hand on her shoulder. "Have no fear, dear one, all will be well. We will do what needs to be done. Do not forget why we live here on Earth. We must endure."

Sumayah lifted her head to give the woman next to her a watery stare. She was right, but she did not think she had what it would take to do what she knew needed to be done.

The woman, about Lhayan's age, put her finger to her lips as a sign for Sumayah to be silent and carefully pointed up.

Sumayah looked with her eyes, being careful not to turn her head, and saw a familiar black-winged shadow disappear down into the shelter of the trees.

Nero. It *had* to be him. What other dragon would come here? She was so excited about his arrival; she did not see the parade of gaily dressed women walking out of the protection of the forest.

A few barbarians whistled and called out, using words she did not understand as the women approached. There were six of them, and they did not wear the normal dress of Lemurian women. Their clothing made music as they walked, and the pieces of gold sewn to their garments flashed brightly in the descending sun. She noticed they also carried drinking vessels.

148

The men grabbed the vessels from the women and drank greedily. Soon more and more of the men joined the gathering; they became loud but very amicable toward the women. They did not treat them as they treated the Lemurian women. They joked and poked at them or gave them an occasional pinch, but that was all.

This perplexed Sumayah, as she watched the women. There was something about them. Their faces were veiled with beautiful iridescent scarves, hiding all but their eyes, yet still, something made her watch them all the more. One in particular caught her sight. She was much taller than the others, and she looked much stronger. Sumayah watched her closely and finally got a good glimpse. She was not as pretty as the other girls, yet the men seem to like her the best. Strange it was, but then again she knew nothing about these men.

The young girl next to her whispered, "The tall girl is getting the most attention, yet she would have been my last choice. Look, they drink too much, and now they sleep."

"There was something different about these girls. I feel as if I know them," replied Sumayah, watching the last of the men nod off to what seemed a comfortable sleep.

As the last one went down, all girls tore off their scarves, hurried to the twenty-six, and began to release them from their constraints.

Recognition set in, and Sumayah cheered. "How on Mother Earth did you get here? I thought you had gone with the rest."

Ryven, looking very odd in his manner of dress, stood with an awkward smile.

Sumayah, so very happy to see him, threw herself into his arms. "I don't know if I should be jealous of you or not," she teased. "Looks as if you won the hearts of all those barbarians."

His face turned crimson. "Sumayah, they were not charmed by my looks; they were charmed by my glamouring."

"Are you sure, Ryven? Looked to be more than glamour to me." She let him squeeze her, taking comfort in his embrace, but this moment was fleeting as the black-eyed stare of Mesha filled her mind, and she pulled away from Ryven.

"Girls, the past days have put me through so many emotions," said Sumayah. "I have felt things I have never knew existed. There is so much sorrow and hurt out there, more than you could ever understand."

Leesabeth came forward and put her arm out to Sumayah. "Sumayah, you forget we are not of Lemuria, so we have been exposed to what you speak of. What is it you need to tell us?"

"Mesha is gone. I did not think it could happen. He was killed..." She choked out her last words, then buried her face into Ryven's chest.

"No, this cannot be," cried out Elspeth, her voice heavy with emotion. "He cannot be..." Riva went to her and put a comforting arm around her.

Sumayah, confused by Elspeth's reaction, looked up at Ryven. He shook his head at her.

"We must leave this place. Mergus granted us two more days before the city is destroyed. Or time is up and we must get back to Agartha," ordered Pennyann, looking around at the other captives. Her eyes then locked on the cage holding the dragon.

"What the—" she said as she walked toward the cage.

"Pennyann, stop," ordered Sumayah. "He is very angry. They have been torturing him. I would not go any closer." She tore herself from Ryven and ran to Pennyann with her eye on the dragon, which suddenly brought Ciara to mind.

"I must find Ciara. She was being held by someone here in charge, to keep me from using my magic. But I think he is in that pile of men. He spoke of a man who came here for me . . ."

"More magic, you have more magic?" interrupted Riva, walking toward her.

"It seems my magic is growing ever stronger...like I am being forced to learn through all of this," she said, circling her arms out and around her, describing all of her tribulations in the past few days.

Ryven rushed toward her, rearranging the bottom half of his clothing, which was threatening to expose what lay underneath.

"Where *is* that feisty mare? It was her that brought us closer to you, but we sent her away, along with Black and the unicorn, to protect them. If you saw her, then where are Black and Elspeth's unicorn?"

Elspeth came to Sumayah's side. "Do they have any other horses kept here?" she asked, worry marring her normally beautiful face.

"We saw where they were keeping them, not very far from here," answered Sumayah, turning to Ryven. "There were more than I could count, and it could very well be they all got captured together. I fear what might have happened to them. This man who wants to keep me is using Ciara as a pawn. If he knows my connection with her, he most likely will know the connection to the others."

The image of a terrified Ciara brought her back to the reality of the moment.

Suddenly a voice from behind one of the tall standing stones said, "Someone looking for a horse?"

CHAPTER 16

CLASH OF THE DRAGONS

☙

Sumayah spun in the direction of the voice and saw him. Her knees went soft. She felt as if things were spinning out of control. Her mind could not make sense of it. He was dead, and yet he stood holding Ciara, his bloodthirsty dagger pressed at her throat.

Elspeth spoke first, stepping closer to Mesha. "Mesha, we thought you had perished. What can we do to help you? Something most certainly is wrong."

"Elspeth, I'm sorry it had to turn out like this," he said, pressing the sharp edge into Ciara's neck where it met her jaw. The mare snorted. Her ears flipped back and forth, trying to figure out her predator.

"Unfortunately your unexpected arrival has changed everything! Now I must rewrite the plan, and how this ends is entirely up to all of you."

Sumayah's confusion turned to anger. She constrained a strong desire to lunge at him.

"Let my mare go, Mesha. You don't need to do this. I don't know what it is you want, bu—"

He cut her off, snapping his reply. "I want the crystal you left with that damn dragon, that's what I want. I thought by pretending to be dead, I

153

could find an outside way to control you…follow you until your moment of weakness so we could reclaim what is ours." His eyes softened, and so did his demeanor. "We were promised to each other, Sumayah."

Her head swam at his words. *What was he talking about?* She shrugged her shoulders and held out her hands to him.

"Mesha, I do not understand. The crystal belongs to the Lemurians from their homeland of Arcturus." She had to think, take him off the trail of that crystal. "You know the crystal is of no use to you without me. But, it has been returned by the dragons. They knew it would be safer out of their keep and back with my father. It is now in Agartha with the one they call Bethia."

Out of the corner of her eye, she saw Elspeth whisper to Ryven. Before she had time to react, Ryven's sword was in his hand—from where, considering his manner of dress, she did not know. The scene before her suddenly slowed. Her world stopped as Ryven lunged for Mesha. Mesha reacted by slicing his dagger at Ciara's throat. The mare screamed, rising up on her hind legs, shaking her head to release the grip of death.

Sumayah willed herself to run, but her legs held fast to the ground. Everything around her stopped except the blood that drained from her beloved mare.

"No!" she screamed, the word sounding slow and foreign to her hears. "No!" The word was barely audible. She watched, unable to move as Ryven sliced his sword through the air, only to be blocked. Mesha, wrenching his sword from the sheath at his side, jabbed at Ryven again and again, sending the Fae into a backward dance.

Sumayah felt hands at her back. She looked up to see Jaylan at her side. "Come, you must save your mare."

Leesabeth and Pennyann struggled to keep the waning mare on her feet, leading her away from the ensuing battle.

Blood, so much blood. Why did it have to be Ciara's? The white sands beneath the mare gorged on the liquid, sucking it deep within. The mare's head hung to the ground, and her eyes began to deepen. It was too late. Her soul was already leaving her body. Sumuyah knew it by the emptiness of her eyes. Trembling uncontrollably, she stumbled to her mare.

"You must do this, Sumayah," pleaded Jaylan. "You are joined…if she dies…"

Sumayah looked around. Ryven and Mesha were still at their sword fight, the clash of iron to iron singing its song of impending death. Riva lay a few yards away, in a fainted heap. Sumayah looked down at her hands that were already on fire.

Fire, that's it! Before she could get her hands on the mare, Ciara suddenly sagged to the ground with a loud moan. Sumayah fell at her side and gripped the gaping wound; blood seeped between her fingers, warm and slick. *We are joined, fire must save us.* Her fingers burned, her hands glowed a fiery yellow, and she stood by her mare, directing the flame through her hand to the wound. The wound sizzled beneath her grasp, and the blood suddenly ceased its flow. She held her hands, letting the energy flow throughout the mare, replenishing what life's energy was lost.

"She's beginning to stir," whispered Jaylan. "I knew you could do it; so did Elspeth."

Feeling the life pour back into her mare, Sumayah turned her head to where the battle continued. Still confused and dazed at the spectacle, she watched as Ryven tripped and almost went down, with Mesha slicing after him, only to be met by Ryven's blade. Their voices carried to her.

"I was right about you," Ryven said, spinning to avoid another of Mesha's expert assaults. With Mesha almost directly behind him, he sliced hard, hitting Mesha's shoulder.

Before the blade could enter all the way, Mesha ducked and spun, swinging his sword low toward Ryven's leg.

Ryven easily sidestepped his thrust. "Nice maneuver Mesha. I did not know a Rep could use a sword in such a manner of expertise."

Grunting with exertion, Mesha replied, "Why, my Fae friend, I have plenty of maneuvers you have yet to see."

"Show me; what I have seen so far has left me unimpressed." With lightning speed Ryven attacked Mesha with a rapid barrage of sword thrusts, connecting with a thick slice to the fleshiest part of Mesha's side. Blood spurted from his tunic.

Wide-eyed, Mesha let out a growl, clamping his hand to his side. "Enough of this child's play. I am through with all of you!" He suddenly let out a roar, his body convulsed, and a black light flashed from every pore of his body.

Ryven backed away in surprise, holding his sword at the ready.

The pinpoints of black light suddenly joined, forming a black thick shadow. The shadow grew taller. Mesha's human form was no longer discernable, and another bellowing roar filled the air around him. The massive blanket of darkness emerged into a perfect, massively muscled dragon formed for one thing. To kill.

Ciara jerked in Sumayah's hand. The mare screamed. The sound, loud and shrill, stung Sumayah's ears. Sumayah had never heard her do this before and looked at her.

"He is a Rep!" yelled Ryven. "I don't think I can hold him off!"

Mesha stood on his back two legs. Sumayah shuddered as she watched the beast slowly stalk toward Ryven, who was dwarfed by the immenseness of the shifted man.

Ryven backed away, holding his sword in front of him. Mesha crouched lower in a sure sign of attack.

The girls huddled close. "What do we do?" asked Pennyann.

Sumayah felt her body smolder with anger, and her hands began to heat. Remembering the phoenix, she willed the heat to spread. As they felt the heat rise from Sumayah, the girls backed way.

Elspeth put her hand on Sumayah, unmindful of the fire. "You cannot battle a beast such as that, Sumayah. Hold steady," she said, pointing to the sky. "Let's see what he does against him."

"Nero," Sumayah muttered under her breath. She was both relieved and distressed to see him. "Ciara must have called him."

Everyone held her breath as Nero flattened his wings against himself and dove right toward Mesha, who still stalked Ryven, unaware that he was now the prey.

Sumayah bit at her lip, tasting the salt. She winced as Nero gained speed, descending closer and closer toward his target.

Ryven dove to the ground at the exact moment of impact. The sound smacked of breaking bones, and Mesha let out a roar in anguish. He quickly regained his composure, summoning strength as Nero latched on to him, taking him into the air. The two joined and entered into the realm of sky, rolling over and over. Nero clamped down on Mesha's much more muscular neck and shook. The two were intertwined, striking and biting every unprotected inch of flesh, with neither getting the advantage. Nero took one behind his shoulder, where the indigo scar flashed. He thundered out a scream of pain and rolled, taking Mesha under him, wrapping his wings around his opponent and dragging him to the earth. Mesha, sensing the impending crash, struggled against the already exhausted Nero.

"They are going to crash! It will kill both of them!" yelled Sumayah gripping Elspeth and Jaylan. "I cannot bear it."

Everyone gasped as the dragons tumbled closer and closer. Suddenly Mesha found the strength needed to push himself off Nero, who had used every last bit of energy he could muster to take Mesha down.

In a frenzy to leave, Mesha flapped away, never even looking back. Nero summoned what bit of strength he had left and tried to lessen the deadly impact of his landing. He hit hard, knocking the roar out of him; over and over he tumbled and came to a fast halt against a tall standing stone. The dragon exhaled a loud moan and lay silent. A few puffs of smoke billowed out of his collapsed nostrils.

Ciara was the first to his side and pushed at the twisted mass of dragon flesh.

The air was filled with the foul smell of blood and dragon scent. It filled Sumayah's nostrils, and she breathed through her mouth to evade it.

She hesitantly approached with Ryven fast at her side.

"He was willing to give his life, Ryven," she whispered. "Why?"

Leesabeth was the one to answer. "There was no love lost between the two. And did you see how Mesha attacked Nero's old sword wound? I think there is more between the two than we know."

Sumayah knelt next to her dragon and held out her trembling hand. As gently as she could, she laid it on his face. The flesh felt cold and damp. She ran her hand down his cheek; tears flooded her eyes and momentarily blocked her vision. Quickly she wiped them away and blinked. Gulping back her emotions, she whispered his name.

"Nero."

Ciara nudged him again and nickered softly.

Ryven knelt next to Sumayah and rested his hand on her shoulder. She welcomed the warmth. His gesture only fueled her already delicate emotions, and she turned into him, letting him embrace her.

"This is all my fault," she sobbed. "He gave his life for me."

"Shh, do not give up hope, Sumayah," Ryven said. "Look, you saved your mare. Why not him too?"

"He is right, Sumayah," said Pennyann, trying to cheer her up. "You must gather your thoughts and push aside these feelings of doom. We do not know how bad he is. He is a dragon after all. They are as tough as they come."

"You are right, you are all right. Just look at Ciara. I will try." With that said Sumayah took a deep breath. *Come on, Nero, don't leave me now. We have too much living to do yet. I need you. I want to know why you came into my life the way you did.* Again she held out her shaking hands, but before she could lay them on him, he began to purr.

"He heard me!"

Everyone laughed as the dragon opened his eye and looked at Sumayah.

The once-silent captives behind them cheered. Some wiped their eyes, and others laughed.

A rush of great relief washed over her and drained away the worry. She patted her dragon and said, "Come on, boy, show them what you are made of and get up."

Slowly the large fellow rose and looked himself over. Ciara nudged at him.

The sudden sound of jangling iron and a low roar took everyone's attention. Nero even perked up at the sound and lumbered over to the silver dragon still anchored within the cage. He nudged at the wooden poles and then looked at Sumayah in question.

"Oh, the poor guy. Come, we must get him out before they awaken," she said, pointing to the man pile still snoring loudly on the ground.

It didn't take them long to let this new dragon out. He was full of wounds and scrapes from his bondage and apparent torture, but he seemed very happy to be out. Blinking his large red-brown eyes, he lowered his head to Sumayah and was promptly given attention by her and everyone who could get close enough.

"He must have been the dragon used to bring the men here," said Ryven. "We got here just in time, for I fear they would have carved him up to—"

"Ryven—stop," ordered Sumayah.

"I apologize. But now we must hurry. Our time has run out." He turned to the crowd of captives. "Do any of you know where they keep the horses?"

"They made an enclosure, and house them not far from here," answered one of the Lemurians, desperately trying to smooth his disheveled appearance, knowing he stood in front of a prince. "It is on the way back to the city."

Remembering his manner of dress, Ryven quickly grabbed a satchel he had brought that had been thrown on the ground during their entertaining of the men. He ripped it open and pulled out his own clothing. He eyed everyone so that he could dress without an audience.

"Catch up when you are finished, Ryven. We must hurry along," yelled Elspeth, leading everyone down the well-worn path to the herd.

Ciara ran ahead as if she knew the way. Both battered dragons took flight. It was not the usual impressive lift-off, but they did catch air and were gliding above them. Their sudden cloaking warned them that other intruders were near.

"We were right," said Ryven as he trotted ahead of everyone. "They come. Look, the dragons are cloaked."

The girls discussed the plan as the encampment came into sight. Nervous and agitated horses milled around, snorting and pawing at the poles that kept them. Black was with them, unhappily snapping at those who came too close.

"Where is my unicorn?" asked Elspeth, her voice heavy with concern.

"We must hurry," ordered Sumayah. "Our door is closing. Quickly, let them out!"

Pennyann pointed beyond the main enclosure, near a tall stand of fir trees. "Elspeth, she is safe there, tethered to those trees." The girls ran over to her and feverishly worked on the ropes that were tied around her bleeding neck.

The ground suddenly trembled, warning everyone the city was descending.

The herd, now free, stormed the opening and left in a billowing cloud of dust. Nero suddenly appeared above them and let out a roar of warning, then lifted back into the safety of the air.

"They are coming! Everyone run!" yelled Leesabeth, dragging the already winded Riva with her. Pennyann grabbed Riva's other arm, and all three took off toward the city.

Ryven sped ahead on Black, with Elspeth on her unicorn. "Ryven, wait!" yelled Sumayah.

"Where do they go? We cannot keep up with them," she said in exasperation, running alongside the girls, with the other captives behind them.

The wind suddenly picked up, making the climb toward the city much more difficult. As they ran against the wind, their legs burned, and their lungs threatened to burst. Some were beginning to lag behind, and Sumayah stopped to yell encouragement to them.

"This is for your lives; if you want to live, you must keep moving. Hurry!" As the last word escaped her parched lips, she saw a black wave of movement coming their way. "They are gaining on us; they are all on horses. We must move now!"

Ryven, where did you go? I know you're up to something. She wanted to run away and save herself too, but looking at all the desperate faces, she knew she could not. She stood her ground until each straggler ran ahead of her. Taking up the rear, she pushed them along.

Just as they felt they could not take another step, they saw a large cloud of dust in front of them. The distinct sound of hooves hitting the dried earth could be heard by everyone. Suddenly Ryven came out of the cloud, returning with horses he had gathered from the fleeing herd to carry everyone to safety. Ciara broke from the pack and raced toward Sumayah with nostrils flaring. Her breath labored, she let out a loud nicker and nervously halted in front of Sumayah. She pawed at the ground, then knelt down on one front knee.

Hearing the noises of the approaching barbarians, Sumayah needed no further instruction and for the first time climbed up and sat upon her mare, grabbing a handful of white-gold mane. Ciara jittered, wanting to charge away.

"Hold on, sweet one," Sumayah crooned. "I was in a hurry too, but we must learn to be patient."

Everyone was seated upon her horse except Riva. Sumayah let out a nervous sigh and urged Ciara toward her sister.

"Sister, we are out of time," she hissed at her.

"You know I don't like horses, and they don't like me," she huffed back at her.

"Well, fine then. Take a look behind you. Would you rather contend with them, or would you rather sit on your horse?" Sumayah waved everyone else away, and they took off at a ground-eating pace. "It's just us against all of them now, sister."

Riva turned and looked behind her. She stiffened with surprise at the impeding wave of destruction. Needing no further encouragement, she jumped up once, but not quite able to get her ample leg up, she slid back down. Taking another quick glance behind her, she took a deep breath and jumped again, holding fast. With a loud moan, she swung her leg over the other side. Before she was even seated, her horse took off.

"Eeek," Riva screamed, gripping at the horse's mane.

"Stay on, Riva; if you fall, I will not come back for you!" Sumayah yelled as Ciara charged forward to catch up to the rest.

The feeling of sitting her mare made her smile widely, even though they were being chased! Ciara surged faster, the wind stinging her eyes. This sudden feeling seemed familiar to Sumayah. She felt as if she had done this before. Something was trapped way back in her mind—a memory, maybe a dream—but it was strong, and she could not shake it.

Finally catching up with the rest, they raced the last mile to the city. No one spoke. The intensity of the moment kept them in a grip of panic, and they knew reaching the city before she was destroyed was their only hope.

Suddenly there she was, her white walls now an amber glow from the setting sun. She was eerily silent and ominous since her desertion, but her beauty still moved Sumayah. The crystalline pillars anchoring the sky were only strides away. And in an instant, they were inside. The earth trembled again so violently, a large crack began to form just outside the gates, spreading and opening farther and farther around the perimeters of the city. It spread like a fast-growing tree, like roots quickly creeping protectively around it.

"We must make it to the circle of stones!" ordered Elspeth. "Mergus wants us all within its circle. We can shift from there."

Sumayah's mind whirled in confusion, as the barbarians charged toward the gates, the ground decayed around them, and the wind...the ceaseless wind. It took away the words she tried to speak, and she barely heard Elspeth's instruction. All anyone could do was follow and do so quickly.

Ahead was the circle of stones, tall and stately, almost as tall as the crystalline pillars at the city gates. The stones were set in a circle formation with one opening, which they quickly pushed their way through. As soon as they got within the circle, the wind could not be heard. The stones acted as a buffer. Everyone quickly dismounted.

Before anyone could speak, the amber-blue sky suddenly crackled, sending tentacles of golden light into the city. Two large, fracturing rays of light hit the pillars of the city, illuminating them. They burned like white fire; the noise was so loud, everyone had to cover their ears.

The barbarians, now at the city gates, tried to jump the protective gorge. Everyone gasped with panic as they landed one by one and rushed the city gate; all that protected them now were the burning pillars blocking the entrance to the circle of stones.

CHAPTER 17

AGARTHA

෮

"Sumayah, you are the one to take us to Agartha," said Jaylan, grabbing Sumayah's arm and turning her.

Horrified at the approaching barbarians, she did not quite hear the words that were coming out of Jaylan's mouth and stood in dumb silence.

Riva reached over with her ample arm and slapped Sumayah hard on the head.

"That's for the horse ride, and now it's time for you to do your job—sister!"

Sumayah's head rattled, and suddenly all became very clear; she saw the anxious looks of all who depended on her. Then she heard a shriek and turned.

The men were at the circle entrance; their horses would not go beyond the billowing pillars of fire. A tentacle reached out from the white flames, striking at the men as they tried to enter. One by one they were unseated, and their horses charged away.

The tight grip of panic that held fast to her throat loosened, and she gasped out, "But what if we go back to the winter lands?"

"Do not think snow!" yelled Pennyann.

"How can I think of a place I have yet to see?" she screamed back.

Her words were drowned out by the lightning clashes from the pillars. Now intensified, the lightning flashed like shattered glass, spreading its glittering shards like a dome blanketing the entire city. The light vibrated at a high rate, and everyone could only watch as the pulsating energy encompassed them.

"We go with the city," yelled Elspeth. "See you in Agartha!"

Sumayah felt Ryven's grasp, and she looked at his half smile, his left cheek twitching on his handsome young face. It was a strange feeling to watch him slowly dissipate, bit by bit. Her last thought before her eyes closed was, *where is Nero?*

Slowly she awakened, too afraid to open her eyes; she groped around, feeling for the biting cold of snow. To her relief she felt only soft warmth, like sand along the shoreline. *What, where am I?* She sat up with a jolt, viewing her new world for the very first time.

The water beyond the gold-white shoreline shone a brilliant blue and soft bright green. Things swam beneath in a large circle; the water broke and rolled toward her. She watched the rounded wave, watched it get bigger and bigger, then suddenly grow a pair of eyes as it arched out of the water, spraying water forward and drenching her. She scrambled to her feet, wiping the dripping water from her face, and blinked until she saw once more.

There it stood, not upright but elongated, on four legs. Its chest was massive and yes, it did have wings, small wings. *This one looks like a swimmer and not a flyer by the size of her wings. Yes, for sure this felt like female energy.* Large doe-like eyes, not red or orange but a piercing pale green, watched her.

"She is a dragon, a water dragon."

Her heart palpitated at the sound of Ryven's voice. She turned to him and saw everyone else was safe, milling around the shoreline like children would explore a new cave.

She hugged him closely. "We made it." Then she pulled back to look at him. "But where are we? Is—is this Agartha?" He smiled broadly at her. A stray lock fell across his forehead. The urge was too strong, and she reached up and brushed it aside.

"It *is* Agartha. The city brought us. I didn't have to take us to the winter lands."

"We believe so," he answered with a laugh.

"Welcome to Agartha. My name is Limitha; I speak for all water dragons here."

Ryven and Sumayah both smiled at what they heard, not by voice but in their minds.

"My name is Sumayah, and this is Ryven. We have come from—"

Limitha cut her off. "I know who you are. I know who all of you are and why you have come. I was told to watch for you in the event things went astray." She blinked and bowed her head. "Which it seems they have...but have no worry, you got here safely."

By now the others had noticed the water dragon and had gathered around.

Elspeth walked out of the crowd. "It is an honor to meet a water dragon. Are there many of you?"

"Why, yes, most of the dragon realm is here," she answered and lifted her head to the amber-blue sky above. "See, even those that once lived in the outer realms are here.

The sky suddenly came alive as dragons, hundreds of dragons, free floated easily in the air. Some dove, spiraling downward, then just before they hit the water, they ascended back up to snag or pull on another dragon's tail in what looked like dragon play.

"Have you seen two dragons?" Sumayah asked excitedly, searching the skies for Nero and Sterling. "One is tall, slender, and sparkling black, the other is the color of polished silver."

"We have many dragons that arrive here almost every day; it is very possible they could be here. It could be they just have not found you yet."

Riva pushed through the crowd. "Where are the Lemurians? I originally shifted here with them, but was sent back to help my sister," she said, pointing to Sumayah.

"They are with the Fae and Bethia's people," Limitha replied with a nod of her large head.

Ryven perked up at the mention of his family. "So all are here now?"

The dragon nodded again. "Yes, all are reunited and are waiting for you to go to them. I will call for assistance." Limitha closed her eyes.

Sumayah's ears picked up a low whistling sound. It changed pitch once, going higher for a second or two, then dropped back down. Limitha re-opened her eyes and pointed toward a mountainous region, jutting skyward about a half-day's walk beyond the shoreline.

"They will lead the way to your family."

Suddenly two dark specks appeared against the great expanse of the green-covered mountains. The specks became larger as they neared.

"Faerie dragons?" Elspeth asked with a laugh.

"Why, yes, they work closely with Bethia and will take you to your new home."

The specks became two smaller dragons, both about two feet in length from tip of nose to end of tail. One was a beautiful shining rose color, and the other was a miniature version of Nero. They squawked excitedly and circled the crowd.

"What else do you have living here?" asked Pennyann.

"There are plenty of beings here," Limitha answered. "This is not like what your outer realm has become. All are safe here; we live together in cooperation and harmony."

"Please tell me there are no long-tooth cats living here," exclaimed Leesabeth.

"I have not seen one in quite a while; they could be up higher in the mountaintops. But fear not, they are not the same as yours; this is a different realm, a different dimension, as you would say. You will be safe enough as you travel to the city of Lyra Shambala. It is the largest city of this realm. That is where you will find your families."

The travelers spent the rest of the day exploring their new world as they followed closely behind the faerie dragons. The air felt much lighter, and walking seemed much simpler, so moving fast was not a hardship here.

"Do any of you feel freer as you walk?" asked Leesabeth. "I feel like I could walk or run all day long and not get winded."

"I do know what you mean," answered Sumayah, watching Ciara catch up to them. The horse ran top speed, jumping a row of orange-and-white speckled mushrooms. Black and Elspeth's unicorn were right behind her. The herd followed but kept their distance, nibbling lightly on succulent herbs. "I am happy we all made it here, but I hope we find Nero and Sterling soon. They were not in the best of health."

Riva bent and picked up a clover-looking plant and laid it on her tongue. "Hmm, this one is even tastier than the ones I've tasted in Faeria. It is quite sweet, with a hint of sour."

"It is Faeria and Lemuria all in one, but one hundred times cleaner, lighter, greener, and safer!" said Pennyann as she reached out to touch a purple flower as tall as herself. She pulled the spiral-looking head toward her and breathed in. "This one is like no other I have seen before. It smells of lavender, but there is spiciness to it."

A tiny elemental popped out of the flower head, poked Pennyann in the nose, and shot back into the head. She laughed and let go. "Just beware the elementals. I think I was just reprimanded by a tiny flower sprite!"

Suddenly Ciara perked up and sent out a warning. Her nostrils flared as she gave one fast blow. The mare took off, tail flying, but then skidded to a halt, spun, and returned to Sumayah. Black was on alert, but then lowered his head to push a tiny golden rabbit off a patch of dewy grass.

"I saw it too. There are more than one," said Ryven. "I cannot make out what they are. But I have seen glowing white-blue eyes." He took a step closer to the stand of trees darkly shadowed by overcrowding.

"I think we will be meeting plenty of new beings here. I have been told that middle earth was the first place to have been colonized," said Elspeth, keeping close pace behind Sumayah, who laughed as the rose dragon tried landing on her head.

Sumayah felt the claws scratching and catching in her hair; she laughed, reaching up, and pulled the squawking little beast down. She held out her arm.

"Here you may ride on my arm, just like Sirius always did."

The small, black dragon turned and circled around the travelers, then changed direction, taking them across a stream that ambled lazily around an outcropping of pink-hued rocks, under a row of long and straight fallen trees, then flowing out of site. Crossing it was not easy. The waters were alive with things that nibbled and pulled at them.

Riva suddenly jumped. "They got me, help, they got me!" she screamed, swinging her arms about and grabbing at her legs, Ryven splashed toward her. "Where? What is it? Stand still!"

"My legs, they got my legs!" she screamed and proceeded to climb poor Ryven's back, to the great amusement of all. Ryven tottered under her weight, her dancing skirt wrapped around his head. Using one arm for balance, he used the other to push away the skirt.

"Riva, it is only a small water toad. Get off me!" he groaned.

Sumayah tramped through the water toward her sister and grabbed at her arm. "Riva, come down from him this instant. Nothing is harming you—a bit curious is all." She pulled her down and smoothed the skirt to cover the generous amount of exposed flesh.

Ryven turned and gave Sumayah a narrow stare. "Remind me next time to keep away."

The travelers broke out in a chorus of laughter. It helped to lighten the mood even more as everyone playfully splashed and skipped through the water.

The herd was right behind them, nosily drinking their fill. Ciara pawed at the stream, sending water up to drip back down on her shimmering white-gold coat.

The lightness of the moment was suddenly silenced as the sound of a strange cry filled the air. Throaty and low, the sound rang out in a beautiful tone, rising up and holding for a few seconds, then lowering slowly and deliberately.

"What a beautiful song," whispered Jaylan, inching closer to Sumayah.

The sound rang out again, accompanied by others just like it.

Ryven pointed to a large ledge of pink- and orange-hued boulders.

"There, something is watching us."

Ciara snorted and stomped her front foot. Sumayah put her hand on her to steady her.

"I have never seen anything like them before, but they are beautiful, they look much like our golden fox, but much larger."

With stealth and sped, the watchers left the ledge and ran out of sight.

The little black dragon, let out a raspy squawk then flew into the cave of trees, then hovered, waiting for all to enter. The trees canopied above, blocking out the two suns that had warmed the sky. The trees creaked and changed position. Sumayah was sure they were watching. She smiled brightly at them as she passed and ran her hand lightly across one of them. It was cool and firm to the touch, but had a velvety texture, which puzzled her.

Strange noises such as tapping and clacking mixed with the forest songs and echoed back and forth within the realm of trees. Elementals tended passionately to all within, and some chattered at them as they passed, warning them to step lightly. It was like stepping into a dream. Though blocked off by most of the sun, the landscape still was illuminated in many shades of green.

"It is the plants themselves that put off the light...look, they glow!" said Jaylan, pointing to a feathery cluster of green foliage. Berries hung like raindrops from many branches, also providing their own light.

Riva picked one and popped it into her mouth. Instantly she was surrounded by a flock of fluttering elementals, obviously perplexed at her unauthorized meal. Wide-eyed, she backed away, profusely apologizing; she quickly took the berry out of her mouth and held it out in her hand. The elementals backed away, shaking their heads and muttering among themselves.

"I think we had better not taste of anything lest we take a chance of upsetting the harmonious balance of this realm," said Elspeth, trying hard to not laugh.

Riva shrugged and tromped on, swiping at a tall fernlike plant that swung back, whacking her on the cheek. She rubbed her cheek but said nothing.

They all kept moving through the cover of the trees, mindful of where they stepped and what they stepped on.

Ryven waited for Sumayah. He tenderly cupped her elbow to help her along the thickly rooted path.

"We are still being watched," he whispered.

"You would know that, wouldn't you, Fae. Does it harbor ill will for us?"

He studied the tunnel of trees, his left cheek twitching. He turned to her and keeping with his serious tone, said, "No, I believe Limitha. We seem to be safe. It is just a little unsettling when you know you are being watched, but have no clue by what."

"If it is the same ones who sang to us, I have no worry, but I would love to get up close to one."

They walked and chatted until the realm of trees began to open to a new realm to explore. Everyone quickened their pace. The forest gave way to a valley of rolling hills, covered waist deep in the lushest grass ever imagined. Each blade was topped with a soft rounded tip.

The stream they had crossed a while back had meandered back to them and now led the way through the valley of grasses. It bubbled and gurgled, rolling and rushing over rocks as it kept its steady pace forward. The banks were home to many interesting species of herbs and flowers, some taller than her and others short and cropped to the ground, holding fast to the smooth, black rocks. There were more colors than she could name, so pleasing to the eye, she could have stood there all day to just admire everything.

Beyond the valley of grass, a lake spread wide and far, traveling beyond sight and seeming to disappear into the neighboring mountains. These mountains were also connected to the ones they just left, but they took a route around the lake.

The herd, excited about the new land, thundered across, racing toward a high knoll. Everyone watched them race to the top, then suddenly halt.

The ridge of the knoll suddenly filled with a new continuous line of horses blending happily with their own herd. There were so many, it was like a giant wave washing to shore, growing higher and wider as it approached.

"We must be close!" yelled Pennyann excitedly. "I have never seen so many horses before."

Ciara, Black, and the unicorn joined the gathering. They went nose to nose introducing themselves, until they were swallowed by the massive congregation.

"I don't think we want to get caught up in the middle of that," said Elspeth, turning more south, away from the herd.

"You are right. It would take us quite a while just to walk through the center of them," answered Sumayah, studying the base of the mountains just beyond the lake, thinking she saw movement.

Suddenly the two faerie dragons took off over the converging herd right to where Sumayah saw the movement.

"Follow the dragons. I see movement," she said, pushing into a run and passing Elspeth.

The closer they traveled to the base of the mountain, the higher it seemed to jut sharply out of the earth. Three enormous waterfalls poured from the dizzying heights of the rocky ledges. It made the air moist and welcoming. The air was so fresh, it was like chewing on a tiny mint leaf. Sumayah's body tingled from the energy created by the falling water. She knew why there would be a city here.

The city, like nothing she had ever seen before, was a combination of Lemurian and Faerian architecture. She wondered about this. Why would a city in another dimension on Earth carry the same style as the two largest cities from her dimension? It was a perfect joining of the two. The structures were nestled against the base of the mountain; each one was tall, anchored upward with the help of the gigantic trees. Crystal pillars also helped to raise the dwellings. The pillars were much like the ones at her city's entrance, but these were not as wide and much taller. She could see the reasoning for this kind of structure. They took up far less space on the ground and were less intrusive to the natural surroundings, blending in and adding to the natural beauty of the land. But what struck her the most were the colors. The crystals of Lemuria were clear and pale, but the crystals here came in every color imaginable. The hues flashed and bounced off the leaves of the trees and petals of the flower; it was as if you were given the most beautiful piece of music ever written and told to build a city inspired by that one piece. The city took her breath away, and the smell—it was like a basin of rose petals, lavender, mint, and snow all in one.

Everyone quickened their paces as throngs of people began pouring out of their dwellings. Sumayah searched the faces for anyone familiar. They were much like the people of her land, so it was hard to tell who was Lemurian, Faerian, or Agarthan. Her eyes rested on a striking woman who walked out of the crowd carrying a long, slender stick intricately carved with symbols she had never seen before. On the top of the tall stick was a crystal that vibrated brightly, sending tiny rays of light up and out around her. This woman held her attention so tightly, she did not even notice her mother standing next to her.

Who is this woman, this handsome, strong woman who seems to be looking right into my very soul? As she studied her, she heard a buzzing sound in her head, and the pictures before her became narrower and narrower until they were replaced by a blanket of darkness. She heard only one word whispered in her ear, before she floated away into her vision. *Bethia.*

CHAPTER 18

CELIO AND SEBASTION

❦

*B*ethia sat smoking her pipe, her eyes locked on the heavens. The somber songs
of the Travelers played softly behind, melding with the song of the night
creatures. It was a natural mixture, both playing together like they had
done for a thousand years.

One child spoke. *"Tell us about the creation of our people. Tell us how the sun
and the moon came together to make us."*

Bethia smiled and puffed vigorously at her pipe. She shifted her weight and leveled her gaze to the wide-eyed children within the circle.

"Tonight I tell you about the Earthkeepers." She paused, turning her ear to the
children. *"What are Earthkeepers, you ask? They are beings that have been on our
Mother Earth from the very beginning of time. They love the Mother very deeply and
all of her natural realms. They live in harmony with the natural realms, believing
that each and every plant, tree, rock, winged, four-legged, crawler, swimmer, and so
on have a soul of their own, just like them."*

"Does my grai *have a soul too?"* one small black-eyed child asked.

"Especially the grai," answered Bethia. *"The grai that the outsiders call* horse
has a very special bond with the Earthkeepers. The horse can take the Earthkeepers

to the otherworld because the grai can live in the otherworld and our world at the same time."

"Will the otherworld be beautiful and kind to us too?" asked a slight girl with unruly red hair.

Before Bethia answered, she took a long drag of her pipe, then blew a long stream of blue-gray smoke out of her mouth. "Yes, most kind and very loving. We will not see any more hardships; we will have a beautiful home that we," she said, pointing her pipe at the children, "helped to create."

"Good," whispered the little girl, wiping a tear that had strayed down her face. "My momma cries every night after they killed Papa here in this world."

Engulphed in listeneing to the storyteller, she snuggled deeper into the one who held her. Feeling the strong arms that embraced her tighten she looked up to see the compassionate stare of Ryven.

Bethia quickly got the story back on track. "Our good and bad memories will all help with the new world. When we go there, it will all be revealed. So, let's get back to the Earthkeepers."

Bethia leaned forward and poked a long stick into the fire. It flickered and shot small sparks into the night, illuminating her face.

"The Earthkeepers have lived lifetime after lifetime watching the Mother, and protecting the natural realms. With each lifetime they lived, they gained more knowledge and more memories. They have had to endure much, and it has been very, very hard for them. They know that what they are doing will be good for all and its creations. They are working for when we all can go to the new world together. But they have a job to do first, and it is very hard."

"What is the hard job?" another child asked, waving her arm at Bethia with excitement.

"With each lifetime the Earthkeepers live, they have to remember who they are so that they may fulfill their sacred mission," Bethia answered, pausing to stare intensely at each and every child as she spoke. "It is like a big game, and in the big game, they are searching for the sacred vision."

"You never told us what their special mission is," said the little red-haired girl.

"Oh well, yes, that is the most important part," stammered Bethia as her pipe left her lips to land in her lap. "They are to awaken all the sleeping people, to prepare them for the Great Shift..."

The words suddenly drifted away, and the vision before her dimmed. She tried to hold on to it but felt the pull of someone calling her name.

"Sumayah, you had another of your visions." It was Lhayan, holding a warm cup of tea to her lips.

Sumayah drank greedily, the taste sweet and refreshing after her journey. Standing next to Lhayan was Bethia. No one needed to introduce her, for Sumayah had just seen her in her vision, but the Bethia standing before her seemed much younger. She could tell by the woman's anxious stare she wanted to know what she had just seen.

"Sumayah, this—"

"Mother, I know who she is. I just saw her in my vision."

Bethia's anxious stare softened; she pushed a strand of ebony hair behind her ear and smiled brightly.

"We are so relieved you all made the shift to Agartha. You had us most worried."

Sumayah instantly liked the woman and felt a strong draw to her. She shifted her weight, retracing the vision in her mind. Then she remembered the pale-green eyes. Ryven was the one in her visions all along. This was their connection, but why? She had so many questions. She turned to Lhayan.

"This last vision let me see the face of the one I have seen before. I looked straight into his eyes, Mother!" She took a deep breath and continued. "It is Ryven."

"Ryven?" questioned Lhayan. "I would have suspected it was Mesha."

The name hit her hard; the lightness of the moment was ripped from her as she let out a heavy sigh and retold the story of Mesha's betrayal.

Bethia spoke. "Did your dragon kill him, Sumayah?"

The emotions of that battle still strong in her mind, all she could do was shake her head no.

"We must make ready for his appearance to our world. He will seek you out, Sumayah, and I fear for you and your sisters, for all of you may know how to wield the power of the crystal key. The keys are the connection to where we all started and carry great power. There is a great plan, and the keys will help us to fulfill this plan."

The woman stood, and her ropes of shiny pieces of gold jangled. She grabbed a strand, holding it out

"This gold is what they seek most of all. They want our whole world under their control for this, and they think the thirteen crystal keys will ensure their continuing ravage of her!" Bethia became silent and tapped her head-high staff on the ground, deep in thought. Her brown eyes narrowed in contemplation. Then her expression softened.

"Sumayah, what else was revealed in your vision?"

Both women sat next to Sumayah as she recounted her dream. When she finished, she sat watching their changing expressions as they absorbed everything.

Bethia was the first to break the silence. "We know that time does not pass as we perceive. So what you have seen, Sumayah, has happened and is happening over and over. Today, tomorrow, and yesterday are here and continue to play out time and again. So I do believe what you have seen is true, and your telling of the Earthkeepers is accurate."

Their conversation was suddenly interrupted by the entrance of the girls. They noisily chatted as they entered freshly washed and back into their normal manner of dress.

"You must come and see the sky," said Jaylan. "We have never seen such color. It is as if the rays of the suns hit a crystal, and the crystal is sending out every color you could imagine."

Riva pushed in front of the girls, sitting heavily next to Sumayah on the large pile of soft cushions. "It is so beautiful here; I cannot imagine ever wanting to leave this place."

Sumayah smiled at the girls. Thinking again of her knowledge of Ryven, she felt her smile broaden.

"There is a strange light in your eye, Sumayah. Do tell us what you have found out," Leesabeth said, pulling her new sage-colored tunic around her sandaled foot.

Sumayah could feel the heat rise in her face, and she lowered her eye-lids. She had a sudden, strange feeling within the pit of her stomach. The knowing made all things different somehow. They were destined to be to-gether. Her questions had been answered—well, most of them anyway.

"Well, give it up, sister, don't leave us hanging," urged Riva, knocking Sumayah from her thoughts with a shove to her shoulder.

"I finally saw the face of the one who frequents my visions." She paused, looking at the round of questioning faces, then blurted out, "It's Ryven!"

All four girls screamed, reaching for Sumayah with excitement. They chatted back and forth, words spilling out one over the other.

Bethia, having enough of the girlish banter, shouted, "Enough! I can-not hear myself think. Remember, girls, the world is never what it seems.

There are things we all will find out about ourselves soon enough. This tidbit of information offered to Sumayah has started her on a new path, a path that includes all of us."

Her last sentence sent all into self-thought. Bethia watched as the smiles were subdued and the eyes turned heavy with wonder. She chuckled.

"We are here to serve, and our role of it will be revealed when the time is true." Bethia put her hand to Lhayan, guiding her away from the girls. Over her shoulder, she said, "We have much work to do. You have much to learn, for our greatest challenge is upon us, and so it begins. We will rejoin at council tonight. There is much to discuss."

The council grounds were similar to the standing stones of Lemuria. There were rows and rows of fallen tree benches, polished so well, they rivaled the feel of glass. The ground rose naturally, creating the perfect setting for all to hear and see. The center of the council ground was marked by a large round slab of what looked to be clear crystal. The circle of quartz vibrated, sending a continuous spiral of energy up and up, continuing until it was out of sight.

"Where have you been?"

A strong rush of warmth enveloped Sumayah as the strong hand grasped hers. She turned to look at him. She could not suppress the deep sigh that left her lips. *He looks different today. Maybe because I now know the truth. Nothing will ever take him from me. I have seen it in my visions.*

Ryven, taken aback by her expression, did not speak. He gave her a questioning smile.

She motioned for him to bend closer to her and whispered, "I will tell you later." She lingered at the nape of his neck before she looked up.

Hand in hand they walked within the grounds. They found their seats next to Rupert and Lhayan, with Bethia standing next to the crystalline circle with none other than the great wizard himself and Nero and Sterling.

Sumayah saw them and it took all she had to not run to Nero.

The wizard held up his arms to quiet everyone, then spoke in a booming voice for all to hear.

"We have all gathered here now, at this time, in answer to Mother Earth. She has called upon us in her great time of need. The original plan has gone astray with the infiltration of the Reps and their kind. Their unlawful coming has inserted a rift in the vision that was planted here from before the beginning of man. Since Earth is the last planetary being in the great expanse of our universe to raise herself to the height of ascension with her new children in tow, it is up to us to help in the making of this great event. The new race of man was to join all races throughout the galaxies. It was to create a world, a world where all could coexist and experience the realm of their dreams. A utopian…"

His last word fizzled, and he strolled behind Bethia and then to where the dragons stood. He extended his hand to Nero, touching him affectionately, then to Sterling, doing the same.

"Nero and Sterling have been with me since the very beginning. They are part of the original plan. They are of the Carian race. They come from the star home Alpha Draconi from the constellation of Orion. They are highly spiritual beings, one of the many types of the Carian race here among us…our sacred bird, the phoenix, still carries the true Carian earth form. Nero and Sterling are of the Carian and the Draconian form together…for a purpose. It was known from the very beginning that one other species, what you also call Reptilian or Rep, would come from the constellation Draco. We always had to be one step ahead of them…and yet they have been a great challenge with the control of man, and joining with the human race to ensure the total reign over Mother Earth. This makes it very difficult for us."

He wiped his brow and ran his hand down his white braid.

Sumayah sat in stunned silence absorbing his words. This was all just too much. Her world had literally collapsed, and now she was hearing this. What had this knowledge to do with her? She looked around the council area. The Fae and Lord Fallonay were seated directly across from them, with the Lemurians next to them and the Agarthans filling all other spaces.

The sky suddenly filled with massive floating shadows; they hovered over the council with ease. She knew them to be more of Nero and Sterling's kind. Then she looked to where her dragon and Sterling stood. She knew Ciara would not be far away. She searched the herd that was in the lush meadows beyond the city. Pulling her line of vision up closer, she finally saw Ciara. The mare had found Black, and they stood as if listening.

The circular crystal slab at the center of the council grounds suddenly illuminated in the color of bright amber, capturing everyone's attention. Bethia walked closer to the glowing center, extending her hand into it. This changed her hand, to the surprise of all, to a subtle but brilliant blue.

The illumination grew and shot up to the Agarthan sky, passing between the twin suns.

Sumayah turned to Ryven and was met with questioning eyes. He squeezed her hand and gave her a half smile.

Bethia held her hand in front of her face, watching it regain its natural form. "Remember what you saw with your very own eyes, for if I had just told you I could do this, you would not have believed me. Our world is not what you think; it is more than what is in front of your eyes. It is more than you could ever imagine or put words to."

She paused as a fowl cry emanated from the cloud high fir trees that held fast to the ragged, boulder-laden perimeter of the lake. The cry sounded again, not a bellow but a tenuous attempt at most. Bethia held out her arm and tapped her staff three times on the earth.

Sumayah sat captivated by the display. The woman had a way of holding one's attention, and Sumayah could not break away, even though Ryven was tickling the palm of her hand with his middle finger. Not wanting to miss a thing, she jerked her hand in warning, just as a beautiful blue bird materialized from thin air upon Bethia's outstretched hand. A singular gasp filled the council air. The bird, as big as the phoenix, also sported head feathers. Its tail extended six feet, with many separate feathers, each ending in a teardrop shape, looking like eyes painted blue, green, and black, and rimmed in gold. The body of the bird was elegantly shaped, and the color a deep indigo blue.

"We all have this ability, this ability to conjure with just a thought," Bethia said. "My thoughts arise from energy, and this energy took form into the beautiful bird. Magic is from the Goddess. We are all merely those thoughts by the Goddess—this beautiful bird, the horses roaming the meadows, the grass beneath your feet, all a great gift from her to us, and all just a projection of her thoughts." She turned and walked back to where Mergus stood and let the beautiful bird take flight.

"What Bethia is trying to demonstrate to you is who we truly are and why we have come here, to Mother Earth," offered Mergus as he strolled to where the Faerians sat. He pointed to Fallonay, who returned his gesture with a quizzical stare.

"Faerians know of their creation," Mergus said. "All are of the four elements, the embodiment of Mother Earth." He smiled at Fallonay who had nodded in agreement, then paused, thinking. "We all have learned and concluded that love is all, and we want to create from love. But there are those here who would stop this creation. They do not know of the love we speak of and can only create through greed and hate. Their creation has broken the balance and has halted the original plan, forcing us to go and do things we have never done before. In a way we have, and will learn more from this adversity. Through adversity we are learning what we do not want as part of our utopian realm. We would have never known the true feeling of love and light without having experienced the darkness."

He smiled, placing his hand on Fallonay's broad shoulder.

"Now is the time to know this fully. This will be our stronghold against those who would possess us and Mother Earth." Mergus's normal jovial, pleasant expression suddenly hardened at his last words. He spun and walked back to his place by Bethia and the dragons.

Sumayah whispered to Ryven, "What was that all about?"

He shrugged, feeling the heated stare from Lhayan.

Suddenly the spiraling light from within the crystalline circle pulsated, creating a melodic sound; the sound grew, vibrating intensely, then dropped to a low hum. Sumayah felt the movement of the sound go through her body making her hair stand.

The sound and vibration slowly lowered until all was silent and still. Standing in the center of the crystal platform were two beings—tall, much taller than Mergus, with flowing hair whiter than white that hung past their slender waists. Sumayah was taken aback by their extreme beauty. Their eyes, slightly larger and almond shaped, held a pale-blue color. Sumayah likened it to the winter lands' snow. But they were not expressing coldness; no, there was no mistaking the deep love that flowed from them, like a mother looking at her newly born child. They smiled brightly at everyone.

Bethia and Mergus approached the two beings.

"Greetings, Celio," said Bethia. "Greetings, Sebastion."

CHAPTER 19

THE DRAGONHORSE

☙

They moved in a fluid motion that seemed strange to Sumayah. They were not like her, she knew that. She wanted to have a look behind them to find wings, for they did resemble the Fae, and yet had Lemurian characteristics. They did not appear solid, not like herself. She could not explain it, but was sure if she walked up to them and put her hand on one, it would easily pass through.

"Greetings to all, our beloved children," said Celio, the taller of the two. "We have vowed to stay at a distance and not intervene with your free will and expressions of learning. But we also want you to know that we have never left your side nor ever will."

Sebastion took one step. "There is a great war occurring around you, and it has been going on for many millennia. The Reps, as you call them, have ignored the quarantine of Earth and have battled their way in. Their intent, as you know, was not part of the original plan. They choose to come at the infancy of man, a time of great vulnerability, and have steered humanity away from their true nature. The Reps have joined with some of the humans to ensure the continuation of their bloodline after they are expelled from Mother Earth. We, of course, will not expel any who still carry the braid of our existence. Thus we must rewrite the plan and journey along a new course."

Sebastion paused a moment, letting his gaze fall upon Sumayah.

She gulped loudly, but was not afraid. She felt the love that still flowed to her heart, but she had a strong desire to know more about them.

"Yes, Sumayah, you do feel it. You see, you are building a new realm for all of us. A place we all can be together, expressing and creating whatever we dream. It will all be based on love, pure love, Sumayah. Love that none of us even at our higher dimension has yet to experience. This is the original plan.

She wondered why Sebastion addressed her and suddenly began to feel a pang of worry in the pit of her stomach.

It was Celio's turn to address them. "We know why you had to destroy Lemuria, and we know how sorrowful it made you feel. But we want to assure you that Lemuria is not gone. Lemuria is waiting for her resurrection, and when she arises, she will be even better than what you destroyed. She is waiting for the time to rise once again, joining and bringing with her Agartha. And to do this, we must ask you, all of you, to embark on a journey back to the outer realm. We must ask for your bravery in ensuring Earth's great and final shift."

The council grounds buzzed with excitement at Celio's words.

"We already have Drakaous and his brothers working for the shift. They have joined with the Reps in order to keep watch over them."

A picture of Mesha suddenly flashed in Sumayah's mind. She wondered if Drakaous was working with him.

Sebastion smiled, nodding, and held up his hand to settle the commotion.

"You will have help in this matter. Some of the human race has stood firmly against the Reps and joined with the Fae and Lemurians centuries ago." With a long, slender arm extended to where Pennyann and Leesabeth sat, Sebastion said, "You are already a creation of the joining. There are more of you, as you already know, and more will be born to help guide those humans who have not been tainted by reptilian blood. It will be up to you to guide and preserve our children—your brothers and sisters."

Bethia walked closer to Celio and Sebastion, her staff tapping the earth with each step then said, "I fear the Reps know of our wise ones—'witches,' the word that is used. They will seek out and murder all of the witches, keeping them from their quest."

"The way will be not easy and will take more than one lifetime, replied Celio. "And as Lemuria will rise once again stronger and truer, so shall *all* who will fall in this quest. We are aware of their plan. Drakaous has already informed us. Our answer to their plan is those three"—Celio pointed to Sumayah and her sisters—"along with all the witches already living on the outer realm."

I knew it, Sumayah fumed, *this involves me.*

Sebastion intervened. "Celio is correct. Those like Sumayah and her sisters, for there are many more on this journey along with the witches, have been and are being prepared through this learning period. And if one should fall, she will rise stronger and truer, but will have the challenge of remembering once again who she is. This is our way of keeping our witches from the Reps. You see, in their state of amnesia, they have no way of being detected, yet their vital energy is still working toward Earth's shift."

Sebastion paused a moment, scanning the council.

"We must also be aware that once again, it will be up to all of you, for *all* are part of the whole. Each one of you has your job, and some of you may change your mind, which can also change the course of events. For we can only *plan* our future…this is why we have given you the thirteen crystals of All Knowledge. This is your connection to us. The Reps know of them and strive to retrieve them, thinking they can stop the shift and the awakening of their slaves. They will do whatever it takes to keep their great deception upon man …" Sebastion stopped, looking at Celio to finish.

"What Sebastion means is, the Reps feed off the sorrows, agony, hatred, and strife of man. Those emotions produce a chaotic form of energy which the Reps devour. So the more separation between realms, the less love that is shared, and the more hatred and division is produced, thus feeding those that control them. Their great deception will lead them and their slaves into justified wars and segregation, all just to feed. They cannot survive without this energy source. And yet the human has no idea how powerful they are. They have the power of their minds, which the Reps do not. With a change in their collective thoughts, they can change the world for their own good and well-being."

This new bit of knowledge enlivened everyone around, and once again whispers echoed back and forth within the council grounds.

Mergus interrupted the chatter. "It has been told to us that men have learned to consume the flesh and blood of others." He shook his clenched fist in anger. "They have eaten the flesh of Carians and our horses, two beings that are no longer safe in the upper realm."

"We have become aware," replied Celio. "This is part of the great deception. The consumption of flesh and blood will become like the gold that they seek. It will control them. It will soon rule the world, and control how they use up Mother Earth's resources to grow and sell and eat of this great lie."

Mergus motioned to Nero and Sterling, and together they moved closer to Celio and Sebastion.

"The continued occupation of the dragon, the Carian dragon, on our planet is tenuous at best, said Mergus. "The reptilian with its aggressive, warlike spirit has turned man against them. There is talk of an uprising of a dominant religion, one that will most assuredly wipe out all witches and dragons from Mother—" His words were drowned out by the sudden thunder of hoofs pounding the earth.

Sumayah laughed as Ciara charged at a full run, her tail streaming behind her, neck and neck with Black. The herd gathered around the council, snorting and pawing. They obviously had much to say. Ciara pranced into the center of the circle and stood next to Nero.

Mergus scanned the crowd until his eyes fell upon Sumayah and smiled. "Sumayah, please come and join us. Demonstrate your special ability to communicate with the horse."

A burst of energy coursed through her body. *What was he talking about? I can't talk with horses, maybe a few pictures here and there, but that was it.*

"Come, come," Mergus urged, motioning with his hand.

Her body trembled as she stood, her face flushed, positive everyone saw her knees knocking. She looked down at Ryven, who gave her a nod and pushed her forward.

Ciara trotted up to Sumayah, giving her a shove and snorted in her face. Sumayah breathed in the sweet scent of Ciara's clover breath. The smell soothed her, and she had the strange urge to blow back into her nostrils.

Mergus continued. "We know that the horse is also from the same realm as the Lemurian. They too have come in service, as all of us have." He walked back and forth in front of the audience, stroking his braided

184

hair. "The Carian dragon has been losing the battle against the Reps. Their devious plan to cloak from men the Carians' true intention and to replace it with an imaginary vision of a bloodthirsty, marauding, killing beast has worked. It is time for the Carian dragon to fade from the upper realm. But I believe we can find a way for the Carian to still help those of mankind who are fighting this war against their enslavement…"

The last word was drawn out as he walked over to Sumayah and rested his hand on her shoulder. He gave her a smile and a wink.

"Sumayah, you know what this is; Ciara has shown you in a dream…"

Dream, I remember no dream. The nauseating assault of panic hit her. Ciara, sensing her discomfort, pressed her head into Sumayah's chest and let out a deep sigh. Sumayah closed her eyes and gently rested her hands on Ciara's head just above her eyes, feeling the steady beat of the mare's heart as blood coursed through her veins beneath her searching hands. She could feel their two separate heartbeats became one.

Sumayah let herself float away, carried on the back of Ciara. The feeling was like standing on the edge of a waterfall and letting go, unafraid, being carried with the rushing water, cradled in the sweet emotion of release. She no longer felt the inquiring stares of those around her. The warmth of Ciara's back was comforting, and the thrill of the ride exhilarating. But in a flash, something changed. The warmth was still there, but the scent of sweet clover was gone, replaced with the pungent scent of sage and lemon. Dragon scent!

Her eyes flew open, and she looked down. *Nero, I'm riding Nero?* She grasped where his wings joined into his shoulders, securing her fingers beneath. A good stronghold. The flap of his mighty wings sent cooling rushes of air, blowing her long tresses behind her. She let out a *woo-hoo,* feeling brave enough to let her stronghold go, swinging her hands above her. Then something hit her, square in the face. She wiped the sting away, hoping she did not kill whatever it was, and was left with a thought. *It all made sense now. The dragon will go to the upper world shifted into a horse! The Reps will never know, I am sure of it. They could still fight this battle side by side.*

Her sudden revelation brought her back to the mundane with a jolt. Her left leg gave out, and she toppled to the ground. Embarrassed, her face flushed once again, she half smiled as Mergus grasped her arm, helping her back up. He grinned at her, then nodded in a manner of knowing.

Feeling much surer of herself, she faced Celio and Sebastion. Their essence seemed to flicker with the vibration of the crystalline energy. The love they exuded filled her, giving her the strength to open her mouth, and so she did.

"It is simple...the dragon will go to the upper world shifted into the horse. We will call them dragonhorse. The dragon and horse will work as one, give and taking of each other's strengths. They will work closely with those of us who volunteer to reemerge to the outer realm. And they will help us, guiding us to remember who we once were time and again, with each lifetime, if need be. They will watch over us and be there in the end for Earth's Great Shift."

The council became abuzz with enthusiasm. It was as if this bit of information gave the tentative volunteers the final push to stand up and say, *I will do it.* One by one all of them stood and agreed, unsure what they were volunteering for, but knowing within their hearts it just had to be. It was for the good of all—not just mankind, but for all. They would do it. They would help man, and most of all, they would help and protect Mother Earth, ensuring her journey upward.

The ebony shadows circling high above the council suddenly descended: the last of the Carian race. They too had heard the call and answered freely. One by one they landed with ease, barely touching the soil. The council area was now overflowing with attendants: horse, Carian, Fae, Agarthan, and Lemurian alike. In cooperation and harmony, they would join and together would tip the balance back to the original plan.

"Then it is done," said Celio, patting Sebastion with excitement. "We return to our cloud ship Athena. There is a battle forming once again in the heavens. Watch the skies above. Know that we go to battle for you as you enter the battle here. You have just caused a great shift within your earthly paradigm, and know that the reptilian race will soon begin to lose their control. They will soon find out, and in their defense, they will strike out with more despair and disease among men, bringing them so low that they will not have the energy to think for themselves. War will be their only driving force, the only reason to rise up each morning, fighting for untruths in order to serve those who bring upon them the great deception."

Bethia walked past Mergus, swatting him with her staff as she passed. Mergus jumped in response. "Mergus and I have much work to do. We will prepare those who have answered the call."

Celio and Sebastion half bowed to the council. "We are just a dimension away, always watching and guiding with love," said Sebastion as the crystalline light flickered and fanned out, once again restored to its previous form of just a circular platform of smooth clear crystal.

Sumayah sat wrapped in the surrounding silence. No one uttered a word, not even a whisper, deep in his own thoughts. It was not to last long, and one by one, the Carian dragons took flight. Sumayah looked for Nero; he was still next to Sterling and Ciara.

Ryven had sidled up to her, grasping her hand. She smiled at his touch and gave him a sideways glance, squeezing his fingers tightly.

"Well, Faerians, who of you will answer the calling?" asked Fallonay, leaving his position and joining Mergus and Bethia.

Rupert followed suit and jumped up and quickly strutted to the group, with Lhayan clutching his arm. "Our daughters have volunteered, as well as most of the Lemurians," he proudly announced, then gave Lhayan a quick peck on her cheek. "My Lhayan and I will also return with our daughters."

Someone gasped out, "What?"

Sumayah smiled, knowing it would be Riva.

Rupert coughed, trying to cover up his daughter's embarrassing outburst, then said, "I think we are all in agreement here. There is no need for verbal confirmation."

"Well then, King Rupert...what do we do next?" asked Fallonay, walking to Ryven and patting his back.

"We plan for the battle that has been already written in the stars," said Bethia.

CHAPTER 20

MESHA

☙

His throat felt charred from the backdraft of his fiery breath; his heart did not just beat, it bludgeoned his chest with each agonizing flap of his wings. With the sight of camp, he felt a slight renewal in strength and willed himself to finish his flight without crashing headlong into the waters beyond the shoreline. He could see a school of those damned mermaids and did not need to be caught in their grasp, not in his present condition. Any other time he could easily rip them tail from head, but not after his battle with Nero. *That blasted Carian; I thought I had killed it.* The last thing he expected was to battle him. And the Fae, oh how he would have loved to end his miserable Earth-worshipping life right in front of Sumayah.

His demeanor softened a bit as her fiery form filled his mind. He wanted her, wanted to possess her and her willful and wild ways. She was special; it was much more than her ability to use the crystal. There was something else; she was an enigma, especially after her newly found display of fire magic. It ignited in him an uncontrollable desire, a desire to mingle fire with fire, flesh with flesh.

He was so deep in thought, he mistook the distance to the ground and nose planted with a muffled *"oof"* and a second *"oof"* as his back end caught up to him and drove his nose deeper into the sand. The sudden jolt of his landing hurried his shift back into his human form, and he rolled over, staring at the big blond peering down at him.

"Anything broken?"

Mesha held out his hand. "Clarron, just help me up!"

Clarron did as he bid and yanked him to a standing position.

"The girl?"

Mesha studied the large young man for a moment, his hair gold as the sun, with eyes a pale, ice blue. He was a big one, even more muscular than Mesha and a good head taller. *They grew them big in the land of the...of...where did he come from?* He suddenly could not remember.

Furrowing his brow he snarled, "She is long gone, along with her merry entourage."

"The dragon?"

"Gone too!" Mesha eyed Clarron, thinking for a split second he saw relief in his eyes.

Suddenly the sound of a horse being ridden hard and fast disturbed Mesha's thoughts. The man ferociously beat at his horse's side with a long strap, *slap, slap, slap*, all the way. He heavily hauled on the face of the horse until it slid to a stop, huffing and puffing, sending bloodied foam from its labored breath.

A fleck of white mingled with crimson hit Mesha on his cheek. He wiped it away and walked forward with clenched fist and slammed it as hard as he could into the horse's already agonizing face. The horse grunted and went straight up in the air, unseating his rider.

Mesha then pointed at the horse, which was struggling to stand. "Butcher that one; he will serve us better on the table tonight!"

Clarron grimaced at his words but quickly cloaked his expression. He grasped the reins of the horse while the rider stood.

"What have you ridden so hard for, to tell me the realm of Lemuria is gone?" asked Mesha.

"Wh—why, yes, there is nothing...it is as if it never were. The land swallowed her up and let the seas rush in and bury her."

"It is as I suspected. They know why we come and have destroyed her or have taken her into middle earth's dimension to keep all from us."

190

Mesha spun, brushing sand off his arm, and stomped off with Clarron in tow.

"This means the way is shut, Mesha. We can go home now."

Mesha slammed to a halt; Clarron narrowly escaped colliding with him. He scowled at Clarron.

"No! We go to Agartha. We will find a way. If they would not have let that dragon loose, he would have been our way. Now I must think."

"Agartha? Do you really want to go...there? I have heard about a wise woman who inhabits that realm, and she is strong and very powerful. There are beings there that make me look the size of—you."

Mesha frowned at his remark. "We have no choice in the matter, if we are to keep control over man; it is what we must do. I *need* that crystal. The rest of them are worth nothing without that thirteenth crys—"

Mesha suddenly smiled, his deep eyes lighting up his face like a torch in a cave. He shook his finger at Clarron. "We might have a way after all. I just bet those Carians that have come to their senses and joined our cause can help us get there. With the war ensuing above us, we have no further contact from our elders. This is all left to us now."

A sudden scream filled the air, horrible and agonizing, ending in a long release of breath. Mesha smiled.

"Ah, we eat! I swear if I didn't have excuses to leave that damned city of tree huggers, I would have starved to death. They consumed nothing but a leaf here or a berry there."

"I like fruit, Mesha, and vegetables are good for you," Clarron chided. "They make you grow big and strong like me."

Mesha glared. "Well, it is one of our largest controlling methods, Clarron. With the consumption and the belief of the need for flesh and blood, we can keep men in our grasp." He stopped to laugh loudly. "In the end, their hunger for flesh will in turn consume them and this planet. What a brilliant plan! The grand, original plan has gone astray; men have not become what was once expected."

"What about the new breed, the ones that are now being called witches? It is said they are not under your control and think for themselves."

"I am very well aware of *witches*; we have a plan already hatched that will take care of them." He studied Clarron, wondering how much he could really trust him. Could he tell this golden mountain eyeing him that soon men would turn against witches in such a matter, it would send a cry throughout the land, causing such fear and anguish, they would bend on knees and worship the false God, and the Goddess would be dead? No, he thought better of it...let him find out in his own time. For this plan could take lifetimes.

"The dragons you speak of are at the mine, I believe," offered Clarron.

Mesha was startled from his daydream. "What...what, they are at the mines, good, good." He extended his arm out to let Clarron tromp ahead. "Then let us go to the mine."

It was not long before they were in the saddle, Clarron on a very large gray and Mesha on his white stallion. Mesha loved his horse, even though he had no problem eating others. He patted his steed affectionately, holding tight to the reins, for his horse was not easy to sit or control. He remembered the day Rupert presented him with the horse, calling him Aragon. Rupert told him the horse was special and had come from a land far away, a land of twin suns.

It was instant admiration for the animal, and Mesha spent many years trying to "join up" with his horse, as the Lemurians would say. The stallion would do Mesha's bidding, but that was all he shared. Mesha could not understand why his beloved pet did not show the same affection that he bestowed up him. But he loved the spirit of the animal, loved the feel of controlling this great beast.

His thoughts strayed to Sumayah, her wild beauty once again filled his mind, how she had bravely pulled his sword out of that damn dragon, her look of triumph, how it heightened her wild beauty all the more. He vowed to do whatever it took to have her back. He would rule the planet with her at his side. If he could control his horse, he could control a mere girl. But then again she was not one of the weak-minded human girls. No, she would never bow down to his rule. He knew that, and that is what excited him. He could feed off of her rebellious energy the rest of his life. But what worried him was her use of fire, and the fact that everyone was still waiting for what other new magic she had hidden within her.

Then Elspeth came to mind. She was lovely to look at and strong in her own tree-hugging way. Ugh, how he hated trees...but if things did not work out with Sumayah, he would take the Fae. He was not immune to her advances; yes, she would also do quite well.

Aragon lunged forward and shook his head, which jolted Mesha from his thoughts. He grasped for his reins and clamped his legs.

"Aragon! That is enough out of you; do you want to end up on the din-
ner table?" But deep inside he could not ever kill his horse. Aragon was an
attention-getter, and Mesha loved the envious stares from his slaves as he
rode by on his prancing stallion. He patted the horse as it pranced. "There,
there, Aragon, I could never do without you."

Clarron ignored Mesha as the mine came into sight. Men rushed in and
out of the cavern, reminiscent of ants on their hill, hurrying and scurrying
in and out. As they approached, one man came forward. He was average
height and had nondescript facial features, but his flaming red hair was
unforgettable. Clarron had never seen such a glaring color before and could
not peel his eyes away.

"Ah, Skully, how is the mine producing?" Mesha asked as he slid from
the back of Aragon, handing the reins to another man, who promptly
turned to lead him and Clarron's horse away.

"See that you don't eat him, or I'll be after your tasty limbs!" warned
Clarron.

The skinny man looked up and down at Clarron's great size, then at his
horse and nodded vigorously. "Aye, sir, I will take good care of him. I'd like
to keep my legs."

They moved closer to the mine, watching as the men-slaves labored.
They had set up a line; each would pass the oncoming sack until the end of
the line, when it was opened and poured into a large wooden contraption
called a sieve. One would pour the bag of dirt and bits of yellow into the
machine, and one would pour a bucket of water on top...the water would
wash away the dirt, leaving the bits of glinting yellow.

They must have hit a good vein, because there was a good layer of
golden sediment ready to be scooped up and bagged once again.

Mesha ran his hands back and forth in the sieve and scooped up a handful
of the freshly mined gold. He squeezed it in his hand and shook it at Clarron.

"This is more precious than my own life. This is why we must keep
control over our slaves. We will live wanting of nothing, in splendor and
luxury. We will have it all; the system is already in place. Even with the
war above our heads, it will begin, and there is nothing any of them can do
to stop it." Mesha paused, letting the wet gold slide from his hand, staring
and watching as if the sight of it would not let him turn away.

"Why do you need the crystal? Why do we need to go to Agartha?"
asked Clarron.

Mesha slowly looked at Clarron; his stare was blank as if he didn't hear him. Then he blinked his eyes and smiled.

"Because they think they can awaken our slaves...they think they have the answer to take their world back. I must have it so that never, ever happens. Besides, if I do not find it, then my life will be forfeit, and I will have to leave Earth." Mesha turned, dismissing Clarron. He cupped his right hand over his left eye to block out the intense sun. "Blast those *Faerians*. When they left this dimension, they took the temperate weather with them." He wiped the sweat from his brow. "Now, where would those Carians be?"

The heat of the day was suddenly swept away by three pair of wings; the dragons, one at a time, set their bodies upon the earth. Drakaous, with his red-orange eye, wearily locked on Mesha's approach.

"I have been informed you seek our council," he said, lowering his head closer to Mesha. "What is it that we may do for you?"

"Drakaous, we need to get to Agartha. We need to find the thirteenth crystal. I know it is there. Sumayah told me it was returned to her father."

Drakaous lifted his head and turned it sideways to glare down at Mesha. He looked over to where Drakemon and Baratheous stood.

"Do either of you know the way to the realm that he speaks of?"

Baratheous strolled forward, his tail slashing the air behind him in annoyance. "I would not suggest you go there, young master. That land is kept by a woman with great power." He paused and turned his head right, then left quickly. "It is told she has spies in every dimension. They are her ears and eyes."

"Baratheous is right," Drakaous said. "She will be waiting for you; she will be ready to do battle. It would be best if you forget about the crystal."

Mesha felt his temperature rise, even in the already searing heat. It traveled up, converging in his head, ready to explode. He clenched his teeth in anger and swiftly pulled his shining sword from its sheath nestled at his thigh. The brilliant blue stone near the hilt glinted in Drakaous's eye.

"You will find us a way or feel the coldness of my blade within your heart."

Drakaous could not get past the stone, that blue stone. He knew then that it was Mesha who had tried to kill Nero; he silently vowed to do whatever he could to stop this tyrant of a young man. He felt his skin tighten as anger surged, carried within the blood of his quickening heart.

"There is no need for bloodshed," replied Drakemon as he walked to Mesha, pushing the blade away. "Are you so positive your swordplay is that which could kill the likes of us?"

"That is enough, Drakemon," ordered Drakaous. "We will help find the crystal. But as far as finding a way to Agartha, that we cannot do. We do not know the way."

Mesha leaned in closer to Drakaous, looking up. "If you cannot find a way, then find me someone who can," he sneered.

Suddenly there was chaotic screaming coming from the cave. The slave-men rushed out, falling over one another.

"They were Knockers!" one yelled, then another.

"What is it?" yelled Mesha as he lost interest in the dragons. He hustled forward toward the cave opening. More men scrambled out. Mesha pushed aside one oncoming man as he edged his way to the opening. "Clarron!"

Clarron bowed to the dragons. "I must go," he said, pivoted on his heel, and ran to Mesha.

Both men waited for their eyes to accustom to the dimness of the belly of the cavern.

"Don't go in there, the Knockers will kill you," a haggard, bug-eyed man screamed as he ran by.

"Stop—what is a Knocker?" Mesha yelled. But the man kept going, huffing noisily all the way out.

Mesha looked at Clarron in question. "What say you, shall we go?" He pulled his sword out of the sheath, and Clarron did the same.

They inched step by step farther into the recesses of the dusty, dimly lit cavern. Mesha heard a ruckus farther back and halted, turning his ear to listen. His curiosity overruled his self-preservation, and he crept closer to the noises. *Angry voices,* he thought, but as they got closer, it seemed as if the voices were from song and dance, which confused him. *Why would they run from this?* With Clarron close on his heel, he flattened himself against the rock and slowly rounded a sharp corner, then carefully peeked his head around to take a look. Jerking his head back, he gave Clarron a grimace.

"They aren't belly dancers," he whispered. "They are heavy on the ugly, and a surly looking bunch."

Clarron itched to take a look and tightened his grip on the hilt of his sword just as he heard the words.

"Get out!"

Mesha looked at Clarron, then held up his sword, giving him a wink. But before he could take a step, something landed with a thud at their feet, then rolled with an unfamiliar squishing sound until it bumped against Mesha's right foot. Mesha looked down, wondering what it was; the face staring up at him was frozen in horror, mouth agape, eyes crossed. Mesha gulped as he moved his foot to push the severed head away and began retracing his steps out of the cave. Clarron walked backward, stumbling on rocks and bumping into the jagged edges of the cave walls.

As soon as they both saw the light of the opening, Mesha shoved Clarron and dove for the outside air. He landed with a grunt and rolled, his sword catching him, slicing at his thigh. He paid it no mind and dug into the sand with his toes to gain momentum up and away.

Clarron passed by him, not looking back. His sword was still in his hand, and his legs were pumping hard, for his great size wielded strength but not speed.

Drakaous stood with his brothers at his back. He eyed the spectacle. He could not hide his look of amusement and heard Baratheous snicker.

Clarron reached the dragons first and knelt, trying to catch his breath. A few seconds later, Mesha joined him.

In between breaths Mesha said, "What...was that? Drakaous, what are...they?"

"Knockers. They live in the earth. They are of the earth and tend to all of the minerals. It is their job to make sure Mother Earth's body is not ravaged and used up."

Mesha straightened and frowned at Drakaous. "How do we get rid of them?"

Drakemon walked forward and answered, "You don't. They can shift and move through walls of dirt, rock, and sand. They are the dirt, the rocks. You will have no choice but to leave that mine."

"Why is this happening now? We have been taking gold from the ground for thousands of years. Why now?" Mesha asked, clasping his hand to his bleeding thigh.

"Because the revolt has begun," answered Drakaous in a matter-of-fact manner. "From now on, it will not be so easy to just take. A price will need to be paid."

Mesha stood in silent anger; his eyes narrowed. In a slow, deliberate voice, he said, "We go to Agartha, I will figure out a way."

CHAPTER 21

THE MESSAGE

ℭℛ

Ryven halted Black and turned to wait for Sumayah, surprised to see her riding today. He watched her sit the fiery mare almost as if they were one. The periodic shadow overhead, like a steady stream of clouds occasionally blocking out the light of the sun, gave Ryven comfort. Nero and Sterling were never far. They watched from the skies as Ryven watched from the land. The Reps had yet to find an entrance into Agartha, and with Mother Earth now in revolt, it was highly unlikely any of them would get past the dark dwarves who kept vigilance over their precious lands. But, then again, with Bethia seemingly in charge he was not sure of anything these days.

"You dally around too much. I am always waiting," he said with a grin as they rode up next to him, Black nipping playfully at Ciara, and Ciara doing the same to Black.

"It is nice to have a break from Mergus and Bethia's teachings. I think I can recite every single plant and its purpose, magical *and* medicinal." She cocked her head and peered at Ryven. "But you know this already. The Fae is of the Earth. It isn't fair that I have to *learn* it."

Ryven laughed, giving Black an affectionate pat. "I know nothing about turning to fire, and I don't think I want to either."

Their conversation was cut short when Sumayah *shushed* Ryven. Ciara, also seeing it, stopped and watched, not in fear but in curiosity.

"There he is again," said Sumayah out of the side of her mouth.

Nero and Sterling hovered above, both coming in closer to give their follower a good look.

"They do not look worried," said Ryven, looking back to Sumayah who had slid from her horse. He turned his head back to where the creature lurked under the canopy of trumpet flowers. Their long, conical flower heads dripped pink nectar that was harvested by Bethia's priestesses and made into a fermented drink called wine, brought out for special occasions and ceremony.

With a heavy sigh, Ryven slid from Black and let him and Ciara nibble at some of the sweet clover flowers. They too seemed uninterested in the elusive creature that shadowed them. But he had to do his job, which was to keep his *priestess* out of trouble.

Sumayah took a few steps closer, then stopped, hoping to let the creature get used to her nearness. She felt it was a he, and he was so beautiful; a wolf is what Bethia called it. She rolled the word around her tongue, then spoke it. His tall, straight ears perked higher as the word traveled to him. He sniffed the air with a square, ebony-colored nose. Sumayah took a step back, noticing one large pearl-white tooth reminiscent of a long-tooth peeking out from under his red-brown lip. *I'm not in Lemuria, he won't eat me. There are no flesh eaters here*, she consoled herself, taking that lost step back. Her hand itched to touch his thick shining coat, curious about how it felt beneath her fingers.

Their moment ended when a wolf cry echoed through the air. The wolf's large expressive eyes left her as he turned his head. He stood, then turned back to her, gave her one more look, spun, and disappeared into the cover of the forest.

Perplexed, she watched the forest a moment longer. She heard Ryven behind her and turned to face him.

"I have been told that no one has ever possessed a wolf, Sumayah. I know what you are thinking, and I would just give it up."

She frowned at him. His words just made her want that wolf all the more.

"We will just see about that. He is just as intrigued with me as I am with him. I feel it in here." She pointed to her heart. "He will not be able to resist me for much longer, Ryven...just like you."

She giggled as he laughed and snatched her up, holding her close to him. The scent of him, a blend of the forest, and a freshly laundered shirt intoxicated her, and she relinquished herself to his embrace. She looked up at him and parted her mouth in invitation, just as a hard knock to the back of her sent her head forward, clanking her tooth hard against Ryven's. Both separated, pressing their hands to their painfully vibrating mouth.

"Ciara!" hollered Sumayah through her fingers. "That hurt."

Ciara flattened her ears back at Ryven, then wheeled around and took off with tail flying high. The moment ruined, Ryven trudged ahead of Sumayah.

"That horse of yours is quite exasperating," he said.

She grabbed at his sword hilt, holding him back, then grasped his hand. "Oh, don't let her ruin our day. Goddess knows what those two will have in store for me when we get back, so let's just enjoy the rest of our time." She took off ahead of him, making him chase her as she wound around more trumpet flowers, dwelling-sized aloes entwined with brilliant, blue morning glory flowers. She breathed in the succulent air, and listened to the chorus of the colorful array of birds and the barely audible ballads of the winged elementals happily doing their jobs.

They soon left the openness of the meadow and headed into a dense ridge of fir trees that were almost as tall as the mountains set behind them. The air cooled slightly as the limbs of the trees parted for her to travel. She thanked them, touching each one softly, feeling their subtle vibration as she went by.

Her entourage did their best to keep up with her.

Ryven trotted to stay with her. "Sumayah, what is the hurry?"

She suddenly stopped where the cover of trees ended and gasped at the sight. Gone was the meadow of fruits and plants, but in its stead was a lake so large, she could not see where it ended. It just went on and on, almost as if she was staring into the waters from the shoreline of Lemuria. The color of the water was a pale lavender. It was so still, so calm, she felt the strange urge to walk on it, as if she could stay right on the top and keep going until she reached the pulsating amber horizon beneath the gaze of the smiling twin suns.

"Oh, it is so beautiful, Ryven. It must go on forever," she said, slipping her soft sandal off to put her toe in. "*Ahh*, as I suspected, not too hot and not too cool."

Nero and Sterling landed without a sound. "How do they do that? It amazes me that something so large can land on the ground in total silence," she said, walking to meet the dragons. Ciara and Black were already splashing their way in, stopping when it got chest deep.

"I think this is the same body of water we came upon when we first shifted here," said Ryven, taking off his calf-high boot to join Sumayah. "We are just on a different shoreline."

Sumayah turned to smile at him as he put his foot in with a deep sigh. She caught a flash of something behind him in the tree line. The figure slowly walked out of the shadow and sat with large dark eyes intent upon her.

"He's baaack."

Ryven turned his head. "Well, looks like we have a new addition to our gang."

"How do I get closer? I itch to touch him."

"I would not rush it. Let him come to you. Look how much closer he is already."

"You are right. We will just go about our day and let him be part of it...from afar."

Suddenly the calm waters began to ripple, traveling toward them and lapping at their feet.

"What is this?" asked Sumayah, looking at Ryven in question. He was already taking a step out of the water.

The ripple became a wave, and the wave grew higher and higher, traveling with great noise toward them. The waves rose above the lake, taking form, and the forms seemed to gallop on top of the waterline, emerging out of the lavender depths. Ciara and Black seemed to love the spectacle and whinnied noisily at the ensuing commotion.

"They are kelpies, do not fear them," said Ryven, holding his hands up against the wet onslaught.

There were eight in all; they looked just like any other horse. Excitedly she waded toward them with hand extended so they could smell her.

"You Fae can call them kelpies, but I will call them water horses."

With great joy she went from one to the other, meeting and greeting, running her hand along their strong top lines to feel the warm, smooth muscles. "They are a strong bunch, are they not?"

"It is told that they helped the merpeople build their aquatic cities. And in gratitude they were given the strength to travel out of the waters and play on land."

Laying her hand on the face of a pretty white mare, she said, "Mergus told us that merpeople were the first inhabitants of the lost realm of Atlantis, that they misused the powers bestowed upon them and were sent into the sea until they learned the true meaning of Earth gifts."

"My father used to tell us the same...but I just figured it was a way to make us listen and be mindful of how we live here on Mother Earth."

"Well, you could be right, Ryven." She paused and gave him a wink. "By the looks of it, it worked."

He smiled sheepishly at her, letting a kelpie sniff at his hair, then take a nibble, chewing, then chewing too hard.

"Hey, that is attached to my head," he scolded, yanking his hair back.

Sumayah suddenly fell silent. Her eyes closed. All around her no longer mattered except the voice in her head.

"We bring you a message, young seeker, said the white kelpie." Know that we speak as one with the Goddess...You are very connected with the many different beings of this world, whether they are winged, four-legged, swimmers, or crawlers. But be warned that like you, all beings here have come for their own purpose, so do not fall into the greedy and self-serving mind-set as those who dwell at the outer realm of our world, for this will bring much strife to those beings that have come in goodwill and service to the Goddess. Remember, all beings here have come to assist one another and are not to be controlled and restrained by human greed.

"It is good that you want to be with the wolf and the dragon and the horse... but be just that. Share with them the great plan of our world. Do not put them in chains and cages, for it will break their spirit, and they will soon forget why they have come, and then they will become just like those who chain them. We want you to know that when you return to the outer realm, you will be greatly challenged. There will be things you must do in order to fulfill your quest, things you could never do here as Sumayah. That is why when you return, you will not be Sumayah. You will change into someone who will be able to live in the realm of men and Reps...you will forget who you were today, yet know who you are today will be with you always.

Bethia will instruct you further in this matter when the time is right. But know that you must do what must be done..."

The mare stepped away from Sumayah. Suddenly feeling present and aware of her surroundings, Sumayah turned to Ryven, who had been watching her intently.

"Another vision?"

"Not a vision, but a message from them and the Goddess." She stroked the green-eyed mare. "Thank you. I will try my best to heed your words." She looked down at her feet, still covered by the crystal waters. "I'm scared, Ryven. I suddenly feel as if my life is not my own. I feel out of control."

Ryven went to her and gathered her in his arms. He tilted her chin up to look down into her eyes.

"Are we ever in control? We must remember the first plan, the original plan. It is hard to remember we did not come here to live for just ourselves. We have come in service. We are being called once again, Sumayah. This is much bigger than just you and me, or you and your dragon. But I feel in the end..." He paused to plant a kiss on her forehead. "In the end, no matter how many millennia it takes, it will all have been worth it, and we will find each other." He planted another kiss on her forehead and whispered into her ear, "I will follow you to the ends of the Earth, no matter who you have become, no matter how many lifetimes it takes."

She searched his face, feeling the tingling effect of his kiss. He was right. It was not about the two of them. It was much more than that. But she did promise herself that she would always find her way back to her Fae. She suddenly felt sad, as if she were saying good-bye to him. She buried her face in his chest, needing to hear his heartbeat, feel the rise and fall as he breathed, take in his earthy scent. She let this moment become forever etched in her mind, willing it to be locked away in a part where it would never be forgotten.

The splashing of forcefully parting water broke the silence. The kelpies turned, having finished their task, and made their way back to the shimmering waters of the underworld.

"I wonder if I will ever see one again," she said aloud.

"They are part of Mother Earth, so yes; you can count on it, just as you can count on me being here for you...eternally."

She thought of the word *eternally* and secretly hoped he was right. For something about this moment changed her. It was time for her to pull away the layer of the little girl and step into the role of priestess, priestess of Lemuria. She vowed that one day she would have her home back and her rightful place in her home.

Feeling a sudden urge to get on with her quest, she stepped out of the water, taking Ryven with her to the shoreline. His strong hand clasped hers, and she found comfort in it, not wanting to ever let him go. Her entourage stood on the low bank of the shoreline, seeming to know what journey lay ahead of them.

CHAPTER 22

THE ALCHEMIST

☙

Mergus caressed his flute while listening to Sumayah. Bethia puffed on her long-stemmed pipe. She exhaled a steady stream of blue smoke that hung in the air, gathering itself into what resembled a dragon entwined with a horse. It slowly floated to Sumayah, and she breathed in. She likened the smell to shaved apple bark and the medicinal pungency of mullein leaf and mugwort. Bethia instructed Sumayah to recite in her head all the magical properties of plants and barks as she saw them. It is one thing to sit in class and learn their proper names and uses, but out in the field, touching, tasting, feeling, and using your intuition to speak with them was how one truly learned. It was getting to the point that whenever Sumayah heard the telltale jingle of Bethia's adornments, she would turn and go the other way.

But this day was not to talk about herbs. It was a time of celebration called MaMa, a time to honor the Goddess and the birth of Mother Earth. It was a day of storytelling and magic sharing. Anyone who had a special story of learning could take this day and tell it to everyone so that this could be remembered and retold, adding to the rest of the history of their benefactor.

Since Mother Earth, MaMa, had been their provider and sustainer of life. Mother Earth was the embodiment of the Goddess, who gave birth to all.

It was Sumayah's turn to tell her story, which was told to her by the kelpie. She felt a tinge of nervousness in her stomach as the council grounds overflowed with anticipation and listeners focusing their eyes on her.

Riva, who sat directly behind her, dug her fat toe in the small of her back. Sumayah smiled as she sent her elbow sharply into the center of Riva's knee. Lhayan, seeing the childish antics, intervened, putting her hand across Sumayah's back and giving Riva a sharp look.

"Please, go ahead, Sumayah, you may begin," said Bethia.

She shifted her weight, searching for the right words. *Come on, just belt it out. Anything has to be better than listening to Mergus drone on.*

"These words were given to me by the kelpie, who told me they were speaking from the Goddess herself."

A few watchers gasped in astonishment, and the hiss of whispers filled the air.

Bethia stood and tapped her staff on the ground. "Please, it is our priestess's time. Let her continue."

"They told me that those in the outer realm have lost the connection to Mother Earth and are misusing her gifts and abusing all other beings. They put them in chains and cages, keeping them for their own greed and purpose. They have lost the knowledge that all beings are here of their own will and purpose."

Fallonay stood in anger at her words. "We have been in Agartha for only one hundred short years, and things have become much worse in the outer realm. I do know what the kelpie speaks of, for it has been told to us from the elementals still brave enough to live out there. The natural realms and beings suffer greatly. Man and his greed are destroying Mother Earth with their growing hatred of one another and for what one possesses over the other."

Mergus set his flute down and strode to the center of the council, making a small circle, his face taut with worry.

"It is much worse than we had anticipated. Not only is the natural realm suffering, but it is also men, for some have not chosen to have their minds enslaved. They fight to awaken their brethren, but to no avail, for the Rep has always been one step ahead of them. Our sisters of the Goddess"— he pointed to Pennyann and Leesabeth—"our sisters and brothers of the

Goddess are being sought and murdered as heretics. They turn one against the other in fear. The Reps have learned that fear is a worthy ally.

Bethia swung her staff, tapping it not too lightly on Mergus's left arm. He frowned at her. She waited until they could once again hear the cascading waterfalls behind the city.

"Even though we are in a different realm, a different dimension, I fear our thoughts and words can travel, feeding the Rep." She paused, scanning the many faces fixated on her. She stomped her foot, and her adornments jingled. "We will do as we said. We *will* help men awaken. We will save Mother Earth from their inevitable destruction. But first we have work to do from here to prepare. We go into unchartered territory, and we have yet to ignite the inherent abilities of our young ones. We need them as much as they need us, for the whole is greater than the sum of its parts. Our young will be ready soon, and I will not send them or any of us until we are ready."

"It is time for our young to reveal what they know on this special day, the birthday of our Mother," said Bethia pointing her staff in the sky. "The phoenix, the sacred bird of Lemuria, has returned to Agartha."

Suddenly the skies became alive with the onslaught of raptors. Their golden-red feathers enhanced the amber glow of the twin suns. Everyone watched the beautiful horde in stilled hush as the creatures' wings silently sliced through the air. There were more than could be counted. Then suddenly they all shifted in one swift motion, and the scrambled mass of wings became one giant phoenix.

"Behold the power of the phoenix! Through cooperation and harmony, they become one!" yelled Bethia.

The giant mass suddenly exploded into flames. Sumayah sat unbelieving; she glanced at Ryven, who had sat down on the other side of her. The flames wildly licked out in every direction, so brightly she had to shield her eyes. Confusion held her.

The flames suddenly began to diminish. The charred remains floated like a black cloud sinking ever so slowly until it crumbled to the earth.

Were they all dead? What sort of magic was this?

"It is time for our people to learn of their inherent strengths," said Bethia, "things imbued into us for this time. But now we must learn the dark side of magic. This was not part of our intention, but the intruders have made it so. We have no choice now except to learn ways of protecting ourselves and our world."

Sumayah felt her flesh prickle at the words. She already had a taste of her dark magic.

Bethia pointed to Sumayah. "You have already shown that you possess magic worthy of battle." She waved her forward. "Come, you will be the first."

Heat coursed through her body, and she felt as if her face were aflame. *I do not want to do this. This was just something that—that happened. I have no control over it.*

"Come, Sumayah, show us," Bethia ordered a little more sternly, tapping her staff on the ground.

She felt the jab of Riva's toe, pushing her out of her seat. Sumayah shot up and spun, glaring at Riva. Riva grinned, then winked at her. *Come, sissy, two can play this game.* Sumayah smiled at her sister and grabbed her by the arm, twisting it to force her to stand. Riva grimaced at the stronghold and reluctantly followed Sumayah toward Bethia.

"I feel my sisters and I all have a certain power of our own. I think I know what power Riva possesses already," said Sumayah, tightening her lips to suppress her smile.

Riva shot her a narrowed look.

Mergus chortled at Sumayah's words and strolled forward, wanting to join in the game. "I think Priestess Sumayah is becoming very intuitive, which is also powerful if not ignored."

Bethia pointed to the charred remains. "Sumayah, do you believe them gone?"

Just great, sure, here we go. She shifted nervously, not wanting to be wrong, especially with her whole family watching. The heat rose once again in her face, and then she caught a glimpse of Nero. His stillness instantly calmed her, and she willed herself to hear him. He is a wielder of fire. He can help me. She closed her eyes and opened her mind, shutting out all else…which did not come easy at first. The constant jingle of golden adornments kept Bethia's questioning stare forefront. Sumayah took a deep breath, and as she let it out, she willed her thoughts to converge with Nero's. To her surprise she heard his voice in her head…

"They can be resurrected; you can return their fire to them, and out of the ashes they will fly. Do not look upon them as bone and feathers. Look upon them as what they truly are, Sumayah."

She had to ponder that a moment. *Without flesh, bone, and feather, they are nothing.*

"You are wrong, Sumayah; look at them without your seeing eyes. Look at them with the Knowledge of All. Do you remember the crystal skull at your priestess ceremony?"

That day suddenly flooded her mind—the crystal, the ladder, her vision. She then remembered...*we are more than flesh and bone. That is just the vessel that keeps us as we live each lifetime here on Mother Earth. A vessel that can change from one dimension to another to carry our very self, the essence of who we truly are!*

"Yes, that's it...they are not dead!" she burst out. "Their true essence is in another realm, another dimension, and they, like all of us, can return over and over."

Bethia smiled broadly. She pushed aside a tendril of her shining black hair. "Well done, my love!"

"But now, Sumayah, the magic is to help them come back," said Mergus, his normal jovial expression clouded by his serious stare.

Sumayah could feel Mergus pulling for her and did not want to disappoint him. She took the ten steps to the charred remains, still in connection with Nero. *Nero, I know the elements are living, and in each of us are all four of the elements; we could not live without them.*

"Yes, Sumayah, you must speak to the fire within yourself, that living element of creation inside of you."

She thought about each of the elements—water, air, earth, and then stopped at fire. She willed herself to feel the heat of it and spoke aloud.

"Salamanders of the elemental realm, I seek your council, and ask that you come forth, illuminating yourself outside my vessel. You are that part of me that keeps me whole, and I ask you now to come forth!"

The sudden gasps of the council told her she was on the right path, and she opened her eyes. She held up her hands, which were not just flesh and bone but feathered. *I now have wings! I turned myself into a phoenix. That was not supposed to happen. Can you hear me, element of air? I did not invoke you! This magic is much, much harder than I had anticipated. And look at Mergus and Bethia looking at me. They are just as dumbfounded as I.*

She quibbled internally, then right on cue, she heard Riva snickering behind her. She turned. *Well, sissy, now is your time to shine. Let's see what you have within yourself.* Sumayah raised up her golden feathered limbs, marveling at how light they felt, and couldn't stop the urge to give them a flap.

Riva's eyes popped as she suddenly understood Sumayah's intention. Riva took two steps back as Sumayah approached with her feathered limbs, which were suddenly in flames.

"Sumayah, stop!" someone yelled.

Ignoring the order Sumayah, waved her flaming feathers at Riva and said, "You mock me, sister!"

Riva took another step back, shaking her head no.

"Come on, sister, I know you have it in you. Let it out, or I might have to burn you," she blurted, then shot her limbs out in front of her, letting her flames flicker ever closer to Riva.

Riva jumped back with a screech, pushing her hand out in front of her. Shooting suddenly up from the solid ground between them was a wall of sparking, flashing energy.

Good girl, Riva, I knew you had it in you. Sumayah let the flames hit her wall, which of course blocked the fiery charge. Hitting the wall forced Sumayah to her original self, and the flames and feathers disappeared.

"Great show!" applauded Mergus. "I knew you could do it—both of you!"

The council erupted in a wave of applause.

Bethia waved her staff and interrupted. "Wait, Sumayah is not yet finished with her challenge."

Sumayah remembered the remains on the ground and focused her fullest attention to them. She stilled her mind and formed pictures of the blackened ground rising up. The swirling mass of burnt remains obeyed and lifted. She watched them swirl and flutter, the ebony pieces darting this way and that. She felt the heat rise in her hands once again and held them out, palm facing forward. She called upon the salamanders, the spirit of form, and then the sylphs, the breath of form. She called upon gnomes, the bones and flesh of form, and then called upon the undines, the blood of form.

Having the vision of all the elements in her mind, she willed them to join with the fluttering, blackened remains. She watched as the elements and the black remains joined, taking shape.

Sumayah suddenly felt dizzy. An earsplitting roar echoed in her head, and her present world soon gave away to another world, another time...

She opened her eyes to chaos. Living, breathing fire surrounded her, the heat so intense, she watched a strand of her hair curl into a wisp of smoke. She had to get out of here, and she imagined her two arms and two legs were now legs of the stag. One leg moved, then the other, faster and faster with each step. Feeling suddenly free she ran with the deer and the rabbits. She ran with the stags. Their strong will to survive became her strong will, and together they forged forward, dodging falling torches and grasses that burst into flames.

Deer crashed into one another, avoiding the flames that leaped at them. A stag, mouth frothing with fear, tried to jump over her; she felt a heavy thud to her head, and a burst of white light blinded her, forcing her face-first down into the crisp, crackling earth. Dirt went up her nose, the smell heavy and sour like vinegar.

After all this, this is how I am to die, *she thought. A tear escaped down her cheek as faces of her coven flashed before her; they were pleading with her. But it was too late; she could not hear their words, and she laid down her head in defeat. Her eyes were heavy, and she let them close.* This is the end, *she thought. But her rasping cough kept her from falling into the abyss long enough to hear a voice...*

"Remember who you are, Shion. Remember the phoenix."

"Bethia, is that you?" Shion whispered hoarsely into the smoldering stench of the earth. "I cannot think. I cannot breathe. Bethia, help me!"

"You can breathe fire! Shion, remember—remember now!"

Summoning all her strength, she lifted her head and heard the sound of hooves pounding the earth. Freia, *she thought. The thick smoke parted enough for her to see the blinding glow of a white horse.*

"Nero!" she sobbed loudly. "You've come back! I knew you would." She shakily stood to meet him, but a searing flame of raging fire separated them. The heat so intense, she could smell the stink of her burning hair. I must get to him, *she thought.*

Then she remembered her magic name ceremony and the stream of fire that shot from the mouth of the dragon.

"I do have the power of the phoenix!" she yelled. "I can breathe fire, I can walk through fire—you cannot stop me!" She envisioned the cloak of red and gold feathers encompassing her body, turning her arms into wings. The pressure in her lungs from the smoke lifted, and she breathed deeply. With amazement the flames parted as she stepped forward. She no longer felt their flickers of death. With one more step, she was next to Nero. He bobbed his head up and down, snorting at her, and then knelt down on one knee so she could climb on his back. She grabbed his long silken mane in her charred black hands and swung herself up. Elation and happiness exploded

within her as she clamped her legs to his side one more time. He turned and cantered through the smoke and flame.

"Thank you, Nero, thank you for saving me," she cried before all went black...

"Ouch!" she cried as a sharp pain from a pinch wakened her from the dark mist. Her eyes sprung open to see Riva smirking at her.

"Where did you go?" Riva asked.

Suddenly her vision overtook her annoyance with her sister, the pain and horror of the fire as it engulfed her. But then she remembered...she spun, searching the council. Then she saw Nero still standing quietly next to Ciara and went to him. She put her hand to his face. Heat radiated into the palm of her hand, and he purred.

"You will be with me, won't you," she whispered. It was not a question, but rather a statement.

The raspy cry of the phoenix stole her attention, and she smiled, watching the new resurrected raptors fill the air as they took flight. Everyone chuckled as the two faerie dragons joined in the antics, dodging and soaring in unison with the magnificent flock.

"So Sumayah has demonstrated one of her powers," said Bethia, leaning on her staff. "As well as Riva. These are powers inherent to you, given to you from the Goddess. All that is needed to use them is the belief. Therein lies the training and instruction."

She took a step to Riva and tapped her index finger to the side of the girl's head. "In here and"—she tapped Riva's heart—"in here is where you will learn from, first the knowledge then the embodiment of that knowledge. But we must remember..." She took a long pause, taking her time to lock eyes with as many gatherers as she could. "Remember that when we return to the outer realm, our knowledge will be locked safely within the chambers of our heart, away from those who would possess it. Our journey there will be to remember our forgotten knowledge, then use it to ensure the Great Shift and resurrect Agartha with Lemuria."

CHAPTER 23

IT'S A WOODWOSE

❧

Nero bent his large head to Sumayah. She patted and stroked him. He purred at her show of affection.

"Oh, so you want me to scratch behind your horn?" She reached up and ran her hand along the right horn. It was cool to the touch but smooth as polished crystal. She scratched with two fingers, feeling the tiny lines that ran in a circular fashion, indicating age. By the feel of the many lines, she could tell Nero was much, much older than she. She was not surprised. She knew of the history of the dragon, the Carian, and how lucky she was to have one as her personal watcher. Especially with her last vision so fresh in her mind. Would life bring her to that moment, and if so, what had transpired to produce such a violent time on Mother Earth?

She looked over her shoulder at Sterling, slumbering peacefully under the shade of one of the towering fir trees. His breath was slow and deep. With each exhalation a tiny whiff of dragon scent filled her nose. She wondered about Sterling, wanting to know more about him, but since the two of them were not on the talkative side, it would probably remain a mystery, unless she could get Mergus alone and in the mood to chat about the old world.

"Sumayah, come, we begin," urged her mother. Reluctantly she left her dragon and joined the girls. It was another lesson day, and though she truly loved making medicine out of plants, she would much rather be with Nero or Ciara.

Elspeth had joined them, bringing her own satchel of fragrant herbs. Jaylan rushed to help her, smelling what she had brought.

"Hmm, Elspeth, do tell, what are they?"

"They are the flower blossoms of the sun-worshipping orange tree. We can make flower water from them called neroli. My mother taught me long ago that neroli can be a great ally during dark times, keeping us cheerful. It can help keep you focused on the deed and keep the mind away from forming any negative outcomes. This will keep our thoughts where they should be, and if things go wrong..." She paused a moment, pulling one blossom to her nose and giving it a twirl. "It has great magic to bring you into your next lifetime—well, for you who are not immortal."

Sumayah interrupted the conversation, hearing Elspeth mention her mother.

"Elspeth, where is your mother?"

Elspeth stared back at Sumayah and gave her a half smile. "She is in the summer lands; she has faded into the west."

"I don't know what the summer lands are."

Bethia barged in, carrying a satchel full of tiny jars that clinked as she walked. "It is a place that I hope you will not want to go to for a long, long time, my little child of the wind." She dropped the satchel, and then dug inside, pulling out a pretty crystalline bottle.

Here were more terms she knew nothing about, so she promptly asked, "Why do you call me child of the wind?"

"Our people were born at the hour of Bavol, the spirit of air. Our people came to Mother Earth when she was in the springtime of her life, riding the tailwinds of the beginning, when things were first born. Not all of us chose to live here in Agartha. Some chose to stay with Lemuria, a bridge to the otherworld, the world of men. Many of our people have crossed that bridge in hopes of bringing their culture to men to teach them the true beginnings of our world."

Sumayah listened intently. Here, finally, were some answers to her many questions.

"Your people have had a very hard life in my world," said Pennyann. "The Reps have taken many of them away from their lands, destroying their culture in such a manner, they could never return to their homeland. They took them as slaves for one hundred years in order to build their cities. During the great wars, the city they helped to build was taken by a great warrior, and your people were released, but they had been gone so long and had committed a great taboo that in the end would not allow them to go home. They were destined to wander the world looking for a new home."

Bethia stuffed a small pinch of dried herb within her pipe, and said, "We are children of the wind and of the phoenix. Fire and air come naturally to us. Working with all the elements comes natural to us just as it is for the Fae." She bent and blew softly at the herb stuffed into the head of her pipe; it suddenly began to smolder, and a tiny wisp of smoke spiraled up and out. Bethia quickly stuck the other end of the pipe in her mouth and sucked loudly until the herb glowed red.

"We are called by another name in the outer world," she said between puffs on her pipe. "They call us gypsies."

"Gypsies?" Sumayah questioned.

"Yes," said Pennyann," after being persecuted to near extinction, your people traveled to a distant land. "The people of that land confused them with the Egyptians, since they had a similar appearance. They welcomed the newcomers, giving them safe haven, and so your people let them think they were Egyptians. But soon the word got out that they were not, and they were forced to leave. The people who had been duped had shortened Egyptian to just *gyp*, saying they were *gyped*…so now they are called *gypsy*."

"This is getting more and more confusing," Sumuyah said. "So there are more of us out there." She pointed toward the skies.

Lhayan laughed. "There is much more to learn about this world, and the worlds within this world, my dear daughter. In time it will all make sense to you, but now we practice our magic, which will be greatly needed when we return to the outer world."

"Speaking of which," said Jaylan, who had been listening quietly, "where is Leesabeth?"

Everyone looked around in question. "I thought she was right behind me," said Elspeth.

Suddenly there was a rustle of the ferns living at the floor of the great fir trees. Nero and Sterling gazed in the direction of the noise, then settled back, uncaring. Ciara came running from the meadow directly behind where Nero laid, her tail flagging behind her and ears flattened against her head. She was making a beeline right for the sound in the ferns. She lunged into the ferns, teeth gnashing.

Elspeth and Sumayah ran toward the commotion.

"Ciara, no!" yelled Sumayah as the horse suddenly burst out of the undergrowth with a black shape running for its life directly in front of her chomping teeth.

"What is it?" yelled Riva, scrambling to stand behind her mother.

The blackened form ran past Sumayah and then darted directly behind Bethia. Bethia threw up her arms at the attacking horse.

"Ciara, that will be enough from you!" she ordered.

Ciara stopped snorting twice and pawed the air.

"No! Now get back. I will take care of this," Bethia scolded again.

Sumayah ran toward Bethia, trying her hardest to conjure a protection spell at the sight of the black long-tooth that crouched behind her. She threw up her arms and began to recite, "As above, so below, energy come, energy flow!"

Again Bethia yelled, her pipe clenched between her teeth, "Enough! Stand down, girl."

The large ebony cat crouched behind Bethia began to shake. The air about it swirled in a sparkling hue of deep blue. The misty cloak covered the entire beast, twirling wildly, then with a sudden *whoosh* it dissipated, leaving the form of a young woman in its stead.

Leesabeth stood up, giving her arms and legs a shake. "That was too close for comfort," she said, turning to Sumayah. "Sumayah, I never thought I would frighten Ciara like I did."

Everyone but Bethia stood silent.

Bethia chuckled. "Who was frightened of whom?" she murmured, sucking on her pipe. "I see you have been practicing your shifting, Leesabeth."

Ciara, now uninterested, left the circle of girls and ran back to the meadow.

Sumayah, still surprised at the protective qualities of her little mare, turned to Leesabeth. "I am sorry she attacked you. I think she was remembering her own battle with the long-tooth."

Elspeth laughed, holding up her orange blossom. "Leesabeth, if she would have sent you to the summer lands, we have all we need right here to help you return." She paused a moment, putting her finger to her upper lip in thought. "I do believe you witches call this reincarnate?"

"Yes," Leesabeth replied. "I have never been to such a ceremony; I am not sure how it is done."

Lhayan stepped forward. "Mind that what you do is only to encourage the soul to return once again to this present world, and to rest first before they returned to help with the original plan."

Sumayah felt her attention wander; she was tired of hearing about the original plan. She had gone from being initiated as priestess of Lemuria and *almost* joining with the one who held her heart, to this, total loss of control over her life. She wished at this very moment she were someone else. She did not want to have these powers. Then she thought, *Maybe going to the outer realm would not be so bad, I would enter in not remembering who I was, then I could live my life as I saw fit.* A vision of Ryven entered her mind. Would he find her, and would they regain what they now have? Her whole life was now nothing but uncertainties and doing the bidding of others.

Mergus stumbled out of the tree line, hefting a large satchel that clunked against his hip, hinting at what lay inside. Carefully packed within were fresh baby carrots, apples, a couple handfuls of mint crushed with just-picked raspberries, and two bottles of the finest honey wine. Ciara was right behind him, snaking her long neck around to grab at the apples. His jovial mood was soon soured as the mare insisted on yanking at his treasures. He swatted at her.

"Sumayah, will you control this beast!" he yelled.

Everyone broke out in a chorus of giggles as the great wizard fended off the little mare.

Ciara ignored his halfhearted slaps, and her nose found an opening to the bag. She pushed in closer to Mergus, taking a bite of his satchel. It became a tug-of-war.

"Stand back I say, you unruly horse!"

Gaining an apple she backed away, munching happily.

"Mergus, so nice of you to join us," Bethia said, walking to the wizard to dig into his satchel, then pulling out one shimmering bottle of wine.

Looking more perplexed than ever, he stomped his foot and said, "I would have expected it from the horse, but you too, *gypsy?*" His glare softened, and he chuckled at his funny.

Bethia stopped in her tracks and spun. She held up her staff and shook it at him. "Mind what you say, you old fool."

Sumayah's dark mood lifted at the interaction. *This was much more entertaining than talk about the summer lands. How interesting it would be to see those two in a battle of magic and wits.* She knew beneath all those white robes and hair, Mergus was nothing but an old softy. Now, Bethia was a different manner. She saw how the woman could stop a man in his tracks with just a look, then smile demurely as he let her pass. No, she had much magic up her sleeve, and Sumayah made a mental note to never be on the receiving end.

Mergus froze in his tracks and held up his satchel. "Old fool, you say. Well, let me tell you, this *old fool* was gracious enough to bring you young women"—he went silent, eyeing Bethia, then cleared his throat—"barring one…sustenance and drink!"

He frowned in exasperation, suddenly feeling another strong tug that ripped the satchel from his grasp. Mergus spun, his patience worn thin and ready to teach the mare a lesson on manners.

His eyes widened in surprise as he stood nose to chest with one very large beast, standing on two legs.

"Mergus, now don't do anything rash," said Bethia. "Just stay calm, and you will be fine." She dragged on her pipe and walked toward Mergus, her hand extended in welcome.

Sumayah took a step back and looked out the corner of her eyes to see what Nero and Sterling were doing. They were alert but content with just watching.

The girls had slowly maneuvered behind Lhayan, afraid to even let out a peep. Riva, much taller than her mother, stood behind Lhayan, holding her in a strong bear hug.

What in our world is this? Sumayah studied the gigantic, bear-like man that towered a good three feet higher than Mergus, who was not a small man by any means. He was covered in a shining, meticulously groomed mass of cinnamon-blond hair. The long mane of hair on his head was neatly tied back with a thin strip of sapling bark. His face looked human, his deep-set, very large, and slightly bulbous, brown eyes twinkled merrily at his new acquisition. He made no aggressive moves, and he didn't look like he had a bad bone in his massive, muscle-bound body. He cradled the satchel in his arms and rocked from side to side.

Bethia put her hand out to stay the approach of Leesabeth. "He is a woodwose and will not harm a soul. He just wants the honey wine. My fault; I gave him some a while back when he found one of my missing birds." She walked to the enormous beast, reached up, and patted his arm. "You can have one of the bottles, but do be kind enough to share the rest with us. Will that be to your liking?" she asked, tapping the head of her long-stemmed pipe on her thigh.

The woodwose's exuberant expression softened a bit, and his brow furrowed. "Hmm," was his reply as he looked into the satchel. He looked up and set his eyes upon each girl, almost as if he was counting, then stopped with his gaze upon Mergus.

Mergus could not help but chuckle at the big fellow, for his demeanor did not fit the great size of him. Mergus nodded to the woodwose and said, "Now be a good woodwose and share with us."

Sumayah wanted to touch him; she had no idea such a being lived here. Walking forward slowly, she put on her brightest smile and opened her hand. Within the center of her palm sat one glistening, indigo crystal. It vibrated sweetly in her hand, sending little tingles up her arm. It was the sapphire given to her by Jaylan, the woodwose might like it in exchange for the satchel. She took another step and stood directly at his belly. Slowly she tilted her head up and caught his questioning gaze.

"Hmm?"

She held out her hand and opened it. The sapphire twinkled merrily in the rays of the twin suns.

"Do you want to trade? I will give you this blue star if you give me the satchel."

The bear-like creature suddenly saw the glinting stone, and his already bulging eyes nearly popped out of his large skull. His mouth widened even further, and he threw the satchel at the unsuspecting Mergus. A strange, high squeal of delight escaped his gaping cave of a mouth. He looked at Sumayah again and reached out with one shovel-size hand, then stopped.

"Hmm?" he asked.

"Yes, it is yours, take it," she answered, then decided to drop the stone in his hand, noticing the large, thick fingers he sported.

When the stone fell into his hand, he let out a little gasp and almost went to his knees, clamping his hand tight. He quickly scanned everyone around them, then reached out with his other hand and patted Sumayah on her head.

The strength of the pat sent her teeth down onto her tongue. She closed her eyes at the twinge of pain. When she opened them again, the bear-like man had already turned and walked back into the dense cover of the fir trees. Sumayah swore she saw another creature like him peering from behind an enormous tree trunk. She quickly turned to the others.

"Did you see it? There was another one waiting for him."

Bethia chuckled. "There are as many woodwose here as there are trees. They choose to stay within the forest, the home that they take care of. They help the dryads tend to the trees. If a tree is ready to die, it is the woodwose who stays with it until the end so it will not fall and crush another being. The woodwose gently glides the tree to the forest floor without harming a soul."

"What else lurks here that we have not seen?" asked Pennyann, flipping her red-gold locks behind her. "I wish I had one of his hair ties."

The girls broke out in laughter at her remark. "Yes, he was kept very well, considering he was all hair," exclaimed Lhayan.

Mergus, holding his satchel once again, said, "Come, let us have some refreshment before we practice spell crafts."

As they all gathered round and sat on the softest patch of moss they could find, Sumayah notice a subtle change in the air. As the others chatted and stuffed their mouths, she watched the sky. There were not as many dragons up there as usual. The few that circled were not playing their dragon games; they seemed preoccupied. They flew as if they were searching for something.

Suddenly the soft hue of amber sky darkened; it was only a flicker of change, but it was enough to catch her full attention. The dragons suddenly dispersed from their search. The silent heavens above echoed with the deep rumble of the roar of the calling dragons.

Nero and Sterling instantly lifted into the air, joining the dragons. Others suddenly appeared out of nowhere. The skies were heavy with dragon flesh, which blocked the warming rays of the twin suns.

"What are they doing?" Sumayah asked.

"Someone is trying to gain entrance to our realm," Bethia answered, relighting her pipe.

The one word slipped from Sumayah's mouth as easily as pouring water from a pitcher. "Mesha."

CHAPTER 24

THE WAY IS SHUT

❦

Mesha stood alone within the darkness of the tent. The smell of the yellow treasure permeated the air with a stench of greed and unearthed soil—soil that was a living part of Mother Earth. Without it she was slowly withering. This decay was manifesting a great anger within her, causing the outer realm to experience her wrath. With most of the Fae gone from her outer world, no one else cared about keeping the balance, and her natural beauty was fading.

Mesha cared not about the Earth. He was there to take what he could as long as he could; the original plan for this world was not of his making or his desire. He opened one large bag and dug into the contents. His hand scooped and dug, absorbing the welcoming feel of the cold pebbles and stones. No, not just stones; this was power, this was control, enough to rule the whole upper world of man. This power would gain him an eternal position at the very top. It did not matter to him that the Rep's were not part of the original plan, or that they had to battle their way there. He did not care that they had lost the battle, and so now the way was shut to any other pioneering Rep. It just meant more for him.

Little did that matter today, for they had devised the most diabolical and devious plan to win this war and rule over all realms of Earth. Granted, it could take generations. Man was easily sucked into the realm of greed and power, not knowing that he was enslaved by his very own thoughts—his incessant belief that riches and power were all he needed to live a fulfilled life. But there was only enough room on this planet for one supreme race to rule, and it was not mankind.

One thing still pecked at Mesha's brain like a flicker tapping on a tree for a meal. Her wild-eyed beauty haunted him night and day. The thought of her, not having her, angered him beyond words. The desire to possess her was just as strong as the desire to possess the iridescent gold powder stuck to his hands. He wiped them on his breeches, cursing those eyes that stayed in his mind every waking moment.

"One day soon, Sumayah my priestess. Soon you will be mine; together we will rule this realm." Which brought another problem before him; he still had not gained entrance to middle earth, the place known as Agartha. It had been weeks and yet nothing. Those dragons either had no idea at all where it was, or they were keeping the way from him on purpose. He was beginning to believe the latter.

Narrowing his black eyes, he spun and marched out of the tent. *Clarron, where is that man? I need him right now!* He walked away from the treasure, grinding the sandy soil with each step. It was later in the day, and the sun was setting, giving some relief to the relentless battering of the heat. A bead of sweat trickled down the nape of his neck, irritating his dark mood all the more.

"Clarron!" He searched the large encampment; it was mostly men leaving their shifts, their faces expressionless as they heavily shuffled off to find a spot to rest, uncaring if it be hard or soft, and slumped to the ground. Mesha surprised himself as he felt a tiny twinge of guilt. Not knowing how to handle this, he just smiled and said, "Great work today. We all will be rich men soon." Then his guilt passed as he thought how easily these men believed this and gave their lives for something they would never achieve. Such easy pickings.

He again hollered for Clarron.

One scruffy, grime-coated man looked up from his seated position on a fallen log. "I think you will find him at the last tunnel."

Mesha just gave him a nod and continued his pace along the beaten path toward the shoreline. He hated walking along the shore; you could never tell when one of those mermaids might be lurking. Hideous creatures they were, crawling out of the water like some fat-bellied seal. He kept a watchful eye for the slightest ripple on the glass-like waters. The cliffs along the shoreline began to heighten, giving way to caverns, eerily dark and unwelcoming to him. He just had to make his way along the shore unscathed. And dragon shifting was a last option. It took too much out of him, like a young rattlesnake that bit, giving up all of its venom, having nothing left when the next predator attacked. Yes, he chose wisely when to turn.

He was not a coward. He just had a very strong sense of preservation, and he had learned long ago that *he* was the only one that would keep *him* safe. He was told he was immortal, but had no reason to believe it and would do whatever he could to not have to find out. This world was a mix of those who could and those who could not. Some had this ability, some had that ability, some had this magic, and many had none. Which brought his mind once again back to his favorite subject: men. They had such abilities, such powerful abilities to make a simple thought a reality; they could manifest whatever they wanted and yet chose to believe only what those in charge preached to them. It was as if they had no desire to think their own thoughts, and it was just much easier to let others think for them. Yes, the great plan was coming along nicely.

A fish jumped nosily out of the water, making him jump and yank his sword out of its sheath. Nervously he eyed the waters. He focused intently and watched. A tiny ripple formed and then swirled around and around. Holding his breath, he watched, waiting. *Better not be a mermaid. I'm ready, and my blade is swift and sure.* Another ripple formed with bubbles popping along the surface. Mesha's eyes were hawklike as they scanned back and forth, back and forth. Then he felt something, something hot and wet on his neck. His heart danced in his chest, a rib-cracking beat. His legs threatened to buckle, and the pit of his stomach lurched. *I'm done; they're behind me!* He felt something clamp on his shoulder, and he spun around with a scream of, "Its fish fry tonight, fresh mermaid over the fire!"

"Damn you!" he yelled, yanking his sword back, then crumpling to the damp sand on his knees. His breath came in heavy rasps, matching the pounding of his heart. He stayed that way for a few moments more while Aragon, his stallion, nibbled at his raven-black head of hair.

"You know how I *hate* mermaids, Aragon..." He slowly stood, putting his sword away, and reached for the strong cheekbone of his horse. "Where have you been? I have been looking for you. That is why I had to take this path *alone*." He could never stay mad at him for very long and lightly pressed his hand to the horse's forehead and rubbed.

"Time we got the move on," he said as he easily swung onto the gleaming white back. Feeling a tad braver on the back of his horse, he urged him into a canter, and they flew along the shoreline, the cooling breeze pulling at his hair. The rocking motion of the long stride calmed him, and he let his legs hang as he found that right spot on the back of his horse, the spot where they became one in motion. This was what got him addicted to horseback riding—this feeling of joining with another. It was not the same as flying, which was singular.

Aragon's steady pace soon ate up the shoreline, and the last tunnel of gold came into sight. The slaves had stopped to switch shifts. Mesha eyed the exchange, remembering the attack of the Knockers. There had been only two other incidents since then, and he hoped tonight would not be a third.

Clarron was easy to distinguish from the rest of the slaves because of his great size. Mesha considered him for a second as Aragon slowed to a walk. Clarron was a handsome sort, with a doe-like expression, but Mesha knew the strength he could muster, and quickly if angered. Yes, he was one to keep at his side and not one to be taken lightly.

Clarron saw them approach; he ran his large dusty hand through his golden crown of hair, smoothing it out of his eyes. The sweat had cooled in the evening, but left streaks of dirt on his handsome features.

"This one is producing well, far better than we had first anticipated." He walked to Mesha, placing his hand on Aragon's neck. Aragon liked Clarron and nibbled lightly at his ear, then pushed on his chest. Clarron laughed, then put the big stallion in a headlock and rubbed briskly on his forehead.

"I know you like this, don't you my boy," he said playfully.

Mesha frowned at the display as he slid from Aragon's back; it did bother him that the horse never showed him that much attention. Mesha slapped the horse on the rump, hard, sending him out of Clarron's arm and toward a small pool of clear blue water.

"Get a drink, and stop playing around," he said before turning to Clarron. "I have grown tired of waiting for Drakaous to find me an entrance. It is time to force the issue...I am beginning to suspect that the Carians might be keeping the way in to themselves."

Clarron frowned. "I was told that the dimension to the middle earth could not be opened unless invited."

"Nevertheless, you will seek out Drakaous. Tell him his time is up. If he does not have a way in, then he and his brothers will be of no further use to me...I think he will understand."

It was the next morning by the time Clarron found the dragons; they had made themselves a home off the cove, not too far from where their original home was. He had heard that they spent most of their time somewhere up in the Amethyst Mountain range, higher than the tree line, where the air was so thin and cold, it could crystalize your breath in an instant, choking you to death. No one else could survive but a fire-breathing dragon. Yes, the weather had changed considerably in the last year, and the winter lands of his home had more snow than he cared for. But up there was no-man's-land.

He walked the last leg to the entrance of a lower cavern they were known to visit when it was too cold up top; it was just off a large, teal-colored pond. A small waterfall dropped from above, the noise of rushing water muffling any other approaching sounds. Clarron was glad for it because Drakaous and his brothers were not easy to deal with as of late. And with the constant badgering from Mesha, he had an idea why.

As he stepped what he thought was *silently* around the pond into the cavern, he was met by Drakaous's red-eyed steely stare.

"Mesha sent you?"

"Aye, Drakaous, he is more insistent upon gaining entrance to the middle earth. He believes you know the way but are hiding it."

Drakaous raised his enormous head and puffed out his glistening silver-black chest. "So he suspects us, does he?"

Clarron found a nice smooth rock about knee height, and he sat with a thud. "Drakaous, if you do not find a way, he has ordered me to go back to the mainland and catch a witch."

Drakaous sucked in his breath at the words. His nostrils flared, and he exhaled a hot stream of air.

"He thinks a witch can gain entrance! No one can enter unless invited, and *I* have not been invited. Bethia is too smart to allow anyone to come and go to the middle lands whenever he pleases..." Drakaous paused and brought one claw up to tap on his right cheekbone. "Yet, the witches might be able to do it if forced; they have magic that has not been seen. They are young in their learning, so we cannot totally rule them out. Ah, that Mesha is much smarter than I have given him credit for." Drakaous thought a moment, his breath deep and steady.

"What of Mesha and his turning? Is that not a new form of magic?"

The words snapped Drakaous back, and he turned his massive head to Clarron. "You have something there, young Clarron. I know not where he has learned it—there is much about him that is shrouded in mystery. We must not underestimate his power."

"There is a way into middle earth," came a voice from within the cavern.

"Dear brother, *the way is shut*; you know that," reminded Drakaous.

Drakemon and Baratheous walked into the light. Standing in the presence of such ominous-looking creatures inflated some of Clarron's self-assuredness. He knew his muscles, as big as they were, were no match. Without even thinking he slid his hand along the hilt of his sword. The cold metal comforted him only slightly.

Baratheous stepped forward, lowering his head, then turning it sideways to peer at Clarron.

"Brother dear, it is time to relinquish our station. We have done our part. I tire of this game. Give them what they seek—besides, if we do give them a way, we can have more control over the situation rather than Mesha finding his own entrance. There is more than one way in, if you remember."

"He does have a point, Drakaous," Drakemon added.

Clarron watched as Drakaous rolled his eyes and let out a huge sigh. "I see I am outnumbered in the matter, and I know you will do this with or without my consent..." Drakaous paused, his tail twitching at the end, displaying his disapproval. He turned and snaked his head toward Baratheous. "Tell me then."

The two dragons seemed enthused by this, and Baratheous quickly spouted, "We have been searching for a subterranean burrow. Many were built by the dwarves." He looked at Clarron. "Not your giant dwarves of the Northland, but kin to the Knockers. They too abhor the pillage of the Earth Mother and build their burrows as gateways between the worlds.

Since the only way in is by permission, certain burrows between the worlds were granted permission from the beginning, but only for the Fae such as the Knockers and dwarves."

"The hard part will be to convince them once we find them to let Mesha pass," Drakemon interjected. "That *is* where you come in, Clarron, cousin to these dwarves."

Clarron stepped back, shaking his head. "My job is just to stay close to Mesha, as his second-in-command, not actually *deliver* him to Agartha."

"Then it is settled," Drakaous said, sounding more convinced. "Clarron, once we find a burrow, it will be up to you to get him there. You will be our eyes and ears."

Clarron swore he heard a snicker come from one of the brothers, but when he looked, they both were expressionless. He did not trust this plan. Things were getting too complicated. If he hadn't been enticed by promises of finally meeting the girl of his dreams, he would not have ever left his homeland. But that face, the face that haunted his dreams since he was a small boy, kept him on this journey. If he hadn't had that encounter with those witches, if they hadn't used magic to get her name, the face would have remained just part of the magical world he had only been told about in the stories handed down from his clansmen—stories about a lost world called Lemuria.

CHAPTER 25

TO TOUCH A WOLF

ℭ

Sumayah loved going into the dark timber. It was like stepping into nighttime, which was not possible in Agartha. The suns never set, and they were always in the same position, no matter when you looked up at them. She and Ryven walked on a spongy layer of emerald mosses that grew everywhere, climbing trees and blanketing rocks, small or large. The largest boulders looked as if they had green heads of hair. Blue-colored birds with long tail feathers colored an iridescent green and purple and spattered with flashes of bright orange and yellow sat high in the trees, staring down at them. The whole realm was eye-catching, and everywhere she looked was something new to behold.

Her favorite were the head-high mushrooms with bright red-orange caps dotted with the yummiest yellow she had ever seen. But the deeper she got within the dark timber, the harder it was to distinguish one color from the other. A cooling vaporous mist floated beneath the lowest-hanging branches of the fir and hardwoods. Both species of tree competed in a race to see which one could reach the twin suns. Looking up, she imagined a whole village built just in one tree. Based on the millions of glowing eyes that watched her pass, she could not help but wonder how many beings did live there. She hurried to catch up to Ryven and slipped her hand in his. The feeling sent a heady tingle throughout her body, their energies joining in harmony.

She could not stop the picture of Mesha that forced its way into her mind, remembering how she felt whenever he touched her, leaving her confused and sometimes uncomfortable. She felt sorry for Elspeth, since she knew Ryven's sister carried a secret attraction for him. She wondered what Elspeth thought now, since finding out about Mesha's betrayal. He had fooled everyone, and especially in the end. The vision of him *turning* would forever be locked in her memory, as would the battle. She wondered if he had survived it.

But nothing he did would surprise her, and she suspected that there would come a time when they would be face-to-face again. She just hoped she had the power or even the courage to stand against him.

A sudden howl took her from her thoughts, and Ryven froze. He turned to her with his finger pressed to his mouth. They stood that way listening in the dense darkness. All of her senses came alive. She slowly inhaled the resinous and pungent air. It was not offensive but clean and earthy, making her want to breathe deeper and deeper, savoring the forest scent. A flutter above caught her attention. She just caught what appeared to be translucent wings, but she could not be sure. There were so many different clans or hierarchies of Fae, you never knew which one you might be looking at.

She leaned into her own Fae, letting his warmth radiate to her. He sneaked an arm around her and whispered, "I think I heard one."

The call sounded again, making her skin prickle, not from fear, but from the beautiful, yet somewhat mournful sound echoing through the trees as if searching, searching, but never finding.

"It sounds so sad. Why would that be?" she whispered, leaning closer to his neck just to be nearer to him, wanting to smell his scent.

He turned his head toward her and looked down, then planted a kiss on the tip of her nose. The sensation flooded through her body straight to her knees. She turned her head up, accepting his invitation, and within the cover of the forest night, they melded. Nothing else at that moment mattered... except the sudden *thunk* on her right shoulder as something dropped from the trees above. She jerked from Ryven and looked up in the trees.

"Looks like we are to be forever kept apart."

Ryven groaned in annoyance. "You are so rig—" Something landed on his shoulder. It hit so hard, he swore it had teeth. He ducked, slapping at his shoulder as if it were on fire.

"I swear it has teeth!"

Sumayah burst out laughing, which made him stop slapping his shoulder. "Ryven, it is just one of Bethia's faerie dragons." She held up her arm so that the rose-colored female could land on her instead.

Ryven looked up. "Where there is one, there is another."

Sumayah searched and saw two green eyes, much larger than the other eyes that had been watching them, so she knew it was the other.

"He's right above your head. Back up a step, and you will see him."

"They must be Bethia's way of watching us, don't you think?" Ryven said, shooing the second one away.

"Ryven, be nice." She petted the little head with her pointer finger, marveling at the silky smoothness of her skin. "She feels different." She peered closer and ran the tip of her finger the opposite way, and the motion lifted what seemed to be tiny, close-fitting feathers. "Why this is interesting. They are feathered."

Another call echoed, accompanied by another, then another. The dragons took flight and settled back in the tree branches.

Ryven took off. "Come on, let's find them."

They quickly followed the chorus, deeper and deeper into the trees until something ahead flickered like many lit candles scattered about the forest floor. The light was not a golden yellow but a silver, the color of a clear crystal laid out to recharge in the cleansing rays of a full moon.

Sumayah's labored breath filled her ears, making it hard to hear. "Ryven, let's slow a little."

In front of them was a curtain of tangled tree branches. The branches hung in long tendrils, intertwined like a shield protecting what lay ahead. Ryven pushed at some, but they held fast. He tried another place, pulling and yanking.

Sumayah searched the branches. *If I were a rabbit and needed to get through, where would I go?* She looked low, rabbit height, ignoring Ryven's manly attack on the great wall of trees, and knelt to look for an opening.

Then suddenly there it was, and she shot through it, leaving Ryven behind. She crawled a few more paces, the soft ground cushioning her knees as she went. Finally far enough through, she stood and gasped at the view before her.

They were at the base of a cavernous mountain ridge; the trees grew up the ridge in layers, one layer taller than the other, reaching through the immense darkness, vying for a touch of any nourishing sunrays. At the base of the mountain ridge was another body of water—not nearly as big as the one that quenched the thirst of those living in Lyra Shambala, but large enough to enter and swim in. More blinking eyes caught her attention, but they were not in tree limbs. They were within the blackness of the many cave openings. The openings were not very tall, but they were large enough for any good-sized animal to dwell within.

The glistening ripple of the small lake beckoned to her, and she could not ignore its call. She tiptoed to the watery edge. Kicking off one of her sandals, she stuck one toe in. It was as she guessed—neither cold nor hot, but just right.

Ryven had found his way in and came at a fast run, stripping off most of his clothing down to a small skirt around his waist that barely came to his upper thigh. He charged toward her, grabbing her by the waist, then easily scooped her up, and together they crashed into the welcoming embrace of the water world.

She held her breath as they went under, then Ryven let her go so they could swim farther out. She loved to swim, and it had always come easy to her. Swimming like one of the pale-white otters that lived along the shoreline of Lemuria, she glided into the water. Ryven was right behind her, and she kicked harder to try to evade his reach. A squeal bubbled out of her mouth as she pushed with feet and hands up toward the surface to suck air before she went under again. Ryven surprised her. She didn't think a Fae could swim. He wasn't an undine, or water elemental, but a land-roving *trooper*.

She swam deeper, leading him in a race. Then just as he grabbed for her foot, she shot up and flipped herself backward, right over his flailing body. He treaded beneath her, then saw her above looking down at him. She spun and headed for the top to break the surface, and as fast as she could, she stroked her way to the shoreline.

Ryven surfaced, and the race was on. She could hear him behind her, and she looked to see how far they were from the shore. She suddenly stopped, just kicking enough with her feet to keep her afloat as Ryven bumped into her.

He grabbed her. "What's the race?" he asked, but was silenced by her dark look.

"It's that wolf again, just sitting and watching us. What should we do?"

Ryven answered by bringing her into him. He pulled her over on his chest as he kicked his long strong legs, floating with her on top.

"Ryven, that is not what I had in mind."

"Well, what would you have us do? The wolf is sitting where our clothes are, so we have no choice but to keep swimming." His smile was wide and enticing.

Suddenly Sumayah's pulse raced as the glowing eyes from the deep recesses of the many caves behind the wolf emerged. One by one they left the cover of darkness to join the lone wolf at the bank of the lake.

"Ryven, we are outnumbered now." She glided from his chest to tread closer to the lake's edge. The urge to join them was strong, and she ignored Ryven's warning as she reached arm over arm to propel herself closer until she felt the sand beneath her.

She stood. The many wolves began to thump their tails, and a chorus of howls filled the air. There was no fear, only intrigue and the need to touch this elusive animal, to feel its fur beneath her wanting fingers. She held out her hand to the one who had been watching her. He sat quietly as she approached. She stopped a few steps from him, and he put up one paw. *Aww, he must be welcoming me.* She took the last step. He was much bigger close up, and when he stood, his head reached her chest. He pressed his large head into her hand, and his tail swished back and forth.

"You are beautiful and so soft. I had never imagined how soft your fur would be," she murmured, stroking his massive head. The others moved in to give her a sniff and a wag. They were in many colors, some a mix of black and white, some pure white, some black like him, and others gray or tan. One pretty white and silver female pushed her way in to get a pat. She bared her teeth at the black wolf, and he backed away.

Ryven stood in the water, watching her in the middle of the pack. "Looks like you have made some new friends."

She laughed, nodding her head. "I think you are right."

Once they all got a chance to greet her, they turned and found a place to lay or sit, basking in their contentment. The black one came back, and Sumayah sat, letting the wolf sit next to her.

Ryven joined them and reached to feel the wolf himself. "They are quite soft, and their fur isn't as thick as I had expected."

"They don't need thick fur; they don't live in the winter lands."

"Quite right," he replied, then narrowed his eyes in thought. "Speaking of winter lands, have you ever figured out how you shifted there? Can you do it again?"

She dug her fingers into the wolf's coat and scowled. "I would never want to go back there, lest we freeze or be eaten by a long-tooth."

"I was just thinking that if you could pop in and out of other realms, it might make our job that much easier when we go to the outer realm."

She contemplated his statement. He was right, but the challenge was so great, and the fear of not having total control over this shifting power made her hesitant.

He winked at her. "If it got too cold, you could set yourself on fire again!"

"Ryven!" She smacked him on the shoulder and laughed, but then went quiet. "What good is it to learn all of this here if we will not remember it there? All of my knowledge will have been forgotten, and I will have to seek it out once again."

"You think too much, simplify it! You must remember, Sumayah, that you are what you are, and it will always be within you." He placed his arm around her bare shoulder and hugged her close to him. "You will never be alone. Even when you think you are in this alone, I will be with you always. I will follow you through every lifetime until the time comes for you to reawaken."

"I don't like the idea that we will not know how long this will take. How many lifetimes must I live without fully remembering you or the others? It will be like a horrible dream playing over and over."

"That is just it, Sumayah. Our job is to awaken as many as we can from their sleep and enslavement. Until that is done..."

She shifted in his arms to face him. A moment of panic overtook her, and she could hear her own heart begin to race. "What if here and now is all we will ever have? What if they *never* awaken? Will we have answered the call for nothing?"

Ryven stared at her; his left cheek muscle began to twitch. He sat quiet for a moment, thinking, then finally said, "They just have to." He pressed his lips to her forehead and murmured again, "They just have to."

Sumayah suddenly felt helpless. She was happy here with her Fae and her horses and dragons. Why did she have to leave all of this to help those she did not even know? What did she owe them? Did they not have a choice in how they chose to live their lives?

The contemplative moment was interrupted by wolf howls. The black wolf next to Sumayah suddenly got up and began to pace. He went from one wolf to the other, licking at their faces. Ryven and Sumayah watched this action.

"What are they doing?" asked Ryven. He looked up into the canopy of trees. "There is something different here. Something does not feel right."

Not wanting to leave this place or this moment, she said lightly, "Oh, that's just Fae talk. I am sure all is well. Maybe it is just song time for them."

The sky suddenly erupted in a thunderous tone, and flashes of light streaked violently across what they could see of the sky through the darkening cover of trees. This sent all wolves back into their caves except the black one. He ran to Sumayah and hugged next to her, his eyes rolling in fear.

Sumayah put her arm around him as best as she could just as the sky opened up once more. A deafening clash of thunder was followed by the weblike streaks of light.

"That sounds like a thunderstorm brewing. Why would there be such weather here?" asked Ryven, pulling Sumayah up. "Come on, we must get from under these trees." He ran in the same direction the wolves had gone and pulled Sumayah into one of the caves, with the frightened wolf hot on her heel.

As soon as they entered and sat, the angry sky went still and silent. Sumayah peeked out.

"I think it has stopped. I have a feeling this has something to do with the outer realm. We better get back to the city."

As they made their way back, the sky opened once more with its magic show of light. The thunderclap sent a melee of faerie dragons in a panic from the cover of the trees. Their raspy screeches filled the air. A group of large dragons swooped down at the tiny dragons, sending them lower, away from the seeking tentacles of light.

"Look, the dragons must know something. They are chasing the little ones out of the sky," Sumayah said, pointing upward. She had never seen so many before and had no idea that many were living in middle earth. She watched with wonder as they maneuvered in the air with ease, expertly gliding and falling, raising and climbing. Their agility left her breathless. Then out of the midst of wings and tails flew Nero and Sterling. They were coming at great speed, their bodies stretched out in a straight line, slicing the air.

"Look at them come!" she said breathlessly.

"What seems to be the hurry?" asked Ryven.

Then with a big *whoosh* of air, they slowed their ascent and landed without a sound. Nero hurried to Sumayah and lowered his head to her so she could put her hand on his face.

"It's Bethia and Mergus. They want us back. It has to do with this strange weather."

"He told you that?"

"Well, sort of. I heard it in my head, saw some pictures. It sounds like Sterling has been watching possible entrances to Agartha and has noticed a change." Sterling took a step closer and nodded his enormous white head.

Sumayah went to him, putting her hand on him. "You are a beauty, aren't you?" She touched him, feeling the beat of his heart through the rush of blood along his jawline. "You're an old one too." She turned to Ryven. "He's even older than Mergus."

Ryven laughed. "No one could possibly be older than that old windbag of a wizard."

The two dragons suddenly lifted into the air, which had cleared again, with all other dragons gone. They flew directly above, keeping close eye on their weary travelers.

It wasn't long before they were safely back. The city bustled with activity. The normal calmness was gone, and the air crackled with excitement. Sumayah was surprised to see not only the normal inhabitants, but also many others: the very tall and broadly built inner-dwelling dwarves had come.

"Why are they not guarding the tunnels of Marantha?" Sumayah asked.

"I'm not sure, but I can guess it has something to do with the storm," Ryven answered, stopping to shake the hand of one of the dwarves.

"Master Ryven of Faeria, it has been a long time. So good to see you."

Ryven lifted his head to study him. The dwarf's nose was strong, a good anchor between hawklike eyes, keen and the color of polished silver. His hair, thick and white blond, hung loose behind, but was plaited on each side in the front with the fibers of a silk flower.

"Clemon, it *has* been a long time. What brings you to the city?"

"There is word that there has been a breach between the realms," he said, leaning down closer to keep his voice lowered. "We have come to inform the queen."

"Well, if I know her, she already knows." Ryven laughed, slapping the big dwarf on his boulder-hard shoulder. "Come, let's find the queen and her wizard."

CHAPTER 26

DEADLY DWYLA

CR

Clarron made his way along the mountain range, alone with his thoughts, thoughts of the one that filled his dreams at night. Where she was now? Was she even alive? But the warm feeling and lightness of his heart whenever he thought of her told him she was. It was his undoing when he had boarded that boat looking for love and had ended up in the wrong place. After the city was swallowed by the waters, he had no choice but to stay with Mesha. In some way he knew it would lead him to her in the end. He was a dwarf after all—well, not all dwarf, but enough to give him a place to call home.

The sudden clunk of a rock on his left shoulder yanked him from his thoughts. He looked up, but nothing was there. Shrugging it off, he pushed on, turning into a natural gulch that had been cut through the mountain. To him, a dwarf of the north, it looked as if the mighty Thor had carved it out himself with his mighty hammer, Mjolnir. He stayed to the bottom, following a stream that crawled along the middle of the gulch. Something flashed out of the corner of his eye, and he snapped his neck to catch it but once again, nothing.

I'm being followed. He gripped the hilt of his broad sword, taking comfort in the chill of its feel.

"Well, whatever it is, I am sure it has never had the pleasure of fighting a Northman and half-dwarf Northman to boot. Double the power!" He consoled himself with his words, keeping to the open and trying to stay in the visible light, even though the sun had already lowered behind the mountain.

The shadows of impending night lengthened. He knew he would have to stop soon. One never knew when a long-tooth would be watching from the top. He naturally began to check the higher rocks, his eyes burning as they studied each formation. Suddenly he had an idea and searched the area for the perfect spot. Not far ahead was a small stand of trees that backed to a steep slope, too steep for any human to climb and too straight and high for a long-tooth to jump from. He made for the trees and yanked off his outer vest; he stooped beneath the trees and then pulled his sweat-laden tunic over his head.

Pulling enough leaves and branches from the lower limbs of the trees, he stuffed them in his tunic and lay the vest over on a nice cozy spot against the trunk of one of the trees. He pulled together enough branches to give the illusion of legs and threw his breeches over them. It was dark enough to hide the fact there was no man, yet light enough to show where a man might be sleeping. Satisfied but feeling a tiny bit exposed, he climbed the tree and waited.

For a while every flicker of light or buzz of elemental put him on alert. With only a sliver of moon in the sky, every shadow looked like a cat. He sat that way, watching the moon slowly glide across the deep purple tops of the mountains. Time was passing, yet no cat, and he was getting darned tired. His fingers cramped, and a calf muscle turned to stone; he tried to switch positions to relieve the deep pounding pain...

Then something moved out there. He focused and watched his breath slow and shallow. Whatever it was crept without a sound around the back side of a row of standing stones, then squatted, disappearing into the opaque shadow. His ears picked up the slight *tink* of something dragging against the stone. *Oh, sloppy, much too sloppy. It tells me you might be more than just a cat, but you move like a cat.*

It darted around the cover of the stones and with lightning speed dove for a clump of ferns, landing without a sound. *Very, very impressive. You have restored my faith in you. Ah, a most worthy opponent you will be. Come closer. See, I haven't even stirred.* Judging from where his clothes lay and the position of the ferns, if talented enough, one could possibly jump onto his sleeping form in one fell swoop. He watched at the ready, every muscle taught, breath coming quicker.

Then it happened. With catlike grace it sprang onto the clothing at the same moment Clarron jumped from his position. He landed as heavily as possible to take his adversary to the ground. *Hmm, much smaller than I would have expected for such stealth,* he thought as he shoved his forearm to the back of the neck of his puny attacker. It yelped and flailed, then spun from under his brute strength, surprising him. The sound of a blade hitting dirt alerted him, and he slashed toward the sound with all his might. He was met with repeated quick thrusts that somehow forced him backward. *What's this? I had better step up the game. This sprite of a thing is almost besting me.*

Back and forth, blow and block, slash and cut, they went at each other. Then Clarron could feel the force of the strikes weaken, which in turn strengthened his game.

"Aha, you tire!" he said aloud. "Now I will cut you to shreds." With his esteem renewed, he lunged forward, slicing air. "What's this?" he said.

A branch snapping sent his gaze upward just in time to feel the weight of his attacker land on his back. He ducked, feeling a tiny blade at his shoulder and in answer grabbed and flung his assailant over his head to land with an "*oof*" to the ground.

Before it could spring up, he pressed his foot to its throat.

"Who are you?" he huffed out, slightly winded. "Reveal yourself, or I will crush your neck."

Its answer was strained and mumbled. Realizing he might be pressing too hard, he let up. "Sorry."

"I'm Dwyla. I live here. I keep watch for the dwarves who dwell within the mountains."

"Keep watch? Watch for whom?"

"For the likes of you—might I ask you the same question? Who are you and why do you search for the entrance?"

He thought a moment, taking in the softness of the voice…then it dawned on him that he was talking to a female and a strong female warrior at that. He lightened his foot after his realization.

"I am Clarron. I am a Northman." He paused, remembering her word, the word *entrance*. Pressing just a tiny bit more, he asked, "What entrance do you guard?"

"Why, everyone here knows what entrance, the entrance to Agartha."

The last word grabbed Clarron's fullest attention. He could have not gotten any luckier.

"If I let you up, will you promise to be good?"

"I am not a child," she said, fuming.

"Well, child or not, what say you?"

"I will not challenge you further. You have bested me."

Content with her answer, he let her up, suddenly remembering his manner of dress. The heat in his face rose, and his strong warrior-like stance fizzled ever so slightly.

She stood and eyed him. Even in the shadow of night, the amusement was plain on her face. But she liked what she saw, not having ever seen such a large man before, or any man, for that matter. He was handsome in a human sort of way, but this one smelled other than just human.

"You say you're a Northman from the realm of men, but I sense something more."

"Yes, interesting. You intrigue me all the more. I am glad I let you live," he said with a chuckle. "Your senses are sharp, for you know the dwarf blood I carry."

Her eyes widened. "You are man and dwarf?"

Seizing the moment of her surprise, he quickly donned his clothes. "Yes, and I don't want to go into it. It seems as though there are plenty of us, or plenty like me, I should say, who are living secretly among men. Some sort of plan to help them, I have been told."

She waved her hand at a figure that had been watching from the steep slope of the mountain not far from where they stood.

"Ah, I see I was outnumbered."

"Yes, you would have had an arrow in the back of your neck," she said smugly, "If I gave the signal."

"Well then, why did you let me keep you in such a—well, such a manner of defeat?"

She laughed; it was soft, much too soft for such a strong one. "I have, or we have, been expecting you. Your coming was no surprise. And we know what you seek and are prepared to show you . . . I just had to be sure I had the right *Northman.*"

"Who told you I was coming?"

"All I can tell you is it was ordered by the Queen."

"Aye, something tells me there is a game of cat and mouse being played out here. I did not think the entrance to the middle realm would be this easy."

He paused a moment as she moved in such a manner that showed her face quite clearly. She reminded him of the one he sought, yes; she was slight of build, but with plenty of curve to her. Her dark hair thickly cascaded in soft waves almost to her waist. But those eyes—yes, he could get very lost in them—keen like a falcon. She looked like a little black, deadly falcon. Her nose, neither too small nor too large, had a slight, pleasing curve to it, and it sat on top of her very inviting lips. A picture of the one who lived in his dreams flashed before him, and he promptly closed his mouth and averted his stare.

"Do you plan to take an army of men with you?" she asked.

"What, me? No. I somehow got caught up in this war. Seems it does not matter where you are." He pointed to the sky. "Above or below, there is war all around. I came looking..." He stopped, thinking she wouldn't want to hear how lovesick he was.

"Ah, you seek someone. A woman, perhaps?" She smiled, giving him a wink.

He buckled his sword sheath and yanked hard, closing it too tight, then let it out a bit. All this just to evade her question, and her stare. *Will she stop looking at me that way?*

"I work only for myself, but my journey brought me to a crossroads, and it was either join or die. And truly, dying was not on the top of my list."

"Really, you, afraid to die? What of your dwarf blood? All Fae and elementals are immortal."

She did have a point, but since he was raised as human, he had never thought he could be immortal. "I was never told either way, and considering I am half man, thus subject to living lifetime after next, I would just as soon keep this lifetime going on for a very long time."

"Well, suit yourself then. But let me tell you, going to the middle earth will not bode well for you...Who *is* wanting to go there?"

"What I believe is just one brainsick ma—" He scratched his chin for a moment. "Well, I couldn't tell you what he is, one of us mixed breeds, but this one is consumed with finding another. And yes, it is a woman, a Lemurian priestess who has one of the crystal keys in her possession. He intends to take her and the crystal in order to rule the whole Earth."

She widened her eyes, then frowned at him. "Well, he *must* be brainsick, for there is something going on that is beyond our knowing—more than we can see with our own eyes. There could be failure at the end of this endeavor."

"Oh, I don't plan on failing, because I have motives of my own, and I couldn't care less about ruling Mother Earth. Not that you could anyway."

She laughed. "Quite right, but there are those who think otherwise and have changed our realm as a result of Mother Earth's deep anger."

He looked beyond her, searching the dark of night for any sign of this entrance. It was much too late to go back now, but what of her?

"It is too late to show you the way; I will take you there in the morning, at first light. But in the meantime, we need to get from under this tree. There are plenty of long-tooth in the area, and they love to climb."

The next morning dawned bright and hot. An intense ray of the sun shining into the small cavern where they slept burned his left cheek, awakening him.

She sat, staring at him, then popped a couple of bright green leaves into her mouth. "I suppose you eat flesh, half-man."

He sat up and stretched, trying to shake the stiffness from his shoulders. "I was raised as a man, so yes, I do eat meat."

"You will have to find it yourself, for I will not and am not capable of it. If you choose to eat, please eat it away from me. You see, Fae and elementals living in this realm can feel the pain of death. Eating flesh would be like taking in the pain and anguish into our own bodies." She narrowed her eyes. "Are you ever unwell after eating flesh?"

Hmm, good question. But, in my line of work and lifestyle, I would not know what being well feels like. He just might have to give it a go one day and see the difference for himself.

To answer her question, he just said, "No."

She shook her head at his reply, muttering, "How could you possibly know otherwise."

After breaking their fast, they hiked about an hour. The entrance to Agartha was not as he thought. It was just another cavern hidden nicely behind a row of standing stones and thickly covered by the braided and gnarled branches of weep trees. It was hard work cutting through them to make a hole large enough for man and beast to enter, because he knew Mesha would not travel without his horse.

Once the opening was made, they cautiously entered, only to be halted by a very tall and wide doorway. It was made of some sort of iron. Clarron knocked on it. The sound was solid and dense.

"They built this one too good. There is no way to battle ram through this," he said, running his hand along the door. "Look, there is something inscribed here...some language I cannot understand." He traced his fingers along the raised inscription. "They are almost like our runes."

Dwyla stepped forward and brushed away the dirt. She pressed her fingers to them. "This is an old language, even older than the language of my people. But it is very similar to our runes also; let me see if I can decipher it in my language." She studied each rune one by one, then turned to him with a wide smile.

"The way is shut."

Clarron roared in laughter. "What joke is this? Well...it sure is on us, is it not? I cannot wait to bring Mesha back here just to read that. "The way is shut."

"I am glad you find this amusing. But I could be interpreting it wrong."

She pushed at a thin branch and rubbed away more dust and dirt. "Wait, there is something else here." She rubbed harder until all runes were exposed. She read it and frowned, cocking her head sideways to read again.

"Open by south, from out of thy mouth."

Clarron roared again. "Looks like we hit a dead end. I am beginning to believe this was all for naught."

"It is a riddle for sure, but one that I do not know the answer to. If this is as old as we think it might be, it was written by those who were here first. Besides the elementals—wait, I might be on to something...If I am right and this was made by the first who came here, the elementals had to be the first."

Clarron looked at her cross-eyed, then shrugged his shoulders.

"The elements, they are what join everything together. Without one, you cannot have the other, and without the whole, nothing can exist!"

"Smart on top of tough. I like you, Dwyla."

She blushed, then turned her attention away. "If it be the elements, south is the salamander, the dragon, the spirit of fire! It's fire!" She jumped up and down and turned to him.

"South is fire, good. But what does mouth stand for?"

"Open by south, from out of the mouth," she said aloud, running her fingers along the runes again. "I got it, Clarron. Who were the first beings here besides the elementals?"

"Um, I wasn't in class that day...but my people spoke of the dragon."

She pointed at him with a wide smile. "Yes, Clarron, if south is fire and salamander is the *being* of fire, then we need a salamander that breaths fire, we need a fire breathing..." Her voice trailed off.

Clarron laughed again. Dwyla shot him a look of annoyance. "What is so amusing now?"

"We need a dragon, right?"

She nodded her head yes.

"Well, I have one, and his name is Mesha. You wait here for us to return if you want to be part of this. If not, I understand. I go now to fetch the dragon." He gave her a strong slap on the shoulder, almost sending her to her knees. "It is sad that things in our world have turned out like they have. I don't think *they* ever imagined dragons with ill intent. It's been good knowing you. You're a strong *warrioress*."

He turned and with a ground-eating pace, walked out of the cave. He then paused and turned to her. "I'll only be gone three days."

She watched him leave. She had her job to finish and had to get word to the queen.

CHAPTER 27

THE TUNNELS OF MARANTHA

☙

Clemon greeted Bethia with a bow of his head. "There is word that a breach has been broken between the realms."

Fallonay stormed forward. "But this is impossible!"

Bethia put her hand to Clemon's arm and gave him a bright smile. "Thank you, Clemon, for coming this far to inform us. I would ask that your people watch the progress of our . . . guests. Use the Carians. If they come through the tunnels of Marantha, send word with them."

Clemon bowed his head, spun, and left the chamber.

"How can you remain so calm when it is obvious they will take over Agartha also?" huffed Fallonay, his face red with rage.

"Come now, Fallonay, not all is lost," consoled Rupert. "If I know my mother, she has already known and is in contact with our elders."

That sentence rang loudly in Sumayah's head. Bethia was her father's mother? She stole a glance at Ryven, who was looking at her calmly. *How can he be so calm? I am the granddaughter to the queen of Agartha and the daughter to the king of Lemuria, a high priestess of Lemuria?* This weighed heavily on her mind. The feel of a warm hand clasping hers comforted her little; it was Jaylan, reminding her she was not alone.

She leaned into her sister and whispered, "Did you hear what Father said?"

"I did, and to think of it, I am not surprised; I had a feeling from the first day we arrived."

The heightened conversation continued, and Mergus entered, shaking his fist in the air and pointing upward. Fallonay stormed back and forth, shaking his head. Rupert calmly nodded and smiled, trying to keep the peace.

Bethia stomped her foot three times before she got their quiet attention.

"It seems as though we have lost some of us to greed and the promise of power. I have eyes and ears keeping watch over Mesha and his doings. I fear some of our Carians in the outer realm are not only doing my bidding, but are doing for themselves also..." Her voice trailed off.

Sumayah felt the grip of fear at the mention of the outer realm. *This means Mesha is still alive and he is looking for me, still thinking I retrieved the crystal when in fact the crystal is still in his realm.* She had brought him here, it was her fault. She looked around at her family, their faces etched with worry and fear. She knew fear was exactly what the Reps fed upon—fear, anger, and hatred. All those emotions that were harmful to her and her people.

She had to stop this. She had to save her people and save Agartha. She had to go to the outer world and find Mesha before he found them. This, she knew, was her destiny. She looked up at Ryven, how handsome he was, and how sad to know their paths were not meant to be a life shared. Suddenly she felt very alone. She was not thinking right. She had to leave, had to think. She had to do this for those she loved, no matter the cost. She fought back the emotion, feeling the burn in her eyes as she watched the telltale sign of frustration in the tick of Ryven's cheek. Something she might never see again.

She leaned into him and whispered, "I have to go to my chamber—wait for me. I will be right back."

He nodded to her, his attention fully on the conversation at hand, and let her go.

Very seldom did she feel the need to sit on Ciara, but the mare graciously offered, which gave her plenty of time to wallow in her sorrows and then produce some sort of plan. Ciara knew what she sought, and so together they traveled the realm of Agartha. The steady cadence of Ciara's trot lulled Sumayah into deep thought. How she would get back to the outer realm, she did not know. She had made it to the winter lands, and she had made it here, so all she had to do was retrace her steps and think.

But this was proving more difficult then she thought. Her mind kept wandering back to Ryven. He would be worried and angry at her for not including him. He was much better off without her, as long as Mesha was after her. What she would do when she found Mesha, she hadn't figured out yet. But time was closing in, and with the breach between the realms, she had to do something.

Maybe she could find the tunnels of Marantha and wait for him to come out. A slight smile crept across her face at the thought of him stepping out to see her standing there. *Not a very good plan, Sumayah. He would shift and take you out. But then again, I could fight fire with fire.* Her hands began to tingle with just the thought of it.

A sudden shadowy figure scampering through the thick stand of head-high ferns caught her eye. Ciara just perked her ears in the direction of the movement, seemingly uninterested.

"Nothing to worry about huh, girl," she said, giving her a pat.

Ciara turned off the path she had been following and veered into a canyon of trees. On both sides the mountains jutted up so high, they blocked out the twin suns, which reminded her of the black timber where she and Ryven met the wolves.

The thought of them made her wonder if that was who followed. It could be the black wolf.

A rustle of leaves and a darting form turned her head. She focused, but saw nothing.

"Whatever it is, it does not want to be seen."

The two of them traveled quickly. Ciara had unending energy. They were entering into lands Sumuyah had never seen before, and she marveled at the expanse of Agartha. She wondered if there were any other cities besides Lyra Shambala, and guessed there probably were. They had left big-water country, which seemed central to Agartha, but many streams and creeks still meandered or rushed along her path. She wondered where the water came from, for it did not rain that often. This world was so very different than her home. She missed Lemuria; she missed the normalcy of her life there.

The lush emerald blanket of moss, herbs, flowers, and grasses seemed to just roll out in front of them as they traveled. The sweet, strong smell of jasmine permeated the air. It grew and filled in every nook and cranny of tree stump and rock crag. The splash of pinks, yellows, and oranges was an eye-pleasing contrast against the black greens of the trees, ferns, and tall grasses.

Ciara stopped at a small brook; the water, only inches deep, lazily meandered out of the base of the mountain. It did not flow from top to bottom as most did, but came right out of the mountain itself. Sumayah slid from the back of Ciara and knelt, scooping the cool liquid into her mouth.

Out of the corner of her eye, she saw again the familiar form; it had peeked out from behind a stand of trees.

Deciding it was time to confront whatever it was, she spoke up.

"I see you behind the trees, and I know you have been watching me. Please do not fear me and come forth so I may see you." She waited a few moments, but nothing happened; shrugging her shoulders, she sat by the edge of the brook to immerse her feet.

"Well, suit yourself, but you are welcome to join me." Reaching into the pocket of her tunic, she grabbed the stones hiding within and pulled them out. She was gifted these from Bethia after she gave her sapphire to the woodwose. She opened her hand, and there lay two purple amethysts and an amber stone. The amber was nothing more than ancient resin, but it carried the energy of the tree it came from. To her it captured the many years of life and experiences of the tree. Even though a tree could not get up and move, she could just imagine what it had witnessed just by standing in that one spot for centuries, letting life happened around it.

Ciara stomped, and Sumayah turned to her. Just as she did, something gently took one of the stones from her hand.

She whipped her head around to see the woodwose squatting next to her with his new possession clutched in his very large hand. He smiled at her with his huge soft eyes, then put his cheek to his left shoulder and held out the amethyst stone to her.

"Hmm?" he said.

She laughed and shook her head. "No, it is yours. You can have it."

Ciara walked over and sniffed the head of the woodwose, then pushed at him. He put his hand to her cheek, almost covering it with just his palm, and chuckled. It was a deep guttural sound.

"She likes you. She usually just puts her ears back at anything that tries to touch her and even takes a bite out of those she disapproves of." Sumuyah got up, feeling refreshed, and slipped her sandals back on. "I am off to find someone who intends to do us harm."

He stood from his squat, towering over her. He smiled, revealing a row of teeth, pointed to the cover of trees, and said, "Hmm."

Looking in the direction he pointed, the trees suddenly became alive with what she suspected to be his family. Out from around almost every tree and standing stone they peaked, some small and some much taller. Some were brown like him, while some were red and others a brown-orange color.

"Why, there are so many of you. Bethia was right. I am so happy to have met your family." The thoughts of the Reps and man coming here and harming these seemingly gentle giants greatly saddened her. She took that emotion and turned it around, letting it make her all the more determined to find Mesha and stop him. His dark brooding eyes filled her mind; she looked down at her hand, feeling it tingle with heat at the very thought of him. Her fingers suddenly flickered with fire, and she rolled her hand sideways as the flames raised higher. You *are* close…

CR

Aragon pranced sideways as Mesha led him up the hill toward the entrance. His mouth frothed as the iron bar in it pressed on the tender flesh inside. He nipped at Mesha.

Mesha yanked on the reins of his bridle. "Steady there, boy, we are almost there."

Clarron had gone ahead and waited. Dwyla was not to be seen, nor were any of her people. Clarron felt a slight twinge of sorrow; he liked her warrior spirit and had hoped she would be waiting.

Mesha finally reached Clarron and handed Aragon's reins to him. "He is in a mood today. Hold him while I inspect this door." He walked the last few feet to the entrance and stopped at the heavy door. He ran his hands along the runes. He could easily read them, and yes, they were as Clarron said.

"Open by south from out of thy mouth. Very, very clever indeed." He stood, looking at the men behind him. There were only a handful of them. He had no desire to war with those in Agartha. He just wanted to reclaim what was his: Sumayah and her crystal. Such a simple and easy plan.

"Everyone, stand clear, for it is I who have the answer to this paltry riddle," Mesha ordered. He took a few steps backward and willed himself to turn. The air suddenly began to move, and it gathered around him, picking up speed and forming a dark cloud of smoke that completely engulfed him. Everyone stood as the swirling black mass of air began to dissipate, and in its place stood the dragon

Aragon pulled back, taking Clarron with him.

"Hold there, boy, he won't eat you...not with me here anyway," he crooned to the stallion. "Let's back up a bit to get out of the way."

Mesha's nostrils flared as he inhaled. With his next exhalation small puffs of gray smoke billowed out of his massive mouth. He swung his enormous head toward the onlookers and glared at them with his bulbous, crimson-red eyes. With one more inhalation, he took another step back and then belched out a streaming flame of fire. Straight as an arrow, the fiery onslaught battered the door, and it only took a moment for it to begin to move. It sounded as if the whole mountain was sliding, sending a spray of rocks tumbling down, barely missing their heads. The door began to slide, as if there was a pocket already tunneled into the side, and it easily disappeared into the mountain.

In an instant Mesha turned back to his manly self. He stood slightly winded, his hands on his knees, grasping for air. Clarron watched him with fascination, for to him it looked like a sign of weakness.

He waved to Clarron. "Bring my horse."

Clarron brought Aragon and helped him up. "Let's go inside...Clarron, you first."

The entrance was tall enough and wide enough to sail one of their ships through it. And it was dark, so dark, Clarron had to order some torches to be lit. He waved the torch in front of him, revealing another world, one he could have never thought existed. Crystals the color of the sea at rest, hung longer than men from the ceiling of the tunnel. The walls were smooth and glowed a brilliant hue of gold. This tunnel was the mother lode of gold, and he turned to see Mesha's expression.

"We mine this one when we get back, hey, Clarron!" he said excitedly. "Why, those crystals alone are worth taking down. You could build a village in here and live off the fat of the land!" Mesha reveled in the idea of living here—him, his gold, and Sumayah. How could he keep this from the dragons or the Reps? There had to be a way. But then he guessed that he was not the first nor would be the last to know about the tunnels of Marantha.

Clarron noticed a small stream of water that ran out of one of the side tunnels. Figuring that water had to run downhill, he chose to follow it, and that is what they did for most of the day.

Mesha urged Aragon closer to Clarron. "Something is not right here. This is far easier than I would have expected. I mean, not even a Knocker or a dwarf has stepped in our way."

Clarron only nodded.

But then the dank, metallic smell of the air suddenly changed. Mesha slumped in his saddle, realizing he had spoke too soon. The strong scent of crushed sage and lemon filled the air.

Clarron turned to see the tunnels behind them begin to fill with dragons and men, but no Reps, for he knew Reps never did their own dirty work.

Mesha searched the army for the familiar faces of Drakaous, Baratheous, and Drakemon, but found none of the three, which took him by surprise. He figured they would have been the first to want to enter into Agartha. But seeing the throngs of followers, the heat of anger built within him, and as it rose, his body tensed.

"This is not part of my plan!" he yelled. "I do not want to be party to any war. Let me get what I want and all will be set in place." He knew his plan was ruined, and he was now just another pawn.

A burly looking man stomped forward. "You have done your part and have gotten us into the tunnels; you are to lead us into the realm of Agartha. Then you may go free."

Free, go free? What was this man talking about? He was never a slave, and he wasn't about to let anyone think otherwise. Kicking Aragon forward, he said to Clarron, "Let's push on."

The tunnels became alive with the echoes of whispers and footfalls that eerily bounced off the high ceilings and hanging crystals. The ceiling seemed to have grown taller with every step. Ladders and stairs were carved out of the walls that led into deep, dark burrows. Clarron watched them also, feeling his skin crawl as blinking green lights seemed to watch their every move. He trotted up closer to Mesha.

"We are being watched."

Mesha snickered. "And you would have thought otherwise? Let's hope whatever they are, they like the taste of dragon flesh much better."

"Better than what?" Clarron murmured, feeling quite outnumbered. "Are we not of flesh? I just hope they only eat grapes and leaves."

Aragon suddenly spooked, almost unsettling Mesha, who grasped at the long white mane. "Damn it, Aragon, what is the matter with you?" The horse jigged and spun, then took a few leaps in the air, this time throwing Mesha to the ground. He lay there catching his breath, wondering what had gotten into that horse. Knowing him like he did, he took it as a sign that something was close. He hoped it was the entrance into Agartha.

Clarron stood above him wearing a half-smile. "Come on, get up. I don't see any blood."

Mesha fumed and grasped his outstretched hand. "If he would just tell me when something is wrong or when something is close, it would be that much easier."

"Do you think we are close?"

"I know we are close. Can't you feel it? It feels as if your hair is standing on end." Mesha stole a glance back at his unwanted entourage, wracking his brain for a way to keep them enclosed in this tomb. A sharp stab of pain shot through his hip. He took a tentative step forward, trying his best to ignore it. *Damn that horse. If I get through this, I think it is time to find a different one.* He limped forward. Each step got better, and he followed behind Clarron.

The tunnel suddenly opened up and widened out in a circular fashion. It was apparent this could have been a council area at one time. In the center of the circle stood a tall altar. Nothing was left on it, but it had the residual feel of something very powerful. Mesha thought it would be wise to leave it alone, not wanting to attract more unwanted energies around them.

Clarron noticed that the ground beneath his feet was etched in thick, circular lines that followed the diameter of the council area. He bent and put his finger in the depression of the line, which indicated the lines were very deep. The circular lines ran through the center of the circle, intersecting at four equal points.

"This looks to be some sort of magic," said Clarron. "It looks to be like an old wheel of the four elements." He suddenly felt a wisp of air come out of the deep lines, making him feel very uneasy. "Let's back away out of these lines."

Mesha suddenly felt the change in energy. Having watched many Lemurian rituals, he knew this was something big. He backed away with Clarron and none too soon, for as soon as they stepped beyond the last quarter, the wisp of air grew into a streaming, vibrating, red-gold beam of energy. It sprang out of the ground and shot toward the ceiling, then back down to the ground and up again in a continuous fashion. The temperature of the tunnel suddenly rose to very uncomfortable.

"I think we found the gateway to Agartha," said Clarron loudly over the crackling sound of the energy.

Aragon's shrill whinny took Mesha's attention. He watched as the horse lunged right for the center of the pulsating show of light and was instantaneously absorbed into it.

"Aragon!" Mesha screamed, not believing what he just saw. "My horse!"

Without thinking he grabbed Clarron by the forearm, and with all his might, yanked both of them onto the same path.

CHAPTER 28

THE BATTLE FOR MIDDLE EARTH

☙

There was a change in the air. Sumayah sensed it. The whole realm of Agartha had been disturbed. The quiet, singsong whispers of the elementals as they worked were replaced by an intense buzz. Mother Earth was preparing for what would come. All her realms were now stepping into a place of darkness, something that was foreign to them. But fight back she would.

The amber-blue sky was empty. Gone from the gentle breezes were the graceful antics of the dragons. Sumayah worried about not seeing the familiar and comforting shapes of Nero and Sterling. Maybe it was for the best. She did not want either of them to be brought into something that was all because of her. This thought pulled on her heartstrings; she was the reason there was a breech. Mesha wanted her. It had turned into a matter of pure possession and nothing more. She felt now that he was incapable of love or empathy. He was out to win, to show Ryven, his adversary, that *he* could have her. The ache in her jaw intensified as she gnashed her teeth together, trying to wipe the image of Ryven from her mind.

Her hands heated at the thought of seeing Mesha. The heat traveled up her arms, and she could feel the almost invisible flicker of flames. This part of her she had mastered. This was her weapon. It gave her strength to meet her aggressor. She smiled, envisioning his shocked expression as he learned of her control over fire. *Let him turn. It will be fire against fire.*

They had been climbing for quite some time. Ciara walked ahead with Sumayah holding on to her tail, which helped to pull her along. As she struggled to stay with the mare's steps, a sudden vision filled her mind. It was Jaylan; she was trying to connect with her. Should she let her sister know where she was, or should she stick to her plan? She chose to listen.

"Sumayah, Ryven is boiling over with rage; he knows you mean to sacrifice yourself. Mother is in a panic. She and Bethia are in the middle of a searching spell to find you. It is only a matter of time before they do, you know, and we will come for you. Hold on, Sumayah, help is on the way. Ryven has already left... You cannot possibly do this on your own. I love you, sister. Be safe..."

A hot tear scaled her cheek as it escaped and pooled at the corner of her mouth, tasting the salty liquid, which seemed more real to her than anything else at this moment. *What are you thinking? How do you think one mere girl could take on so much alone, even with the help of magic?* Her strong resolve began to fizzle.

Ciara took the last few steps. By no means were they at the complete top, but they were halfway, and the land flattened out and ran as far as one could see. The grass was short, a rich, succulent green that blanketed the ground, muffling any sound as she walked. She felt as if she had already shifted into the upper dimension. But it was far too beautiful here to be the realm of man. To her left in the distance, another lake lay like a sheet of glass, calm and crystalline. Beyond the lake the mountains again continued the last leg of their journey to reach the embrace of the pale-blue and amber sky.

She stood, looking about her. "Well, now what?" she asked Ciara, who was milling around sampling the sweet grass. She picked up her head, nickered to her, then resumed her nibbling.

"Thanks, girl, but I guess you earned a little treat. You dragged me up to this point." She felt compelled to travel to the right, and continue on to where the mountain once again reached for the sky. *Always follow your inner self*, Mother would say, and so that is what she did.

She took one more look behind her, angry at herself for hoping to see Ryven's smiling face and flashing pale-green eyes. *It was not meant to be, my love. The path we have chosen forsakes the heart. You were right, it is much bigger than us.* She slowly turned and continued walking toward the mountainside.

The mountain seemed much closer, but she felt like all she was doing was walking. She knew Ciara was just as tired and didn't even bother to ask for a ride. She didn't even want the mare here, but the mare had a mind of her own, and she pretty much did what she wanted. The thought brought a smile to her lips, which helped her take the rest of the steps.

Trees started once again, but there was no sound coming from them. They silently watched as she walked beneath them. She wondered how many of the trees concealed woodwose and hoped all of them did.

Suddenly Ciara bolted straight for her; she flattened her ears and gnashed her teeth. Shocked by her actions, Sumayah jumped back.

"What's the matter, girl?" Then she remembered her attack by the long-tooth and how Ciara had acted in the same manner. She steadily kept stepping back, feeling the wind suddenly pick up. It started in the treetops and grew, blocking all other sound as it threatened to break limbs and lifted bits of branches and grasses, sending them swirling, stinging everything in its path.

Her hair whipped around, covering her eyes and filling her mouth. Panic gripped her, and the emotion lodged in her throat. She tried to call out for Ciara. Then as quickly as the wind started, it stopped.

She crept around in a circle to see what it might have blown in. Ciara stood, intently watching in front of them, where a cavernous opening had been revealed. The wind must have taken away branches that would have otherwise kept it hidden from sight. The mare's ears twitched forward and back. Her muscles bulged, ready to react. She stomped once and snorted.

"What is it, girl, is something in there?" she asked, her voice wavering. Her eyes watered with the effort of trying to see what was in the cavern. The cavern itself was very large, large enough for a whole army to come through. Her skin suddenly prickled. *Oh, oh.* She rubbed her bare arms, mind racing. *Is this it? Is this the entrance? Will Mesha suddenly walk out of it?*

Ciara jumped and spun in a 360-degree circle as the black hole suddenly exploded with sound. Sumayah's heart thumped against her chest. She covered her ears to block the high-pitched screeches.

She had the urge to run, to save herself. Ciara snorted again and trotted back and forth in front of her, her tail flagging behind her.

"Ciara, come here—get out of the way!"

To her great annoyance, the mare just ignored her. "Dammit, do you want to get eaten?"

That caught her attention, and the mare slammed to a halt in mid-stride. She spun and looked at Sumayah; she blinked at her and tossed her head.

"That's it, girl," Sumayah crooned. "Come on, girl."

The screeching escalated, and a large, black, swirling mass erupted from the opening. It was tiny, winged elementals being chased from their home. The solid mass, like a swarm of honeybees, flew up and out, then scattered to the winds.

"Hold on, girl, something is coming. You better be ready!" Sumayah wiped her sweating palms on her travel-smeared tunic and waited.

Something caught her attention from the corner of her left eye. It was the black wolf standing beneath a low-hanging branch, lips in a snarl and eyes glowing.

What was he doing here?

Suddenly the sound of galloping echoed loudly, bouncing off the interior walls.

What is this? Could it be horses from the upper realm? The sound got louder and louder until it burst from the cave's entrance.

A beautiful white stallion lunged out of the cave and thundered away at a ground eating pace.

There was no mistaking him. It was Aragon, and he seemed driven. This told her what she needed to know, and the very thought of Mesha again sent heat flaming up her arms. She bit down hard on her lips, tasting blood.

And then it happened, just like she pictured. *He* walked out of the cave; she had forgotten how handsome he was, with that ravenlike appeal. His flashing ebony eyes locked on hers. Time froze, and she felt a rush in her head as she was taken back to Lemuria, a time when he was the catch of all and belonged to her. *No, no, no!* She shook her head, erasing the lie that clouded her vision. He had been a lie all this time. The anger welled within, and her hands clenched, fingernails biting into flesh.

Ciara reared, and a shrill whinny escaped her throat. She landed and flattened her ears, standing between the two as they sized each other up.

Sumayah frowned as another form exited the cave. He was young and blond and very tall. For a split second, the image of Clemon flashed in her mind.

"I see that filly of yours still has her sweet disposition," Mesha said, mocking her with a sadistic smile. "Give her to me, Sumayah, and I will show you what we do with unruly beasts such as her."

The mare charged him, and like lightning his sword flashed before her, making her stop a few feet in front of him.

"Call her off, or I will run her through."

Sumayah's mind exploded with all the horrible ways she would make him pay. Her hands burst into flames, and she held them up.

"You will not touch her, or you will feel the burn of my wrath!" she snarled, spitting out the last word.

"Tut-tut, Sumayah, I haven't come to kill your beloved horse. I have merely come for you and the crystal key. Once I have both, we can leave peacefully and without any bloodshed." Mesha opened his palms to her as if in a peace offering.

The offer was tempting. *Isn't this what she had come for? To find him and stop all of this madness?* It was that simple. Leave with him, letting him think she knew where the crystal key was—for she had no idea where Drakaous had hid it—and all would be well.

A vicious snarl behind her reminded her she had plenty of help if she chose to do battle. She agonized over what to do. She wanted to take him on, show him what she was made of, and stop him here and now. But she saw Ciara so bravely standing guard, ready to die for her. No, she would not let anyone die for her. This was between her and Mesha. She would leave with him and then plan his demise. It would be all the sweeter to see the look on his face when she sent him the final blow. With that triumphant thought, her hands cooled, and she let them rest at her sides.

"Ah, good show! I knew you couldn't let a single drop of blood be shed over you. Brave, strong Sumayah, my priestess." He walked toward her, waving his gleaming sword at Ciara; the mare took a step back and halted.

Something blue glinted on the sword; it was the sapphire, the same blue that was savagely slashed into Nero. The vision of the man so deviously, so apathetically thrusting his sword into the side of her dragon made her pause and rethink her decision.

"It was you all this time. You were the man in my visions. You tried to kill Nero."

The wolf behind her growled as Mesha shrugged and took another step toward Sumayah. All the while Clarron stood in the background; he had pulled out his sword and kept looking behind him. He took a step farther into the sunlight.

"Mesha, we are running out of time," Clarron said. "They could come through the entrance at any moment."

Mesha frowned at the reminder. With a deep sigh, he said, "Sumayah, come to me now, and let's avoid being caught up in the hailstorm that threatens to rain down, for it is the most unpleasant storm you will have ever been in."

She had no idea what he was talking about and could stall no longer. With a heavy sigh, she walked toward Mesha.

Mesha turned his head and said, "Catch Aragon. I will not be walking back through this entrance."

"He could be long gone, Mesha. We haven't the time to get him. Can't you whistle for him?"

Mesha gave him a look of exasperation. "I saw him just over there. At least go that far."

But before Clarron could take one step, the entrance to the cavern once again came alive as the darkness became filled with a multitude of dragons and men.

Sumayah froze in her tracks, staying far enough away from Mesha so that he couldn't get his hands on her. The wolf moved forward, snapping in warning. *This is it; they have come to destroy the beautiful Agartha.*

Ryven's desperate look as he searched for her filled her mind, and something in her snapped. It was too late now to give herself up. Her mind ran rampant. She was unable to think. Then a small rock tumbled from the mountainside, catching her attention. She looked up to see a beautiful girl hidden behind a small outcropping of large red boulders. Both she and the boulders clung to the side of the mountain. This girl looked like she meant business. She was not dressed in a silken tunic like herself. No, she was dressed like Ryven, ready for action, with a crisscrossing of weaponry hanging from her back. Behind her, also clinging precariously from crags and crooks in the rock outcropping, were more like her.

This is most encouraging. What will pop out of the camouflage of Mother Earth next?

"Mesha, we want to thank you for helping us through the entrance," said the deep guttural voice of one of the dragons that had just stepped into the light. This one was large and muscular, reminiscent of how Mesha looked when he turned.

"I have no quarrel with you," said the red-faced Mesha. "I just want that girl."

"I'm truly sorry, Mesha, but it is not that simple, for we want the girl too. And her sisters, for they carry within their blood the key to stop what we have worked so many millennia for." He proceeded toward Mesha; his steps were light, considering his lumbering size. His minions followed him, one by one.

Well, it just went from bad to much worse, Sumayah thought. And she wasn't about to stand here and take a beating. She shook her hands, setting them ablaze; she willed the flames further with just a thought. They leaped at Mesha, who bellowed with rage.

"Then take her sisters, but leave her to..." Before the last word came out of his mouth, he began to violently shake. A swirling blackness suddenly appeared around him, and in the blink of an eye, he turned, eyeing Sumayah in the most menacing way.

Her hair stood on end. Gulping, she sent her flames around him in response. And that is when the sky blackened, and the air swirled with dragon scent.

Carians descended to the earth at breakneck speed, grabbing an opponent and carrying it back in an entanglement of death. One would live and one would die, for this dance was to the end.

Sumayah tried to evade the approaching Mesha as she searched for Nero and Sterling. *They just had to be there.* Her searching eyes took her off Mesha, and he pounced toward her.

The black wolf, with lightning speed, lunged at Mesha's exposed neck. Mesha roared and shook his massive head as the wolf ripped at the black flesh.

Clarron, unsure whom to attack, for this was not his battle, just tried to keep anything from attacking him. He backed farther away from the heaviest of the fighting as more and more dragons exited the cave, only to be preyed upon by those waiting above. Clarron smiled when he caught a glimpse of Dwyla. Her speed amazed him as she sliced and dodged without getting a scratch. He would fight with her, and let out a war whoop and jumped into the battle, slashing and thrusting his way toward the little girl who was deadlier than a poisonous snake under the bedcovers.

Mesha gave a mighty twist of his neck, sending the wolf into the air. The dragon spun, slashing his tail with deadly intent at the wolf. The wolf screamed once, went down with a heavy thud, and did not move.

Sickened by the sight, Sumayah fought back the bile that rose in her throat. Her eyes felt as if they were ablaze, and she screamed, charging Mesha and sending a torrent of flames at him. *I will kill you if it is the last thing on this earth I ever do.* But before she could join the black beast in full contact, she was grabbed by her shoulders and swept up into the air.

CHAPTER 29

THE DARK ONE

❦

As Sumayah hung precariously from Nero, she could see Sterling behind them, acting as buffer to whatever challenge came their way.

Nero gently swung her on his back, where she anchored her two legs behind his wings and held tight. She looked at the battleground below. Lemurians, Fae, and Agarthans had found the intruders, and were all locked in the fight. She tried to find Ryven in the cloud of war but could not. The sky was so riddled with warring dragons, droplets of blood splattered her face as they flew too close. She agonized over the many lifeless forms plummeting to the earth.

Wiping the tears from her face, she tried to focus on her course ahead, but heard Sterling roar from behind. Two dragons were fast on his tail and gaining. She felt helpless as she clung to Nero.

"Nero, they are after Sterling. We must do something!" She knew how futile those words were before they even left her mouth. She knew Nero was saving her at all costs, and she buried her head rather than watch the two dragons take Sterling to the ground. She was lost in a sea of emotion, which filled her to near suffocation. She couldn't bear it, and the sobs poured out of her. She was so lost in her sorrow, she was not prepared for the hit that almost sent her off Nero. Grappling in desperation, she dug her nails into Nero's flesh as he nosedived. The deathly shadow of their attacker loomed above them, trying to cut them off. Nero swerved sharply to the right and rolled, narrowly avoiding the jaws that still dripped blood from a previous kill.

Sumayah knew these dragons had gone to the dark side. It was as if she was caught in a struggle of good versus evil, but of the worst kind. She caught the look of pure darkness as it gained on them, its large, blood-red eye wide with frenzy. Suddenly the thought *snow* came to mind, and in response her world went gray as the horizon before a storm. She clung to Nero in hopes that she had accomplished her wish. The sudden change of temperature sent her into a fit of shaking, and she knew she had taken them to the winter lands.

CR

Ryven watched helplessly from the ground below as the dragon hit Nero. He felt it just as if it had happened to him. In agony he watched Nero desperately try to evade the relentless attack. But caught in the midst of his own battle, Ryven had to turn away to stay the thrust of a sword, for not only did dragons come out of that cave, but also with them came men working on the side of their keeper.

To Ryven's surprise this one was proving to be a worthy opponent and met strike with strike. Out of the corner of his eye, he saw Elspeth, clad in the newly made garb for war. The thin chain-mail tunic fashioned from a new metal just mined from the dwarves was proving to be strong as stone. She was showing her prowess for battle and easily kept pace with Ryven in pushing back her attackers.

Ryven stole a quick glance to the sky to see it empty. His heart sank, but his heartbreak would have to wait as another warrior charged his way. The fire burning in his attacker's eye matched the fire within himself, and he easily stepped to the left just before the impact. With lightning speed he spun and thrust with all his might, sending his sword into the opponent's

268

shoulder and taking him down. Without another look he moved to his next opponent.

Men kept pouring out of the black hole of the cave. *Something has to close that entrance*, he thought, and he battled his way toward the opening. He noticed a new band of dwarves fighting nearby; some were still dropping from crags and crevices above the opening. Two fighters battling side by side caught his eye. The speed and ease of movement from the girl left him in awe. She matched the skill of her giant-sized partner, who closely resembled Clemon. The two noticed Ryven's advance and quickly took care of the two they were fighting and went to him.

"My name is Dwyla, Master Ryven," she said breathlessly, bowing her head to him. "We are honored to fight by your side."

Ryven held up his hand. "Please, none of that, but I see your people are watching the entrance. We need to close it somehow, and I might have a plan." He jerked his head to the stand of dark timber. "If we can get the woodwose to help close it up, we might have a chance."

The man who resembled Clemon put his broad hand on Ryven's shoulder. "I am Clarron, and I will get it done," he said with a reassuring wink. "I hear they are gentle beasts, but stronger than twenty oxen together."

Ryven smiled and gave them a nod of appreciation. "May the Goddess protect you," he said and disappeared into the storm, searching for the one he should have finished off long before this. He took in a deep breath and centered his thoughts on Mesha.

Overlooking the carnage below stood Mergus, Bethia, and Lhayan, with Pennyann, Leesabeth, Jaylan, and Riva. They were also searching for the one—the one who had brought this butchery upon them. Lhayan busily prepared the circle to ensnare their captive once they had them in their grips.

Everyone in the battle was instructed to find Mesha and single him out. They suspected he would be fighting in dragon form, which would make it more difficult. With Ryven, Elspeth, and Clemon leading the warriors, they were certain to get him.

"Is the circle ready?" asked Bethia, stroking Aragon's white silken mane. "You did your job well, my boy. I am proud of you!" She then pushed on him. "Now off with you. Be safe and take Ciara with you. Without the help of you both, we would not have made it here so quickly. Now away!" The stallion snorted and spun. He bit at Ciara, who released a quick kick at him, then lunged forward and tore away.

"Yes, the circle is ready; we just need to bring him to us. I am worried about Sumayah, Bethia," said Lhayan, wringing her hands nervously.

Mergus, keeping a keen eye on the battle in the sky and below, spoke in a soft tone. "We have just lost Sterling. He was defending Nero and Sumayah. Two attackers were just more than he could handle, and he... well." His eyes filling with tears, could not finish his sentence.

Bethia stomped to him and promptly slapped him on the head. His face registered a look of shock, and he frowned at her.

"Mergus, what sort of wizard are you, hey? Have you forgotten?" she asked now, poking him with her staff.

He cleared his throat, pushing the stick away. "I haven't forgotten... yet to see them fall, well, it does not get easier with each time. I do know this: Sumayah and Nero, though we cannot see them, are still with us." His body shook, and he wrapped his arms around himself. "They have gone somewhere very cold." As he finished the word *cold*, a stream of frost exited his mouth.

"The winter lands!" all four girls said at once.

"She has taken them back to the frozen land," said Riva, "No one would dare follow them there!"

"She knows how to control fire," said Leesabeth. "It will keep them warm. Between her and Nero, they will be safe until we retrieve them. But for me, I am having a hard time standing up here when I could shift and join the battle below."

Jaylan jumped up and pointed. "Look, there he is! Father and Lord Fallonay are closing in on him."

"Let us prepare for the binding," ordered Bethia. "We have only a short window of time."

Everyone ran to her position around the large drawn circle, with Pennyann at the east, Jaylan at the south, Riva at the west, Leesabeth at the north, and Bethia and Mergus standing at the God and Goddess position. Each took her turn calling in the elemental of the direction they stood. Lhayan, with her athame pointing outward, walked around the circle, drawing the protective energies. Her athame shot a stream of blue that wrapped around the entire circle. It shot up, enclosing the entire sphere of the circle above, and then did the same below. The large circle was now filled with the aspects of all elements, and looking with the inner eye, you could see the swirling entities in their perspective colors of yellow, red, blue, and green. Bethia called in the assisting energies of the Goddess, and Mergus called in the God. A swirling mist suddenly appeared within the center of the circle.

"The circle is complete," Bethia said. "We bind to us the darkness called Mesha. He will now become my eyes and ears; this battle today is only the beginning of the war. He is bound to us, and in doing us harm, he is doing himself harm. Though he may try, he can never overpower the combination of our powers."

"Let us hold this cone of creation for the one we seek, and hold it until it is delivered to us rightfully so!" chimed in Mergus.

And so they all stood holding the energies, until Mesha was within their grasp. They watched with anticipation as those below closed in on him.

Ryven watched as the woodwose emerged from the dark cover of their trees.

"Thank you, Clarron, thank you, Dwyla," he whispered as they closed in on the entrance of the cave. Each carried with him a boulder or a tree trunk, whatever he could grab that could block the entrance. Some fought bravely against the men, unmindful of their bloodletting swords, holding them back with their great size and strength. And so slowly the entrance to Agartha was once again closed to the outer realm.

Now I seek out Mesha, Ryven thought. He sidestepped a grunting and groaning duo as they met sword thrust with sword thrust. The Fae, a far better swordsman than the man, soon overpowered him. The dark dragons, were more difficult to defeat, yet the great speed and tenacity of the dwarves surprised him—even the women, for they took on the great bulk of the dragons two or three at a time, slicing and jabbing, angering them into confusion until one by one, they began to fall.

He suddenly saw his father closing in on Mesha, who was still in dragon form. With renewed strength, he pushed his way toward his father, who was now joined by Rupert.

Both king and lord, filled with the fever of the hunt, came alive. Their eyes expressed the fire of the moment as they closed in on their prey.

"We got him surrounded now, my boy!" yelled Fallonay as he expertly swung his sword from one hand to the next.

"Now that we got him, how do we get him up that ridge?" bellowed Rupert.

Ryven lunged into the midst and yelled, "I will kill him first!"

"Nay, son," yelled Fallonay. "The queen wants him alive."

Mesha, feeling impending doom, roared and began sucking in air.

"Watch him, he conjures fire!" warned Rupert.

Mesha let out an earsplitting roar in his defense, his blood-red eyes widened with rage. He swung his tail, narrowly missing Fallonay, and sucked in more air.

"Get ready!" yelled Ryven. "When his fire is spent, he will be at his weakest point. We need to get him to change back—then we take him."

All kept a healthy distance, jabbing and yelling at Mesha to provoke him. They poked and jabbed and catcalled. With one last bellow, Mesha prepared to let loose of his fiery flames, but before he could, he was hit with a mighty blow to his exposed throat. It happened so quickly, all around him exclaimed in surprise.

The wolf had sprung out of nowhere and lunged for Mesha's throat. This time he clamped down with all his might and did not let go. Mesha could only snarl as his throat was caught in the death grip of the raging wolf.

"Don't let him kill him!" yelled Ryven.

"Well, what the hell do you want us to do?" Fallonay hollered, trying to jump in, but the speed and action between wolf and dragon was too much.

"We have no choice but to kill that wolf before he kills Mesha," said Rupert, advancing on them.

Ryven knew how much Sumayah loved that wolf and rushed forward. "Rupert, you cannot kill it. It belongs to your daughter."

Rupert froze in his tracks and looked at Ryven. His eyes spoke of his great love for his daughter.

"That, that wolf is hers?" he asked, pointing his sword at the massive struggle that still ensued.

Before Ryven could answer, a woodwose charged into the fray with amazing speed and grabbed the wolf, yanking it by the scruff of its neck and throwing it aside. The wolf yelped as it hit the ground with a thud.

Before Mesha could react to his freedom, the woodwose clamped his mighty, muscle-laden arms around his neck and began to squeeze.

All three watched in fascinated horror as the woodwose held his ground. Mesha flopped helplessly, and suddenly the dragon succumbed to its lesser form. The woodwose stood, holding the man.

"Great work!" roared Fallonay. "Let's get him to the ridge before he awakens and regains his strength."

The wolf had clamored to a standing position and went to Ryven. "Great job, my friend. Sumayah will be very thankful for your assistance."

The wolf replied with a deep "*woof*," then spun and sprang back into the dark timber.

Ryven looked around him. The deafening noise of clashing swords, screaming, and yelling had lessened. All around him lay the vestiges of the senseless battle. His heart sank, and the smell of fresh blood would be forever imprinted in his mind. Dead and dying from both sides lay all around him. Many were lost today, and the bodies lay strewn for miles around. He feared Sumayah was among them, but something deep in his heart told him otherwise. She lived. It was more than a hope or a wish. They were one, and if she had perished from this lifetime, he knew he would surely feel it. The woodwose, having finished their job of sealing the entrance, disappeared back to their forests. The sudden grasp of a large hand on his shoulder startled him.

"Looks like you got him, Ryven." It was Clemon. He had a sword wound to the side of his face that dripped blood, and he seemed drained of strength, but he was alive.

Ryven, so happy to see him, hugged the big blond. "Yes, with the help of many, we got him and showed the Rep's we will not be controlled."

They were joined by those who still stood, hands grasping in thanks, joyful recognition, giving backslaps of victory. Or was it? For all around them lay those who had sacrificed their lives to keep alive what they believed in. A way of life that was in danger of being taken away from them, a change they did not want.

Clarron and Dwyla caught up to them as they ascended the ridge. Both were battle weary, and the climb was not easy. Dwyla had a sword wound to her upper thigh that made her journey all the more difficult.

Ryven stopped to lend her a hand. "You fight like no other."

She smiled, her face blushing. "I have been trained from the very beginning for this day. When he"—she pointed to Clarron—"appeared looking for the entrance to Agartha, I knew my time had come, along with those like me who had prepared their whole lives."

Ryven was confused by her words and frowned at her. "You knew this day would come?"

She just nodded, hobbling farther up the ridge, then pointed to Clarron, who had grasped her other arm. "He was born for this also. It was no mistake that he looked for another, and his searching brought him to Mesha."

Clarron laughed long and loud. "Looks like you and I, Ryven, have been duped into a performance that was already written in the stars."

Ryven chuckled. Instantly, the big guy reminded him again of Clemon, which made him look for the other big blond. He spied him with Elspeth. She had slipped from his mind during the battle, and he was not surprised to see her still standing, for he knew she was just as good a warrior as little Dwyla.

Elspeth felt her brother's stare and glanced at him, flashing him a weary smile. Although she was coated with the coverings of battle, she had not a scratch on her.

She walked to him with Clemon at her side, and all made the last steps to the impatiently waiting circle of witches, wizard, and priestesses.

The woodwose still had his grip on the unconscious Mesha, with Fallonay and Rupert closely guarding them just in case he awoke.

All who had survived the battle now arrived, watching as the magic began. Lhayan used her athame to cut a door in the circle of light, allowing only for the transfer of Mesha into the center of the circle, where the swirling mist of Goddess energy wrapped around him to hold him.

Bethia stepped closer to Mesha and gave him a look of sympathy. She rose up her arms, gathering energy from all aspects within. A great ball of rainbow light swirled within the center of her hands. She willed it bigger, and it grew.

"The battle unwinding, yet the war has just begun. By our binding, Mesha is now one. With us he will always be connected, and every thought and move, will have been expected."

Everyone in the circle repeated her words three times, and each time they spoke it, they spoke louder. The ball of energy in Bethia's hand grew wider and bigger with each word, and as the last word was spoken, she threw the ball of binding at Mesha. It hit him so hard, it took him off the ground, and he convulsed three times.

Opening his eyes, he moaned. As everything around him came into focus, he realized where he was and screamed out one word.

"Sumayah!"

In desperation he screamed it over and over trying to shift into his greater form.

Those watching backed up, unsure of the outcome. Some murmured his name, while others looked on him with compassion, even though he was part of what lay around them.

"You will keep your position with those who would try to destroy us and our Mother Earth," commanded Mergus. "For you will work for us now. Through your eyes and ears we will know their every move. We will in the end save our mother, and restore her to the original plan."

Mergus gave the four girls a nod, and they clasped hands, intensifying the power flowing around them in a great show of blue and violet light. The girls became one circle of binding energy and stepped closer to Mesha, letting their flashing energies encompass him.

Mesha bellowed, his body convulsing chaotically, then turned black. All around gasped, fearful of the emerging dragon.

The girls held tight, not letting go, unable to take their eyes off the turning body.

"That's it, girls, keep him," ordered Bethia. "Bind him. Do not let him go!"

The black form of the dragon never materialized. Instead, it remained a swirling, chaotic black mist. The cry that came from it was eerie and horrifying, and one bony hand reached out, the only thing that was left of the true expression of Mesha.

Bethia raised her staff. "Mesha, you will leave our world and enter into the outer realm to do our bidding. We release you for you can do us no harm. We release the circle. We release all those who have joined and brought their powers, for the binding spelling is complete. Hail and farewell!"

Everyone in the circle swung up her arms and released all energies within, along with the pathetic mist of the dark one that dissipated from sight...

CHAPTER 30

WAITING FOR TOMORROW

❧

S umayah felt Nero's draining strength, and he wavered in flight. His moan rumbled in her ears. The cold air made flight difficult, and they headed for land. Looking behind, the empty, gray sky told her they were alone. Sterling's hopeless attempt to keep them out of harm's way was still fresh in her mind. Her heartbeat fluttered uncontrollably, as if he had taken a piece of it with him. The vision of so many fallen had taken its toll. Drowning in her own misery, she did not even realize they had hit ground, and hard. She tumbled over and over, landing in the biting snow a few yards from Nero. She had forgotten how cold cold was, and she scolded herself for bringing them here.

As she wallowed in the snow, something red caught her attention. Slowly she looked down. It was blood and lots of it. She checked herself and found no wounds. Comprehension did not register at first. She refused to believe it, and she crawled to Nero and gently laid one arm across his still and very cold body.

He tried to lift his head to look at her.

She scrambled around to his head. "It's going to be just fine, Nero. I am right here. I won't leave you." Hot tears froze in the biting cold, and her hands began to numb. She willed fire, and the heat warmed them immediately. She willed the flames higher, warming herself and trying desperately to warm Nero. She searched for his wound and sat in stunned horror as blood poured from the indigo scar. *The hit he received was at the right place. How did that dragon know where to hit him—unless it was Mesha.*

She tried to summon the healing energy but it would not come. She lay by his neck, listening to his labored breath. Her love for this great creature poured from her as steadily as the blood that left a growing pool around them. The contrast of crimson and white was like the contrast between life and death. She sobbed in his neck and tried to be brave for him, but even so, her heartbeat waned.

"You were so very brave today; I thank you for all that you have done. We both had a great journey, did we not?"

His reply was a soft purr. Then his words formed in her mind, "Do not save this body Sumayah. I must go. Remember the dragonhorse, for that is how I shall return to you."

She understood his words which brought a slight smile to her face. Celio, Sebation's and Bethia's words about living more than one lifetime flooded her mind. Their words stilled her, and she lay with him until he took his last breath, until she heard his final heartbeat.

Her world closed in. She willed herself to go with him, to join with him in the new life. And her heartbeat slowed. She lay there waiting, waiting to follow...

CR

The swirling black mist screamed inaudibly as it approached the lifeless forms in the snow. Was he too late? Mesha screamed again in anger as the opaqueness of his being deepened and pulsated. He thrust out his arm, surprised to see only pale bone ending in thin, calcified appendages once resembling fingers.

"Sumayah!" he rasped, letting the cold wind carry the word to the lifeless form.

Deep within the bleakness of her mind, she heard her name. *Is someone calling me?* She blinked her eyes and heard her name again. Slowly she rolled from her dragon's neck and was met by the gruesome mist that hovered above her.

Is this what death is to be? Am I to be pursued in death as I was in life? What trickery is this?

"Yes, this is death, Sumayah. It is all around you. Look, your beloved Nero is dead, and all those that fought in *your* battle, the battle to save *you,* are all gone. The mare Ciara is dead, and my men are dining on her as we speak!"

She covered her ears to escape the words. *No…they could not be gone. I left. I ran so they would be safe.*

"No, you are wrong; all have perished because of you!"

She looked into the black cloak of darkness and knew whom she faced. The knowledge of defeat, and the sight of his grotesque form ripped at her heart as if he had reached into her chest and pulled it out himself. She envisioned it in his outstretched hand, the beats slower and slower. With each beat she willed it to stop. *Wait for me Nero, I want to follow.*

"You have lost everyone, Sumayah. Most of all, your Ryven was a lie all along. Your Ryven worked alongside me, thrusting his sword into those who would fight for you…"

As Mesha spoke his last word, so did her heart beat its last.

She felt herself leaving the darkness, up and up she went, pulling away from this lifetime. Slowly she stood and looked down at her lifeless form. How strange it feels she thought. And for a second she hesitated not wanting to leave, but something called to her. She stepped away, leaving the body in the snow.

Suddenly, warmth and a bright golden light radiated behind her, and she turned to see Nero waiting, and heard his words in her mind.

"Its time for us to go, we are being called Sumayah," he said. She climbed on his back, and together they lifted into the loving golden light.

ॐ

The sky had turned a pale, muddy orange, and there was heaviness in the air. The joyous song of the elementals as they tended to Mother Earth was gone. The silence permeated everyone, settling within them, dragging them down in the wallows of their sorrow for loved ones lost.

Bethia waved her staff, letting the crystal at the top blink brightly, like a beacon of hope in the midst of such despair. The blinking light grew brighter and wider, then shot out in a steady stream of energy, connecting with each and every survivor. The light was meant to heal as best it could, helping to bring them from the pit of sadness.

"We have won the battle. Yet it is only the beginning of what is ahead. We must remember our calling, and the sacrifices we have made to save those who are enslaved. We have chosen to restore our Mother back to the world we envisioned from the very beginning. Be not sad for those who have lost this life, for we know we must go on, as they will too. Need I remind you, death is never the end. It is but a time to rest and begin anew, rising up better and stronger."

Fallonay pushed forward, disheveled from battle. "Bethia is right; this is not the end, but only the beginning. We have shown today that we do have the power and the will to push forward, no matter the consequences. I am proud of all of my people and all of those who have joined in this great feat, going against what they believe to recapture what we had started."

Riva stormed forward in anger. "I don't want to hear any speeches about heroics and sacrifice. What of my sister? What happened to her? And what of them!" she cried, pointing to the fallen. "What happens to them? What do we do with..." She buried her face in Jaylan's chest, and sobbed out, "Jaylan, I want my sister back."

"My sister is right," replied Jaylan. "We do not know of our sister's plight. Can we now search for her and take care of the fallen as best we can?"

Clarron, hearing the name Jaylan, pushed toward the center of the gathering. He rushed to where he could see her and froze. It was the one he sought. She was not just a dream, *the queen was right*, he thought. With a wide smile he turned to Bethia and gave her a nod.

Bethia noticed Clarron's advance with a half smile.

Ryven suddenly felt his heart stop, and then it beat again, then skipped a beat. His hands suddenly went cold and began to turn blue.

Elspeth, seeing her brother's ashen expression, sidled up to him and whispered, "It is Sumayah. She is gone from this lifetime."

Ryven looked down at his sister and saw her mouth move, but did not hear her words over the loud buzzing in his head. He suddenly saw

Sumayah slumped over the lifeless body of her dragon, he knew then she had taken them back to the winter lands. *She is so cold and so alone. She needs me.*

"I must go to her!" he yelled, pushing aside Elspeth.

"She is alone. She—she cannot go alone!" His mind whirled. *How do I get back to her? Nero is gone, so he cannot lead me to her.* He stormed from the crowd with all intentions of finding a way.

"Master Ryven, stop!" bellowed Mergus.

Ryven ignored him and saw Ciara off in the distance with a familiar white stallion. *Ciara will take me to her.* He lengthened his stride to go to the mare.

But two sets of strong hands stayed him. He struggled with all his might, unseeing, unhearing. His only mission was to go to her—to gather her up in his arms so she would not be alone. He agonized over the thought of her lying in that cold, unforgiving land.

"Ryven—please," grunted Clemon, trying his best to hold the wiry Fae. Both Clemon and Clarron had all they could do to handle the battle-weary Ryven, who suddenly slumped against Clemon's massive chest.

"I am finished," Ryven rasped out, the tone of defeat in his voice. "I care not."

"Bring him to me," ordered Bethia. As they half carried him forward, the mud-orange sky suddenly opened, letting in a cylinder-shaped beam of iridescent golden light. The light danced and snapped as it descended to the ground. Once it landed, it spread a warming, comforting glow through everyone.

After a few minutes, the light faded, and the beautiful Celio and Sebastion stood in its place.

Bethia and Mergus quickly made their way to the duo with greetings.

Celio spoke first. "We have come to remind you as a mother would counsel her daughter or son. We come to tell you that your world is much more than what you see. There are worlds within your world and worlds outside of your world, and all of them are part of a greater realm. You toil in sorrow at what you think is lost. But it is not lost; it is the ultimate show of love, the love for another and the love of self, for if we do not love ourselves first, how could we possibly love another. For that is all there truly is in the end."

Sebastion intervened. "Love is what all have desired, and it is the spark of life within all of us. Love is the original plan for your world, for Mother Earth, and as long as there is one here who can hold the light of love within himself, he will also hold the light for all. Many of you have shown that within you is carried that light, and so all those who have fallen today are not truly lost. If you believe in that light, then they are still with you and still have much work to do. Yes, they have come to a crossroads, but it is only a place to rest and grow from this experience. See, they go now to that place of rest and reflection."

Sebastion pointed to the fallen around them.

The crowd gasped as the air around them filled with a brilliant golden-white light. It swirled and tumbled like tendrils of golden hair blowing in the breeze. The tendrils reached out and went to each and every fallen, including the fallen from the outer realm, touching them, reawakening the love-light within each. That love-light rose from each and mingled with the rest of the light, until all had risen and had joined into one expanded expression of love.

Awes and oohs filled the air as everyone watched the great show of light dance and twirl, rising higher and higher in the sky until it disappeared beyond the mud-orange horizon.

Then a great wind picked up, bringing with it a gust of indigo and violet air. It spread across the land, enveloping all in its light. Then, as suddenly as the wind had picked up, it ceased, and all was silent.

Ryven looked around to see that all had been restored. The crimson-stained landscape was back to its original beauty, and the joyous songs of the elementals filled the air once again. The mud-orange of the horizon was restored to its original amber-blue hue, with the twin suns brightly shining down upon them. All trace of the battle was gone.

Celio and Sebastion smiled, their large, blue eyes twinkling with know-ing and radiated love.

"You see, even those who fought against us have been taken," said Sebastion. "They will, go to their place to rest, and relive their life on Earth. They will have a chance to grow from their experience here.

Celio turned, letting her gaze fall upon Ryven. "Your love will restore her, Ryven. She and the rest of them will be with us, in the otherworld... until the time when they are ready to once again set their feet upon the path of this journey. Listen for the sound of thunder in the earth and watch for the thrill of the run, when you see it, you will understand what I speak of. That will be your sign to look for her, Ryven. Do not harden your heart, Ryven, for it was her heart that took her this time. Her heart could not withstand the test of deep sorrow, but rest assured when she returns; she will be all the more stronger, as will the rest of them."

With her last words, the cylinder of iridescent gold light once again came down and shrouded their form, then ascended back to the horizon and beyond.

Ryven looked at Clemon, then at Clarron. Trying to lighten his previous mood, he jokingly asked, "Might you two be twins?"

Clemon laughed and looked at Clarron. His laughter abruptly stopped and lodged in his throat, and he sputtered and coughed. Clarron reached over and slapped him hard on the back, almost sending him to the ground, which sent Ryven into a fit of laughter.

"Well, I'll be dipped in honey," said Clarron. "He does carry a *small* resemblance."

"Small?" asked Dwyla, walking to Clarron and giving him a little jab in the ribs with her elbow. "I would say *spitting* image." She leaned into him and whispered, "I see you found her."

Ryven caught her words with much interest. "Tell me more. Who did you find?"

Clarron's face blossomed into a deep shade of blush.

"Yes, tell him more," chided Dwyla just as Jaylan and her entourage approached.

She walked right up to Clarron and looked him in his eyes. "I am Jaylan, the one you seek."

Pennyann and Leesabeth gave Clarron a look of recognition. "We never thought you would have found her after we revealed her name!" replied Leesabeth. "With us leaving Lemuria and coming here, we had totally forgotten about you."

She turned to Ryven. "He was on the ship with us that brought all of us to Lemuria. He told us of his vision, and we helped him with a finding spell. At that time we had no idea who Jaylan was."

Clarron pointed to Bethia as she approached and said, "Was her that brought me the rest of the way."

Mergus came up behind Bethia and wrapped his arms around her and said, "There is much more to this *gypsy*, then we will ever know."

Bethia spun out of his embrace and poked him with her pipe that she was just getting ready to light, "Mind your manners wizard, or I will turn you into a toad!"

Mergus frowned at her and said, "You can do that?"

The lightness of the mood did little to help Ryven, as he saw the haunting images of Sumayah bravely pulling that long-sword out of Nero, her expression of surprise when he found her in that cave with her dragon, and the first time she touched a wolf. Looking back on her lifetime, he acknowledged and witnessed her growth. It did nothing to lessen the void in his heart, and yet he knew she was still with him.

Lhayan and Rupert found Ryven, and Lhayan grabbed him, hugging him close. "She chose this, Ryven, as did you. There is no going back now, only moving forward. We too feel the void. But together we will all await their return."

Rupert squeezed Ryven's shoulder. "When she returns, Master Ryven, be prepared, for she will return much harder to handle than before."

Ryven could not help but smile at his remark. He looked up at those who were still standing around, the many faces who would be waiting for a return, just as he would. How long it would take, no one knew. But he hoped it was tomorrow...

CHAPTER 31

SEEKERS OF THE FORGOTTEN KNOWLEDGE

೧೪

Tomorrow came and went; many tomorrows came and went. Ryven spent those days alone with his thoughts, and each day dragged on. Ciara had become his and Black's constant companion. It was if she knew something, and she waited too.

She did not seem to grieve over Sumayah's loss as he did. The mare tried her best to keep him entertained during Sumayah's absence. Her new and favorite thing to do was to sneak up on that old wizard and pull at his beard, then spin and take off with her tail flagging behind her. Ryven figured she singled out the wizard to lighten his days, because as wise and ancient as he was, he mourned the loss of his two dragons, Nero and Sterling. It was almost as if he didn't believe his own magic anymore, as if he thought it had run out, and there was never to be a return. Ryven hoped that was wrong, but as each day passed, it was getting harder and harder.

Another month had lazily rolled by, and Ryven decided to leave the city. Every time he saw Jaylan and Clarron together it just reminded him of his loss. But he knew their time together would be cut short. They also had volunteered to return to the outerworld and would have to find one another again. He needed time away from it all, time to ponder his life and time to awaken from his horrible dream. So he climbed aboard Black, and with Ciara in tow, they left the city.

His thoughts took him back to the spot where he saw Sumayah pulling the long-sword from Nero. As he relived that time in his mind, he rode around the shoreline of the lake, then felt drawn to a small ridge that was not a hard climb. Once at the top, it overlooked the whole valley below. There he sat alone, trying hard to recapture more memories of his time with Sumayah. Black and Ciara nibbled the lush grasses not far from him, and he just sat, opening his mind and allowing her image to come in. But to his dismay, this moment was to be different. There were no more images of Sumayah. Hard as he tried, nothing would come forth, and he jabbed the ground with his fist in anger. Was he forgetting her? If he forgot her, it would mean she never existed. But the steady beat of his heart reminded him that locked in a chamber within was his love for her. That love he knew kept her alive.

Ciara suddenly picked up her head and stared at the valley below. Her ears twitched back and forth, listening. Ryven listened, wondering what she heard. Black picked up his head, then lowered it again to resume his munching. Ciara let out a loud whinny, then turned to Ryven and nickered at him.

"What is it, girl, what do you hear?" He stood to go to her, but she spun and tore off down the ridge. He stood, mouth open, watching her run like he had never seen her run before.

The thrill of the run.

The words rang in his head. Was it too much to hope for? And yet his heart pounded in his chest, *thump, thump, thump, thump.* He put his hand on his chest to steady it. *Stop it, Ryven, it is only a high-spirited mare off on a chase.*

He sat down and pulled on a long blade of grass. As it gave way, the ground beneath him suddenly rumbled. He scrambled to his feet, stopping his breath, and listened. It came again, the sound of distant thunder, and it grew louder and louder until the earth shook beneath him.

His excitement sent him into a flat-out run as he scrambled, slid, and rolled down the ridge with Black right behind him. He reached the bottom as they came into sight. The beauty of it caused his flesh to rise. A single tear slipped down his cheek.

These horses were not just Rupert's and Bethia's horses coming. This was much, much bigger, because in their shadows he could see the shapes of the dragons. This was the thunder in the earth, the thrill of the run. This was the dragonhorse.

The excitement of the moment was so strong; he yelled the word, "Dragonhorses!" With a loud *whoop,* he tore across the meadow, racing after the thundering cloud of dust. He ran and ran until his heart threatened to burst.

As they came closer in sight, the sound awakened and revived him. It was more than magnificent. A million dragonhorses thundered through the valley, with Ciara running neck and neck with her Nero and Sterling. He knew it was them, even though they had taken the body of the horse. *Oh, would Mergus be excited to see this.* With another *whoop* of excitement, he whistled for Black.

Together they raced in the tail wind of the dragonhorses. When they got nearer to Lyra Shambala, he could see throngs of people pouring out of their homes and gathering to watch the arrival. He heard their cheers of excitement. Mergus stood in the front of the crowd. Ryven could see his wide smile as he caught sight of Nero and Sterling.

Ryven stopped in front of Mergus, his breath coming in excited puffs. Mergus walked forward and slapped Ryven on his shoulder.

"It is a grand day today, is it not, Master Ryven," he said as Nero and Sterling cantered forward.

The whole city was there to marvel at the dragonhorses, dragons in the form of the horse.

"Well, Nero, how do you like having these legs to run versus wings to fly?" asked Bethia, coming forward and puffing excitedly on her pipe, a cloud of sweet herbs following her.

Nero nodded his head up and down.

"Looks like he approves, but it is very strange to see two white horses standing here that were once black and silver dragons!" she said with a laugh.

The rest of that day, everyone celebrated and chatted about the coming event. It would be time for those who chose to return to the upper world to leave, taking the dragonhorses with them and once again finding those that were lost in the battle who would have also returned.

Later that night, Bethia sat in the middle of the council grounds. She was beaming; her silken, black hair was polished and gleamed, except one long strand of silver that hung closest to her cheek and eye.

"The time has come," Bethia began. "We prepare to go to the upper realm. The times of men have brought them into a dark age, and they need our help more than ever. Many are awakening from their dream and realizing they have been kept in bondage far too long. . . The time has come for Mother Earth's shift, so that she can shed herself of those who rape and pillage her."

Ryven sat in excited silence; he did not hear any of Bethia's words, for he knew them well. He had sacrificed much, and so had Sumayah. Their time was returning, and that was all he could think about.

"Master Ryven, you think of Sumayah," Bethia said. "She and all like her are ready to return and once again continue their journey. They will be placed in the upper realms by their parents, with the mothers staying nearby to guide and watch over them. The fathers will place them in homes that have already been prepared for them. But know this, they come with no memory of this." She pointed around the city. "They must be free of any memory of who they truly are to keep them safe from those who would seek them out and stop them."

Hearing Bethia's words took away some of his excitement. *She will look upon me as a stranger. I waited all this time, and she will return not knowing me.*

Bethia's eyes bored into Ryven. He felt her stare and glanced at her.

"I know what you think, Master Ryven, but do not worry, for in the end she will be with you once again. When Agartha has risen and joined with Lemuria, then and only then will all of her memories return. It must be this way."

Ryven felt a hand grasp his and looked to see Elspeth; her look of sympathy helped him only slightly, for he remembered she pined for something that was now pure darkness.

Mergus stood and joined Bethia. "With the return of the dragonhorses, it is now time for us to move forward and restore the original plan for our world. Parents of loved ones lost, your waiting is over, and the return to the upper world is at hand. Time for their resurrection."

Leaving Agartha and returning to the upper realm was an easy task for Ryven. Almost everyone who heeded the call had returned and had taken on their roles, except for those who were still needed in Middle Earth. Nero and Sterling both melded with the humans as horses, waiting for the time when Sumayah would find them. Ciara, whose name had been changed to Freia, once again became Sumayah's favorite mount.

As for Sumayah's sisters, they too would appear in the upper realm when the time was right and would join with Pennyann and Leesabeth. Everyone had a role.

Ryven would return to Sumayah's life and protect her, for even though Mesha was bound to the witches, no one knew when or how he would return, or if ever.

And so, Ryven's time had come to join in the great play, and ease himself once again into Sumayah's world. The word came from Lhayan, who had taken residence in an old cobby belonging to an old farmer in Westenhill. She would wait for Sumayah to find her and once again reacquaint her with magic and guide her on her quest. Ryven had taken the identity of a stag hunter, a role that would not draw attention, and gain him access to Sumayah when the time was right.

And so his day had come, the day he would set his eyes upon her. His anticipation had transferred to Black, who pranced through the woods toward the home where Sumayah now lived.

He had to remember that she went by a different name.

"Shion," he said aloud. It felt foreign and different to him. But the world he had entered was now foreign. Men had long since lost the memory of their true origin and were under the control of the Rep's, who were masquerading as holy men, magistrates, kings and queens They built temples to worship their deity, calling them churches, and tortured and killed anyone who showed the least bit of indifference to their cause.

The world was much different now. All that he had known before had changed, and it was going to be work to fit in. He would play this game in order to keep Sumayah and all like her here alive. He would wait for the time when they were reunited, back to the place they started and back to the truth about who they really were.

He felt a waver in his heartbeat. She was close, and his thoughts flew from his mind. Catching sight of something in the meadow beyond the cover of the forest, he halted Black and watched. His heart lurched, and his body tensed with excitement; it was Sumayah. He fought hard to contain his emotions, wanting nothing more than to run to her and gather her into his arms where she belonged, and awaken her from this horrible dream.

He watched with a smile and longing in his heart as she danced beneath the threatening sky. She was the same wild beauty, but more so. He hoped that she had kept part of him and what they had, locked away in her heart.

The thunder rolled, and lightning flashed, suddenly releasing a torrent of rain upon her. As he suspected, it fazed her none but seemed to energize her. Yes, she was alive. His Sumayah was alive.

Black stomped the ground impatiently. "Soon, boy, soon," he reassured him and reluctantly turned him back into the woods until it was time to enter fully once again into her life.

$$\text{\CR}$$

And so, like the phoenix out of the ashes, Shion had risen. And their lives together began anew—the seekers of the forgotten knowledge.

The End

If you would like to know more about the true inspiration behind the characters and story of the Dragonhorse Saga, and to learn more about the author Denice Garrou, go to her website.
www.denicegarrou-dragonhorse.com

Made in the USA
Charleston, SC
11 June 2014